CONNIE MASON

New York Times
Bestselling Author

The Pirate Prince

CAPTIVE DESIRE

Dariq lurched from the bed and glared down at her, stunned by his loss of control. The woman was dangerous. The sooner he placed her in Ibrahim's keeping the better.

"That will not happen again, lady. You will cease using your wiles on me."

Willow rolled to her feet. "You are mad if you think I wanted you to...to attack me. All I want from you is my freedom."

"What you ask is impossible." So saying, Dariq turned and strode from the cabin.

Willow sank down upon the bed, shaking from her horrified reaction to Dariq's words. She would never resign herself to becoming a sex slave to a heathen Turk.

She touched her lips. They felt swollen; so did her breast where Dariq had touched it. The pirate was the devil incarnate, and far too handsome for her peace of mind.

The Pirate Prince

CONNIE MASON

LEISURE BOOKS NEW YORK CITY

A LEISURE BOOK®

November 2004

Published by

Dorchester Publishing Co., Inc.
200 Madison Avenue
New York, NY 10016

ISBN 0-8439-5234-2

The name "Leisure Books" and the stylized "L" with design are trademarks of Dorchester Publishing Co., Inc.

Printed in the United States of America.

Visit us on the web at www.dorchesterpub.com.

Prologue

Istanbul, Turkey, 1562

Death stalked the marble halls of Sultan Ibrahim's seraglio.

Prince Dariq, second son of Murad, the recently deceased ruler of the Ottoman Empire, slept peacefully beside his concubine, his body sated and his mind at ease. Since his plush chambers were far removed from the main part of the palace, the prince remained blissfully unaware of his older brother Ibrahim's vile scheme to slay his male siblings. Killing all the other male heirs would assure him that no one would be left alive to challenge his claim to the sultanate.

Suddenly a secret panel leading into Dariq's private bedchamber slid open; a woman stepped inside. The woman pulled Dariq's concubine from his arms.

"Go, Fatima," Saliha Sultana whispered, giving the startled girl a push toward the secret passage. "Return to the harem immediately."

Startled awake by the commotion, Prince Dariq rose up on his elbow. When he saw his mother urging his concubine into the secret passage, he knew mischief was afoot. His mother rarely left the harem and never entered his chambers in the dead of night.

"Hurry, my son," Saliha urged. "Get dressed. You must leave immediately. Ibrahim has slain his brothers. Even as we speak janizaries loyal to Ibrahim are on their way here to murder you."

Horror darkened Dariq's gray eyes. "My brothers are dead? All of them?"

"Aye, my son, even young Alkbar is gone."

Dariq pulled on baggy trousers and shirt, stomped his feet into boots and reached for his scimitar. "I will avenge their deaths, Mother."

"Do not be foolish, Dariq," Saliha Sultana chided. "You will be cut down the moment you leave your chambers. You must flee. I know your ship is due to sail soon. Flee to the harbor and sail far away, where Ibrahim cannot find you."

Even as Saliha spoke, Dariq heard footsteps echoing through the deserted hallways. They were coming for him.

"Here," Saliha said, offering Dariq a heavy cloth bag. "Take this. Inside are the gold and precious gems your father gave me while he was alive. I cannot bear that you should go away with nothing."

"I cannot take them, Mother. They are yours."

"I have no further use for them, son."

The door opened. Dariq grasped his scimitar, prepared to kill as many of Ibrahim's janizaries as he could before he himself was slain. Mustafa, the captain of Dariq's personal guard, a giant of a man with eyes as black as his flowing beard, entered the chamber.

"Your loyal guardsmen are stationed outside the door, Prince," Mustafa reported. "We will hold off the janizaries while you make good your escape."

Saliha thrust the cloth bag of valuables into Dariq's hands. "Leave nothing of value behind," she advised, casting a glance around the elegantly appointed bedchamber.

Moving swiftly, she gathered up gold plate and silver, gem-encrusted bowls, and anything else of value she saw, and dropped them into a satin pillowcase. She thrust the pillowcase into Dariq's hands and pushed him toward a door opening onto a narrow balcony.

"You can escape over the rooftops and through the alleys to the harbor. Go with God, my son."

Dariq's handsome features settled into stubborn lines. "I am not leaving without you, Mother."

Saliha Sultana sent her son a stern look. "You will do as I say. I do not fear Ibrahim. He needs me to keep peace in the harem. Even as we speak, your father's concubines are mourning their slain sons. I must stay with them."

"Nay, Mother, you must come—"

"Listen to your mother," Mustafa interrupted. "Kamel will see that no harm comes to her. He is the most powerful eunuch within the seraglio. He has the ear of Selim Pasha, the Grand Vizier. Trust him to keep Lady Saliha safe. You must live to avenge your slain brothers."

The thunder of footsteps and jangle of weapons grew louder, louder even than the heartrending cries drifting through the seraglio from the harem as mothers mourned their children. "How many men are still loyal to me?" Dariq asked.

"Of your twelve personal guardsmen, none has deserted you," Mustafa said. "They will hold off the janizaries as long as they can. Their lives are naught compared to yours, my prince."

"Nay!" Dariq cried. "No more deaths. Summon them inside. I wish to speak to them."

"Dariq, please," Saliha begged. "There is no time."

Mustafa opened the door and motioned for the armed guardsmen to enter the crowded bedchamber.

"You have proven your loyalty to me," Dariq began, "but I do not want you to lose your lives on my behalf. Flee while there is still time."

Saliha Sultana knew by the determined look on Dariq's face that he intended to fight Ibrahim's janizaries alone. She knew her son well. To his way of thinking, running was the coward's choice. She glanced at Mustafa and knew by his expression that he had come to the same conclusion. A slight nod of Saliha's head was all Mustafa needed to act.

Dariq was still urging his guardsmen to flee when Mustafa raised his scimitar and brought the handle down on Dariq's head. Mustafa caught him before he fell and hoisted his prince over his massive shoulder.

"Hurry," Saliha urged. "Take my son, and as many guardsmen as are willing to join him in exile, to his ship. I trust you to protect him, Mustafa."

"Aye, my lady. Fear not, I will keep Prince Dariq safe."

To a man, Dariq's guardsmen agreed to accompany him wherever he might lead, even to the ends of the earth.

A loud banging sounded on the door. "They are here, Mustafa," Saliha Sultana hissed. "Kamel's cousin Hassan is a carpet seller. He has a stall in the souk. Tell Dariq to contact Hassan whenever he is able. He will pass your message on to Kamel and Kamel will tell me."

With a sob, she tore herself away and slipped into the secret passage, closing the panel behind her.

"Lock and barricade the door," Mustafa ordered as he stepped onto the balcony and leaped over to an adjacent roof with an unconscious Dariq slung over one broad shoulder, "and bring the pillowcase." One guardsman snatched up the pillowcase stuffed with valuables while another barricaded the door; then they all followed Mustafa over the rooftops.

Jumping from rooftop to rooftop, Mustafa and the guardsmen made their way to the high wall surrounding the seraglio. One by one each man slid down a tiled roof overhanging the wall and jumped the few feet to the ground. Mustafa handed Dariq down to a man on the ground before leaping himself and once again taking Dariq over his shoulder. The janizaries were not far behind; their shouts spurred Dariq's men on as they sprinted toward the harbor.

Unerringly Mustafa led them through the city and into the maze of alleyways stretching through the souk. But they weren't safe yet. Judging from the noise of crashing stalls, loud shouting, and pounding footsteps, the entire Turkish army was hard on their heels. As long as Dariq lived, he would always present a threat to the sultanate. Nothing short of Dariq's death would satisfy Ibrahim.

As they raced through the sleeping city, Dariq struggled back to consciousness. "Put me down!" he roared.

Mustafa set him on his feet.

"What have you done?"

"Saved your life, master. We must hurry; the janizaries are not far behind."

Realizing that he had no choice now but to flee, Dariq led his loyal followers to the docks. His ship, *Sultana*, was due to sail with the midnight tide. Dariq had no idea whether the midnight hour had come and gone, so he prayed that his ship had not yet left. Without the *Sultana*, he and his men would never live to see the light of day.

When they reached the docks, Dariq let out a shout of joy. The *Sultana* was still docked, though frantic preparations were under way for imminent departure. Dariq made a dash for the long stone pier as the gangplank was being raised. He shouted until someone aboard the ship heard him. He ordered the gangplank to be lowered. Nothing happened until the captain appeared at the railing.

"Who is there?" the captain asked in a booming voice.

"Prince Dariq. Lower the gangplank. My men and I wish to come aboard. And hurry. My brother's janizaries are hard on our heels."

The gangplank was lowered immediately; Dariq and his men scrambled aboard. "Pull up the gangplank! Quickly," Dariq ordered.

The anchor was raised, and the sails filled with wind as the janizaries charged down the pier. Dariq took the wheel, easing the *Sultana* away from the pier and into the Sea of Marmara. Beyond the Bosporos Straits and the Aegean Sea, a new life awaited him.

Chapter One

Two Years Later—Somewhere in the Mediterranean Sea

His legs balanced against the motion of the ship, Prince Dariq stood on the deck of his frigate, renamed the *Revenge* after his escape from Istanbul, staring at the endless blue sea stretched out before him. Mustafa, his right-hand man and first mate, stood at his side.

The weather was perfect; a brisk breeze filled the sails, sending the *Revenge* scudding across the water. The frigate extended two decks high and was well equipped with forty cannon, employed for a good cause.

The ship rode high in the water, hunting prey and riches to fill her hold. Turkish ships were particularly vulnerable to Dariq's Brotherhood of pirates.

Though Dariq had fled Istanbul to escape certain death, he had managed to slip in and out of the city several times during the past two years to contact friends loyal to him. He had risked his life more than once to inquire about his mother's welfare and to learn what Ibrahim was up to, but he had also used his clandestine trips into Istanbul to bring his men's loved ones out of the city to their stronghold on the island of Lipsi, forty miles off the southern coast of Turkey.

"Perhaps the *Ottoman* never left Algiers," Mustafa suggested. "We have seen no sign of the ship since learning that a treasure of great value was being transported to Istanbul aboard it. Perhaps your information was false."

"Nay," Dariq said. "Kamel has never given his cousin Hassan wrong information. The ship will follow the same course as all Ibrahim's ships sailing from Algeria. We will find it, and when we do, we will steal Ibrahim's treasure." He thrust his fist in the air to emphasize his words. "By Allah, Ibrahim will not have it!"

Dariq's nostrils flared. He looked like a demon bent on mayhem. Thick black hair, tousled into curls by the damp sea air, fell over his forehead. His jutting jaw was strong and dark with the beginning of a beard, and every visible muscle in his face and neck was pulled taut. His tense body and well-developed form were hardened by hard labor. Nothing about Prince Dariq looked soft.

Dariq wasn't the same man he had been two years before. The murder of his brothers had turned him into a vengeful man with dark depths, a man on a mission to avenge those cruel deaths. A man who refused to rest until his innocent brothers had been avenged and Ibrahim made to suffer.

"Hassan said the treasure Ibrahim expects is extremely valuable," Mustafa mused.

Dariq nodded. "Valuable enough, I hope, for its loss to annoy Ibrahim. Unfortunately, Hassan could tell me nothing more about the treasure, for Kamel hadn't enlightened him. I had to leave the city before receiving detailed information from Kamel; there were janizaries everywhere. Hassan said that Ibrahim is aware that I enter the city incognito and wants to put an end to it." He laughed—a bitter sound that held a world of hatred. "Ibrahim fears me, and with good reason."

"The men are eager for a good fight, Prince," Mustafa said, gesturing to the motley crew of pirates who had followed Dariq from Istanbul into the Brotherhood.

"So am I," Dariq replied. "We fight now to survive, to rob Ibrahim of his riches, and to protect our loved ones."

"They would gladly die for you, Prince. You brought their wives and families to Lipsi and created a safe haven for them."

"They followed me into exile when all seemed lost," Dariq replied. " 'Twas the least I could do."

Dariq tensed as an expression of watchful anticipation slid over his handsome features. "Hand me the glass, Mustafa."

Mustafa placed the spyglass in Dariq's hand. Dariq held it to his eye, adjusting it until an object came into view.

"There she is!" Dariq shouted gleefully. "The *Ottoman*. Bring the *Revenge* about, Mustafa. We will lay in wait for her."

Mustafa took the wheel and brought the ship about. After a shouted order from Dariq, the deck erupted with activity. As the *Ottoman* approached, the *Revenge's* guns were being primed and readied for battle and weapons distributed to eager pirates.

"She's using evasive action," Dariq bit out. "She'll never outrun us. Pile on the canvas!"

Wind whipped into the sails, sending the *Revenge* crashing through the waves at top speed. It didn't take long for the ship to overtake the slower, clumsier *Ottoman*.

Once they were in range, Dariq shouted, "Bring her about and fire a warning shot across the *Ottoman's* bow!"

Dariq's crewmen responded smoothly, having made

similar attacks many times in the past two years. Piracy was their game and they played it well.

The first volley of shots sailed over the *Ottoman's* bow, but she didn't stop. She tacked to the left, but it soon became apparent that she couldn't escape. The *Revenge* was relentless in its pursuit.

"Fire the port cannons!" Excitement bit deep into Dariq's gut. The mysterious treasure would never reach Istanbul or Ibrahim if he had his way.

A volley of shots from the port side snapped the *Ottoman's* mizzenmast. Utter chaos reigned aboard the beleaguered ship. Dariq could see crewmen scurrying about to repair the damage done by the *Revenge's* guns.

"Bring her about, Mustafa," Dariq ordered, "then give the wheel over to Omar. Break out the grappling hooks and ready the boarding planks. I want them in place the moment we come abreast."

Mustafa hurried off to do Dariq's bidding while Dariq continued to watch the drama taking place aboard the *Ottoman*. He was acquainted with Captain Juad, the master of the *Ottoman*, and hoped he would surrender his ship and give up the treasure without loss of life.

The *Ottoman* made a half-hearted attempt to fire its starboard cannon. The shot went wide, and then the battle was over. The pirates secured the grappling hooks, bringing the two ships together. Dariq was the first to leap atop the boarding plank, feet wide apart and sword at the ready. Mustafa was close behind him, towering over Dariq, while pirates from the *Revenge* grabbed lines to swing aboard the *Ottoman*, eager to share in the plunder.

"Surrender!" Dariq shouted as he jumped down upon the rolling deck of the *Ottoman*.

Captain Juad raced across the deck toward him. "I want bloodshed no more than you do, Prince Dariq."

None of the Turkish sailors seemed eager to meet the Pirate Prince in armed combat, and Captain Juad was wise enough to realize his crewmen would fight a losing battle against cutthroat pirates, who lived and fought for the promise of riches.

Dariq watched through narrowed lids as Juad seemed to wage a battle with himself. Dariq knew the captain to be brave and honorable, and that he valued the life of his men, but Dariq wondered if the good captain valued the treasure he carried more than his own life.

"Do you promise to spare my men?" Juad asked. "I know what it is to have my decks run slippery with blood."

"Surrender your ship and your treasure and you may leave with your lives intact."

Juad eyed the pirates lined up behind Mustafa with distrust. "Will your men obey you?"

Dariq threw back his head and laughed. "My pirates always obey me. All they care about is the treasure you carry."

Juad's heavy dark brows shot up. "What do you know about the treasure, Prince Dariq?"

While appearing to be relaxed, Dariq was drawn taut as a bowstring. "Not a great deal, except that its arrival is eagerly awaited by Ibrahim. He will not have it, however, for I shall claim it."

"Come to my cabin," Juad invited. "We should speak in private about the treasure."

"Do you surrender all to me?"

Juad laughed. "Oh, aye, the treasure is yours, such as it is. I wish you joy of it."

Captain Juad snapped out curt orders to his men, informing them that he was surrendering the ship and its treasure to Prince Dariq. Their reaction was not what

Dariq had expected. Some men laughed outright, while others sent him sly smiles. Though there were a few grumbles, most seemed relieved to be rid of the sultan's treasure.

"Secure the ship," Dariq told Mustafa. The knot of men parted as Dariq followed the captain to his cabin. Some of the *Ottoman's* sailors clapped him on the back, while others wished him good luck. A few even asked to join the Brotherhood.

"Down with Ibrahim the murderer!" a Turkish sailor shouted, followed by a chorus of ayes.

Dariq entered the captain's cabin and closed the door behind him.

"Sit down, Prince," Juad invited. "'Tis a long time since we have spoken." He sighed. "The days of the great Murad's rule are long past. I must answer to Ibrahim now, whether I like it or not."

Dariq took the seat Juad offered. "I hoped you would surrender, Juad. I have naught against you personally and would spare your life for my father's sake, for he loved you well."

"I am glad to hear that, Prince. I but do Ibrahim's bidding. I consider myself lucky to have avoided you on the high seas thus far. Ibrahim is a murderer; few of his subjects hold him in high regard. He is nothing like his father. He even tried to convince the Grand Vizier that you had a hand in killing your brothers. Selim did not believe him. You are admired by all for your courage and perseverance against your brother's evil machinations."

"Thank you for confiding that to me, Juad." He pushed himself out of his chair. "All the same, I still must relieve you of your cargo. What is it? Gold? Silver? Aye, tell me what my brother is so eager to possess."

Juad straightened his turban and cleared his throat. "The treasure is not what you think, Prince."

Dariq's face settled into harsh lines. "Describe the treasure to me."

"Better yet, I will show you. Come, my friend. Follow me and you shall see for yourself the treasure Sultan Ibrahim is eagerly awaiting."

"I know how greedy Ibrahim can be when he wants something," Dariq said, following Juad out the door, "so I'm quite anxious to see his treasure. Depriving Ibrahim of something he desires is my sole purpose in life. 'Tis the reason I turned to piracy."

Juad sighed and shook his head. A frisson of disquiet slid down Dariq's spine. Why was Juad being so evasive? Perhaps there *was* no treasure and he had been deliberately misled.

He stopped abruptly and hauled Juad around to face him. "Something is wrong, Juad. Is the treasure aboard another ship?"

Juad shrugged. "There is treasure and there is treasure. You must judge its worth by your own standards."

Dariq's scowl deepened. He was beginning to worry now. Captain Juad was talking in riddles. A treasure was a treasure no matter what a man's standards. Dariq was hoping to take something from Ibrahim that he valued, something he desired, but Juad's attitude was making him intensely uneasy.

Dariq followed Captain Juad down a narrow companionway. He expected to be taken to the hold, where cargo is usually stored, but obviously this treasure was too valuable to be left in damp quarters. That thought raised his spirits a bit but didn't entirely ease his misgivings.

Juad stopped before a door at the end of the companionway. Dariq's dark brows rose when he saw a burly sailor standing guard. "You keep Ibrahim's treasure here, under guard?"

"Aye. You will see why in a moment."

Juad dismissed the guard and opened the door. "Behold the sultan's treasure, Prince Dariq. Make of it what you will for it now belongs to you. Truthfully, I am glad to be done with it. It has caused me a great deal of trouble."

Somewhat wary, Dariq stepped inside. He ducked just in time to avoid a missile that sailed past his head and crashed to the deck.

Then, with shock and a great deal of dismay, he saw her.

Ibrahim's treasure.

A woman.

Willow Foxburn glared at the fierce pirate who had barged into the cabin, ready to defend herself should the need arise. He appeared startled to see her, his ferocious glower causing her to gulp back a cry. He had dangerous eyes, she thought. Mesmerizing gray eyes. They locked with hers and held, but she didn't look away.

Did he speak English? she wondered.

He said nothing, merely fixed her with that intense silver gaze. She held her breath, suddenly aware that this man presented a new king of danger. Though the man was dressed as a Turk, there was something about him that set him apart from Captain Juad's sailors.

He was handsome. Impossibly so. Terrifyingly so. Clearly, he was Turkish, but his silver-gray eyes softened his features and suggested he was not all Turk. She had never seen a man quite like him before.

"Who are you?" she asked, refusing to back away from his intimidating presence. "I heard the sound of cannon. Is the *Ottoman* under attack? Are you a pirate?"

She gave a little start as his glittering gaze swept over her, his curiosity as obvious as hers.

"Do you speak English?" Willow asked.

The responsive flicker in his silver eyes might have been surprise, but his expression remained unreadable.

Dariq was too shocked to speak. It had never crossed his mind that Ibrahim's treasure could be a woman. Not just any woman, but a woman with hair of pure gold, eyes as green as emeralds, skin like silk and cheeks tinted with roses. His mind failed to accept what his eyes beheld. Dariq had always known that Ibrahim preferred golden-haired women but had yet to find such a woman . . . until now. The woman standing before him now was likely to satisfy all his brother's desires.

And with good reason. She would satisfy a stone if it had a cock. Thinking back, Dariq couldn't recall one golden-haired concubine in the harem. Even his mother had dark hair, and she was English. It was from Saliha Sultana that he had inherited his silver-gray eyes.

Dariq's gaze slid over the young woman, assessing her worth as only a connoisseur of beautiful females could. She wore a short vest and sheer skirts that concealed little of her charms. An aba, the robe meant to hide her curvaceous body from the eyes of the world, lay across the bed.

Dariq looked his fill, memorizing every lush line of her lithe form, from the short veil that fell over her head and shoulders to the soft slippers on her dainty feet.

"Who is she?" Dariq asked Captain Juad, who hovered behind him. He could tell from the woman's puzzled expression that she could not speak his language.

"She is Lady Willow Foxburn, an Englishwoman. Quite a beauty, is she not?"

"How did she get here?"

"Mehmed the slave master had the good fortune to buy her from Barbary pirates who had attacked her ship. The ship was sailing from Marseilles to England when it was stopped and boarded. The woman was taken to Algiers and sold to Mehmed. Apparently, the slave master realized she matched the description of a woman Ibrahim had been searching for, and offered her to him at a hefty price.

"Though her price was exorbitant, Ibrahim paid it gladly and sent me to fetch her," Juad continued. He shot Willow a stern look. "She has been a problem from the moment she came aboard. Ibrahim won't make a pet of this one. She has a fiery temper."

"I know you are talking about me. What are you saying?" Willow demanded impatiently. "Do either of you know what happened to my maid?"

Dariq glanced at Juad. Juad shrugged and said, "Mehmed sold the maid to a minor pasha. Felah is old and known for his gentle ways. The maid will not suffer."

"Leave us," Dariq ordered. "I wish to speak to the woman alone."

"You speak her language?"

"Aye. My mother is English and taught me her language. She was Murad's true and only wife. He married her in a Christian ceremony. I speak both languages fluently and have knowledge of her Christian God as well as Allah.

"Ibrahim was born to Father's favorite concubine before he wed Mother," Dariq continued. "My six half-brothers are younger, products of Father's liaisons with other concubines. Despite his Christian marriage, Father followed the dictates of Islam."

"Aye, I remember the story now. Your mother's father

was sent to Istanbul on a diplomatic mission; he brought his wife and daughter. Murad fell in love with your mother at first sight and asked for her hand."

"Mother must have shared his feelings, for she begged her parents for permission to wed Murad. My grandfather consented to the marriage only when Murad agreed to let Saliha Sultana practice her Christian faith for as long as she lived.

"Mother loved my father," Dariq murmured. "His death was a blow to us." His expression hardened. "Ibrahim will not have this woman without paying a price."

Jurad darted a glance at Willow. "Be careful with this one. She cannot be trusted. When you are finished here, I wish to know what your intentions are for my ship and men."

The door shut firmly behind Juad. Arms crossed over his massive chest, Dariq turned his attention to the woman.

"I do not understand your barbaric language," Willow spat. "What is going to happen to me? Who are you? What happened to my maid? Where are my clothes? What I'm wearing is indecent. Someone will pay for this indignity when my papa hears of it."

"I am Prince Dariq. Your maid was purchased by an elderly pasha known for his gentleness."

Willow nearly collapsed with relief. "Thank God you speak English. Did Papa send you to rescue me?"

Dariq laughed, the sound rich and deep. "Did no one tell you that you were purchased by a Turkish sultan?"

"The slave master spoke a smattering of French. He said a Sultan Ibrahim purchased me for his harem."

"I am Dariq, the pirate prince. Ibrahim is my brother."

She drew back in horror. "Pirate! This nightmare goes from bad to worse . . . a horrible dream that won't end. I heard cannon fire. Have you captured the ship? If you take me to England, my father will reward you. He is a marquis with high connections."

Dariq adroitly changed the subject. He would most definitely not take her to England. "Captain Juad said your name is Willow. Willow is a tree, is it not? Or is my English faulty?"

"Your English is perfect, and you know it. Willow also means freedom. I want to be free."

"I cannot free you. You are now my prisoner."

"Prisoner! Never say you want me for *your* harem!"

"The idea has merit, but 'tis not what I want from you."

"Then why . . ."

" 'Tis a long story. Suffice it to say, my brother and I are at odds. I misunderstood the nature of the valuable treasure he was expecting. It seems, lady, you are the treasure I set out to steal from Ibrahim. Although you are not what I expected, you will do."

"What role am I to play in your games with your brother?"

Dariq's silver eyes glittered as it suddenly occurred to him how he could make use of Willow. "I have dedicated my life to punishing Ibrahim for past sins. You, lady, will help me accomplish that goal. I shall trade you to Ibrahim for someone dear to me."

Dariq thought of his mother, whom he hadn't seen in two years. Though offers had been made for his mother's release, Ibrahim had refused to let her go. The last message to reach Dariq from the seraglio had made him desperate to free his mother from Ibrahim's control. His brother had threatened to kill Saliha Sultana if Dariq didn't surrender. Dariq had hoped to trade Ibrahim's treasure for his mother's release without surrendering himself. Perhaps that plan would still work.

Willow regarded Dariq with disbelief. "What makes you think your brother will agree to a trade? You give me too much significance, pirate. A woman's life is of little value in your culture. I am no good to you. Return me to England."

"You are wrong, lady. Ibrahim lusts after you even without having seen you. I will use his lust to my advantage."

"Don't expect me to cooperate," Willow spat. "I've been held captive, probed, prodded, humiliated beyond endurance, dressed indecently and sold like a prize mare to the highest bidder." She stamped her foot. "I demand that you take me home!"

Dariq grinned. "You have been wrongly named, Willow. A willow tree bends in the wind, but I doubt you will ever bend. Come, it is time to leave."

"Leave? Where are you taking me?"

"To my ship. Captain Juad will carry my terms for your ransom to the sultan. Put on your aba. Your beauty must be covered."

Willow harrumphed. "Why? My beauty seems to have little effect on you."

Dariq didn't dare tell her how wrong she was. He went hard just looking at her. " 'Tis the custom," he said gruffly. "Women must remain hidden from everyone except their immediate family members. The robe will protect you from unwanted male attention."

Grumbling, Willow pulled on the robe. Dariq reached out to fasten the piece of cloth that would cover all her face but for her incredible green eyes. Their gazes met. Dariq's hand froze, then slid onto her cheek. "So soft," he murmured. "I wonder . . . Are your lips as soft as your skin?"

"Don't touch me!" Willow hissed, neatly avoiding him as he bent to taste her lips.

Dariq stiffened, his voice devoid of emotion. "You are right, of course. Ibrahim expects a virgin. If I take you, you are worthless to me." He searched her face. "You *are* untouched, are you not?"

Willow's breath caught in her throat. "I believe that has already been proven. The slave master had me examined before he offered me to the sultan." She shuddered. "It was not a pleasant experience."

Dariq's face remained carefully blank. Compassion had no place in his profession. Trying not to think about Ibrahim taking Willow's virginity, Dariq fastened her veil and ushered her out the door.

She stepped out onto the deck and froze. "Your men are a ferocious lot, I do not like them."

Dariq supposed his crew of pirates did indeed appear a savage lot to a highborn English lady. Most were bearded and wore turbans upon their heads. They carried scimitars and an assortment of weapons; their clothing was a mixture of scruffy Arab and Western wear.

"They will not harm you," Dariq informed her.

Captain Juad joined Dariq and Willow. "I have spoken with my men and they wish to join the Brotherhood. Are you agreeable?"

"That depends," Dariq replied. "I could use another ship in my small fleet. The more ships and men under my control, the better able I am to harass Ibrahim's merchantmen. Are your crewmen's wishes also your own?"

"You and I both know what Ibrahim will do to me when he learns I lost his treasure. He will order my death without a moment's remorse. I prefer life, Prince."

"I had hoped you would carry my ransom terms to Ibrahim, but I will contact him through the usual channels. Your ship will be renamed and sail under my flag. You will be answerable to me in all matters. You can stop any ship you please on the high seas and divide the plunder among your men, minus my twenty percent, of course. But your main purpose will be to attack and plunder ships bearing the Turkish flag. Do you accept my terms?"

"Aye, I accept," Juad replied.

"Good. I will arrange to have your wives, children, and concubines brought out of Turkey to my stronghold on Lipsi."

"Lipsi. A good choice for a stronghold," Juad allowed, "as long as the Greeks do not interfere. The island belongs to them, you know."

"Aye, but Lipsi and its handful of inhabitants have long been ignored by Greece. And Turkey has little interest in it either. I intend to take Lady Willow to Lipsi immediately. There is a deep-water bay and pier on the south shore where we can anchor our ships. Your ship will make five in my fleet. How long will it take to repair your ship?"

Captain Juad surveyed the damage done by the *Revenge*. "Not long. A few days at most. I will inform my men of your decision to accept us into the Brotherhood." So saying, he left Juad to confer with his own men.

"What was that about?" Willow asked.

"You should make an effort to learn Turkish," Dariq advised. "It will be to your advantage once you reside inside the harem."

Willow bristled. "I will *not* become a sex slave to a sultan! Papa will find me and bring me home. I have no desire to learn your heathenish language."

A muscle clenched in Dariq's jaw. The Lady Willow would have to learn to watch her tongue if she hoped to live to a ripe old age. Once she was safely on Lipsi, he would teach her about palace intrigue, and what she must do in order to survive. That was the best he could do before sending her to his brother. It wasn't that he wished her ill; he merely needed something to trade for his mother. Ibrahim wanted this blond goddess, and Dariq wanted his mother out of harm's way.

Sweeping Willow into his strong arms, Dariq strode across the deck, leaped onto the boarding plank and carried her to the *Revenge*.

Dariq set Willow on her feet and then promptly ignored her, his attention now on his ship and men, all of whom had followed him to the *Revenge*.

"Release the grappling hooks!" Dariq shouted. "Bring in the boarding planks and unfurl the sails! Helmsman, set the course for Lipsi."

Chapter Two

Dariq stomped back and forth, barking orders, while his men scurried about Willow, paying her scant heed. Once the *Revenge* was under way, Mustafa turned to confront Dariq, his face dark with fury.

"I cannot believe you took a woman off the ship and left the treasure behind. Of what worth is a woman when 'tis valuables we sought? What happened to the treasure? Was Kamel's information false?"

Dariq gestured in Willow's direction. "I brought the treasure aboard the *Revenge*. *She* is the treasure. Her name is Willow. She claims her father in an English marquis."

Mustafa's black eyes widened with disbelief. "Surely you jest, my lord. What is so special about this woman?"

"Ibrahim happens to desire this particular Englishwoman and parted with a great deal of gold to purchase her for his harem."

Mustafa sent Willow a fierce scowl, then recoiled in shock when she met his gaze without flinching. Few men, let alone women, had the courage to defy Mustafa.

"Tell me what makes this woman special so I can better understand Ibrahim's obsession with her," Mustafa said.

Dariq hesitated a moment to collect his thoughts. A quick glance into Willow's defiant green eyes reminded him of everything he had found desirable about her. He grew breathless as he searched for words to describe her to Mustafa.

"She is a jewel among women, brighter than the moon and stars. Her hair shines like newly minted gold, and her skin is as smooth and iridescent as an exquisite pearl. Her lips are lush and pink, designed expressly for kissing . . . and more erotic purposes."

Dariq felt his body swell, felt his manhood rise, and shifted uncomfortably. He could not deny the fact that he wanted the English slave in his bed.

"Go on," Mustafa said eagerly.

"Her body is perfection, her skin as smooth as silk, and her breasts large enough to fill my hands without over-flowing them."

Dariq wished he could have seen her nipples, but they hadn't been visible beneath her brief vest. "She is indeed a treasure," he admitted. "Ibrahim can enjoy her at his leisure, after he releases my mother."

Mustafa rubbed his scruffy beard. "Ibrahim won't want her after you've had her."

"I do not intend to touch her," Dariq said with a hint of regret. "I will spare her maidenhead for my mother's sake."

Mustafa grinned, and then broke out into a belly laugh. "We shall see, Prince, we shall see." He wiped his mirthful tears away with the back of a very large hand. "Why didn't you sink the *Ottoman?* Or at the very least put a skeleton crew aboard to repair her mizzenmast and sail her to our home port? A ship of her quality would enhance our fleet."

"Captain Juad and his crew asked to join the Brotherhood. He will sail the *Ottoman* to Lipsi after temporary repairs are made."

"Why would he do that when he has a secure place in Ibrahim's fleet?"

"Think about it, my friend. Ibrahim is a cruel man. If the *Ottoman* should return without the woman, Ibrahim would feel betrayed and have Juad and his crewmen executed. Juad is a not a stupid man. He prefers life to death, and the Brotherhood offers him and his men a safe haven."

"You had best confine the woman to her cabin if she is as beautiful as you say," Mustafa warned.

"The lady is not easily controlled," Dariq admitted. "Perhaps I should place her in your keeping."

His face a mask of horror, Mustafa backed away. "Nay, my prince, she is your responsibility. I am sure you can protect her better than I. How will you let Ibrahim know that you have the woman and wish to trade her for Saliha Sultana?"

"Through the usual channels. The news will reach Kamel, and he will see that it reaches Ibrahim. I cannot risk showing myself in Istanbul at this time, and your great height is far too recognizable, so I will ask Ahmed to sail to the secret cove near Istanbul. With the help of friends, he can secure a horse and ride to the city to relay my message to Hassan."

"The logistics of the trade will be difficult and the negotiations lengthy," Mustafa warned. "If Ibrahim agrees, how will the exchange be arranged?"

"I will demand that the exchange take place on the high seas, just my ship and Ibrahim's," Dariq mused.

"Ibrahim is no fool. He will attempt to lure me to Istanbul where he can kill me."

"You have been to Istanbul many times in the past two years," Mustafa reminded him.

"Aye, but well disguised, if you recall. I will have a few weeks to refine my plan." He glanced at Willow. "See to the ship while I escort Lady Willow to my cabin."

Mustafa's dark brows shot upward. "Your cabin, Prince? Is that wise?"

"Aye. Willow is my guest and deserves the best my ship has to offer. I will find quarters elsewhere."

"As you wish, master," Mustafa said, bowing deeply.

As she sweltered beneath the suffocating black aba, Willow's temper rose with her body temperature. She hadn't understood a word spoken by the prince or his underling. She knew that at one point they had been discussing her and wondered if they had already settled her fate.

Did the prince mean her harm? He looked so fierce that she wanted to shrink away from him when he turned to study her through those startling silver eyes. But she held her ground, her own green gaze unwavering.

"I will show you to your cabin," Dariq said.

"Where is your ship taking me?"

"To my stronghold on the island of Lipsi. You will not be harmed during the weeks or months it will take to work out the details of the trade."

"With whom am I being traded?"

" 'Tis none of your concern," Dariq said sharply.

Willow didn't need to be told that she was being exchanged for Dariq's wife or a favorite concubine; it was obvious.

"Follow me," Dariq said crisply.

When Willow merely stared at him, Dariq grasped her

26

elbow and ushered her toward a cabin nestled beneath the quarterdeck. He opened the door, hauled her inside and closed the door behind them.

Familiar with ships, Willow knew immediately that the luxurious cabin belonged to the pirate prince, but she asked anyway. "Whose cabin is this?"

"Mine."

Willow stiffened. "Where will *you* sleep?"

"In a small sleeping chamber reached through that door," Dariq said, pointing to a narrow panel. " 'Tis normally occupied by my cabin boy, but he can sleep elsewhere."

Willow had no reason to trust Dariq, yet he was all she had to protect her from his fellow pirates.

"You can take off your aba while inside this cabin," Dariq instructed.

With a sigh of relief, Willow whipped off the aba and tossed it aside. "Am I confined to this cabin? Or may I walk out on deck?"

Several speechless minutes passed as Dariq's appreciative gaze roamed over Willow's thinly clad body. If it weren't for his need to deliver her untouched to Ibrahim, he would put all his considerable skills to seducing her.

"This cabin is the only place you will be safe," Dariq warned.

"Am I safe from you?" Willow challenged. "I trust you no more than I do your comrades."

"A wise move," Dariq said, nodding. "A woman as lovely as you should trust no man with her virtue. Are you aware of your great beauty, my lady? Your lush curves would tempt a saint. Your hair is pure sunshine, and your body is flawless."

His words stunned Willow. She had heard pretty words from London dandies, but they were unexpected from this fierce pirate. Aware of her near nudity, she reached for her aba and held it before her. "What do you know of saints, my lord prince? You are a heathen."

"My mother is English," Dariq revealed, "and a Christian."

That bit of information stunned Willow, but not for long. "Then you must know how wrong it is to imprison women in a harem! It is against God's teachings."

"But not against Allah's. If you please Ibrahim, you will be petted and pampered and lavished with gifts. For your own well-being, I suggest you try to please him."

Lips clenched tightly together, Willow gave a stubborn shake of her head. "I will *not* become your brother's plaything. Nor will I accept such a fate without a fight."

Dariq pinned her with his hard gaze. "You have no choice, my lady. If I hadn't interfered, you would still be Ibrahim's newest concubine. Though you have gained a short reprieve, the ultimate outcome will be the same."

"My father—"

"Your father can do naught. You are already lost to him. Why did he allow you to travel alone in dangerous waters?"

"I wasn't alone. My maid accompanied me. I was visiting my mother in Marseilles. She and Father have lived apart for a number of years, and I chose to remain with father in England. I have visited Mama every year without mishap. My father owns the ship upon which I travel; this is the first time the *Fairwind* has encountered pirates."

"There is always the first time," Dariq said, "as you just recently learned. Resign yourself, my lady. You'll never see your father or England again."

Rage seethed through Willow. "All is not lost. The *Fairwind* was allowed to proceed after I was taken off the ship. Papa will search for me, even to the ends of the earth."

The thought of being hidden behind harem walls the rest of her life was more than Willow could bear. Throwing caution to the wind, she flung herself at Dariq, pummeling his chest with clenched fists.

"I won't listen to you! I cannot! Let me go, damn you! Take me to England, or Marseilles, if England is too far. What kind of demon would condemn a woman to a life of sexual abuse?"

Grasping her wrists, Dariq pulled her arms behind her back. She arched against him, bringing her body flush against his. He felt her nipples tauten against his chest and went instantly hard. He groaned. He had been at sea too long. He needed to get back to Lipsi and Safiye.

With Willow in his arms, he couldn't even recall what Safiye looked like, except that her hair was black, not gold, and her eyes did not glow like precious emeralds. His body ached for Willow, and he usually took what he wanted. Slowly he backed her up against the oversized bed, falling with her upon it when her knees hit the edge and buckled beneath her.

Her eyes widened; she opened her mouth to scream. Too far gone in lust, Dariq forgot everything but the soft lips so close to his and the sweet breath fanning his cheek. The scream never left Willow's throat as his mouth covered hers. Even the gurgling in her throat ceased when Dariq deepened the kiss, filling her mouth with his tongue.

Willow stilled beneath him. She had been kissed before, but never like this. She whimpered as his tongue thrust deep inside her mouth, tasting, teasing. She felt the pull of something strange and titillating reach down into the most private part of her body. She shouldn't feel like this with a murderous pirate. She couldn't even guess at the number of people he had hurt in the name of piracy.

Willow didn't realize Dariq had released her hands until she felt his fingers stroking her breast. Dear God, he was going to ravish her!

Struggling free of his mouth, she cried, "You said you wouldn't harm me."

Dariq blinked. What in the name of Allah was he doing? The woman had bewitched him. No matter how badly he wanted her, he must not touch her. If he took her virginity, Ibrahim would reject her. His bargaining power would be lost, and with it his mother or his own life.

Dariq lurched from the bed and glared down at her, stunned by his loss of control. The woman was dangerous. The sooner he placed her in Ibrahim's keeping, the better.

"That will not happen again, lady. You will cease using your wiles on me."

Willow rolled to her feet. "You are mad if you think I wanted you to . . . to attack me. All I want from you is my freedom."

"What you ask is impossible. Resign yourself to the inevitable. You will become Ibrahim's concubine as soon as I can get rid of you." So saying, Dariq turned and strode from the cabin.

Willow sank down upon the bed, shaking from her horrified reaction to Dariq's words. She would never resign herself to becoming a sex slave to a heathen Turk.

She touched her lips. They felt swollen; so did her breast where Dariq had touched it. The pirate was the devil incarnate, and far too handsome for her peace of mind. Was he really a prince? It made no sense. Why would a prince become a pirate?

Most likely he was a fraud. She recalled the dark intensity of his gaze while he'd held her pinned to the bed. His silver eyes glittered with what she believed was sexual hunger. She had barely escaped his lust this time. Would there be a next time?

A shudder passed through her. Would she rather be ravished by the devil she knew or the devil she didn't know? She would prefer not to be ravished at all. But the way her life was going, her wishes would probably be ignored. What truly frightened her was the possibility of never seeing her parents again.

A tear slid from the corner of her eye, tunneling down her cheek. She dashed it away with the back of her hand. Her father had always said she was stubborn and willful, and she supposed she was, but she had never considered herself particularly brave. Bravery, she decided, was something she had to find within herself, and very, very soon. And she would, she vowed. She would need a great deal of courage if she was ever to find her way out of this horrible situation.

"Is the woman settled in your quarters?" Mustafa asked when Dariq reappeared on the deck. "You were gone a long time."

"The woman is troublesome," Dariq grumbled.

"Ah," Mustafa said, as if further explanation was unnecessary.

"Have you determined if she is still virginal?"

"If you're asking whether I took her maidenhead, no, I did not, though it was a struggle not to. Her beauty is luminous, her body lush and ripe. I would have ravished her had I not come to my senses in time. Ibrahim will be pleased with her."

Mustafa chuckled. "I'm surprised you were able to control yourself, master. It has been a long time since either of us tasted a woman's sweet flesh. 'Tis good we are returning to Lipsi. Where will you keep Ibrahim's woman?"

Ibrahim's woman. Somehow the words bothered Dariq. "Willow will reside in my harem with Safiye. She will be safe there until she is placed in Ibrahim's keeping."

"Who is going to keep her safe from you, my lord prince? Or from Safiye, for that matter. Your concubine will not welcome another woman to the harem. She has had you to herself too long."

"Do not imagine trouble where none exists," Dariq groused. "Safiye will abide by my wishes once she realizes I have no sexual interest in Willow."

"As you say," Mustafa said disbelievingly.

Willow paced the cabin, searching for a weapon she could use to defend herself. The washbowl and pitcher offered possibilities, as did a heavy globe and letter opener sitting on the desk. She hoped there would be no need for violence, but she didn't trust the pirate prince. While his lips said one thing, his wicked silver eyes promised another.

Though her situation seemed hopeless, she hadn't given up. If Dariq could be believed, she had several weeks to change his mind about sending her to the sultan.

Willow paced to the large set of windows overlooking the stern of the ship and gazed at the gentle waves slapping against the hull. Her thoughts traveled backward to Marseilles, remembering the wonderful weeks she had spent with her mother, and how she looked forward to returning home to her father and friends in London. Her cozy world had shattered when a vile pirate had captured her ship and taken her and her maid prisoner.

She thanked God that they hadn't been hurt physically. She and Kitty had hovered together in the small cabin they had been given until they were dragged out and sold to a slave master in Algiers. It still hurt that she and Kitty had been separated soon afterward. Though Willow had learned her fate early on, she hadn't known what had happened to Kitty, until Dariq told her.

Willow knew nothing about the island of Lipsi. In fact, she'd never heard of it. But one thing she did know. If there was a way to escape, she would find it.

That night a young cabin boy brought Willow's dinner on a tray. When she attempted to speak to him, he lowered his eyes and quickly departed. It was obvious he neither understood nor spoke English.

Willow picked without appetite at the spicy rice and lamb dish, and then went to bed fully clothed. Though she tried to stay awake and watchful, exhaustion conquered her good intentions. She was sleeping soundly when Dariq entered the cabin.

Dariq walked to the bed and stared down at her. Moonbeams streamed through the stern windows and fell across the bed. He sucked in a quick breath. Willow's hair, gilded by moonlight, was spread across the pillow like a golden cloak. She had shifted in her sleep, exposing her breasts above the low neckline of her vest.

Dariq's thoughts ran amok when he saw two coral nipples peeking out at him. His first inclination was to take a succulent bud into his mouth and suckle it. His head lowered and his mouth opened. Fortunately, his wits returned and he started to back away. Willow chose that moment to open her eyes. She gave a little shriek and scooted up into a sitting position, unaware of the fetching sight she made with her breasts bared.

"What do you want?"

"Naught," Dariq replied. "Go back to sleep."

Dragging his gaze from her rosy nipples, he continued on to the small room where he intended to sleep during the remainder of the voyage.

But sleep eluded Dariq. His body reminded him in the most elemental way that he hadn't had a woman in a very long time, and that a desirable woman lay but steps away . . . a woman he could not touch.

Rolling over on his stomach, Dariq cast aside his lustful thoughts and opened his mind to sleep.

Willow awakened the following morning to brilliant sunshine streaming through the windows. The vessel was rolling gently from side to side, and for a moment she thought she was still aboard her father's ship. Her rude awakening came when she recognized the pirate prince's cabin aboard the *Revenge*.

Willow rose, spied a tray sitting on the table and approached it gingerly. It contained a breakfast of dried fruit, hard biscuits and rice. A water pitcher and pile of clean cloths next to it caught her eye next. She walked over to it, discovered it held hot water and poured some into the bowl. Keeping an eye on the door, she washed herself and cleaned her teeth with a cloth dipped in water. Then she ate sparingly of her breakfast.

Willow wanted to go out on deck to enjoy the sunshine and fresh sea air but hated wearing the suffocating aba. She was embarrassed by the vest and sheer skirts she had been forced to don and wanted something less revealing so she could appear in public without the aba.

Hoping the pirate kept clothing in his cabin, Willow

began a thorough search of his trunk. She was rewarded when she discovered a neat stack of clean clothing. She removed a pair of baggy canvas trousers, a white shirt with long billowing sleeves and a red sash.

Keeping an eye on the door, she removed her revealing clothing and stepped into the trousers, rolling up the legs several times so she wouldn't trip over them. The waist was way too big, but Willow used the sash to cinch it in. The shirt sagged at the shoulders, but she made do by rolling up the sleeves and buttoning the front as far as it would go and tucking the excess material into the waist-band of the trousers.

Willow was so pleased with the results that she decided to get rid of the hated harem outfit and aba for good. Gathering up all her discarded clothing but for the soft slippers she had been wearing, she walked to the window, pushed it open and tossed the bundle into the sea. Her small act of rebellion brought a smile to her lips as she watched the offending cloth sink beneath the water's surface.

Gathering her courage, Willow opened the cabin door and stepped out onto the deck. She remained in the shadow of the quarterdeck a long moment before dragging in a deep breath and boldly walking to the ship's rail.

Willow felt dozens of pairs of eyes upon her in the stunned silence that followed. Then everyone began speaking in their heathen tongue and pointing at her. Comprehension dawned, and her hands flew to her head. She should have covered her hair with one of the knit caps she'd seen in the prince's trunk.

She was aware of his vibrant presence before he reached her. Rage emanated from him like an inferno. "Have you lost your mind?" he said with quiet menace. "I warned you about exposing your beauty, did I not? How am I to control my men when you brazenly display yourself before them?"

"Brazen?" she challenged. "I am covered from neck to toe in cloth. Your clothing is so large on me, I am all but enveloped in it."

His gaze was riveted on her face. "Your face, lady, and your golden hair; to look upon you is to want you. Return to your cabin. If you put on your aba, I will accompany you on a turn around the deck."

Willow's chin lifted. "I tossed the aba overboard."

"You what?"

His clenched fists and harsh features warned Willow that she might have gone too far. "I am English, not Turkish, and Englishwomen are allowed to speak their minds and bare their faces in public."

"Ibrahim will have you beaten if you defy the laws of Islam. Have you never heard of the bastinado?" Willow shook her head. " 'Tis a thick rod, an instrument of torture applied to the soles of the feet. 'Tis unbearably painful; you would not like it. I advise you to curb your tongue and willful nature."

"Why should I do anything you say?"

"It will make your life easier if you understand the rules. Contrary to your belief, I wish you no harm. I would take you as my own concubine if I had not a better use for you."

"I do not want to be anyone's concubine. I have a fiancé at home in England."

"Forget him and your former life. Ibrahim's concubines are expected to devote their lives to pleasing him. Once your fiancé recognizes the fact that you will never return, he will find another woman."

Willow had little doubt that Dariq spoke the truth. Percy, Viscount Dimpleton, needed a wife to bear his heir and would doubtless seek another bride despite her father's objections. But Willow wasn't about to voice her doubts to the arrogant pirate prince.

"Percy and Father will join forces to find me."

"You are delusional, lady." He grasped her arm. "Come, I will escort you back to your cabin. Now that my men have looked upon your face, I must guard you well."

Willow was propelled inside the cabin. Dariq entered behind her and closed the door.

"Am I to be confined to this cabin until we reach your island?"

"Without your aba, I see no alternative. You should not have acted so impulsively."

Willow stared at Dariq, more aware of him as a desirable male than she had ever been with anyone. He was magnificently masculine and imposing in a harsh way. His tanned chest, exposed by the open neck of his shirt, rippled with muscles. His legs, encased in baggy trousers thrust into boots, were as sturdy as oak trees, and his arms beneath the rolled-up sleeves of his shirt were thick and browned by the sun. But it was his face that was most arresting.

Unlike his fellow pirates, he was clean-shaven, his longish black hair tied back with a leather thong. But it was his mesmerizing silver eyes that held her captive. Forcing her eyes from his face, her gaze slid down his body, noting with alarm the assortment of weapons he wore upon his person. A scimitar hung from a wide leather belt at his waist, and thrust into the belt were a dagger and a pistol.

"Keep looking at me like that and you will find yourself on your back beneath me," Dariq warned in a low growl.

Willow looked away, her face tinged with red. "I did not mean . . . that is . . . I was just sizing up my enemy."

A slow grin spread across Dariq's face. The golden-haired houri was staring at him as if he were anything but her enemy, as if she wanted to devour him. Not even Safiye, in their most intimate moments, had looked at him like that. A great shudder passed through him, and he had to forcibly restrain himself from pushing her onto her back and making her his.

"I am not your enemy, little one. Tonight, when my men are sleeping, I will take you for a stroll around the deck. But first you must find something to cover your hair." He opened the door. "Next time you want to do something so foolish, think twice about the consequences."

Dariq left the cabin in a strange mood. No wonder Captain Juad was happy to be rid of Willow. The woman obeyed no one, following only her own dictates. Like his mother, Willow was obstinate and willful. His mother had willingly entered the harem as Murad's wife and never regretted it because she had loved her husband. But Dariq knew that Willow would never love Ibrahim; what woman could love a man capable of killing his own brothers?

"Damn obstinate woman," Dariq muttered.

"The houri has you talking to yourself," Mustafa laughed. "You should have let Captain Juad keep her on his ship since you are both sailing to the same port."

"Aye, I should have," Dariq allowed, "except I felt the need to keep my eye on her."

"I pity Ibrahim."

"Nay, I pity Lady Willow. She will never conform to harem life and will suffer for it."

"That is not your concern, my lord. Nothing matters except your life and Saliha Sultana's safety. Allah placed Lady Willow in your path for a reason. She will make it possible to bargain for your mother's life without sacrific-ing your own."

Dariq sent Mustafa a censorious glare. "Mother should have come with me when I was forcibly carried from the seraglio. You know I would not have left without her had I been conscious."

"Had you been conscious, you would not have gotten out of the seraglio alive. I would not have struck you if your mother had not given me permission."

Dariq sighed. "We've gone over this a thousand times, Mustafa. No matter what you and Mother agreed upon, I would have stayed and fought to avenge my brothers."

"Your mother's life was not in danger; yours was."

Dariq did not reply. His mind was still on the tempting blond houri inside his cabin.

Could he survive weeks upon weeks without touching Willow?

Would she leave his stronghold a virgin?

Those were questions he could not truthfully answer.

Chapter Three

Willow didn't see Dariq again until he returned later that evening to escort her on deck. Recalling his warning about covering her hair, she pulled a knit cap she found in his trunk over her head and stuffed her hair beneath it.

"Good, you are ready," Dariq said when he arrived.

He held the door open. With the eagerness of a child, Willow stepped onto the deck and walked to the rail. Moonlight illuminated her features as she lifted her face to the warm breeze and inhaled deeply of the fresh, salt-scented air.

"The stars are so bright I can almost reach out and touch them," Willow said. "And look at the moon! It's magnificent."

"Aye, magnificent," Dariq replied, his gaze riveted on her face. "Shall we stroll? The exercise will do you good."

He wound her arm through his and proceeded along the deck. When they approached the night watch, the man deliberately looked away. Willow couldn't help wondering at this strange religion that wouldn't allow a man to look upon a woman's face.

"Who is the large man you call Mustafa?" Willow asked curiously.

"Mustafa was the captain of my personal guard. Now he is much more than that. I would not be alive today and master of the *Revenge* if not for him."

"What an odd name for a ship."

"Perhaps, but the name suits my purpose. Seeking revenge for Ibrahim's sins against those I held dear is my soul purpose in life."

"What did Ibrahim do?"

Dariq came to an abrupt halt. His face was stark, as if beset by painful memories he'd rather forget. " 'Tis best you do not know the worst about Ibrahim." He started walking again.

Willow wanted to know what Ibrahim had done to earn Dariq's hatred but realized Dariq would tell her nothing more. Instead, she said, "This is a large ship."

"She carries forty guns," Dariq said proudly. "The *Revenge* is the flagship of my pirate fleet."

"Why did you become a pirate? It seems an unlikely life for a prince."

"My reasons are none of your concern. Suffice it to say, I had little choice. I escaped the seraglio with my life, a few loyal men and little else except for a bag of gold and gems my mother gave me from her own coffers."

"Who threatened your life?"

"You ask too many questions, my curious little houri."

"I'm merely making conversation. Why did you call me a houri? What does it mean?"

Dariq grinned, his white teeth gleaming in the moonlight. "A houri is one of the beautiful maidens who plea-sure men in a Muslim paradise."

Willow's mouth opened and then snapped shut. Stop-ping abruptly, she pivoted to confront Dariq. "Do not call me that again."

Seeing her face upturned and her eyes spitting fire, Dariq thought the word houri had been invented to de-scribe Willow. Curling his fingers around her narrow shoulders, he pulled her against him. His right arm slid around her as his left hand lifted her chin to receive his kiss. Then his mouth clamped down over hers.

She tasted sweet, her natural scent deliciously arous-ing. Through the heavy canvas fabric they both wore he could feel her heat, feel his own arousal respond to it. He was tempted to throw caution to the wind, carry her back to the cabin and teach her the meaning of pleasure.

His hands found her breasts, so perfect against his palms that he could not resist gently kneading the tender mounds. He heard her breath catch and drank deeply from her mouth, his tongue searching out her sweetness. And he tasted heaven.

"A lovely evening, is it not, my lord?" The voice came from behind him.

Mustafa!

Dariq ended the kiss abruptly and pushed Willow away. "What are you doing here, Mustafa?" he asked in their language. "It is not your watch."

"I am admiring the beauty of the night, just as you are." His voice was ripe with censure. "What you are do-ing is not wise, my friend."

"You are right, of course. Perhaps you should escort Lady Willow on her walk. I cannot be trusted."

He turned to Willow. "I am needed elsewhere. Mustafa

43

will accompany you until you are tired and wish to return to your cabin."

"But I cannot talk to him," Willow protested. "I do not speak his language."

" 'Twas exercise you wanted, not conversation," Dariq growled. He walked away and was quickly swallowed by the darkness.

Willow sent Mustafa an uncertain look and continued her stroll. Mustafa trailed behind, his disapproving silence mute testimony to his low opinion of her. After several turns around the deck, she returned to her cabin, no longer as excited about taking the air as she had been.

During the following days, Willow saw little of Prince Dariq. She was asleep when he returned to the cabin at night, and he was gone in the morning before she awakened. Mustafa arrived promptly after dark each day to escort her on deck. Being unable to converse with anyone but Dariq made her life extremely boring. In fact, Willow found it intolerable and decided to complain to Dariq.

One day she caught a glimpse of him at the wheel during her evening walk. When she headed in his direction, Mustafa grunted a warning, but she ignored him. Before he could stop her, she climbed the stairs to the quarterdeck to confront the elusive pirate. He looked up and scowled at her.

"Can't you control her?" Dariq said to Mustafa in Turkish.

"No more than you could," Mustafa answered.

"Very well, I will speak to her."

He turned his gaze to Willow. "You wish to speak with me?"

"I most certainly do. I find my situation intolerable."

Dariq's dark brows lifted. "Whatever do you mean? Are you not well fed? Are you not treated with courtesy?"

"Yes, but—"

"Then you have naught to complain about."

"On the contrary, my lord pirate," Willow sniffed. "I suffer from lack of human contact and lively conversation. No one except you understands or speaks English or French. Am I your prisoner or your guest?"

"My guest, of course. No harm will come to you in my care."

"Then treat me like a guest. Since I have no maid or companion, the least you could do is talk to me."

"You do not know what you are asking," Dariq warned.

She squared her shoulders. "I am asking to be treated like a human being. I have never"—she swallowed the lump forming in her throat—"felt so alone in my entire life."

"You will have plenty of company in Ibrahim's harem. You will be surrounded by women."

"No! I will fight that fate with my dying breath."

Dariq stared at her, his eyes opaque, unreadable. "If everything goes as planned, you *will* become Ibrahim's concubine, perhaps even his wife. However, I understand why you feel isolated. It will be the same in the harem if you cannot understand or speak Turkish. Starting tomorrow, I will endeavor to teach you the language."

Willow felt as if she had won a small victory. Once she learned Turkish, all kinds of possibilities would open to her. If she hoped to escape Ibrahim's harem, being able to speak the language of the land would benefit her greatly.

Willow nodded eagerly. "I shall look forward to learning your language. I bid you good night, pirate."

"You may call me Dariq."

"It pleases me to call you pirate." Head held high, she turned on her heel and made her way back to her cabin with Mustafa following in her wake.

After her nightly exercise on deck, Willow crawled into bed and fell asleep immediately. But she awakened in the middle of the night in a panic. She felt as if the cabin were closing in on her. Nightmares had crowded her dreams. She saw Ibrahim leering at her, his guards holding her down while he had his way with her. Stifling a scream, she jerked upright. She was shaking and sweating profusely. Fear of her fate loomed over her, large and uncertain.

Willow rose stiffly; she needed fresh air to chase away the nightmares. She opened the door and was immediately buffeted by a freshening wind that rocked the ship and filled the sails.

When she started to pull on the knit cap, an errant breeze caught it up and whirled it away. Deciding that darkness would disguise her hair should anyone be about at this time of night, Willow moved cautiously toward the railing. Raising her head, she closed her eyes and sucked in refreshing draughts of salt-laden air.

A half-moon hung high in a star-studded sky, beaming down at her. She spread her legs against the motion of the ship and stared at the heavens, thinking she had never seen an English sky equal to tonight's glittering display.

Willow was so engrossed in gazing at the stars that she failed to hear approaching footsteps. She did, however, sense a presence seconds before a heavy hand gripped her shoulder. Whirling about, she went straight into the arms of a fierce pirate. He said something to her she didn't understand. She shook her head and opened her mouth to scream for help.

She caught the odor of onions and unwashed flesh as

his hand came over her mouth, stifling her cry. He crowded her against the rail, stroking her hair with his free hand. She struggled against the assault, but the pirate was huge and muscular, easily overwhelming her. His hand left her hair, tore open her shirt and covered her breast, kneading hurtfully with thick, blunt fingers.

He spoke again, his voice as rough as the seas had suddenly become. Then she felt his hand work its way beneath the waistband of her trousers. Shaking her head from side to side, she tried to dislodge his hand so she could call for help, but he was too strong and determined.

The ship gave a sudden lurch, and his hand slipped just enough for her to yelp. He growled in her ear and started to drag her into the shadows, where no doubt he intended to ravish her. When he found the place he was seeking, he lowered her to a coil of ropes and fell on top of her, stealing her breath. Her mouth was free, but she had no air left in her lungs to make a sound, much less scream.

He clawed at her shirt, managing to bare her breasts to his filthy hands. She knew she would bear marks on her tender skin from his rough handling, but that was the least of her worries. Why had she come out on deck alone? Dariq had warned her about his men, and she hadn't heeded him. If only he were here now.

An enraged roar shook the air around her; it sounded like a wild animal about to pounce on its prey. Then her attacker was gone, flung away like a sack of potatoes, blood streaming from his mouth and nose. Dariq roared again; Mustafa came running to join him. After a few short, stabbing sentences from Dariq, Mustafa dragged the hapless pirate away.

Willow was still fighting for air when Dariq picked her up and carried her back to the cabin. He laid her on the bed and turned away to strike a light to a candle. His face, defined in the flickering light, looked so fierce that Willow recoiled in fear. His eyes were the gray of storm clouds, his mouth flat and unsmiling.

"Are you hurt?" he asked.

She shook her head, unable to find the breath or words to answer.

He held the candle aloft so he could observe her more closely. Hot color flooded her face as he stared at the purple bruises on her breasts.

"I will kill him," he ground out.

He set the candle down and walked to the washstand. He returned shortly with a wet cloth and pot of salve. Her gaze never left his face as he washed the scratches marring her pale breasts.

"The scratches won't leave a scar," he said through clenched teeth. "Such loveliness should not be abused. Abdul shall feel the bite of the whip for this night's infamy."

His fingers upon her were gentle. His touch warmed her skin, sending bolts of feeling clear down to her toes.

"Whatever possessed you to leave the cabin tonight? Obviously, I failed to impress upon you the danger that exists from my crewmen. They haven't had a woman in months."

"I did not think," she whispered. "I awakened after a threatening dream and needed air. The hour was late. I thought no one would be on deck to see me."

His voice was ripe with reproach. "There is always someone about." His silver gaze lingered on her breasts. "Are you bruised elsewhere?"

Her face reddened. "I d-d-do not think so."

His heated gaze swept over her. Suddenly his expression tautened and he brought the candle closer. Before Willow could protest, he loosened the scarf that held up her trousers and pushed them down far enough to expose the scratches Abdul had put on her stomach.

His eyes blazed with raw fury. "Do you realize how close you came to being raped? What good would you be to me then?"

Willow's wits returned, and with it her anger. "What about my feelings, my pain? Do they mean nothing to you? You measure my worth in terms of my usefulness to you. I am only important to you because I can be bartered for someone you care about."

Dariq's hands shook as he applied salve to the abrasions on Willow's stomach and breasts. Her flesh was warm and firm beneath his fingertips; the thought that her soft white flesh had been defiled by one of his men brought a kind of madness to him. Such beauty was not for the eyes of a common man like Abdul.

With marked reluctance, he brought the sheet up to Willow's neck, bade her good night and turned toward the door.

"Where are you going?"

"To see to Abdul's punishment."

"Tonight?"

"I see no need to wait."

She swallowed hard. "Stay with me until I fall sleep."

Dariq searched her face. "You are frightened." It was a statement, not a question.

"I . . . suppose. I am not a coward, but—"

He interrupted before she finished her sentence. "I never thought you were." He came closer. "Very well. I will sit with you until you fall asleep. Abdul can wait until tomorrow. This incident proves that women do not belong on a pirate ship," he muttered as he settled down in a chair.

Willow turned on her side to face him. "I agree. If you

set me ashore at the nearest port, I will find my own way home."

"I would if I could, beauty, but I need you."

Willow glared at him and rolled over, facing the wall. Dariq's gaze traced the enticing curve of her back and hip beneath the light cover and wished himself in bed with her. Covering her scratches with salve had nearly unmanned him. The woman was truly a houri. She lured him with her delicate scent, her beauty and her innocence—an innocence he was beginning to deplore. If she were not untouched, he would have her now, this instant. Gritting his teeth, Dariq reminded himself again why Willow's innocence was important to him and tried to ignore her.

Willow woke before dawn. The candle had burned out, leaving the cabin in eerie predawn light. A tall, broadshouldered figure rose from a chair. With the languid grace of a sleek tiger, Dariq stretched his lanky frame.

The shadows draping him parted as he stalked toward the bed. She watched him approach; there was a commanding power inherent in each long, prowling step.

His eyes were heavy-lidded and glinted silver beneath dark, sweeping brows. He looked pure Turk and terrifying, until she looked into his eyes. A hint of something tender lurked within those silver depths.

His lips were full and boldly sensual, and his luxuriant lashes softened his angular face. His lips were pursed now, as if she were a puzzle he couldn't quite figure out. She caught her breath as he leaned over her and then quickly straightened. She heard him mutter something beneath his breath.

She stared up at him. "Is something wrong?"

"Nay." He stroked her cheek. "Your skin is as soft as rose petals." He studied her in silent contemplation. "There is an old crone in Istanbul who is said to be able to repair a woman's hymen and return her to a state of virginity."

Willow blinked.

He sat on the edge of the bed. "I have been watching you all night. You have no idea how badly I want you." His hand stroked downward, sweeping over her breasts. "I am going to kill Abdul for touching you. 'Tis a just punishment."

She shuddered. "Isn't that a bit drastic?"

" 'Tis no more than he deserves."

"Can you not show him mercy?"

"You ask mercy for a cur that nearly raped you?"

"Death seems so cruel."

"Very well, for you I will be merciful. I will sever the hand that defiled you."

"Cut off his hand?"

"Aye, and he will thank me for it."

His hand paused near the top button of her shirt.

She grabbed his wrist. "Don't."

"I merely wish to see if your scratches are festering."

"I can check them myself."

His hand rose to her hair, stroking gently. He lifted a shiny strand and brought it to his mouth. The finest silk paled in comparison to the softness of Willow's hair. He inhaled deeply of the scent of roses, then let the tress slip through his fingers.

"The scent of your innocence tempts me beyond endurance."

He removed the sheet shielding her from him. If he couldn't have her, he would at least look his fill. He had spent the night in agony. He had never lacked willpower until he crossed paths with this green-eyed houri who stole his wits and made him forget his purpose.

"What are you doing?" Willow cried, tugging the sheet from his hand.

He dragged the linen to the foot of the bed. "I want to undress you, to fill my eyes with your beauty. I want to see for myself the treasure I am preserving. This has not been a pleasant night for me. You will have your revenge upon Abdul, but I cannot have what I desire."

The dawn of a new day chased away the shadows, revealing Willow's stunned expression. "Why do you desire me? I am sure you have seen women more beautiful than I."

Dariq could not stifle his groan. It took little imagination to envision Willow's nipple in his mouth, rising against the stroking of his tongue. He could even imagine the taste of her skin. Fighting the force of his need, he dragged his eyes from her body and his mind from the pit of lust.

"Only a fool or a eunuch would not want you. You do yourself no credit by denying your beauty. Englishmen must be blind if they do not see what I see."

"Proper English gentlemen speak of beauty without offending a woman's sensibilities. They write poetry to her eyebrows, or the sweetness of her voice."

Dariq laughed. "Pray Allah I will never become a gentleman." His voice took on a husky quality. "I could make love to you without breaching your maidenhead. I could teach you things that Ibrahim would thank me for. The body is a sensitive instrument made to give and receive pleasure. We could spend hours, nay, days in bed and you would still go to Ibrahim a virgin, technically speaking."

Willow shrank away from him. "You speak of sinful

things I do not understand. Pray do not touch me, sir. Prince or nay, no one has a right to my body except the man I marry, and then for the purpose of procreation only."

Dariq gave a bark of laughter. "Infidels have strange customs. They view their bodies as something shameful. I can teach you that bodies are instruments of pleasure as well as vessels for procreation. This I vow, sweet Willow. Before you leave me, you will be well versed in the many ways to give and receive pleasure, and you will enjoy every moment of the learning process."

"Go away! I refuse to listen to you. 'Tis Satan talking."

"You think me possessed by the devil?"

"You *are* the devil."

"You know naught of devils, beauty. Ibrahim is the devil, not I. I do not envy you his attention."

"Why give me to the devil if you feel that way?"

Dariq looked away. "There is no alternative. I am not the coldhearted bastard you think I am. With Kamel to look after you, you will survive. The one I hope to barter you for needs my protection more than you do."

"Who is Kamel?"

"The keeper of the harem. He is the most powerful eunuch within the seraglio. He will teach you the ways of the harem and protect you. Your survival depends on how well you please Ibrahim. And you must try to make no enemies in the harem. I will explain all that you do not understand before you leave Lipsi."

Willow scooted out of bed and backed away from him. "I understand more than you think. Your culture imprisons women behind walls and makes them into playthings. I want no part of the sinful pleasures you described. I will not become a willing slave."

Dariq sighed. "You will do what you must once you re-

Connie Mason

alize that your life depends upon Ibrahim's whims; unfortunately, his whims can be capricious."

Willow searched his face. "What did Ibrahim do to you? Why are you a pirate instead of a pampered prince living in a palace?"

His expression turned thoughtful. At length he said, "That, my beauty, is a story for another time. Perhaps 'tis better left untold."

He sent her a cocky grin. "One day soon, you will beg me to pleasure you."

"Not in this life," Willow sniffed. "I do not intend to remain your prisoner. I am nothing if not resourceful."

A smile stretched his sensual lips. "I look forward to your resourcefulness, beauty. Meanwhile, after last night's attack upon your person, I must insist that you remain inside your cabin unless escorted by either myself or Mustafa. You are to trust no one else."

"After my experience last night, I have no desire to venture outside my cabin alone."

"Then we are in agreement. As much as I would like to stay here and spar with you, I must see to Abdul's punishment."

The cabin seemed much larger after Dariq left. His commanding presence filled the space with animal magnetism and made the cabin seem smaller.

But Willow was no weak-livered female without a will of her own or a brain. Though she might wonder about and secretly long for those sinful things Dariq had mentioned, she had the will to resist his seduction and the gumption to escape when the opportunity presented itself.

She had always believed she would marry a proper English gentleman, raise the children of that union and follow the strict rules of English society.

Although that life sounded dull, Willow knew it was

her destiny. A sudden thought occurred. Was boredom the reason her unconventional French mother had fled England after nearly fifteen years of marriage to a staid English marquis?

Willow loved her father and her life in England, but during the time she had spent with her mother, she'd begun to believe that Frenchwomen were much freer than their English counterparts. Monique had begged Willow to remain with her, but Willow felt more connected with England than with France and had refused.

Willow realized that her engagement to Percy would not result in marriage even if she was lucky enough to return to England, for the scandal of her unfortunate experience would turn him away from her. If she wished to wed, her father would be forced to buy her a husband. France was beginning to look like a better choice once she escaped, for Willow knew that her mother would welcome her unconditionally.

Piercing screams interrupted Willow's reverie, and she knew immediately that Abdul's punishment had begun. Had Dariq severed his hand as he'd threatened? Or had he relented and shown mercy? The screams continued too long for Willow's peace of mind, then stopped abruptly.

Some time later Dariq returned to the cabin. His face was grim, his mood tense and unreadable.

" 'Tis done," he said tonelessly.

"What did you do to him?"

Dariq grimaced. "I do not enjoy maiming a man who needs his limbs to survive. In the heat of anger, I did consider taking his hand for touching you, but in a saner moment I decided a whipping would suffice. Abdul will recover to serve me again, but he will think twice before breaking my rules."

"I am glad you did not maim him," Willow said. "You are not as brutal as you pretend."

Dariq's dark eyebrows shot upward. "I am not a cruel man by nature. Events outside my control have forced me to make difficult choices. I have done things contrary to my nature in order to survive."

"Is holding me against my will against your nature?"

"Aye. Women are made to be cherished and loved. Abusing women is against Allah's teaching as well as God's. I adore women. Giving them pleasure is one of my favorite pastimes. One day you will experience my passion and judge for yourself. My plans for your future are necessary to save someone I love and honor above all others."

"Tell me about her. Is she very beautiful?"

"To me, she is."

"Is she in danger?"

"I have every reason to believe she is."

"From Ibrahim?"

"Aye. He is furious because I allow few of his ships to reach their destinations. He has threatened my loved one if I do not give myself up to him."

"I am sorry that I cannot help you. I do not know what happened between you and your brother, but I am not the solution to the problem."

Dariq reached her in two long strides and pulled her against him. "You are wrong, sweet Willow. You are exactly what I need to barter for my moth . . . loved one."

Then he kissed her.

Chapter Four

Dariq slid his hands onto Willow's cheeks and pulled her to meet his mouth. Her hands went to his chest, intending to push him away, but she hesitated when she felt the strong beat of his heart and the warmth of his skin through the fine linen of his shirt. The sensation was so thrilling, she felt her will drain away. His lips brushed hers once, twice, then claimed them with a fierceness that stirred her senses.

When his tongue searched for hers, she let him take it. As her hands slid over the contours of his muscles, the sharp intake of his breath returned her scattered wits. She gasped and pushed away from him, flinging her hand over her mouth. He searched her face, his expression inscrutable.

"You caught me off guard," she said. "I did not want this to happen. Besides," she added, "I was quite unaffected by your kiss."

Dariq chuckled. "Tell that to someone who will believe you. Mark my words, beauty, one day we will fully explore our passion in ways you cannot begin to imagine."

He gave her a slow, burning look, then took his leave.

* * *

Mustafa was waiting for Dariq when he arrived on deck.

"How does the lady fare after Abdul's attack? Did the cur hurt her?"

"She bears a few scratches, but no serious harm was done."

"It would be wise to keep her confined to her cabin until she is safely ensconced in your harem. Your crewmen are too woman-hungry to be trusted."

"Though it may seem the wisest course, I cannot do that to Willow. She would rebel."

Mustafa scowled. "She must accept her lot if she is to survive in Ibrahim's harem. Foreign women are given too much freedom."

"I agree, but as my guest, Willow will be allowed a certain degree of freedom aboard ship. She has agreed not to walk out on deck until either you or I can accompany her. Meanwhile, I intend to teach her Turkish."

Mustafa eyed him narrowly. "You are becoming too involved. I do not like it. You must remember why she is aboard your ship."

"Do not preach to me, my friend. I know where my duty lies. My mother is not safe in Ibrahim's seraglio." He clasped Mustafa's shoulder. "Come, Mustafa, let us see to the running of the ship."

Willow prowled the cabin for lack of anything better to do. Though she'd found several books in Dariq's cabin, they were written in Turkish. She hoped Dariq had meant what he'd said about teaching her his language, for she'd die of boredom if she didn't at least have that to look forward to.

Dariq did indeed keep his word. He appeared in the cabin after the noon meal to begin Willow's lessons . . .

and every day after that. The language was difficult, but Dariq was an excellent teacher. Within two weeks they were conversing in short sentences. With nothing else to do but study, Willow learned quickly.

To Willow's relief, Dariq made no attempt to seduce her during those teaching sessions. The last time he had kissed her, she had been tempted to the point of allowing whatever he wanted to do to her or with her. Though she knew he wouldn't take her virginity, he had hinted at other ways of finding pleasure; pleasure of which she knew nothing.

One stifling afternoon as she waited for Dariq to arrive for her lesson, she heard a commotion outside the cabin. Pounding feet, loud shouting and the metallic clanging of weapons drifted to her through the closed door. She wanted to rush out to see what was happening, but hesitated when she recalled her promise to Dariq. But, oh, it was so hard to remain inside while something terrible might be happening, something that could affect her future.

Willow couldn't resist cracking open the door and peeking through the opening. The cabin was situated beneath the quarterdeck, making it difficult to see anything but a small section of the deck. Disappointed, Willow stepped away from the door seconds before it banged open. Dariq loomed large and frightening in the doorway. He was fully armed for battle, his countenance fierce.

"What is it? What is happening?" Willow cried.

"We spotted one of Ibrahim's merchant ships. She's riding low in the water, a clear indication that her hold is full. I intend to take it. You are to remain in the cabin until the battle is over."

Willow blanched. "Why must you attack the ship? There are bound to be deaths."

Dariq shrugged. "There always are. I know the ship and

its captain. Hamid is Ibrahim's man; he won't give up his ship or cargo without a fight. Sighting the *Mahmed* is a stroke of good luck. Once the ship is relieved of her cargo, I shall send her on her way with word of your capture and my terms for your return."

"What if you lose?"

Dariq gave her an incredulous look. "We will not lose. My men and I have never lost a battle and don't intend to now."

"Perhaps I can be of some help. I can tend the wounded."

"Nay! You are to remain out of sight. I will return when it is safe." His face settled into harsh lines. "Obey me in this, Lady Willow." He strode out of the cabin, giving Willow no time to voice a protest.

The tumult on deck intensified. Willow heard the roar of cannon and clapped her hands over her ears. Several rounds were fired before the big guns fell ominously silent. Minutes later she felt a tremendous bump and staggered against the bulkhead. Rushing to the window, she saw that the two ships were being hauled together with grappling hooks, and that the *Mahmed's* crewmen were preparing to meet the pirates pouring across the boarding planks and swinging between the ships on ropes.

Dariq was one of the first men to board the *Mahmed*. His scimitar slashed wildly as he was immediately engaged in hand-to-hand combat. The battle was brutal, for the *Mahmed's* crewmen were exceptionally fierce and determined.

Dariq felled one man, but not before suffering a slash high on his thigh. Another man came up behind him and would have sent Dariq to eternity if Mustafa hadn't beheaded him with one swift stroke of his scimitar. Dariq barely had time to smile his thanks before two burly Turks attacked him and Mustafa.

Elsewhere the battle raged as men struggled for their lives, the deck running red with blood. Dariq and Mustafa fought on, quickly finding other prey. Both men were covered with blood, some from minor wounds of their own and the rest from their foes.

Dariq cursed each time he saw one of his men fall and renewed his effort to fight his way to the captain. Once the captain was killed or captured, Dariq believed his crewmen would lose heart and surrender. Dariq saw Captain Hamid standing on the quarterdeck and slowly fought his way to him; as always, Mustafa protected Dariq's back.

Dariq fought with easy grace, wielding both scimitar and knife with equal dexterity. When he reached the quarterdeck, he lunged at the captain.

"Surrender your ship!" Dariq shouted above the din of battle.

"Never!" Captain Hamid yelled back.

"Surrender before you are left with no men to sail your ship back to Istanbul."

Hamid gave Dariq a blank look. "You intend to let me keep my ship? Why? I know how you work. Not only do you steal cargo, but you add all captured ships to your pirate fleet."

"Not this time," Dariq promised. "If you surrender, your cargo will be confiscated, but your ship will be left intact to return to Istanbul."

"If I surrender my ship, do you promise not to slaughter my men?"

"I thought I made myself clear. You will need crewmen to sail your ship to Istanbul so that you can deliver a message from me to my brother."

Captain Hamid looked at his bloody scimitar and then at the dead and wounded littering the deck, his expression bleak when he noted there were more pirates standing than his crewmen.

"Your answer, Captain," Dariq growled, gripping his scimitar in a threatening manner. "You know I can slay you in combat with little effort."

Hamid wiped blood-tinged sweat from his forehead and glared at Dariq. Dariq could tell that the captain was still in the throes of blood lust, and that he was weighing his thirst to engage in battle against Dariq's superior strength. Finally Hamid lowered his head and let his sword fall to the deck.

"You win, Prince. I surrender my ship to you. I hope your black soul burns in eternal hell."

"I won't argue that point with you, Hamid, for hell is likely where I will end up. Tell your men you have surrendered the ship."

Hamid ordered his men to lay down their weapons, shouting that he had surrendered his ship to the pirate prince. The sound of weapons falling to the deck sounded like thunder, and the battle was disengaged. A triumphant roar filled the air as Dariq's men claimed victory.

Mustafa herded the *Mahmed's* captain and crew to one end of the deck while Dariq climbed into the hold to inspect the cargo. He found a veritable treasure trove of spices, silk and other valuable commodities. He returned from the hold smiling, and immediately set his men to work transferring the cargo to the *Revenge's* empty hold.

Dariq approached the sullen captain. "While my men are transferring your cargo, I will tell you what I wish you to say to Ibrahim when you return to Istanbul. We will speak privately in your cabin."

Dariq motioned Hamid to lead the way. He ached from more than a dozen wounds but brushed the pain aside in order to conclude his business. When they entered the captain's cabin, which had suffered only slight damage from one of the *Revenge's* cannonballs, Dariq came right to the point.

"Your ship suffered minimal damage, Captain Hamid, so you should have no difficulty continuing your journey to Istanbul."

"Without my cargo," Hamid groused.

Dariq shrugged, and then winced when a particularly deep cut above his eyebrow caused a twinge of pain. "Sit down, Captain, and listen closely while I give you the message you are to convey to Ibrahim. You are to say that I have his 'treasure,' and that she is everything and more than he could wish for. Tell him I will return her to him— untouched, of course—in exchange for my mother."

Hamid frowned. "I have heard that Ibrahim's long-anticipated treasure is a woman but did not credit it. Is that all?"

"Nay, there is more. Tell Ibrahim that I want Kamel to act as contact between us, and that arrangements for the exchange will be made through him. And tell him his 'treasure' is more beautiful than the moon and stars, well worth the price he paid."

"Very well, I will tell the sultan everything you have said. He will not like it, but I will tell him."

"There is one more thing. Wait here. I will return shortly with something for you to give Ibrahim to prove my claim."

Dariq left the cabin and strode swiftly across the deck. Grabbing a dangling line, he swung across the divide to the *Revenge*. Once aboard his ship, he went directly to his cabin. He found Willow pacing the room, her face white, her eyes glazed with fear. She halted in mid step, then raced toward him, gasping when she saw his bloody clothing.

"You're hurt! Do you have a surgeon aboard? Tell me what to do."

"Easy," Dariq said, "'tis just blood. Some of it's mine and some not. I have suffered worse than this in my life."

"Is it over? The fighting sounded fierce."

"'Tis over," Dariq replied. "My men are transferring the *Mahmed*'s cargo to the *Revenge*. Then she'll be free to proceed."

Willow nearly collapsed in relief, glad that the bloodshed had ended. Never would she understand men and their thirst for violence. She glanced up at Dariq to tell him what she thought of him and the violent life he led, and nearly stopped breathing when she saw that he held a knife in his hand.

She recoiled, raising her hand to protect herself when he raised the blade toward her. "Nay! Why do you want to kill me?"

Dariq staggered backward. "You think I meant to kill you? There are many things I wish to do to you, but killing is not one of them."

"You raised your knife to me."

"I merely want a lock of your hair to send to Ibrahim. Once he sees it, he will believe that you are my captive. The good captain has agreed to carry my terms for your ransom to my brother. Now hold still while I cut off a hank of your hair."

Willow stood still as a statue while Dariq lifted a long strand of hair and sawed off a portion from the end. Then he rummaged in his desk until he found a narrow leather thong to tie around the lock of hair. Next he produced a cloth pouch, placed Willow's hair in it and pulled the strings tight. Without another word, he turned and strode toward the door.

"Wait!"

He paused, glancing over his shoulder.

"What about your wounds? Who will see to them?"

"Are you worried about me, beauty?"

"I . . . I, no, of course not. No more than I would worry about any wounded human being."

"Fear not, I will survive. Mustafa knows more about healing than any surgeon. He will see to my wounds."

Despite the throbbing of multiple cuts and bruises, Dariq couldn't help smiling. No matter how much his captive denied it, she was interested enough in him to care about his well-being. He could scarcely wait for the day he would teach her about pleasure, and ways to gain it without breaching her maidenhead.

Willow would be far from innocent when she went to Ibrahim. He counted the ways he could take her—with his mouth, his tongue, his hands—and she would enjoy them all. He would even teach her to give him pleasure.

His mind turned away from erotic thoughts to the business at hand as he returned to the *Mahmed*, where Mustafa was awaiting further instructions.

"Send our wounded back to the *Revenge*," he ordered Mustafa. "After the cargo is transferred, have the men gather up the sailors' weapons. I will join you aboard the *Revenge* as soon as my business with Captain Hamid is concluded."

Captain Hamid waited nearby for Dariq, his expression churlish. "What besides your message do you want me to give to the sultan?"

Dariq pulled open the pouch, removed the lock of hair and dangled it before Hamid. The captain's eyes widened as he gazed at the golden strands in Dariq's hands.

"You are to give this to Ibrahim," Dariq said, dropping the lock of hair into the cloth pouch and pulling the strings tight. "'Tis all the proof he needs to know that I am not lying. Tell him his 'treasure' is as safe with me as I expect mine to be with him. I wish you fair winds and a safe journey to Istanbul, Captain."

Willow couldn't stand the waiting. There was a great deal of activity taking place on deck, and she felt an overwhelming need to see what was going on. She knew there would be casualties and wanted to help, despite the fact that she owed Dariq and his pirates naught but her contempt.

Throwing caution to the wind, Willow pulled on a knit cap, stuffed her hair beneath it and stepped outside, hovering near the door as her gaze swept the deck. She saw men carrying bundles and bales from one ship to another, then disappearing down into the hold of the *Revenge*. Then she saw the wounded; some were lying flat, while others were sitting, blood oozing from various parts of their bodies. Mustafa moved among them, inspecting wounds and treating them with salves and bandages he took from a small casket he carried under his arm.

Willow's soft heart wept when she saw Mustafa bandaging the stump of a man's severed hand. When she saw Dariq striding across the deck toward the wounded, she stepped from her concealment.

Dariq didn't see her until she made her presence known to him. She touched his arm. "How can I help?"

Dariq whirled, fury emanating from him. "I thought I told you to remain inside the cabin."

Willow's chin jutted out stubbornly. "I am not one of your concubines. Though there are rules Englishwomen must follow, living behind walls or closed doors is not one of them. Now, tell me what I can do to help."

"Mustafa and I can handle whatever needs to be done here. This is not woman's work. Your constitution is too delicate."

Willow snorted. "Obviously, you do not know me very well."

"What does she want?" Mustafa asked in rapid Turkish.

"She wants to help."

Mustafa's keen gaze passed over Dariq. "You are wounded, my lord." He returned his gaze to Willow, and using simple Turkish words, he said, "The prince is in need of attention. Take him to his cabin and see to his wounds."

He thrust a jar of salve and some clean cloths into her hand. "You will find needle and thread in the cabin for the more serious of his wounds."

Dariq glared at Mustafa. "That is not necessary. I have suffered worse wounds than these."

"Wounds fester quickly in the heat," Willow pointed out. Grasping his arm, she urged him toward the cabin.

"Are you giving me orders, my lady?"

"I'm but following Mustafa's orders. Are you coming with me or not?"

Dariq was on the verge of refusing when Mustafa said, "I do not need you, my lord. I am quite capable of seeing to the wounded myself. The lady is right. Wounds, even small ones, can fester."

"Very well," Dariq muttered reluctantly. "As soon as my wounds are seen to, I shall return to help you."

He stomped off toward the cabin. Willow hurried to keep up with him. Once they were inside, she pushed him down into a chair. Then she poured fresh water from a pitcher into a bowl and returned to Dariq. She inspected the cut above his eye first, carefully washing away the blood.

"This one does not need stitching," she said as she spread salve on the cut with her fingertips.

"I told you," Dariq said grumpily.

She stared at him a moment, swallowed hard, then said, "Take off your shirt."

A slow smile lit Dariq's dark features. "You want me to undress?"

She sent him an exasperated look. "Just your shirt."

Still grinning, Dariq pulled off his shirt. Willow's breath caught in her throat. Though she had seen him on a daily basis since being taken aboard the *Revenge*, never had she seen the ropes of muscles on his arms, or realized that his chest was so broad or dusted with black hair. The wet cloth hung limply from her hand as she stared at him.

"Is something wrong?" Dariq asked blandly.

The devil knew exactly what was wrong, but Willow refused to acknowledge how profoundly the sight of his bare chest affected her. Pretending no interest, she examined the numerous cuts on his torso and arms. Most had stopped bleeding, and none needed stitching. With forced detachment, she washed the cuts and spread salve on them. When she was done, she backed away.

"Aren't you going to finish?"

His words startled her. "I thought I had."

Dariq stretched out his leg. "This one is more serious than the others."

Willow gasped and covered her mouth when she saw the blood on his trouser leg. "Perhaps you should ask Mustafa to take care of that one."

"It could fester before Mustafa can get to it. Come, my lady, I thought you weren't like pampered Muslim women. Are you too squeamish to treat my wound?"

"I am not squeamish," Willow denied. She held out her hand. "Give me your knife."

Dariq stared at her hand, and then lifted his gaze to hers. The incredible sensuality of the man, the intimacy of the situation, made her a little reckless.

"Are you afraid to arm me?" Willow challenged.

"I fear no one," Dariq said, carefully placing his knife in her hand.

Willow closed her hand around the hilt and stared at the razor-sharp blade. If she planned to harm Dariq, now was the time to do it. He was wounded and at a disadvantage. But Dariq had trusted her enough to put a weapon in her hand, she found she wanted to earn that trust.

She dropped to her knees, grasped his trouser leg and slit it from hip to hem. When she saw the seriousness of his wound, she sat back on her heels and dragged in a shaky breath. His flesh was lacerated from thigh to knee.

"How could you still be walking with a wound like that?"

He shrugged off her question. "Can you sew it?"

"I suppose. I have always been good with thread and needle." She rose. "I'll need some fresh water from the pitcher."

She returned shortly with a basin of clean water and several cloths. The wound had stopped bleeding, which was a good sign. Once she cleaned the long gash, she realized that Dariq was right, the wound did indeed need stitching.

"Where are the needle and thread?"

"In the desk drawer. If you are going to be digging a needle into my flesh, perhaps you should pour me a glass of brandy first. You'll find a bottle and glass in the cabinet."

Willow filled a glass with brandy and brought it to Dariq. He drank it in one gulp as she rummaged in the desk drawer for a needle and thread.

"Pour a drop of brandy over the needle," Dariq said.

Willow did as he suggested, then threaded the needle. "Are you ready? I shall endeavor to make the stitches as neat as possible."

"I am not in the least worried. If I trusted you with a knife, I surely can trust you with a needle. Do your worst, beauty."

Worrying her bottom lip between her teeth, Willow bent over Dariq's leg and proceeded to sew the edges of his wound together with neat stitches. Dariq didn't move, didn't say a word; he just stared at her with a steady, unreadable gaze. By the time she'd finished, she was sweating profusely, her hand shaking with the release of tension. She sat back on her heels and studied her handiwork.

"Are you finished?"

"Aye, after I apply salve and a bandage."

Dariq observed Willow through narrowed lids. His eyes never changed; they merely observed and waited. Like a predator's eyes, his were avid, hungry.

Willow shifted nervously beneath the intensity of his gaze, feeling heat rise up her neck to her cheeks. With shaking hands she tied off the bandage and backed away, trying to avoid looking at his naked chest.

Reaching out, he trapped her between his muscular arms and dragged her onto his lap.

"What are you doing? Why can't you act like a civilized gentleman?"

He laughed. "I am not a gentleman, and I am definitely not civilized. I am a pirate, remember?" His arms tightened around her.

Willow realized she was as close to peril as she had ever been. Danger poured from him in dizzying waves. His every gesture exuded arrogant power. He was sexual in a way that made women think of sinful things.

Willow's thoughts scattered when his mouth claimed hers. He kissed her deeply, greedily, sweeping the breath from her with the vastness of his need. Heat was building up inside her, igniting her skin. No! It wasn't heat igniting her skin, it was *him*, the pirate. His hands had somehow found the bare flesh of her breasts. She tried to protest, but his tongue was thrusting in and out of her mouth, stealing her voice along with her breath.

She began squirming to escape with such vigor that she must have inadvertently hurt his freshly stitched wound, for his hands fell away from her and he howled in pain.

"What is it? Have I hurt you?"

"No more than I deserve," Dariq muttered.

She started to rise. Dariq pulled her back onto his lap. "Try to relax. I won't hurt you. I promise you will go to Ibrahim a virgin."

"Why must you send me to Ibrahim? Can you not find another way to convince your brother to release your loved one?"

"You talk too much," Dariq said as his mouth descended on hers, molding, coaxing, until, with a gasp of pleasure, she parted her lips. The tip of his tongue stroked the edge of her teeth, ventured further, brushing the inside of her cheek in a burning, delicate exploration.

She felt the intimate bulge of his sex press against her bottom and squirmed, unaware that her movements were intensely arousing to a man in the throes of lust. A harsh breath escaped him as his mouth possessed hers with wicked skill. Even in her innocence, Willow sensed a wealth of experience in his kiss.

Though she tried to resist, she could not. Slipping her arms around his neck, she opened her mouth to his erotic exploration. Her shirt slipped off her shoulders, revealing the white gleam of her skin against his dark hand. He groaned as his hand eased over her breast. Her soft nipple puckered against the callused pads of his fingers, the peak growing hard and taut beneath his expert stroking.

Willow pressed her face into the crook of his neck. She had to stop him now, before her will was completely destroyed. Dariq acted before she could put her thoughts into action.

"This is neither the time nor place," he said, breaking off the kiss. His hand slid from her breast and he set her away from him. "My men have need of me. When we explore pleasure together, I want to make your first taste of passion memorable for you."

Willow could scarcely think. Her body thrummed and her mind whirled with sensations previously unknown to her. Though she knew it was wrong, she wanted to curl up in his lap and absorb his warmth and vitality, taste his passion.

She realized she had been staring at him when he said, "Did I frighten you?"

"I have frightened myself. I cannot believe I let you touch me improperly and did nothing to stop you."

Dariq stood and pulled on his shirt. "One day, you will let me do more than that, beauty. Count on it."

"You can wait till doomsday, pirate."

Favoring his wounded leg, Dariq couldn't stop grinning as he limped from the cabin. Willow picked up his shaving cup and flung it at the door scant seconds after it closed.

Arrogant pirate!

Chapter Five

Willow woke several days after the *Revenge* had attacked the *Mahmed* to an exceptionally blue and cloudless morning. She stretched and climbed out of bed. A soft linen shirt she had found in Dariq's chest made a fine sleeping garment, far more comfortable than the scratchy canvas shirt and trousers.

As was his habit, the cabin boy had brought a pitcher of hot water before she awakened. Willow washed quickly and reached for her clothing, not surprised to find that young Osman had washed and pressed her trousers and shirt. They lay folded neatly at the foot of the bed.

Willow had just finished dressing when there came a discreet knock on the door. Wishing to practice her Turkish, she bade her caller to enter in her newly acquired language. Osman walked in with her breakfast, grinning broadly.

"You speak our language well for a foreigner," he complimented.

"I had a good teacher," Willow pronounced slowly and

carefully. "I am very happy to be able to converse with you. When will we reach your master's stronghold?"

"We are close, my lady. We should see land in a few days if the winds are fair. You will like Lipsi."

"What can you tell me about the island?"

"It lies close to Turkey, but it belongs to Greece. It has been largely forgotten by both countries, for it has little value. There are more goats than people on the island. The Greek peasants are friendly toward us; they provide the Brotherhood with fresh meat and produce."

Willow accepted his explanation with a nod. "Tell me about your master. Does he keep a harem? Does he have many concubines? Who is the loved one in Ibrahim's seraglio that Prince Dariq intends to trade me for?"

"You may return to your duties, Osman."

Startled, Willow lifted her gaze, her heart skipping a beat when she saw Dariq standing in the open doorway, his frown directed at the hapless cabin boy. Osman sidled past Dariq, then broke into a run as soon as he was out the door. Dariq advanced into the cabin.

"I did not teach you Turkish so that you could question my cabin boy about my personal life."

"I was merely making conversation. I do get lonely, you know."

"You won't be lonely much longer," Dariq informed her. "Osman was right about our proximity to Lipsi, except that he was off by a day or two. We should reach the island in about five days."

"I will be happy to set foot on solid ground," Willow said. "Will I stay at your home?"

Dariq grinned. "You'll find my home pleasing. My harem is small but sumptuous, thanks to Ibrahim's taste for luxury. All the furnishings in my seraglio as well as the building materials were taken from Turkish ships."

"You have a palace?"

"Indeed."

"And a harem?"

"Did I not just say so?"

"Your women won't welcome me," Willow predicted. "They will view me as a contender for your attention, even though we both know that is not so."

"I only have one woman," Dariq revealed. "Safiye may be jealous at first, but once she learns you are intended for Ibrahim, she will welcome you. Besides, Ali Hara will let no harm come to you."

"Who is Ali Hara?"

"A eunuch and keeper of my harem. I smuggled him out of Ibrahim's seraglio on one of my covert visits to Istanbul. He will welcome another woman into his keeping, for I imagine his days are dull with only Safiye to look after."

A jolt of unwelcome jealousy surged through Willow. How could that be when she didn't care a fig about her captor? He was a bloodthirsty pirate without a conscience.

"How long must I remain in your harem?"

Dariq shrugged. "As long as it takes. When we drop anchor at Lipsi, I will dispatch Ahmed to Istanbul to arrange an exchange through my contact. Any more questions?"

"Is Safiye your wife or your concubine?"

"My concubine."

"Is the loved one you left behind in Istanbul your wife?"

"I have no wife." He made an impatient gesture with his hand. "Your breakfast grows cold. I merely came to warn you that a storm is brewing."

Disbelief colored Willow's words. "A storm? How can that be, when I have never seen a more perfect day?"

"Too perfect. Dark storm clouds are gathering in the west. The storm should arrive before nightfall. Even as we speak, the crew is lashing down cargo in the hold so it won't shift. I came now to warn you while I still had time. I'll send Osman with a rope. Use it to bind yourself to something solid, like the bedpost, if the storm becomes violent."

Willow blanched. "What makes you think the storm will become violent?"

"Instinct. I have seen that kind of sky often enough to know to prepare for the worst. Don't worry, the *Revenge* will ride it out and take us home safely."

Home, Willow thought after Dariq left. How she wished that were true. She would give anything to be home now. Her father had decided she would be safer traveling over water to Marseilles because of the high incidence of robberies and kidnappings on French roads. Little did he imagine her ship would be attacked by pirates.

Willow's thoughts turned inward as she picked at her breakfast of biscuits, cheese and lamb the cook had slaughtered the day before. She recalled how uneventful the voyage from England to Marseilles had been, and wondered what had gone wrong on the return trip. The pirate ship had come out of nowhere, and only she and her maid had been taken off the *Fairwind* after it surrendered. The *Fairwind* had sustained minimal damage and was allowed to continue after being stripped of her valuable cargo, including Willow and her maid.

The days following her capture had passed in a blur. She and Polly hadn't been harmed, much to their surprise and relief, and they'd had each other for company. But once they reached Algiers and learned their fate, fear had become Willow's constant companion. The idea of a future living behind walls, denied contact with society while awaiting the sultan's pleasure, was a horrible one.

Willow wouldn't, couldn't allow that to happen. Osman had said that Greek peasants lived on Lipsi. Perhaps they could be persuaded to help her escape. She knew Dariq meant her no harm, but he was determined to send her to his brother.

By midday the winds had begun to howl, though the weather could not yet be described as a storm. Willow would call it a freshening breeze. She walked to the windows and peered up at the sky. She could still see the sun, but it appeared to be sliding behind some peculiar-looking clouds.

Osman brought her midday meal, and with it the rope Dariq had promised. He departed too quickly for her to ask him any more questions. Willow suspected that Dariq had given him a severe tongue-lashing for talking too much.

Willow toyed with the unappetizing food on her plate, longing for a piece of fresh fruit, or a slice of warm bread dripping with butter and honey. She did manage to eat most of the meal, for once the storm struck, she knew no one would be thinking about food.

Willow's observation had been correct. Suppertime came and went with no food forthcoming. The sun had disappeared and the sky had turned an ugly shade of purple, an ominous portent of what was to come. The wind howled outside her cabin, and the ship began to dip and sway front to back and side to side. Willow sat on the bed and clung to the bedpost, trying to ignore the waves of nausea that threatened to overwhelm her. Normally she didn't suffer seasickness, but this tossing was beyond anything she had experienced in the past.

Then the eerie purple clouds snuffed out the light of day. A distant rumble of thunder could be heard over the wailing wind, accompanied by streaks of lightning. The temperature began to drop. Willow felt the chill in the air and burrowed beneath the blankets on the bed. She didn't feel any safer there, but at least she was warm.

The storm struck with savage fury. Thunder boomed, lightning slashed across a sky that had changed from purple to black, and the seas rose up as if trying to swallow the ship. Willow heard naught over the howling wind. For all she knew, everyone on the ship had been swept overboard.

When the *Revenge* continued to pitch violently, Willow realized it was time to use the rope. Crawling from the bed, she wrapped a blanket around herself and found the rope Osman had left. Then she bound herself to a bedpost, knotting the rope in front of her so she could release it quickly if she needed to make a quick escape.

Willow had no idea how long the storm outside the cabin raged. Time seemed to stand still as she fought both nausea and vertigo, due to the violent pitching of the ship. During those desperate hours she saw no one. It was as if she had been forgotten in a world gone wild.

It was at her lowest point that she heard shouting above the howling wind.

"Man overboard!"

Willow's first thought was that she wasn't alone on the ship. Her second was more terrifying. What if Dariq had been swept overboard? Without Dariq, she had no protection from his crewmen. She knew she couldn't rely on Mustafa, for he didn't like her. Her last and most sobering thought was that she didn't want Dariq to die.

Disregarding her own safety, Willow worked free of her bonds and inched toward the door. The ship made a sudden violent roll to one side. She fell, hard. Recovering quickly, she ignored her aching body and crawled to the door. Clinging to the panel, she slowly, carefully lifted herself to her feet. Gathering her strength, she pulled open the door. It was immediately taken from her by a fierce gust of wind and flung wide.

The wind literally stole the breath from her, and the pounding rain slashed against her skin like stinging needles. Peering through the solid curtain of water, Willow saw a knot of men standing near the rail. Was that where the man had gone overboard?

Willow's heart sank when she realized that the wind would sweep her away if she stepped out from her shelter beneath the quarterdeck, but her hopes soared when she saw the line strung across the deck. If she hung on to the line, she should be able to make her way to the railing. She had to find out who had gone overboard. Her very life depended upon it.

Dragging in a steadying breath, she lurched toward the line, which was but a few feet from where she stood. Grasping it firmly, she inched her way across the open deck. She stumbled twice and would have been swept away if not for her deathlike grip on the slippery line. She knew she should turn back to the relative safety of her cabin, but she had to learn whether Dariq was lost to her.

Suddenly the ship lurched up and then down. Willow's feet slipped out from under her, and then the worst thing that could happen did. The line snapped. Willow screamed as she slid across the wet deck. No one heard her. She knew real fear when a wave higher than the ship surged over the sides, lifting Willow and carrying her toward a watery grave.

Willow said a short prayer, closed her eyes and prepared to die. She cheated death by scant seconds when something hard and unyielding caught her flailing legs, bringing her slide into eternity to an abrupt halt.

She was dragged backward against the pull of the water, inch by painful inch. After what seemed an eternity, she was hauled to her feet and shoved into her cabin. Breath heaving in and out of her chest, Willow struggled to control her trembling. She wiped the water from her eyes and stared up at her savior. Her trembling increased when she looked into the eyes of hell in all its fury.

"Are you mad?" Dariq shouted. "Whatever possessed you to leave the cabin?"

Willow swallowed hard, recoiling against Dariq's rage. "I . . . I feared you had gone overboard."

Her words stopped Dariq in his tracks, but after a moment's hesitation, his rage regained its momentum. "Have you lost your senses, lady? There was nothing you could have done had I been the hapless man tossed overboard. If I hadn't seen you hurtling to your death, you would be food for the fish by now."

Willow shuddered and lowered her head. Dariq couldn't have been more blunt. She shouldn't have left the cabin, she knew that now. But at the time it seemed the right thing to do.

She looked at him through a fringe of lush golden lashes. "Thank you for saving my life. I know I acted rashly. I do not know what I would have done if you had been swept overboard. Without your protection, I would be fair game for your men. Mustafa would be of no help, for he doesn't like me."

The ship lurched up and came down hard. Dariq was able to remain upright, but Willow went flying, straight into his strong arms. His feet braced wide against the violent roll of the wave, he held Willow's shivering body until the ship righted itself.

"We are going to sink," Willow whispered. "The ship is going to be swamped."

"Nay, the *Revenge* is sturdily built; she won't sink. You are shivering. Take off your wet clothes and climb into bed. I'll lash you down so you can't fall out. Hurry—I must return to my men."

Willow hesitated. She wore nothing beneath the shirt and trousers and couldn't bring herself to undress with Dariq watching. Sensing her dilemma, Dariq grasped her wet shirt and whipped it over her head. A few swift motions and her trousers followed it to the floor.

Dariq's breath caught in his throat. Instant arousal was not something that happened to him often, but rarely was a body as perfect as Willow's. Not even Safiye's voluptuous curves could compare with Willow's sleek body. The only thing marring Willow's perfection was the body hair that he was not accustomed to seeing, although he had to admit the blond fuzz on her mound was enticing. Turkish women's bodies were shaved and plucked clean of all body hair, a custom foreign women had yet to embrace.

Regret colored Dariq's words. "Get into bed; you are shivering."

His words released her from some strange trance as Willow crawled into bed and pulled the covers up to her neck. Working against the roll of the ship, Dariq managed to bind the rope around her blanketed form and tie the loose ends to the bedposts.

"That should hold you," he said. "The storm should blow itself out soon. I'll release you when the danger is over."

He stared at her a moment, wishing he could join her in the bed. He was soaked clear through to his skin and couldn't do anything about it until the storm abated and the damage was assessed.

"Why are you looking at me like that?" Willow asked.

"I was thinking how much I would like to join you and warm your body with my hands, my mouth and my tongue. Your body was made for love. Think on that, beauty, for one day it will come to pass."

The arousing vision of Willow's body remained imprinted upon his brain as Dariq walked out of the cabin into the raging storm. Glancing up at the dark, angry sky, he saw no visible sign that the storm was abating, despite his optimistic words to Willow. The storm still had its teeth, and he would need all his skill to bring the ship safely to port. He had no idea how far off course the ship was being blown, and wouldn't know until he could see the stars to take a reading.

Dariq saw that the line had been reattached and started across the deck, hand over hand, his body braced against the force of the wind. He reached the rail, where Mustafa and several crewmen were peering into the swirling water.

"Who went overboard?" Dariq asked.

"Tarrif," Mustafa replied.

"Is he gone?"

"Aye. No man could survive long in that cauldron."

"How great is the damage to the ship?"

"The mizzenmast is gone. Other than that, the damage appears minimal. The *Revenge* will ride out the storm. Where have you been? I saw you with the woman. What happened?"

"Lady Willow did something foolish, as usual," Dariq shouted over the howling wind. "She left the cabin. Had I not seen her, she would have been swept overboard. But, fortunately, I caught her and hauled her to safety."

"Foolish woman," Mustafa growled.

"She will cause no more trouble, I have seen to that. I am confident the storm will blow itself out soon."

Willow was finally warm again. Cocooned in the blanket, she felt nothing but pity for the men forced to endure the elements at the height of their fury. As often as she had sailed aboard her father's ships, she had never experienced anything like this before.

Incredibly, her nausea abated and she managed to doze, lulled by the motion of the ship. She awoke to weak light filtering through the windows and the gentle rocking of the ship.

Was the storm finally over? Where was Dariq? Until he returned to release her, she was forced to remain bound to the bed. Squirming only pulled the ropes tighter.

Dariq returned to the cabin a short time later, feet dragging, shoulders bent and his face gray with exhaustion.

"Is it over?" Willow asked.

"Aye. Mustafa is assessing the damage."

"Untie me."

He slumped down on the bed and pulled off his boots. "L-l-let me remove my wet clothing first."

Willow feared for his health when she realized he was shivering violently. "Hurry, before you catch your death. Wrap yourself in a blanket."

Removing his clothing seemed almost too much effort for Dariq. His fingers fumbled with buttons and ties as he peeled away his wet shirt and trousers. Willow tried not to stare at him, but her weak will betrayed her. He was all virile male, from his handsome face to his large . . . My goodness, his male parts were beyond breathtaking. She'd seen pictures of Greek statues in books, but the dull flatness of pictures held little resemblance to the magnificent planes and valleys of Dariq's body.

She watched through lowered lashes as he untied the rope binding her and flopped down on the bed. Shock shuddered through her when he crawled beneath the covers and pulled her naked body against his.

"I need your warmth," he said through chattering teeth. "Do not worry, beauty, I am too tired to do you any harm."

Before Willow could gather her wits to voice a protest, Dariq was sound asleep. His body was frigid against hers, and she could almost forgive him for seeking her warmth, for she had been warm and cozy while he had been buffeted by cold winds and chilling rain. She attempted to ease out of bed.

The moment she moved, his arm tightened around her, holding her captive against his hard body. It took all her willpower to ignore the pleasant pressure of his chest against her back and his lower body spooned against hers. Unable to move, she gave in to exhaustion and slept.

Dariq awoke hours later, feeling refreshed and deliciously warm. The female body pressed intimately against his contributed to the heat slowly rising through his veins. How glorious to wake up with Safiye in his arms. Her warm, fragrant body stirred awake in his arms as he nuzzled her neck.

His cock had grown hard the instant he felt the softness of her backside pressed against his loins. Beautiful sloe-eyed, dark-haired Safiye knew exactly how to please him. His hand crept around to her breast, cupping it fully. He frowned and opened his eyes when he realized that, unlike the tender mound now nestled against his palm, Safiye's breast usually overflowed his hand.

He recalled where he was and who he was with when he saw a wild tangle of golden tresses spilling over the pillow. He picked up a lock of her hair, holding it, feeling the softness of it, silk against his palm.

"Willow," he whispered against her ear.

Willow burrowed against him but did not open her eyes. He wondered what she was thinking.

"Willow, are you awake? Turn around, beauty."

Willow awoke with a jerk. "What are you doing?"

"Touching you. Do you like it?"

"No! Take your hands off me."

Ignoring her, his fingers sought out her nipple and squeezed gently. "I was too exhausted last night to do more than fall into a dark void of sleep. But I am rested now, and since we are in bed naked, we should take advantage of the situation and begin to explore passion together."

Dariq turned her onto her back. Willow struggled to escape; he placed a leg over hers to hold her in place.

"Shall we start by kissing?" Dariq asked. "We can progress from there at our leisure."

"No, I—"

Her words gurgled to a halt as Dariq's mouth claimed hers lips. The surge of primal heat shocked Willow's body into stillness. He broke off the kiss and stared at her. The hot darkness of his gaze filled her with memories of how he'd looked naked. His face was now harsh with emotion, savage with demand. He was a beautiful animal, infinitely dangerous, infinitely sexual. He terrorized and fascinated her in equal parts.

Suddenly she became aware of his hands moving over her, touching her, finding places that made her jerk with awareness. She tensed, and then arched against the jolting heat of his caresses. The feeling was so intense, she was afraid to acknowledge its existence.

"Does that feel good?" Dariq whispered.

"No. I hate it."

"Liar. Perhaps you'll like this better."

His hand moved slowly down her body, his callused palm creating a pleasant friction against her inflamed skin. Then she felt him reach between her thighs. She stiffened and gazed up at him. He wasn't smiling. His silver eyes were rapt, a look of such intense ardor in them that she had to fight to catch her breath.

He found her lips; he tasted of untamed things, wicked things, and sin. She gasped against his mouth.

"Be easy," he whispered. "I won't hurt you."

His hand moved along the inside of her leg in a caressing stroke. She jerked in response. "What are you doing?"

"I did not want it to be here, but lust dictates the time and place, not I. I wanted silken sheets and perfumed oils, but you are here and I am here, so the time must be now."

His lips moved downward, licking a little pool of sweat from the hollow of her throat. His mouth trekked lower, pausing to suckle a pert nipple before moving on. Willow tried to shift away from his questing mouth, but the weight of his big body held her securely in place. When his tongue dipped into her navel, her breath left her lungs in a loud whoosh.

"Dariq, please do not do this to me."

He lifted his head and gave her a beguiling look filled with sensual promise. "You will leave this bed a virgin; that I promise. Now be quiet and let me kiss you."

His promise gave her scant comfort. She scarcely had time to form a coherent thought when Dariq shoved her legs apart and settled between them. She felt him pressing her swollen folds open; lightning flashed through her when she realized where he intended to kiss her.

She rose up on her elbows. "You cannot do that! 'Tis wicked!"

"Who is to say what is wicked and what is not? I want to taste your sweet nectar."

His tongue found her, stroking gently, touching something so sensitive that her thinking process closed down. Her elbows collapsed beneath her and she fell back on the mattress, staring blindly down at his dark head between her legs. Oh, God, he was *licking* her, in long, sinuous laps that made her body quiver with uncontrollable excitement.

Try though she might, Willow could not control the motion of her hips, rising upward to match her rhythm to his stroking tongue. She felt detached from her body, as if she were floating above it on a cloud of incredible pleasure. Her nerves were stretched taut; she floated higher, reaching for an unattainable peak dangling just out of her reach.

A heartbeat later, she felt his fingers open her and his tongue slide deep inside her. She lurched and cried out his name. His scent mingled with that of her own arousal, filling her senses. As if needing more of her, he hooked his arms under her thighs and draped her legs over his shoulders. His tongue was a slice of dark magic, licking, savoring, thrusting in and out of her tight passage, driving her toward a place she had never been before.

She arched up against his hot mouth, pushed by a wildness building inside her; the growing sounds of frenzy in her throat filled the silence of the cabin. A few moments more of this and she would shatter.

Then she did shatter, her throbbing body dissolving in a pool of pleasure so intense she feared she would drown in it.

She screamed Dariq's name.

The sound brought Dariq surging upward to watch her. "Beautiful," he whispered. "The loveliest sight in the world is a woman in the throes of ecstasy."

"What happened?" Willow asked breathlessly.

"You experienced an orgasm. 'Tis the greatest pleasure you will ever know."

"Did you . . . ?"

"Nay." He grasped her hand, placing it over his groin. "My cock is still rock hard."

"Did you receive no pleasure?"

"My pleasure was watching yours." His silver gaze glittered. "There is something you can do for me, however." He curled her fingers around his manhood and slowly moved them up and down, teaching her a rhythm as old as mankind.

His flesh beneath her hand was hard, hot and slick. She didn't want to touch him like this, but she couldn't find the will to stop. She curled her fingers around him, moving them up and down the way he had shown her. She felt his body grow taut and his manhood grow even larger. He kept his need in check, but she could feel it, a power coiling out of him and surrounding her.

"Faster," he panted. "I'm almost there."

His head fell back, his teeth were bared, and he looked as if he were suffering intense pain. Suddenly he lurched upward, shouting his pleasure as he reached his peak. She stared at him. Their eyes locked as the tension drained from his face.

Willow scooted away, shocked at what had just taken place between them. She had never imagined, never dreamed such things were possible between a man and a woman.

And she was still technically a virgin.

Chapter Six

Reaching for her temper to ease her conscience, Willow shoved Dariq so hard he fell out of bed. Legs sprawled, arms akimbo, he glared up at her. "Why did you do that?"

"You had no right to do what you did to me."

Dariq picked himself up off the floor, not in the least embarrassed by his nudity. "Perhaps not, but you cannot deny that you enjoyed it."

Her chin rose. "You forced me. I had no idea what you were doing. Never touch me like that again."

As he stood there with his hands on sturdy hips, his legs spread wide, Willow watched in dismay as his manhood sprang up from the nest of dark hair at his groin. She swallowed hard and looked away.

"You have no say in the matter," Dariq said. "You are my captive; I can use you in whatever manner I please."

"I thought I was your guest."

"Aye, a very special guest. I will personally see that you have everything your heart desires . . . including pleasure." He placed a knee on the bed. "There is still time for another lesson."

There came a knock on the door. Grateful for the reprieve, Willow heaved a sigh. Dariq reached for his trousers and pulled them on.

"Who is it?"

"Osman. I bring fresh water."

Dariq sent Willow a look lush with sensual promise before bidding Osman to enter.

"Do you wish to shave, master?" Osman asked, looking anywhere but at the rumpled bed.

"Aye. Take the water into my sleeping quarters. Then fetch another pitcher for the lady."

"He knows," Willow hissed after Osman scooted out the door.

Dariq shrugged. "What does it matter? You are a woman, and women are made to give and receive pleasure. 'Tis a natural thing."

"Not to me. I had a proper English upbringing. 'Tis sinful and improper for a woman to enjoy"—she blushed—"sex."

"You said your mother is French. Are those her sentiments?"

"Mama marches to her own drummer. English society was too restrictive for her, but it suits me very well."

A slow grin spread over Dariq's face. "You liked what we did."

Her face turned even redder. "I . . . I . . . You are too experienced for me. I did not know how to protect myself against your sensual nature."

"Why would you want to?"

Osman's arrival saved Willow from replying. The lad placed the pitcher of hot water on the washstand and left.

"I shall leave you to your ablutions while I perform mine," Dariq said as he crossed the room to his sleeping chamber.

The moment the door closed behind Dariq, Willow climbed from bed, wrapped a sheet around herself and padded to the washstand. Taking up cloth and soap, She scrubbed all the places Dariq had touched her with his mouth, his hands and his tongue. Then she scrambled into her clothing, ready to face the day.

Dariq exited his small sleeping chamber a few minutes later, freshly shaved and dressed in loose trousers and shirt.

"If cook was able to fire up the brazier, you should have a hot meal soon. Try to entertain yourself while I inspect the ship for damage. If the *Revenge* fared well in the storm, we will continue our journey to Lipsi."

Dariq was halfway out the door when Willow said, "I want to come with you. I shall go mad if I'm forced to remain cooped up another day."

"You are to remain here," Dariq answered. Then he was gone, leaving Willow fuming in impotent rage.

Dariq saw Mustafa standing near the broken mast and hurried over to join him.

"How long will it take to repair it?" Dariq asked.

"A day or two," Mustafa replied. "Ripped sails and broken lines are being repaired as we speak."

"I intend to take a reading tonight to see how far we were blown off course."

"I did that last night while you slept. As luck would have it, we were blown toward Lipsi, not away from it."

"That is good news indeed, Mustafa. What would I do without you?"

"That is something you need never worry about, Prince, for I shall always be at your side."

Dariq clapped Mustafa on the back and went in search of something to eat.

* * *

Osman arrived a short while later with Willow's breakfast. She was hungry and ate every bite. With nothing to do but ponder her dismal future, she prowled the narrow confines of the cabin. She longed to step outside into the sunshine, to raise her face to the rain-washed air and fill her lungs with it.

"I refuse to stay in here a moment longer," she muttered to herself.

She found another woolen cap in Dariq's chest, pulled it down over her ears and stuffed her hair underneath it. Then she opened the door and stepped outside. She lifted her face and sniffed appreciatively. The air smelled of sunshine and freshness.

The deck was a beehive of activity as men rushed about their duties. Willow saw men sewing ripped sails, working on the mainmast, and clearing debris from the deck. Gazing up, she noticed several bare-chested men repairing broken lines. Blushing, she started to turn away. Then she spied Dariq dangling precariously from a mast high above the deck. Had her life depended upon it, she could not have looked away.

He appeared to slip; she clapped a hand over her mouth to stifle a cry. But the surefooted pirate did not fall. He merely grasped another line, steadied himself and continued his work.

Willow spied an overturned barrel, righted it and sat down so she could watch the activity without getting in the way. The soothing warmth of the sun after the intense drama of the storm made her drowsy, and she closed her eyes. Immediately her thoughts drifted to the wondrous, startling and embarrassing things Dariq had done to her.

The bubble burst when a pair of strong hands grasped

her shoulders and heaved her up until her feet were dangling inches above the deck. She looked straight into Dariq's glittering eyes, and to her credit, she didn't flinch.

"By the beard of Allah, don't you ever do as you are told?"

"Sometimes I do, but only when it pleases me. Let me stay on deck, Dariq. I wasn't bothering anyone, and no one paid me the slightest heed until you drew attention to me."

Dariq plopped her down onto the barrel. "Sit there and don't move or say anything. I don't want you getting in the way. Is that clear?"

Willow smiled. She had won another concession, and each one was precious to her. "Perfectly."

Willow remained on deck, watching the activity until late afternoon, when shadows began to gather and she grew tired of her hard perch. Then she quietly returned to her cabin, pleased with her afternoon of freedom.

Willow didn't see Dariq again until late that night, when he tiptoed through the cabin to find his bed. He stopped abruptly beside her bed and stared down at her. Light from the guttering candle made the stark planes of his face appear dark and dangerous.

"You must be exhausted," she murmured.

Dariq jumped away as if startled. "You should be asleep."

"Was the ship badly damaged?"

"Nay. The repairs should take but a day or two."

"Were we blown off course?"

"Mustafa said we were blown toward Lipsi, not away from it. We should see land in three days, barring another storm. It cannot be too soon for me. The *Revenge* has been at sea many months; the men miss their women."

He sat on the edge of the bed. Wary of his intentions,

Willow scooted back. "I did not know your men had wives." Somehow Willow couldn't picture these fierce pirates with wives.

Dariq chuckled. "Most of the men keep concubines. A few have taken wives from among Lipsi's Greek inhabitants."

Willow could think of no response. "Good night, Prince Dariq."

Dariq stared at Willow several long moments before rising. "You are right to dismiss me, sweet Willow. Your next lesson in passion should take place on satin sheets, in a room that will complement your beauty. Sleep well."

Willow trembled at the thought of Dariq touching her again. How could she bear it?

Land appeared off the bow three days later, just as Dariq had predicted. The *Revenge* entered a deep-water bay and sailed gracefully toward a long stone jetty, where a crowd had gathered to await the return of their prince. The deck bustled with activity as sails were furled and lines trimmed. Through an expert feat of maneuvering, the *Revenge* slid gracefully up to the jetty and dropped anchor.

Willow spied two ships anchored in the bay a short distance from shore and assumed they were part of Dariq's pirate fleet. A shout of welcome greeted Dariq when he appeared on deck.

Not long after the docking, Dariq returned to the cabin. "Welcome to Lipsi," he said. "I hope you will be happy here while negotiations with Ibrahim are in progress."

"I won't be happy anywhere but home, but I will be glad to get off this ship."

"I sent one of my men to my seraglio for an aba. As

soon as you are properly covered, I will escort you to my home."

Willow balked. "None of the women I saw from the windows wore abas."

"Women on Lipsi are free to do as they please, but you are not. Do not argue, Willow, for this is the way it must be."

Willow hated the thought of wearing an aba but knew she could not avoid it. Dariq left, and a short time later Osman delivered the robe to her cabin, informing her that the prince awaited her on deck.

Willow donned the robe, groaning as its voluminous folds all but swallowed her. She would surely die of suffocation before she reached Dariq's seraglio.

Willow exited the cabin, anxious to feel solid ground beneath her feet once again. Dariq was waiting for her. He grasped her elbow and escorted her down the gangplank onto the jetty. She wobbled slightly, then found her land legs as she proceeded with Dariq through the crowd of fierce-looking pirates, most of whom Dariq greeted by name.

An Arabian gelding was led to the end of the jetty. Dariq mounted, then nodded at Mustafa to hand Willow up. Moments later, she found herself seated across Dariq's legs atop the prancing horse. They took off in a cloud of dust. Mustafa remained behind; she supposed to oversee the unloading of the cargo.

" 'Tis but a short ride," Dariq said as he reined the horse away from the cove. "Every comfort will be made available to you at my seraglio."

As they rode through the lush green landscape, Willow saw signs of life beyond the pirate community clustered around the docking area. She noticed a young boy driving a large herd of goats toward what looked like a village in the distance. That information could come in handy when she planned her escape.

She lost her train of thought when a glittering palace at the end of a long drive paved with seashells rose up before her. She suspected it was smaller than most palaces, but what it lacked in size, it made up for in elegance. Surrounded by swaying trees and blooming flowers, the palace resembled a perfect jewel in an opulent setting.

They rode into a tiled courtyard, so lovely it nearly took her breath away. At its center was a fountain in the shape of a dolphin that spouted water into a blue-green reflecting pool.

Dariq dismounted; he reached up and Willow slid down into his arms. A young man appeared to lead the horse off as Dariq ushered her into the dim coolness of the entranceway. A very tall, very intimidating guard greeted them. Dressed in balloon trousers, flowing shirt and boots, and armed with a scimitar that hung from his wide belt, he looked ready for battle. The large turban crowning his head made him seem even taller.

"Welcome home, Prince. All is in readiness for you." Though the servant did not turn to look at the black-clad woman at Dariq's side, his gaze kept straying to Willow.

"Lady Willow, this is Haroun, the captain of my personal guard. Haroun, this is Lady Willow. She will be my guest for an indefinite period of time. Please take her to the harem. Tell Ali Hara to take good care of her, and that I will explain her presence as soon as I have a spare moment. Baba will know what to do."

He touched Willow's black-clad shoulder. "Go with Haroun, Willow."

Willow stiffened. "Who is Baba?"

"The mistress of my harem. You have naught to fear from her. She will see to your comfort."

Dariq strode off down a white and green marble corridor; Willow had no choice but to follow the gigantic Turk. After several twists and turns, they arrived at a wide double door embellished with leaves and flowers of pure gold. Haroun's knock was answered immediately by an ebony-faced man whose size exceeded that of Haroun.

"I bring you our master's new concubine," Haroun announced importantly. "You and Baba are to see to her comfort."

"Welcome, lady. I am Ali Hara," the eunuch said, bowing before Willow. " 'Tis time my master brought another concubine to his harem. Safiye has been the sole occupant far too long. I know you do not understand our language, but nevertheless, I wish you welcome."

Curving his fingers around her arm, he gently guided Willow inside the harem. When she heard the door close behind her, she panicked, shouting in English, "No! Let me out! I do not belong here."

An elderly gray-haired woman wearing a caftan in muted colors came hurrying up to them. "Who is this woman, Ali Hara?"

"She is Prince Dariq's new concubine."

Willow sought words to convey her displeasure in Turkish. "No, I am most definitely not! Please, open the door and let me out."

"You speak our language," Baba said, clapping her hands in delight. "I wondered how we would communicate with you. How do you know our language, my lady?"

"Prince Dariq taught me."

"Are you Frankish?"

"I am English," Willow replied, choosing to claim her

English heritage rather than her French. "I am Lady Willow Foxburn."

"You may remove your aba, my lady; you have no need of it here."

"Gladly," Willow said, whipping off the dark robe.

"Oh, my lady," Baba gasped. "What monstrosity are you wearing? You should be dressed in the finest silks and satins." Baba took Willow's arm, gently leading her away from the door. "Come with me, my lady. I am Baba. I shall take good care of you for my master."

Since she had no choice, Willow followed Baba, her gaze taking in every detail of the large, elegant chamber. It was like no room she had ever seen before. She walked upon green and white marble floors across a room whose walls were composed of colorful tiles. Willow was intrigued by the oval-shaped pool in the center of the room, and the statue of a naked young man pouring water from a pitcher into the pool. Several marble benches were scattered about the pool, but it was the low couches piled high with colorful pillows that caught Willow's attention. The windows were open, admitting a soft sea breeze that fluttered the filmy curtains.

Judging from the size of the harem, Willow assumed that Dariq intended to fill it with women. Her attention sharpened when Baba opened a door and ushered her into a sleeping chamber.

"I hope you will be comfortable here, my lady. You may rest while preparations are being made for your bath." She inspected Willow with a critical eye. "You must be properly groomed and clothed before you go to Prince Dariq. Ali Hara will bring you food and something refreshing to drink."

Willow didn't bother to correct Baba's assumption that

she was here to pleasure Dariq, for she supposed Dariq would inform Ali Hara of his plans for her in his own good time.

Once Willow was alone, she made a thorough perusal of her sleeping quarters. The room was small but elegantly appointed with a silk-covered bed, table, dressing table, chest and several cushioned chairs. The walls were hung with silk in muted shades of peach and turquoise, and a thick carpet covered the marble floor. The window looked out over a small garden, exquisite with blooming roses and other exotic flowers. It was like another world.

Ali Hara arrived with a tray of fresh fruit, freshly baked flatbread and a pot of honey, a bowl of hot soup with pieces of lamb floating in it, and a drink that blended several fruits. Everything looked delicious after the ship's fare she'd become accustomed to.

Willow picked up a piece of flatbread, spread it with honey and bit into it. It was so good she devoured it in minutes. Then she lifted the bowl of soup and sipped the hot liquid, relishing the spicy taste.

She was just starting on her second piece of bread when the door burst open, admitting a whirlwind of vivid color and grating sound. Her visitor was a woman, a very beautiful olive-skinned, dark-haired, sloe-eyed woman with generous curves. Her beaded vest of scarlet brocade and transparent skirts consisting of several layers of filmy chiffon left little to the imagination.

"Ali Hara said Prince Dariq had purchased a new concubine for his harem." Hands on ample hips, the woman glared at Willow. "Why are you wearing men's clothing? You look ridiculous." She searched Willow's face. "You are too pallid, too unremarkable for Prince Dariq's taste. He likes women with lush curves and golden skin. Do not expect to take my place in his bed, for I will not allow it. He has had no other woman since he purchased me at a slave market."

"You must be Safiye," Willow said. "Please speak slowly, for your language is new to me. Dariq told me about you. I am Lady Willow. You have naught to fear from me; I will never become Dariq's lover."

Safiye's eyes narrowed. "I am no fool, lady. My lord would not bring you here if he did not want you in his bed. Just remember, I am the favorite, and you must answer to my authority. Once I bear Lord Dariq a child, he will make me his wife and you will be naught but a slave."

"I am naught to him now. Believe me, Safiye, I am not here by choice. I was captured by pirates and sold to—"

"Bah. Whatever he paid for you was too much. Has Lord Dariq bedded you yet?" Willow remained mute. "Never say you are still untouched."

Willow blushed. While technically she was a virgin, she couldn't claim to be untouched.

"Hah! 'Tis just as I thought," Safiye spat. "He will tire of you once the novelty wears off." She preened for Willow's benefit. "Prince Dariq will send for me tonight, not you, and I will please him as I always do."

"You are welcome to him," Willow snapped. She was growing weary of Safiye's boasting.

Her eyes spitting dark fire, Safiye looked as if she intended to launch herself at Willow. Willow prepared for the attack that never came, stopped abruptly by Ali Hara, who had just entered the chamber.

"What are you doing here, Safiye?"

Safiye's cat-eyes glittered with barely concealed malice. "I was merely welcoming our lord's newest concubine. A pallid little thing, is she not? And whatever is she wearing? I cannot imagine what Prince Dariq sees in her. The only thing appealing about her is her hair."

"You may leave," Ali Hara said. "The master wants Lady Willow properly groomed, and there is a great deal to do before she is ready to go to him."

"It will take more than grooming to make her presentable," Safiye sniffed. Turning on her heel, she stomped off.

"Follow me, lady," Ali Hara said to Willow. "Baba awaits you in the *hammam*."

Willow knew the *hammam* was the bath and went forth eagerly, for she was in desperate need of a good wash. She expected to be taken to the pool in the main chamber but instead was led to a smaller room at the end of a short hallway. Baba, wearing a white robe belted at the waist, awaited her there.

The *hammam* held a large sunken tub, a marble bench, ewers filled with water and a table laden with vials and clay pots. Willow headed for the tub.

"Nay, my lady, you are not yet ready to immerse yourself in the bath."

"What else is there?"

"Remove your clothing and lie down on the bench. All traces of body hair must be plucked and scraped from your skin before we can proceed to the next step."

"Is that necessary? It is simply not done in my country."

"You are in Prince Dariq's harem, lady. He is a Turk and follows the teachings of Allah. You cannot go to him unclean."

"I will not go to him at all," Willow protested. "I do not belong here."

"You would be much happier if you accepted your fate," Baba scolded. " 'Tis a good life, one you should embrace. You will be pampered and showered with gifts if you please our master. Since he is away at sea for long periods of time, you will not be overly taxed by his attentions. Please lie down so that I may attend you, my lady."

Willow didn't argue with the old woman; it would be futile to do so. Obviously, Dariq hadn't told Baba that she wasn't intended to be his concubine. Disgruntled, she stripped and stretched out on the marble bench.

The first thing Baba did was dip her fingers into a clay pot and spread a pink cream over Willow's groin area, her legs, her arms, and all the places that hair appeared on her body. Baba busied herself elsewhere for at least a half hour before returning with a ewer of water. Using a rough cloth, Baba proceeded to scrub the cream from Willow's body, taking away hair along with the cream and leaving Willow's body as smooth as silk. Then she bade Willow to sit up.

From another pot Baba scooped a double handful of soft soap and rubbed it over Willow's body. Then she took a flat tool and scraped away dirt and soap until Willow's skin felt cleaner than it had in weeks.

"Now you may get into the bath, my lady."

Willow rose and stepped into the pool, surprised to find the water warm and soothing. While she soaked the soap from her body, Baba applied soap to her hair and gave it a thorough scrubbing. Then she rinsed it with clean water from a ewer. It was so wonderfully refreshing that Willow hated to leave the *hammam* when Baba told her to do so.

Exclaiming over the color of her hair, Baba dried Willow with a large linen drying cloth. When Willow's skin was glowing, Baba told her to lie on her stomach on the bench. Willow had no idea what was coming next until Baba poured a stream of fragrant oil on her back and buttocks. She rested her head on her crossed arms as strong hands began massaging oil into her shoulders, back and buttocks, and down her legs to her feet. It felt wonderfully decadent and sinful.

"Turn over, lady."

Willow stiffened and looked over her shoulder, stunned to see Ali Hara's hands on her. She groped for the drying cloth but it had been taken away.

"Where is Baba?"

"She will return when I am finished."

"No! You should not . . . it isn't right. You're a man."

Ali Hara gave an impatient snort. "I am a eunuch, lady, not a man in the true sense of the word. Turn around so that I may finish."

Blushing bright red, Willow turned onto her back and closed her eyes. In her world, if a man looked like a man, he was a man. But the bored look on Ali Hara's face confirmed what he had just said to her. Her naked body meant naught to him. She closed her eyes and tried not to picture Ali Hara as a man.

Ali Hara lifted his hands a moment, and when they returned they somehow felt rougher, callused even, but so wonderfully relaxing. Then those talented hands sought out a place so intimate that Willow's eyes flew open and she reared up, shouting, "Stop it, Ali Hara!"

She blinked, and her mouth dropped open when she saw Dariq leaning over her, his hand slick with oil. He wore a simple white robe, baggy trousers, and a white turban that covered his black hair.

"How did you get here? Where is Ali Hara? Where is Baba?"

"I dismissed them. As for how I got here, I go where I please, when I please." He pointed to a partition of latticework across the room. "I watched you at your bath from there. Lie back, I am not finished yet."

"You most certainly are finished," Willow huffed. She lurched off the bench. "Where are my clothes?"

"Baba is fetching them for you."

She covered her breasts with her hands and gave him her back. "Go away! I am naked."

He laughed. "So you are." His silver gaze traveled the length of her elegant back and dimpled buttocks. "You please me very much, beauty. Were it possible, I would keep you for myself."

He stalked toward her. She retreated. He reached for her, pulling her hard against him.

"Kiss me, beauty."

She turned her head away, though she knew she fought a losing battle. There was no way she could stop Dariq from doing as he pleased. He turned her head toward him and kissed her, using his skillful mouth and tongue to work their erotic magic on her. His kiss went on and on, until her legs turned to jelly and her will to resist eroded. She felt a melting inside her and whether by choice or need, leaned into his kiss, molding herself against his hard body. Then she felt herself floating as he scooped her into his arms.

"Where are you taking me?"

"To my chamber. 'Tis time for another lesson in passion."

"No! You cannot. Have you forgotten why I am here?"

"I won't ruin you for Ibrahim, if that's what you are worried about. Your virginity is too important to me. There are other things we can do to give us pleasure."

"Stop! I am naked! You cannot carry me off like this."

"A small problem easily solved. Ali Hara!" The eunuch appeared instantly. "Bring a caftan for Lady Willow."

Ali Hara disappeared and reappeared a few moments later with a rose-colored caftan trimmed in gold tassels draped over his arm. Dariq set Willow on her feet and slipped the silken robe over her head.

Suddenly a whirlwind flew into the room. "My dear lord, I have been waiting for you!" Safiye cried as she flung herself into Dariq's arms.

In her eagerness to reach Dariq, Safiye shoved Willow so hard that she fell backward, landing on her rump. Then Safiye treated her to a display of passion so sexually charged it made Willow's face flame bright red. Ali Hara rushed to help her to her feet. Refusing to watch Safiye make love to Dariq where he stood, Willow fled from the room.

Chapter Seven

Dariq uttered a curse as he peeled Safiye off of him. She was clinging to him so tightly, he could feel her distended nipples and the moist heat of her woman's mound pressing against him.

"Why do you not touch me, master?" Safiye asked sulkily. She grasped his hand and brought it between her thighs. "Can you feel how wet I am for you through my skirts? Must I wait until tonight for your attention?"

From the corner of his eye, Dariq saw Willow flee into her chamber. He supposed he owed Safiye an explanation for Willow's presence in his seraglio and wondered how much he should reveal. Safiye was merely his concubine, not his wife, and he didn't need to explain anything to her. He had bought Safiye several months before, after his seraglio had been completed, and until he'd encountered Willow he had been content. She had served his needs well.

Safiye's sultry gaze turned petulant when Dariq remained silent. "Never say you intend to take the pale foreigner to your bed tonight. How can you abide her? She is ugly, and I am willing to wager she is ignorant in the art of pleasing a man."

A wry grin tipped up the corners of Dariq's mouth. Willow's sexual knowledge was indeed limited, but he intended to remedy that situation. Her sexual education would strain his control, but he felt confident he could contain his lust.

He gazed down at Safiye, suddenly aware of her possessiveness. He wondered why he hadn't noticed it before. The gleam in her dark eyes was almost predatory as she fondled his cock. Being a virile man, his body reacted noticeably to her intimate handling.

Rising up on her toes, she whispered against his mouth, "Take me now, master. Right here, where everyone can see I am yours and you are mine."

Dariq knew exactly what Safiye intended. She wanted to make Willow jealous. Safiye had never had reason to be jealous before and couldn't bear the thought that Willow might take her place in Dariq's bed. Would Safiye hurt Willow if she thought she was being replaced in Dariq's affections? He intended to quash any such thoughts here and now.

He gave Safiye a little shake. "Safiye, listen to me. Willow is no threat to you. She is merely staying in my harem until Ibrahim agrees to the trade I've proposed. I plan to exchange Lady Willow for my mother."

Safiye snorted in disbelief. "I hardly think Ibrahim will want her after you take her virginity."

"Willow is still innocent, and I intend for her to remain that way. If you have jealous thoughts about Willow, forget them."

Safiye looked perplexed. "How can that be? You were

together aboard your ship, and you have been without a woman a long time."

"I am not a lad who cannot control himself. Willow is too important to me as a hostage. As you say, Ibrahim will not agree to the exchange if I take her virginity."

Safiye gave him a flirtatious smile. "You must be in great need, master. Let me ease you."

She knelt before him and searched for his cock through the opening of his trousers. Dariq pulled her hands away and lifted her to her feet.

"Not now, my passionate little dove. I have too much to do."

"Do you swear you won't take Lady Willow to your bed?"

Dariq frowned. "I make no promises, Safiye, for what I do is none of your concern."

Safiye's full lips turned down. "Will you send for me tonight?"

"Perhaps," Dariq muttered distractedly. He was thinking not of Safiye but of Willow, whose supple body he longed to explore upon silken sheets. She consumed all his thoughts. He desired something he could not have, and it was driving him mad.

Dariq walked away from Safiye, leaving the fiery concubine fuming in impotent rage. Safiye recognized obsession when she saw it, and Lord Dariq was obviously obsessed with the pale Englishwoman. Though Safiye had no idea how long his self-control with Willow would prevail, she knew with a certainty that one day it would snap, and probably sooner rather than later.

If Willow was still innocent, which Safiye seriously doubted, she wouldn't be for much longer. Safiye made a silent vow to prevent the inevitable. Whatever it took,

Safiye was determined to preserve her position as the prince's favorite.

Willow kept to her chamber the rest of the day. Baba brought her clothing similar to Safiye's, consisting of a colorful beaded vest that barely covered her breasts, a skirt of several layers of gauzy material, soft slippers and a golden girdle studded with jewels. Since she had nothing else to wear, Willow removed her caftan and donned the clothing, even though she considered it far too revealing.

As evening approached, Willow became aware that she was hungry. She wondered when someone would bring her supper. Eventually Ali Hara appeared without her dinner, carrying a colorful garment over his arm.

"Am I to go to bed hungry?" Willow asked.

"Nay, lady. Prince Dariq commands your presence in his chamber."

Willow went still. "What does he want?"

"He did not confide in me, lady." He handed her a hooded caftan of varying shades of green. "Put this on and follow me."

Willow wondered what would happen if she refused. She eyed Ali Hara warily. If his size was any indication of his strength, he would have no problem forcing her to obey Dariq's summons.

What did the pirate want? Willow wondered. Didn't he realize that paying attention to her and not Safiye would antagonize his concubine? Why did he not summon his concubine to his chamber? As Safiye pointed out, Dariq had been many months without a woman and should be eager to bed his lovely concubine.

Sighing with resignation, Willow pulled on the caftan and followed Ali Hara. To her chagrin, Safiye was waiting near the door, her teeth bared in a feral snarl. Boldly Safiye placed herself in Willow's path.

"What did you do to him?" she hissed.

Willow sent her a startled look. "If you mean Prince Dariq, I did naught."

"Prince Dariq sent for you, did he not? He wants to bed you. He lied to me. He said he did not bring you here for his pleasure, and that you were to go untouched to Ibrahim."

"Prince Dariq spoke the truth," Willow contended.

Safiye gave a snort of disbelief. "Then why did he summon you tonight?"

"I have no idea," Willow said truthfully.

"Move aside, Safiye," Ali Hara commanded. "My master awaits Lady Willow, and he is not a patient man."

Safiye moved away, but not before snarling one last insult at Willow. "I know the prince well. He is a lusty man. He will have you if it pleases him."

Willow sincerely hoped not, but she trusted Dariq no more than she did Safiye. Not for the first time, she wondered about the loved one Dariq had left behind in Istanbul. He or she must mean a great deal to him.

Ali Hara led her down a long green and white marble corridor, turned a corner into another corridor, and stopped before a solid brass door polished to a high sheen. A guard opened the door. Ali Hara gently pushed her forward. When she glanced over her shoulder at him, all she saw was his retreating back. Willow wanted to flee with him but was frozen in place by the opulent chamber that looked like something right out of a fantasy.

She stood in the open doorway, gawking like a fool at silk-covered walls, slender columns of creamy white and gold marble, and filmy curtains floating around a bed piled high with colorful cushions. Candlelight bathed the chamber in varying shades of gold.

At first glance Willow thought the chamber was unoccupied. Then she saw him, lounging upon a pile of cushions scattered on the floor around a low table. He lifted his hand, and with a lazy motion, beckoned her forward.

Willow hesitated. She wanted to turn and run, but the sound of the heavy door closing behind her and her own curiosity carried her forward. Her steps may have dragged a little as she approached Dariq, but her courage did not waver.

"What do you want? Why did you send for me?"

"I wish to share my meal with you," Dariq purred in a voice so blatantly sexual that her steps faltered. "Are you afraid of me, beauty?"

"Nay. Should I be?" Her quivering voice belied her words.

Uncoiling his body in one graceful motion, Dariq rose. Willow stared at him. He was every woman's dream. Dressed in unadorned white, he wore his shirt open nearly to his navel and his baggy trousers thrust into black leather boots. His black hair was loose and rather long, just brushing his shoulders. The predatory gleam in his silver eyes could have melted stone, and Willow was far more malleable than stone.

Reaching out, Dariq whipped off her caftan and tossed it aside. His breath seized as he stared at her. His gaze roamed over her thinly clad body, from the top of her glorious head to her feet shod in soft slippers. Her hair rippled down her shoulders like a golden cloak; he had seen nothing to compare with it in all his travels. Her legs, visible through the sheer material of her skirts, were long and shapely. Her breasts were barely contained beneath her short vest, and the jewel-studded girdle that draped her hips accentuated the smallness of her waist and the graceful curves flowing beneath the diaphanous fabric of her skirts. She was breathtakingly exquisite; perfect in every way.

Grasping her elbow, he led her over to the cushions and eased her down. Then he sat down beside her and clapped his hands.

The door swung open. A servant entered and bowed.

"You may bring our food now, Haroun," Dariq ordered. The servant bowed again and departed.

Dariq smiled when he saw Willow sitting stiffly beside him, her face wearing a wary expression. "Relax, beauty, I merely wish to share a meal with you." The husky sound of his voice coated her with warmth.

"Why me when you have Safiye?"

Dariq frowned. Why indeed? "Had I wanted Safiye, I would have sent for her."

A discreet knock and then the door opened. Haroun entered carrying an enormous tray. Another servant bearing gold-trimmed plates, cups and eating utensils entered behind him. Haroun eased the tray down on the table, placed the plates and eating utensils in precise order and quietly departed.

Dariq uncovered dishes of steaming rice, a savory dish of lamb and vegetables, fish, bowls of soup fragrant with mint, rounds of flatbread and mounds of butter. Accompanying the meal were a pot of tea and a bowl of fresh peaches, dates and figs. Dariq filled a plate for Willow and one for himself.

When Willow made no move to eat, Dariq picked up a succulent piece of lamb with his fingers and held it to her lips. He chuckled when he heard Willow's stomach growl.

"Open your mouth, beauty. You will find this food far superior to any you had aboard the *Revenge*. Superior to anything you had in England, too, I'll wager."

He nodded his approval when Willow opened her mouth. He popped in the piece of lamb and watched her chew, purposely licking his fingers as she chewed. She must have found the food to her liking, for she picked up her fork and began to eat. Satisfied that Willow did not mean to starve herself, Dariq gave his own plate the attention it deserved. When they had both eaten their fill, Dariq picked up a peach, peeled it and offered Willow a slice.

She opened her mouth to accept his offering, but instead of letting go of the peach, he let Willow's mouth close over his fingers. She started violently when he slowly moved his fingers in and out of her mouth before releasing the fruit. A trickle of juice slid down her chin. Before she could wipe it away, Dariq leaned over and licked her chin and then her lips with his tongue.

"Delicious," he murmured. "Would you like another slice?"

He took her silence for assent, though she appeared somewhat wary. He pared another piece of peach and held it to her mouth. As he'd done before, he thrust two fingers into her mouth with the peach.

He did not even try to suppress his groan as Willow's tongue flicked over his fingers, licking the peach juice from them. The sensation was so erotic, he feared his cock would burst. Needing to defuse the volatile situation before he lost control, he removed his fingers and popped a slice of peach into his own mouth.

After they finished the peach, he clapped his hands. The door opened on silent hinges. "Take this away," he ordered, gesturing to the remains of their meal. "See that we are not disturbed by anyone." His glittering gaze remained on Willow the entire time he spoke.

"I should return to the harem," Willow said. She started to rise.

Dariq dragged her back down. "No, beauty, you cannot leave yet. I have been thinking about you in this setting all day—nay, since I first clapped eyes on you."

Willow scooted away from him. "Why, when I cannot give you what you need? Why did you not summon Safiye? She is eager to . . . to pleasure you. You have been at sea a long time and need the comfort of a willing woman."

Dariq himself wondered why he hadn't summoned Safiye. Safiye could give him everything he needed from a woman, but it wasn't Safiye he wanted. Willow intrigued him beyond endurance. It wasn't just her beauty, which was considerable, or her extraordinary golden hair and lovely green eyes. Nay, it was something less easily defined, something difficult to explain.

Her spirit was indomitable, her nature unflaggingly optimistic despite the situation in which she had been thrust. He knew she hoped to escape her fate, but what she didn't know was that escape was impossible. Once she left his protection, she would belong to Ibrahim, body and soul.

That thought brought a frown to Dariq's handsome face and a pain in the vicinity of his heart. Ibrahim was not known for his gentle nature. Most of his concubines feared him, and with good reason. His brother was a difficult man, one who had his concubines beaten with the bastinado when they displeased him. Dariq couldn't bear the thought of any part of Willow's silken flesh being bruised.

"Why are you frowning?" Willow asked.

"I just had an unpleasant thought." He pushed those thoughts aside. It would be a long time before Ahmed returned with Ibrahim's reply to his terms for the trade. "But 'tis gone now; you have my undivided attention."

He reached for her. She flinched away, but the thought that she couldn't escape him made him smile. He wanted to give her pleasure even if he had to deny his own. He had no idea why he was willing to put himself through that kind of torture, except that he adored the look on Willow's face when she peaked. He had seen it once and wanted to see it again . . . and yet again. Her pleasure was his pleasure.

"I am going to remove your vest," Dariq murmured.

He smothered her protests with a kiss while he effortlessly removed her vest and tossed it aside. She went still beneath him, which he took as a good sign. He didn't want to frighten her; he just wanted to love her in every way except the one way he couldn't.

Willow tried to shield her breasts, but Dariq wouldn't allow it. He bore her down against the cushions and held her wrists above her head with one hand while he nibbled and suckled her nipples. He trembled with excitement and need. Just touching Willow like this drove him mad with wanting. It took all of his willpower to recall why she must remain virginal.

He unfastened her girdle and tossed it aside. He kissed her deeply, his tongue thrusting inside her mouth in imitation of what he really wanted to do to her. He groaned as his cock lifted and filled with blood.

Suddenly he yelped and reared back. "Why in the name of Allah did you bite me?"

She gave him a smug smile. "I wanted you to know I am not a willing participant in what you are doing."

"Do you know what would happen if you did that to Ibrahim?"

"He would not want me, which would suit me just fine."

"You are naive if you think that. He would have you beaten, and then he would take you while you were too weak to resist. Or he would drug you into compliance."

"Drug me?" Willow whispered. "He would do that?"

"Aye, he would, beauty. You would be fed something to make you so desperate for a man, you would beg for his attention. You would welcome him with open arms . . . and legs," he added crudely.

Willow gasped, her eyes bright with fright, though Dariq knew from experience that she didn't frighten easily. She was a woman who deserved better than what he intended for her. The least he could do was give her a taste of pleasure before she was used so ruthlessly by Ibrahim.

"I did not mean to frighten you, beauty," Dariq apologized, "but 'tis best that you do not go to Ibrahim ignorant of his cruel nature or his methods of controlling a woman's rebelliousness. It will go easier on you if you accept your fate."

Willow shuddered. "Never! Have you no compassion? No conscience? I beg you, send me home. Do not give me to a man you despise—a man who abuses his women."

Even if Dariq chose not to send Willow to Ibrahim, he knew he wouldn't send her home. He would keep her for himself. The thought had crossed his mind more than once, despite the knowledge that keeping her would spell his mother's doom.

"You will learn to survive," Dariq said, keeping his voice deliberately passionless despite the turmoil roiling inside him.

"If you insist on sending me to Ibrahim, the least you can do is tell me for whom I am being exchanged."

"Aye," Dariq said thoughtfully, "I suppose you are right. But first you should know more about my brother than I have told you. He is our father's eldest son. My mother was Father's only wife, but he had many concubines with whom he had sons and daughters. Ibrahim was born before Father met and wed my mother in a Christian ceremony. Mother is known as Saliha Sultana. When Father died three years ago, the sultanate passed to Ibrahim. It mattered not to me, for I never wanted what rightfully belonged to my brother.

"Two years ago, Ibrahim went on a rampage, killing all of Father's male heirs. He feared that one day the heirs would rise up and overthrow him. He was coming to kill me when Mother warned me of his intent. She begged me to flee. I wanted to take her with me, but she refused. She said the mothers of the slain children needed her.

"When I refused to leave without her, Mustafa, the captain of my personal guard at the time, knocked me unconscious and carried me to my ship. For a while, Mother lived in the harem without fear of harm, but I began to hear rumors about her safety that led me to ask Ibrahim, through an emissary, for her release into my custody. Thus far, Ibrahim has refused.

"You see, my brother wants me to stop interfering with his shipping and has threatened to slay my mother if I do not surrender myself to him. I dare not go to Istanbul, for Ibrahim's janizaries have orders to kill me on sight."

"Your mother," Willow whispered shakily. "Now I understand why you are so determined to negotiate a trade."

"I cannot allow Ibrahim to kill my mother. She is very dear to me."

Willow moved restlessly against him; he felt the erotic

friction of her breasts against his chest, and his randy cock reminded him why he had summoned the blond beauty to his chamber. It certainly wasn't to discuss his problems.

"Do you remember what I said about pleasuring you on silken sheets?"

He felt her shudder. Scooping her into his arms, he carried her to his bed. The bed had already been turned down; he placed her on rose-colored silk sheets and whipped off her skirts, the only piece of clothing left to her. Then he began to strip off his own clothing, his piercing silver gaze daring her to watch.

Willow wanted to look away but could not. Dariq was magnificent, every part of him masculine and virile, all corded muscles and rippling tendons. His skin appeared as if warmed by the sun; his features were sharply defined, as if honed in granite. While ropes of muscles sculpted his torso, his slim waist and hips gave the impression of pantherlike sleekness. His bronze flesh and black hair made him look exotic, but his features and silver eyes proclaimed his English blood.

Her gaze slid over him, then skittered away when she saw his manhood springing up from the dark forest between his legs. Her gaze immediately returned to his face.

"There is naught to be afraid of," Dariq said. "Roll over, beauty, you are too tense. Let me help you relax."

Willow's breath caught when Dariq placed his hands on her hip and shoulder and turned her onto her stomach. "What are you going to do?"

He reached into a basket on the nightstand and retrieved a vial of liquid, rubbing it between his palms to warm it. Then he removed the stopper and poured a small amount into his palm; he rubbed his hands together to distribute the liquid equally.

"What is that?"

Connie Mason

"Fragrant oil—can you smell it? 'Tis very soothing. Breathe deeply of the scent while I massage it into your skin."

When his palms flattened on her back, she stiffened. Then her skin began to tingle. Heat followed the erotic path of his hands as they moved in slow, sensuous circles over her shoulders, back and buttocks. Not only did Willow begin to relax, but the oil's aroma was having a strange effect on her.

She felt herself drifting on a sensual fog. Her skin became so sensitive that his lightest touch was pure torture. When he began massaging the insides of her thighs, Willow couldn't stop the tiny moan that escaped her lips. Then he touched her more intimately, his fingers slipping into the division between her buttocks and following it to the swollen lips of her sex.

Willow summoned a protest, but her voice was suddenly too weak to voice it. She knew that what Dariq was doing to her was sinful, and the way it made her feel was wicked, but she couldn't help herself. Her mind and body were no longer hers to command. The oil intensified the sensations of her body while its aroma addled her brain.

Dariq eased her over on her back, dribbled more oil onto his hands and began to massage her breasts, giving her pouting nipples special attention. By the time his hands left her breasts and slid over her stomach, Willow was writhing and moaning beneath him, the movement of her hips begging for his intimate touch.

"Your skin is like silk," Dariq whispered. His palm cupped her smooth mound, and then he kissed her there. "Especially here." He spread her thighs, kissing her between them. "How do you feel?" he asked.

Willow stirred. Dariq's voice sounded as if it came

from a great distance. "What did you do to me? Did you drug me?"

"Nay, beauty, it's the aroma of the oil. It can be overpowering to one unaccustomed to the scent. It makes you feel wonderfully relaxed, does it not?"

"I feel . . . strange."

"I know. Open your legs for me; I can make you feel better."

Willow obeyed even though she knew she should not. He slid down her body, opened the petals of her sex and touched her with his tongue. She nearly jumped off the bed.

"Did you feel pleasure?" he murmured.

"I feel like my skin is on fire and my bones are melting," she gasped.

He lowered his head and laved the slick folds of her sex with his mouth and tongue. He played her body like a finely tuned instrument while she helplessly responded to the strains of his melody. This couldn't be happening to her. She'd never known she was capable of feeling the kind of intense pleasure Dariq was giving her. It overwhelmed her to the point of madness. When Dariq reached up to fondle her nipples, she exploded, her orgasm so strong, she feared she would shatter into a thousand pieces.

Slowly Willow regained her wits, disturbingly aware of another erotic sensation. She opened her eyes to find Dariq lying beside her, a predatory grin spreading across his face as he tickled her breasts with a peacock feather. She could feel his extremely hard, exceedingly thick manhood prodding her leg.

She wanted to touch him . . . badly, and that shocked her. She had never been shy or retiring, but neither had she been overbold about sexual matters. It had to be the oil that was making her long for things she shouldn't.

"Go ahead, touch me," Dariq said, as if reading her mind.

Was that a quiver she heard in his voice? She dared a glance at his staff; it was erect and growing. That couldn't be comfortable. She recalled how she had touched him aboard the *Revenge*, and how his seed had spewed forth when his excitement reached its peak. Some perverse devil inside her wanted to do that to him again.

She heard him suck in his breath when she reached over and curled her fingers around him. He was hard yet soft, firm yet yielding, and so enormous her fingers didn't reach around him. She started to release him but he grabbed her wrist, holding it in place so she couldn't move her hand away. Willow had no choice but to begin the motion that she knew would give Dariq pleasure.

She worked her hand up and down, watching his face grow tense, feeling his body harden. She was waiting for the eruption she knew was inevitable when he flung her hand aside and mounted her.

"The hell with Ibrahim," he growled. "I will perish if I cannot have you."

She felt his staff prodding the entrance of her sex and attempted to push him away. "Dariq . . . !"

He kissed her into silence. His mouth was soft and persuasive, his tongue an erotic force thrusting into her mouth. She was growing dizzy, drunk on the excitement of Dariq's seduction. His body was heavy upon hers, but she welcomed the weight; somehow it seemed right. Her bones were melting; she wanted him inside her but couldn't find the courage to express her sinful wishes.

She moved her hips in blatant invitation; she felt him push inside her a little ways and then stop. He touched his forehead to hers, his chest heaving as if he had run a great distance.

"Allah help me. I never meant for this to happen." His voice was a ragged plea that fell upon deaf ears.

A sudden, desperate thought came to Willow. If Dariq took her virginity, Ibrahim would not want her, and perhaps, just perhaps, Dariq would send her home. Her resistance melted with that thought and she relaxed.

Dariq flexed his hips, preparing for the final thrust that would destroy her virginity, when a loud knock shattered the moment.

Lifting his head, Dariq frowned at the door. "Go away!"

"I've brought Safiye to you, my lord," Mustafa shouted through the panel.

"Go away!" Dariq repeated.

"But, master, Safiye can satisfy your needs."

"If you do not go away, Mustafa, I will have your head lopped off."

Silence.

"Master, it is I, Safiye. Send the English houri away and let me pleasure you."

A low growl formed in Dariq's throat. "Leave immediately, Safiye, and take Mustafa with you!"

The sound of retreating footsteps grew distant, and then disappeared. Dariq gazed into Willow's eyes, thrust his hips forward and completed the act. A sharp pain tore into her, through her, and she screamed. Dariq covered her mouth with his, swallowing her cries until she grew quiet and began to kiss him back.

He was panting hard when he finally came up for air. "Did I hurt you?"

"You could have warned me. I . . . had no idea. Is it always like that?"

"Nay, just this one time. I never intended for this to happen. This is the first time I've ever lost control with a woman. Lust is a powerful emotion, but with you I fear it is more than that." He began to move inside her. "Does it still hurt?"

"A little."

But it didn't hurt for long. As Dariq moved inside her the pain disappeared, replaced by a sensation like nothing she had ever felt before. At first it was a tingling where they were joined. Then heat spread through her body, unbearable, throbbing heat that surged through her veins. She wanted to feel him deeper, feel him harder, feel him melt into her, become a part of her. Then she shattered; the pleasure was so intense, she lost the ability to think. She was nearly in an insensate state when she heard Dariq call her name and felt his hot seed splash against her womb.

Dariq's last thought was that his unquenchable lust for Willow could very well mean his mother's death.

Chapter Eight

Dariq rolled onto his back and flung an arm over his eyes. He had just made the biggest mistake of his life, and there was no way to rectify it. He had acted like an irresponsible fool, putting his own pleasure before his mother's life.

"I'm worthless to you now," Willow said hopefully.

Dariq lowered his arm and stared at her, a thoughtful look on his face. "Perhaps all is not lost. You are still as tight as a virgin, and there's a way to substitute virgin's blood where there is none."

Willow's expression was one of stunned disbelief. "You mean you still intend to give me to Ibrahim?"

"I love my mother," he said simply. "I cannot let her die."

Willow pulled the sheet over her nude body. A heavy silence throbbed between them.

When Dariq spoke next, his voice was devoid of all emotion. "If I trade my own life for my mother's, there is no guarantee Ibrahim would let my mother live once I am dead."

"You would sacrifice yourself?"

"Aye, if I must."

Willow chewed thoughtfully on her lower lip. "Perhaps there is another way."

"Aye, I will think on it. Perhaps Ibrahim will not know your maidenhead is missing. Then again, he might insist that one of his physicians examine you before the trade is completed. My brother trusts me no more than I trust him, and with good reason."

"All will be lost if a physician examines me."

"I would not let it go that far," Dariq said fiercely.

"I am sorry," Willow said. She should have fought harder against Dariq's sensual assault, but she had hoped her lack of virginity would lead to her release. She should have known better.

"I hold myself responsible for what happened," Dariq replied. "I must now make things right. Go now, before I take you again. One time with you has but whetted my appetite. I must not take you again, and I cannot I trust myself alone with you." He turned away from her. "My lack of self-control is unforgivable. You emasculate me, beauty. You test my control as no woman ever has before."

He surged from the bed in one fluid motion and dragged on his trousers. Willow arose also, looking for her discarded clothing. Dariq plucked her caftan from the floor and dropped it over her head. Then he gathered her clothes and thrust them into her arms. Turning away, he shouted for Mustafa. The giant burst into the chamber immediately, as if he had been waiting outside the door for Dariq's summons.

Mustafa shot Willow an assessing glance before turning his attention to Dariq. "What is your wish, master?"

"Return Lady Willow to the harem and then attend me in my chamber."

His expression grim, Mustafa bowed and ushered Willow from the chamber. He returned a short time later to find Dariq prowling his chamber like a caged animal.

"I warned you, did I not?" Mustafa reproached. "I hope she was worth it."

"You don't know what happened; you can only surmise."

"I know you, my lord prince, better than you know yourself. When you summoned Lady Willow to your chamber, I knew how it would end, even if you did not. You must send her away, for she is useless to you now."

Dariq disagreed. "Why would I do that? She can still be useful."

Mustafa searched Dariq's face. "Do you intend to keep her for yourself?"

Dariq shifted uncomfortably. "Although that option is still open to me, there is another."

Mustafa's dark brows knitted. "What would that be, master?"

Dariq poured himself a tumbler of water from a pitcher and drank thirstily. "Sending Willow to Ibrahim is still possible. I cannot replace her maidenhead, but there are ways to simulate innocence. I'm sure Baba could teach her about such things."

He began to pace again. "The problem, Mustafa, is that I cannot bear to part with Willow. She pleases me beyond understanding. The thought of Ibrahim abusing her is repugnant to me."

Mustafa groaned and rolled his eyes. "You are thinking with your cock, my lord. You still have Safiye. You adore Safiye."

"I adore what she does for me, but I have no feelings

127

beyond mild affection for her. I am a sexual creature, Mustafa, but I am also a discerning one. I know when a woman pleases me beyond mere physical satisfaction."

"Do you mean that Lady Willow is the woman you need to make you happy?"

Dariq scoffed. "I do not need a woman to make me happy, merely one to satisfy my sexual needs. Raiding Ibrahim's ships makes me happy." He shook his head. "I truly do not know what to do, Mustafa, aside from wanting to keep Willow for myself. But I cannot." A horrifying thought occurred to him. "What if she conceived my child tonight? For the first time in my life, I cannot trust myself with a woman. What does that say about me?"

"It says, Prince Dariq, that you are a man with a divided heart. Worry not, 'tis unlikely the lady conceived tonight, but if she did, Baba knows how to rid her of your unwanted seed. I will see that it is taken care of."

"Nay! I do not want Willow harmed."

"You are besotted."

Dariq made an impatient gesture. "You know not what you talk about, my friend. I have no heart. I satisfy my sexual urges where and with whom I please; women mean naught to me but a moment's pleasure."

Mustafa sent him a skeptical look.

"I refuse to succumb to weakness of the flesh," Dariq declared. A determined look hardened his features. "I know what I must do, Mustafa. Despite her lack of maidenhead, Willow is my only hope of saving Mother. My plans for Willow will follow their original course."

"Is that your final word, my lord?"

"Aye, Mustafa." His voice thickened with resolve. "I will not seek Willow's company while my willpower to resist her is so low. I suspect my desire for her will wane if I keep my distance. Instruct Baba to watch for Willow's courses. I will decide what to do should she quicken with my child."

He turned away, but his thoughts were still with Willow. *Out of sight, out of mind doesn't always work*, a little voice in his head whispered. Could he banish Willow from his mind? He had to, for his mother's sake. No matter his personal feelings for her, Willow was destined to become Ibrahim's concubine.

Despite the late hour, Safiye accosted Willow the moment she returned from Dariq's chamber, verbally venting her venom. "He bedded you!" she accused. "Do not deny it."

"I am in no mood to argue with you," Willow replied tiredly. She wanted to be alone. She was exhausted and in need of a bath.

"You reek of sex," Safiye blasted as she followed Willow to her chamber.

Willow blocked her entrance. "Go to bed, Safiye, 'tis late."

Safiye's scathing gaze fell on the bundle of clothing in Willow's arms. She gave a bitter laugh. "I knew it! You did not please him. He sent you from his bed in disgrace."

Willow had heard enough. Safiye's taunts were more than she could bear. She wanted to be alone to think. "Ali Hara!" she shouted, and then waited for the ebony giant to appear.

He arrived moments later, naked to the waist, his feet bare. "What is it, my lady? Are you hurt? Is there aught you desire?"

"Aye, Ali Hara. I desire Safiye to leave my chamber. I grow tired of her insults."

The eunuch sent Safiye a censuring look. "You should be abed, lady. Come, I will escort you to your chamber."

Safiye gave Willow a scathing glance and flounced off. "I will sleep outside Safiye's door to make sure she does not return, my lady," Ali Hara whispered.

Willow heaved an enormous sigh as she closed the door behind Safiye and Ali Hara. She looked longingly at the bed, but as much as she wanted to give in to exhaustion she knew Safiye was right. She *did* reek of sex. She could smell Dariq's seed on her. She opened her door once again and peered out. The harem was silent. Quietly she made her way to the *hammam*. She needed to be alone to think about everything that had happened tonight and the ultimate consequences.

The halls were deserted and the *hammam* dark but for a single wall sconce, creating disturbing patterns of light and dark. Ignoring the grotesque display dancing upon the walls, Willow drew off her caftan and lowered herself into the sunken tub.

A blissful sigh escaped her throat as she sank down into the warm water. She closed her eyes, letting the warmth soothe away her troubles. What had happened between her and Dariq tonight had caused more problems for her. Did Dariq blame her for his loss of control? She thought he did. And in a way, she *was* responsible.

She had stopped resisting Dariq, mistakenly believing that her loss of virginity would foil his plans to give her to Ibrahim. She'd assumed that once she had been defiled, Dariq would return her to her father . . . perhaps for ransom. But her assumptions had been wrong.

Willow saw the pot of soap lying on the rim of the tub and scooped out a handful, using it to scrub Dariq's scent from her. Only then did she feel fresh and clean again. Unfortunately, nothing could restore her virginity. Even if Dariq returned her to her father, she was ruined for marriage to anyone else. She would be ruined even if

Dariq hadn't corrupted her. The scandal would scare off prospective suitors despite her generous portion.

Gossip would travel to France and beyond, so it would make no difference if she decided to live in her mother's country. Scandal would follow her wherever she went.

A terrifying thought abruptly occurred to her. What if she had conceived Dariq's child? She wasn't ignorant. She knew that one time was all it took to catch a babe. Would Dariq still send her to Ibrahim if she carried his child?

Would he sacrifice his own child to save his mother?

Willow stepped out of the tub and reached for a drying cloth, depression weighing heavily on her. A dismal future lay before her no matter where fate led her.

Sleep eluded Dariq. Willow's fate was in his hands, and he didn't know what to do. Bedding Willow hadn't been a smart move, but he had been desperate to have her. Never had his self-control been so thoroughly compromised. His moment of uncontrollable lust was likely to have dire consequences, and he had no idea now how to rectify it.

Should he go ahead with his original plans to exchange Willow for his mother? Would Ibrahim punish Willow for her lack of virginity? Or should he abandon that plan for another? He had sneaked into Istanbul before; perhaps he could attempt it again, this time to spirit his mother out of Ibrahim's harem. He had a wonderful ally in Kamel, but his brother's janizaries would be difficult to elude, especially inside the seraglio.

An untamed urge to have Willow again clawed at Dariq's innards, torturing him to the point that he wanted to burst into the harem and carry her back to his chamber. His loins throbbed, and he rolled over on his stomach, fighting his need for a blond houri who tempted him beyond redemption.

Bedding Willow had been a mistake, but a powerful hunger for her had created a temporary madness in him. He should be content after satisfying his lust, but he wasn't. The sad fact remained that one time with Willow would never be enough.

Perhaps he should summon Safiye, Dariq thought. The dark-haired beauty had the expertise and stamina to exhaust his body until it accepted sleep.

He didn't want Safiye.

By Allah's beard! What had Willow done to him? All he could think about was her soft white skin, the fragrance of her hair, and the silken tightness of her feminine sheath as he drove them both to climax.

Aye, he was mad. There was no other explanation.

The following two weeks passed with boring similarity. Willow hadn't seen Dariq since the night he had taken her virginity. Though she found it difficult to explain, she missed him. She was ably served by both Baba and Ali Hara, but they hardly provided the stimulating conversation she enjoyed with Dariq. Safiye had kept her distance. The concubine seemed to come and go at will, often leaving the harem without permission. There seemed to be no rules where Safiye was concerned. Where she went on her outings, Willow had no idea.

One day Willow was in the *hammam* enjoying a bath when she sensed someone watching her. She called Baba, but the old woman must not have heard her, for she didn't answer the summons. She remembered the peephole and turned her head toward the latticework behind which Dariq had once watched her bathe.

"Dariq, is that you? Are you spying on me?"

Willow saw a shadow move behind the lattice, and then it was gone, and with it the feeling that she was being spied upon.

Later that day, Willow was sitting on a bench in the small garden, bored and restless. She would surely perish if she had to spend the rest of her days imprisoned by walls. It was time to flee, despite the fact that scant opportunity existed for a successful escape.

Willow stifled a groan when Safiye entered the garden and glided languidly toward her. Safiye was the last person Willow wanted to talk to. She suspected that the other women had been occupying Dariq's bed these past two weeks, and the thought didn't please her.

"You look unhappy," Safiye said as she fluttered down beside Willow, "while I am deliriously happy." She stifled a yawn. "Prince Dariq summoned me to his bed last night. He is a tireless lover, but you already know that."

"I am thrilled for you," Willow muttered sourly. "I am not here by choice, or to serve Prince Dariq's needs." She started to rise.

"No, do not go," Safiye said. "If you wish to leave, perhaps I can help you."

Willow settled down again beside Safiye. "How can you help me?"

"Unlike you, I am not confined to the harem. I have few restrictions, except that I must wear a caftan and veil when I go abroad."

"Where do you go?"

"The pirates and their women live in Pirate Town, a small village hugging the docks. The women sell trinkets and such in the marketplace—items they no longer want or need. I sometimes visit the souk to look over their wares. Everyone knows I belong to their prince, and no one harms me."

"Does Dariq know you leave the harem?"

"The prince knows and approves. This is Lipsi, not Istanbul, and he is quite lenient where I am concerned. Sometimes Ali Hara accompanies me, and sometimes I go alone."

Willow's fine brows knitted. "How does that help me? Dariq would never allow me to leave the harem, not for any reason."

"Sometimes I visit Lipsi Town, a small Greek village where most of the islanders live. I am friendly with the inhabitants. Perhaps I can hire someone with a sturdy boat to take you to the Greek mainland. You could book passage to England from there."

Hope stirred in Willow's breast. "But I have no money or valuables."

"I will give you money. Prince Dariq is a generous lover. He gives me jewels and coin from his own portion of the booty taken from Turkish ships." She shrugged. "Since I have little use for coin, you are welcome to it."

Safiye's offer sounded too good to be true. Why would Dariq's concubine help her?

"Why should I trust you?"

Safiye sent her an exasperated look. "Think you I want you here? My master is obsessed with you. I would do anything to make you disappear from his life."

"How soon can you make arrangements for my departure?"

Safiye's smile was genuine. "It will not take long. When you leave here, you will be wearing my caftan and veil. Everyone will think I am out on one of my jaunts."

"What about Ali Hara? Won't he be suspicious?"

"I often go out and about alone. The island is small, with few inhabitants. Prince Dariq's harem is not a prison."

Willow scoffed. "To me it is."

"Your situation is different. The prince keeps you under guard for a reason."

"Won't Dariq be angry with you for helping me flee?"

Safiye shrugged. "I will deny any knowledge of your escape. You could have discovered the garden gate on your own, stolen money from me and bought your own passage to Greece. Anything is possible for a resourceful woman."

"There's a garden gate?" Willow asked, scanning the high walls surrounding the garden for the gateway to freedom. "Point it out to me."

"I will show you, but not yet. You will fail if you attempt to leave before the arrangements are all in place. You cannot do this on your own, lady; you will be caught and returned, which neither of us wants."

"Very well, but please hurry. I shall need clothes, too. I cannot go about in public in harem clothing."

"Agreed," Safiye said. "I will purchase a Greek peasant costume for you in the souk."

After Safiye left, Willow remained behind, contemplating the fish swimming in the small pond. For the first time in ages, she felt hope. She didn't trust Safiye, but she trusted the woman's jealousy. Safiye wanted her gone as badly as she wanted to leave.

Willow recalled the garden gate Safiye had mentioned and decided to investigate on her own, just in case something should go wrong with Safiye's plans. Pretending to study the plants as she strolled amid the foliage, Willow casually inspected the three walls surrounding the garden. At first she saw nothing to indicate a gate. On her second pass around the perimeter of the garden, she pushed aside dense shrubbery and found what she was looking for: an ivy-covered gate that blended with the surrounding greenery. Had she not been looking for it, she would never have noticed it. She tried the handle and was surprised when the door gave. But she didn't push it open. Being of a practical mind, she decided to wait for Safiye to pave the way for her. With no money or proper clothing, she wouldn't get very far. And her blond hair would surely arouse suspicion.

The next few days were pure agony for Willow. Anticipation made her restless and irritable. When Dariq appeared in the harem, Willow was certain Safiye's plan had gone awry. She was alone in the garden when he sought her out. It was the first time she had seen him since that fateful night in his chamber.

"Baba told me I would find you out here," Dariq said.

"It's peaceful in the garden," Willow replied without looking at him. She didn't want him to see how powerfully his presence affected her; just being near him made her skin tingle and her blood heat.

"I am glad you've found a place you could enjoy."

She looked at him then. "Why are you here?"

Why, indeed? Dariq wondered. He couldn't tell her he missed her, that he hadn't bedded Safiye after their night together because he couldn't bear the thought of another woman in his arms. Nor could he admit that he hungered for the sight of her. Baba had told him her courses had arrived, so he had no worry on that score.

"I wanted to check on your welfare. You are important to me, Willow. Ali Hara tells me you are unhappy."

"I have naught to be happy about. You still intend to trade me to Ibrahim, do you not? Or have you come to tell me you are making plans to take me home?"

"I cannot take you home. Plans for the exchange are already in progress; I cannot stop them now. If Ibrahim thought I was lying about holding you hostage, he would kill my mother."

"So there is no hope for me."

She stiffened when he grasped her shoulders and pulled her close. "Even if negotiations with Ibrahim should fail, I would not let you go."

His voice was low and harsh and his expression fierce; he looked and sounded as if parting with her would bring him pain. But that was ridiculous. She was merely a pawn in his games with his brother.

"I still want you, Willow," Dariq admitted. "You would be in my bed every night if I could claim you for myself."

"I thought Safiye was satisfying your needs."

Dariq's brow furrowed. "I haven't . . . she hasn't . . ." His sentence fell off.

Willow searched his face. His denial sounded false, but why would he lie? She meant naught to him.

Reaching out, he tipped up her face, his lips hovering over hers. She stared into his eyes and saw something she hadn't expected to see. Regret? Sadness? She had scant time to analyze his expression as he brushed her mouth with soft kisses, and then played more seductively, his mouth rough and tender at the same time.

His kisses held a note of desperation as his arms tightened around her, his fingers digging into the soft flesh of her shoulders. To her consternation, Dariq seated himself on the bench and dragged her onto his lap. Their mouths were still fused, but his hands had left her shoulders and were now fondling her breasts beneath her brief vest.

Lost in his kiss, Willow felt his erection pulse hard and hot against her bottom. This was as close to ecstasy as she could get without actually having Dariq inside her. And, God help her, she *did* want him inside her. He had already ruined her, so he might as well repeat the act and satisfy them both. Once she left here, she would never see the arrogant pirate again, and good riddance to him, she thought. But deep in her heart she knew she was lying to herself. She would miss Dariq even though he didn't care for her.

Excitement raced through her when she felt him push her skirts up, felt his hands on her thighs, lifting her upon his—

"Prince Dariq!"

Dariq groaned. Leave it to Safiye to appear at the wrong time. He should be grateful to her, for had she not appeared, he would have made love to Willow on the garden bench, and he didn't need another reminder of his inexplicable obsession with the blond beauty.

Hastily he straightened his clothing and returned Willow to the bench. Once he regained his composure, he stood and greeted Safiye.

"Why did you not tell me you were here, my lord?" Safiye pouted. She sidled close to him, her full breasts brushing his arm in blatant invitation.

Dariq glanced at Willow. Her face flushed. Was she jealous? Did he want her to be jealous? The devil inside him made him lower his head and kiss Safiye. He compared her taste to Willow's and found it lacking. What was the matter with him? Willow was a woman like any other. What hold did she have over him?

"Please excuse me, I do not wish to intrude," Willow said, edging past Dariq and his concubine.

Dariq watched her leave with a sense of loss, wondering what sending her away would do to his emotions. He suspected he would be devastated, though he had difficulty admitting it, for though he loved women, he had never shown partiality.

"My lord, what is wrong?" Safiye asked. "Why are you so distant? I beg you, do not let the blond houri distract you. She is not worth it."

She glanced down at his groin, smiling when she saw his manhood stir restlessly beneath his trousers, unaware that his arousal was the result of his encounter with Willow. "Come to my chamber, my lord." Her hand slid downward, her fingers curling around his cock.

Unconsciously Dariq brushed her hand aside. His gaze followed Willow's swaying hips until she disappeared inside the harem. His cock thickened and hardened. He spit out a curse and turned away from Safiye.

"I have business elsewhere," he said gruffly. "I have no time for you now."

"You never have time for me. Not since you brought that blond *houri* here."

"You go too far, Safiye," Dariq warned. "When Willow is gone, everything will return to normal. Meanwhile, you will have to accept things the way they are." Turning on his heel, he strode away.

"I will *not* accept your lack of attention," Safiye muttered beneath her breath. "And the *houri* who has taken you from me will soon be gone from your life."

Her jaw firm with purpose, Safiye set out to find her rival. She located Willow in her chamber. Willow's brows rose in surprise when Safiye barged unannounced into her room.

" 'Tis time," Safiye said. "The arrangements have been made. I purchased native Greek clothing and hired a fisherman to carry you across the water to Greece."

"Today?" Now that the time had come to leave, Willow felt a strange emptiness. She blamed it on anticipation, even though she knew the sensation had more to do with loss.

"Tomorrow. The weather promises to be fair, and Ali Hara mentioned that Prince Dariq plans to meet with the captains of his ships. He will be occupied most of the day. I will come for you after breakfast."

After Safiye took her leave, Willow sank down on the bed. This was what she wanted, wasn't it? Perhaps not what she wanted, but what she had to do. Dariq showed no sign of softening his position about her future as Ibrahim's concubine, and she resented him for remaining firm despite the intimacy they had shared. So she would leave and not look back, but she would always remember Dariq. Perhaps with fondness, but also as the man who'd stolen her innocence and abandoned her.

She would also remember him as the man who'd awakened her sensuality and found his way into her heart.

Chapter Nine

The minutes dragged by the following morning as Willow waited for Safiye to appear. She'd seen little of the concubine since the day before. Had Safiye lied to her? Time was running out. As soon as word from Ibrahim arrived, she would be sent away. Dariq had left her no option but to flee this intolerable situation.

The door opened and Safiye slipped inside, her arms filled with a bundle of clothing.

"'Tis time," the concubine said, thrusting the bundle into Willow's arms. "Here is the caftan and veil I usually wear when I leave the seraglio. No one will interfere with you as long as you are wearing it. And this," she said, "is a Greek peasant outfit. Wear it beneath the caftan."

Willow shook out the caftan and set it aside while she inspected Safiye's offering. There were several petticoats, a black skirt, a white blouse with a drawstring closing at the neck, an apron and a white cap. In addition, Safiye had included black slippers and cotton stockings. Apparently she had thought of everything.

Willow quickly shed her revealing harem outfit and

141

donned the peasant clothing, feeling more comfortable than she had in a long time. She placed the white cap in her pocket until she needed it, then donned the colorful caftan and placed the veil on her head, holding it in place with a thin silver circlet.

"I'm ready," she said, drawing a shaky breath.

Safiye placed a small sack of coins in Willow's hands, then stepped back to inspect her. "Aye, 'tis perfect. No one will suspect. Listen carefully while I explain what you are to do."

Willow leaned close so as not to miss a word of Safiye's instructions.

"I will take you to the garden gate and point out the path to a deserted beach, where you will find the fisherman I paid to carry you to Greece."

"I do not know how to thank you," Willow said sincerely.

A sly smile crept across Safiye's face, one that should have warned Willow to be on her guard.

"Your absence from Dariq's life will be thanks enough." She opened the door and peered out. " 'Tis safe—no one is about."

Willow released a breath she hadn't realized she'd been holding when Safiye beckoned to her. Making sure her disguise was in place, Willow followed Safiye into the garden.

Safiye led her to the gate she had already discovered on her own. The concubine pushed open the gate and stood aside as Willow slipped through.

"The path to the beach begins beyond the orchard," Safiye pointed out. "Good luck."

"Does the fisherman speak Turkish?"

"A little, but you needn't worry; he has his instructions."

"But what if . . ."

Her words stuttered to a halt as Safiye closed the gate

in her face. Willow had no choice but to go forward and pray that fate would be kind to her.

So far so good, Willow thought as she hastened toward the orchard and the path to freedom. She saw no one, a good sign that the path was little used. Still, her relief was heartfelt when she entered the orchard and the protection it offered. The ground beneath the trees was dappled with shadows and sunlight, providing a cool and peaceful sanctuary. But Willow was too intent upon finding the path to notice.

She came out of the shadows into sunshine and stifled a cry of joy when she saw a narrow dirt track. She followed it only a short distance before she smelled the sea and knew she was close to her destination. She waded through the river of sea grass that stood between her and the water's edge, oblivious to the stalks of grass that tore at her caftan as she hurried forward.

Panic raced through her when she couldn't find the skiff that was supposed to carry her to Greece. And then she saw it, rounding the beachhead. She waved frantically and waited for it to reach her. When the skiff got hung up on a sandbar, she splashed out to it and was dragged inside by the fisherman.

"Thank you," she said. The fisherman grunted but did not reply. Willow settled down on the wooden seat and removed her veil and caftan, stashing them under the seat. If all went well, she'd have no further use for them.

The fisherman, his face obscured by the floppy-brimmed hat he wore, brought the skiff around toward open water.

A shiver of excitement raced through Willow. Free at last! Never again would she have to look at Dariq's handsome face and virile body and wish for sinful things. Once she returned home, she would retire to the country and live a spinster's life, sustained by dreams of her one and only time of being loved by a prince.

Willow tried to hate Dariq, but couldn't summon that emotion. The only emotion she felt when she thought about him was . . . No, she wouldn't allow herself to think of Dariq as anything but a heartless pirate.

"How long will it take to reach Greece?" Willow asked in Turkish and then in English when the fisherman failed to answer. He didn't even look at her. She'd heard fishermen were a taciturn lot, but this was ridiculous. She didn't pursue conversation, however. It was enough to know she was on her way to freedom.

Sweet freedom; she could almost taste it.

His face wearing a puzzled expression, Ali Hara confronted Safiye when she returned from the garden. "I thought you had left. I saw you leave through the garden gate."

Safiye sent Ali Hara a beguiling smile. She'd been so certain no one had seen Willow leave through the gate, she'd been silently congratulating herself for her cleverness in getting rid of the woman who held Dariq's affection. Safiye wasn't stupid. Despite his denial, her prince was infatuated with the pale Englishwoman, and Safiye had arranged to get rid of Willow in such a way that no one would ever find her.

"You must have been imagining things, Ali Hara. As you can see, I am here."

Ali Hara did not believe her. He knew Safiye too well and recognized a lie when he heard one. He grasped her shoulders in his thick fingers and gave her a warning shake.

"You are lying, lady. Do not leave the harem. I go to fetch the master."

"Nay, do not!" Safiye pleaded. Her plans were going awry, and there was naught she could do about it except continue to spin a web of lies.

Ali Hara sent her a look over his shoulder that did not bode well for her as he hurried off.

Safiye cursed her bad luck. She had been eagerly anticipating her reunion with Prince Dariq, but now she had no choice but to deny all knowledge of Willow's absence. If she had her way, her prince would spend scant time lamenting his loss. Once Safiye returned to his bed, she would see that he forgot the pale Englishwoman.

At that moment Dariq charged into the harem with Ali Hara hard on his heels. "What have you done, Safiye?"

Safiye flinched but held her ground against Dariq's fury. "I have done naught, master."

"Ali Hara informs me otherwise. Where is Willow?"

She shrugged. "I know not, my lord."

"Search the harem, Ali Hara. Find Baba and see if Willow is with her."

Dariq fixed Safiye with a piercing look meant to intimidate. "Who left the harem wearing your clothing?"

"I know not." She smiled up at him. "Ali Hara lies. What did he tell you? Of what am I accused, master?"

Ali Hara returned with Baba. "Lady Willow is not in the harem," the eunuch reported. "I fear she is gone, master. You may lop off my head if you wish, for I have failed you."

Dariq made an impatient gesture. "If anyone is to be punished, it's Safiye. She provided Willow with the means to escape."

"Nay, master," Safiye pleaded. "I had naught to do with Lady Willow's disappearance. Mayhap she stole my caftan and veil and—"

145

"Enough!" Dariq growled. "The truth, Safiye—I will have it from you. If you lie to me, I will beat you."

Safiye shuddered. This wasn't supposed to be happening. She hadn't planned it this way. All she'd wanted was to get rid of Willow . . . permanently.

"Fetch the bastinado, Baba," Darig ordered.

The bastinado! Safiye began to tremble. She'd heard the pain was unbearable, and that those who were punished in that manner couldn't walk for weeks. Safiye realized she couldn't withstand that kind of pain.

She fell to her knees before Dariq, clutching the hem of his robe. "Please, master, do not beat me. I will tell you everything." Her words came out in a rush. "Lady Willow was unhappy here, so I offered to help her leave. I gave her clothing and money, showed her the garden gate and set her on the path to the beach. A fisherman was to meet her there and carry her to Greece in his skiff."

"I assume you arranged for the skiff," Dariq bit out.

"Aye, I did, but only because I felt sorry for Lady Willow. Sultan Ibrahim is not a good man. She would not have fared well in his harem."

"Where was the skiff supposed to pick her up?"

"The north beach. No one ever goes there."

Dariq observed Safiye closely. Had she really been concerned about Willow's welfare? Was compassion the emotion that had driven her to disobey him? Probably jealousy, he decided. As the harem's sole occupant, Safiye had become spoiled and willful. Still more unsettling was the realization that she wasn't above committing murder to get her own way. He needed to find Willow before . . . before what? The direction of his thoughts was too terrifying to consider.

"Don't let Safiye out of your sight, Ali Hara," he ordered as he headed out the door. "I was far too lenient."

"Where are you going?" Safiye cried.

"To find Willow, and you had better start praying that I find her hale and hearty."

Fifteen minutes later, Dariq and Mustafa sailed from the harbor in a skiff that belonged to the prince. Dariq set a course for the north beach, praying he would be in time to intercept the skiff carrying Willow away, perhaps to her death.

The island grew smaller and smaller as the skiff flew with the wind. Willow began to relax and pay more attention to the fisherman. Though he was wearing the garb of a fisherman, something about him bothered her. He studiously avoided eye contact, which wasn't a good sign.

"How long will it take to reach the mainland?" Willow asked in Turkish.

The fisherman grunted.

"Do you understand anything I am saying?"

Another grunt.

Disappointed, Willow returned to her silent ruminations. She felt uneasy about not being able to speak Greek, since Greece was where she was headed. She had no idea how she would manage once she reached her destination, but thanks to Safiye, at least she had money. Idly Willow gazed behind her toward the distant shoreline and gasped aloud when she saw another skiff coming at them at a fast clip.

"Look!" Willow cried, pointing out the sail to the fisherman.

Apparently he understood her well enough, for he glanced in the direction in which she was pointing. Then he spat out a curse in a language Willow recognized as Turkish. What was going on here? Why had the fisherman pretended not to understand her?

The fisherman took a spyglass from somewhere on his person and held it up to his eye. This time he spat a whole string of curses.

"What is it?" Willow cried.

"'Tis the prince's skiff," the fisherman said in perfect Turkish, startling Willow.

"Who are you?"

He didn't answer. She watched in horror as he left the tiller unattended and reached for her.

Her voice rose on a note of panic. "What are you doing?"

"I hoped to be farther from land, but this will have to do. If Prince Dariq recognizes me, I am a dead man."

When she finally caught a glimpse of his face, Willow knew she had been betrayed. His eyes were dark with desperation beneath thick, bushy eyebrows, and Willow knew immediately that he was a Turk. The fisherman was no fisherman at all; he was a pirate paid to . . . what? Kill her?

"Why do you want to kill me?"

"I was paid a great deal of money . . . and more. Do not fight it. It must be done quickly, before the prince reaches us."

Crowding her against the side of the boat, the pirate pulled a knife from his belt. Willow had no intention of dying without a fight. She cast a hopeful glance at Dariq's skiff, and her heart sank. There was no way he could reach her in time. She had no one to depend upon but herself. When the pirate came at her with his knife, she could think of only one thing to do. Right or wrong, she flung herself overboard, hitting the icy water with a splash.

Hampered by her heavy skirts, she sank beneath the water. The last thing she heard was the pirate's laughter.

* * *

Dariq held the spyglass to his eye, and his heart nearly stopped when he saw a struggle taking place on the skiff.

"What the devil is going on?" Dariq wondered aloud.

"What is happening?" Mustafa asked.

"A bundle of rags just went overboard," Dariq replied. A chill of apprehension slid down his spine as he watched the rags slowly sink beneath the water.

"Dear God!" he cried, invoking his mother's Christian deity. "The bastard tossed Willow overboard and left her to drown! Allah, fill our sails," Dariq prayed. "We must reach her before she drowns, Mustafa."

"Perhaps it is already too late."

Furious, Dariq rounded on him. "Do not say that! I cannot lose her!"

Willow was an excellent swimmer. She had learned in the lake near her father's country estate. But the water was so cold, she could barely move her arms to propel herself to the surface. Her lungs bursting, she kicked her legs and made some headway, but her heavy petticoats were dragging her down.

Somehow desperation and the strong will to live gave her the strength to loosen her petticoats and kick them off. The urge to breathe was so strong, she had to fight it with every last bit of her willpower. But willpower wasn't good enough; she had to breathe. She dragged in a breath, expecting water to fill her tortured lungs. Instead, she drew in deep gulps of tangy salt-tinged air. She had reached the surface.

Unencumbered by petticoats, Willow began swimming toward the approaching skiff, praying it would reach her before she froze to death or grew too weary to continue.

She swam until her arms grew heavy and her legs felt like lead. A wave washed over her. She swallowed water and choked. And still she swam, until she could no longer feel her body and her lungs burned.

She was tired—so very tired. How long could she go on before her arms no longer worked and her legs became dead weights? Not nearly long enough, she realized as she began to sink below the surface.

"Do you see her?" Mustafa asked anxiously.

"Nay." A tense silence throbbed between them. "Aye, there she is, floating portside!" Dariq cried. He leaned over the side and reached out to her. "Willow, grab my hand!"

"She cannot hear you, Prince."

"She is sinking! I cannot let her die, Mustafa. Trim the sail; I'm going in."

He handed the spyglass to Mustafa, peeled off his shirt, kicked off his boots and dove into the water. When Willow began drifting away from him and then went under, he swam with sure, steady strokes toward the place where he had last seen her. He saw her head bob to the surface again and then disappear. The fear that she might drown sent adrenaline surging through him. Sucking in a lungful of air, he plunged beneath the choppy surface, down . . . down . . . down . . .

Dariq saw naught but fish and murky water. He swam around until his breath was gone, then spiraled upward, sucked in another deep breath and dove down again. Giving up wasn't an option. Then he saw her. She was drifting toward him, her blond hair floating eerily about her face and shoulders. Grasping a long lock of hair and wrapping it around his hand, he dragged her up . . . up . . . up . . .

They broke the surface together. Gasping for air, he slowly towed her toward the skiff. Mustafa stood by to pull her in. Once Willow was safely aboard, Dariq heaved himself out of the water and into the skiff.

"Is she breathing?" Dariq asked from between chattering teeth.

"Nay, Prince."

Dariq knelt over her, more frightened than he had ever been in his life. He would not let her die. She didn't deserve to die. She was an innocent pawn in his game with Ibrahim.

"Press the water from her lungs," Mustafa urged. "Then breathe life into her. I saw it done once. Open her mouth and give her your breath."

Desperate, Dariq did as Mustafa suggested. First he turned Willow onto her stomach and gently pressed his palms to her back several times until water spewed from her mouth. Then he turned her over, lifted her head and breathed into her mouth.

A tiny gasp. A subtle breath, and then another, and yet another, until her chest rose and fell in regular intervals and she began taking shallow breaths on her own. But she was so pale and still that Dariq feared for her life.

"We must get her back to the seraglio," Dariq said. He wrapped his dry shirt around her and pulled her into his arms in order to share what little body warmth he had left after his frigid dip into the sea.

Mustafa turned the skiff about and steered toward the harbor. They rounded the beachhead, reaching the pier below Pirate Town soon afterward.

Dariq paid little heed to the curious onlookers as Mustafa tied the skiff to the pier. The moment it was secured, he leapt ashore with Willow in his arms and ran all the way to the seraglio, watching every tortured breath that wheezed from her lungs. If she died, he'd banish Safiye to the darkest corner of hell.

Dariq sprinted into the seraglio with Willow in his arms and Mustafa close on his heels. He carried her directly to his chamber.

"Fetch Baba!" he shouted to Mustafa over his shoulder. The big Turk hurried off to do his master's bidding.

A servant opened the door to his chamber and Dariq pushed past him. Willow was shivering so hard, her whole body shook. With an efficiency of motion, he stripped off her wet clothing, pulled back the covers and tucked her into bed. Moments later, Baba rushed into the chamber, her expression grim when she saw Willow's white face. A manservant entered behind her, carrying a small casket.

"What happened to her?" the old woman asked.

"I pulled her out of the sea," Dariq explained.

Baba's rheumy eyes widened. "Ali Hara said Safiye was responsible for Lady Willow leaving the harem."

Dariq's expression turned hard. "Safiye said she was merely helping Willow leave, but I fear her intentions were evil. Can you help Willow?"

"Move aside, my lord," Baba said, pushing Dariq away from the bed. The manservant placed the casket on the side table and departed, but Dariq hovered over Baba as she examined Willow.

Baba thumped Willow's chest, then turned her over and did the same to her back.

"She has no water in her lungs," Baba announced in a cautiously optimistic voice.

"I pressed it out. Mustafa had seen it done before and explained the process to me. I'm more worried about con-

NAME: _____

ADDRESS: _____

_____

_____

TELEPHONE: _____

E-MAIL: _____

_____ I want to pay by credit card.

__ Visa   __ MasterCard   __ Discover

Account Number: _____

Expiration date: _____

SIGNATURE: _____

Send this form, along with $2.00 shipping and handling for your FREE books, to:

Historical Romance Book Club
20 Academy Street
Norwalk, CT 06850-4032

Or fax (must include credit card information!) to: 610.995.9274.
You can also sign up on the Web at www.dorchesterpub.com.

Offer open to residents of the U.S. and
Canada only. Canadian residents, please
call 1.800.481.9191 for pricing information.

gestion in her lungs. The water was cold, and I had no blanket to wrap her in after I pulled her out."

"I will do what I can, master. I can prepare herbal remedies to relieve the congestion, and others to ward off fever. Light the brazier and then summon Ali Hara. He can assist me."

"But—"

"Go, my lord Prince, I will not let your lady die. This I vow."

Reluctantly Dariq left the chamber. He had to trust Baba, for there was no one else.

He entered the harem, barking for Ali Hara to attend him. The eunuch appeared instantly in answer to his master's frantic summons.

"What happened, master? Mustafa told me naught when he came to fetch Baba, except to say that you pulled Lady Willow from the sea. Thank Allah I summoned you in time to save her."

"Baba assures me Willow will live. Go to Baba; she needs you to assist her. You will find her in my chamber with Willow. Where is Safiye?"

"In her chamber, master."

Dariq's rage was simmering out of control as he stormed off to confront Safiye. She had planned the death of an innocent woman and must answer for her treachery.

Apparently Safiye had been expecting Dariq, for she had arrayed herself for maximum effect upon her sleeping couch, her voluptuous body covered by a minimum of diaphanous clothing. She rose on one elbow and smiled tremulously at Dariq.

"Forgive me, my lord. I meant no harm."

A muscle twitched in Dariq's jaw. "Which one of your sins do you regret?"

She blinked. "I am sorry about Lady Willow's death. She is dead, is she not?"

Dariq considered Safiye with barely concealed contempt, but losing his temper before extracting the information he sought would defeat his purpose.

"I pulled her out of the sea," he confided without giving specifics.

Safiye sighed. "'Tis a sad thing. I trusted the fisherman who offered to take Lady Willow safely to Greece." She spread her plump arms in blatant invitation. "Let me give you comfort, my lord." The movement caused her brief vest to rise, exposing well-rounded breasts and coral nipples.

Dariq was unimpressed. His voice hardened, along with his expression. "The fisherman's name—I want it."

Safiye's expression went blank. "I do not know his name."

"You paid the man to take Willow to Greece, did you not?"

She swallowed hard. "Aye, I did, but he was naught but a fisherman I met in Lipsi Town. I did not ask his name." She raised her leg and spread her thighs, affording Dariq a glimpse of her naked mound and the glistening lips of her sex.

Dariq glanced at her undeniable charms and looked away, uninterested in what she had to offer. He wanted but one thing from her. "You are lying, Safiye. Admit it. You arranged for Willow's death."

Safiye refused to meet his gaze. "Nay, I did not." She gulped audibly. "What does it matter? The lady is dead and I am alive. You are clever. You will find another way to rescue your mother. Let me give you what Willow cannot."

Dariq's rage exploded. It took considerable restraint to say quietly, "Willow lives. Your scheme did not work. She was alive when I pulled her from the sea. Tell me the name of the fisherman you paid to drown her. We both know Willow wasn't supposed to reach Greece. A skiff is not sturdy enough to sail great distances on the open sea."

Leaping from the couch, Safiye threw herself at Dariq's feet, hugging his knees and sobbing pitifully. "I did not want Lady Willow's death, my dear lord. What do I know about sailing vessels? I truly thought she would reach Greece. I trusted the fisherman, 'tis not my fault he did not honor our agreement."

"What agreement was that?" Dariq asked with quiet menace.

"I paid the fisherman a small fortune to take Lady Willow to Greece, and even gave her money to purchase transportation to England."

Dariq's hands fisted at his sides. "I do not believe your lies. You never expected Willow to reach Greece."

Safiye gazed imploringly at Dariq. "You accuse me falsely, master. I but wanted to help a woman who did not belong here."

Grasping her arms, Dariq pulled her to her feet. "Do not lie to me! You feared Willow would supplant you in my affections and wanted her out of the way."

Her eyes blazing with untamed fury, Safiye accused, "You were besotted with Willow! Obsessed with her. I admit I was jealous and wanted her gone, but I would not—"

He shook her hard. "Wouldn't you? Tell me the fisherman's name so I can see to his punishment."

Safiye shook her head. "I do not know his name. We both preferred it that way."

"I cannot believe that a fisherman or anyone else from

Lipsi Town would agree to your reprehensible scheme. With or without your help, I will find the man and punish him."

Safiye bit her bottom lip, her eyes revealing her terror. "Am I to be punished?"

Dariq's edict was temporarily forestalled when Ali Hara rushed into Safiye's chamber. "Come quickly, master. Lady Willow—"

Dariq didn't wait to hear the rest. Turning on his heel, he raced from the chamber. "Guard Safiye well," he called over his shoulder. "I will deal with her later."

Fury drained from Dariq, replaced by sheer terror. Had Willow's condition worsened? Was she . . . ? Nay, he refused to think along those lines.

Dariq burst into his chamber and skidded to a halt when he saw Willow sitting up in bed, still pale but alive. "You're not dead!" he cried. "I imagined the worst when Ali Hara summoned me."

"Give me some credit, my lord," Baba huffed. "Did I not promise you she would live?"

"Aye, but I feared . . ." He approached the bed. "Are you truly well, beauty?"

A shiver passed through Willow. "Aye, thanks to you. Baba said you pressed the water from my lungs." She shivered again. "The water was so cold, and my clothing dragged me down." She paused before continuing. "The fisherman tried to kill me, but he wasn't really a fisherman. He was a Turk."

Dariq motioned for Baba to leave the chamber.

"Are you sure?" Dariq asked once they were alone. "Did you see his face?"

"I did, but not until he attempted to kill me. He wore a hat with a brim pulled low over his forehead and did not look directly at me. Nor did he speak, until he saw your skiff. Then he drew his knife and came for me. He was a pirate; I'd stake my life on it. He feared your reprisal."

"As well he should. How did you end up in the sea? Did he push you overboard?"

"I did not fancy being stabbed, so I jumped into the water. It seemed the lesser of two evils. I know how to swim, but my clothing dragged me down. Thank God you reached me in time."

"Thank Allah and God and all His saints," Dariq said reverently.

"I asked Baba to send for you because I needed to tell you something," Willow said. "The Turk said I was not supposed to reach Greece."

She blinked away a tear. "I think Safiye wanted me dead. I am sorry, Dariq."

Dariq sat on the edge of the bed. "Don't be sorry. I should have known Safiye would be jealous and attempt something like this. Are you truly all right?"

"Baba could find no congestion in my chest, and if I don't develop a fever, I will recover quickly. She thinks I should stay in bed a day or two, drink hot liquids and rest."

"Baba is usually right; listen to her."

Willow sighed and snuggled down into the pillows. "I should return to the harem."

"Not yet. There's still Safiye to deal with, but all in good time." He stroked her forehead, trailing his fingers down her cheek. Their gazes met and locked; for the first time in his life, Dariq knew what heaven looked like.

Propelled by a desperate need, he lowered his head and kissed her.

Chapter Ten

Dariq kissed her with all the passion in his heart, until her mouth relaxed beneath his. When his tongue probed against her lips, they opened to him. Pressing his advantage, he thrust his tongue inside, drinking of her unique taste like a man dying of thirst.

When he heard her whimper, he drew away and searched her face. "I must be mad to want you like this, but I cannot help myself."

Willow stroked his face; Dariq's body hardened in response. She shivered. "Are you still cold, beauty?"

She shook her head. How could she be cold with heat rolling off Dariq like a newly stoked fire?

He bent to kiss her ear, the tip of his tongue exploring the tender whirl of flesh while his teeth worried the plump lobe. Then he pushed the long strands of her hair aside and began to kiss down her throat.

"*Oh!* That feels . . . It makes me . . ."

"Do you want me to stop?"

"No." Her reply was so soft, it could scarcely be heard.

He sighed and started to rise. "You're still weak. I should let you rest."

"I . . . suppose so." She shivered again.

He didn't leave, instead he stripped off his damp clothing and climbed into bed. "You're cold. Let me warm you." He brought her into his arms and pressed her against his naked body. Willow gasped, seared by the heat of his flesh. Heaving a sigh, she snuggled close, burrowing into his comforting warmth.

He stroked her back, up and then down, dragging his fingers along the crease separating her buttocks. Willow trembled, but not from cold. Just when she began to enjoy the soothing warmth and sensation of his talented fingers, Dariq grasped the taut mounds and pulled her hard against his loins. She felt his erection prodding against her stomach and knew she was in danger of succumbing again to his seduction.

Did she have the strength to resist him?

Did she want to?

Obviously not, for she merely sighed when he said, "I want to make love to you, beauty. If you do not want me or feel too weak to respond, tell me now, while I can still stop."

"I . . ." Words failed her. It wasn't weakness she felt, but desire. She couldn't deny the heat permeating her body where Dariq touched her, any more than she could deny her body's response to his touch.

Accepting her silence for acquiescence, Dariq groaned her name and turned her over on her stomach. Baba must have sponged her body in warm water mixed with the essence of flowers, for she smelled delicious. The intoxicating fragrance sent his pulse racing out of control.

He pushed the drying mass of her hair aside and kissed the nape of her neck. He was encouraged when Willow gasped his name. But when he grasped her hand and licked her palm and sucked each of her fingers, she tried to pull her hand away, as if having second thoughts.

"Dariq, perhaps we shouldn't. I am not a wanton. Your touch muddles my mind and makes me crave wicked things. I shouldn't feel like this."

"You are wrong, beauty. Physical attraction between man and woman is a natural thing, sanctioned by both your God and mine. Do not fight it. You know how wonderful it can be between us. I want to love you in all the ways a man can love a woman. Before you leave me, I want to introduce you to pleasure so powerful you will yearn for my touch upon your flesh."

Before you leave me. Would nothing change his mind? "You still intend to send me to Ibrahim?"

Sadly he answered, "I have no choice."

"But I am no longer virginal. Ibrahim will reject me."

"Once he looks upon you, he will want you despite your lack of maidenhead. No man alive could resist you, and I am very much alive. I am a man who takes what he wants, and I want you."

Willow couldn't deny that her body yearned for Dariq's touch, for his loving. She was no longer an innocent virgin, so what did it matter if he made love to her? She had lived with restrictions all her life, and the wicked promise of Dariq's loving was too tempting to resist.

She wasn't ill, nor did she feel weak; she felt empowered by Dariq's passion. Naught was wrong with her except the desperate need gnawing at her, driving her to madness.

Madness, thy name is Dariq.

Then she lost the ability to think as Dariq licked down her spine in long, leisurely strokes, murmuring love words in Turkish and English, doing deliciously sinful things to her body.

Willow stifled a cry when he reached the crevice at the bottom of her spine. "What are you doing?"

"Trying to love you if you will be quiet and let me do what I do best. Open your mind to what I am doing; try to think of naught but the way my hands and mouth feel on your skin."

He laved each mound of her buttocks with his tongue, then trailed his mouth down her legs, clear to her toes. He glanced at her once before sucking one pink digit into his mouth and then each one in turn. Willow had never suspected such an outlandish act could be so erotic. Could not even imagine why a man would wish to do such a thing. But Dariq seemed to know no boundaries. Whatever he did made her yearn for more.

The "more" came when Dariq turned her over and laved her breasts with his tongue and suckled her nipples. She felt her flesh swelling and her nipples puckering as if they had been touched with ice.

Her breathing accelerated; she was panting heavily, her body tense, waiting for Dariq's next move.

He gazed into her eyes. "Your flesh is a drug I cannot get enough of."

His words were like an opiate; she wanted to partake of whatever erotic pleasure he offered.

"Are you still cold?" Dariq asked.

"I am afire."

He grinned. "'Tis what I intended." He caught her hand. "Touch me. I ache for your hands upon my skin."

She stretched her hand out to his chest, curling her fingers in the mat of hair she found there. His flesh beneath her hand felt hard and soft at the same time. He let her fingers roam over his torso, and then covered her hand with his own, carrying it downward, curling her fingers around his arousal. She tried to pull away, but he held her hand firmly against him.

"Explore me, beauty. Feel me."

Mindlessly she obeyed, mesmerized by the intoxicating sound of his voice. She couldn't have disobeyed if her life depended upon it. She remembered how huge he had felt inside her, and was surprised when he grew thicker and harder in her hand than she recalled.

"Caress my jewels," he murmured in a voice thick with desire.

"Your jewels?" Willow choked out.

"The sacs that hold my seed. Touch them. Hold them in your hands."

Her hand closed gently around a sac, felt it harden, saw his sex jerk in response. He groaned as if in pain. She released him instantly. He groaned louder and returned her hand to his manhood. He felt satiny warm, yet hard as stone, every incredible inch of him throbbing with life. Driven by curiosity and her own need, Willow caressed up and down his great length. His breath quickened, becoming harsh gasps that thundered in and out of his chest.

"Stop now, beauty, before you ruin both your pleasure and mine. Turkish men take great pride in giving their women pleasure."

"Their *women*," Willow repeated. "Why do Turkish men feel they need more than one woman?"

"Because 'tis not natural for a man to confine himself to one woman. It takes many women to satisfy a virile man. In my world, a man's virility is measured by the number of concubines he owns. But we please our women as no English or Frankish man can, as I shall prove to you."

Would her fiancé have been able to satisfy her? Willow wondered. Somehow she doubted it. But before she'd met Dariq she wouldn't have known the difference. She would have been content with the crumbs of her husband's affection, unaware of what she was missing.

After experiencing Dariq's passion, she knew that no other man would ever satisfy her, so why not enjoy what he offered while she could?

Willow's thoughts scattered when Dariq's mouth came down hungrily on hers, his tongue pushing past her lips, sending her senses soaring.

Suddenly she pulled back, searching Dariq's face. "I do want your passion, my lord Prince. Give me enough pleasure to last the rest of my life."

He grasped her face between his large hands and stared into her eyes. "My passion can be a fierce thing, Willow. Are you ready to accept it?"

Burgeoning excitement shot through her. Beyond speech, she nodded.

Dariq began to kiss her face softly, gently. Her lips. Each of her cheeks. The tip of her nose. Her chin. Her closed eyes. After he had showered her face with kisses, he slowly caressed her body, smoothing his hands over her shoulders, her breasts, her stomach, her buttocks. He fondled the firm mounds until Willow wanted to scream at him to hurry, to continue with his sweet torture.

Dariq could have caressed Willow till eternity. She was sweetly curved with a narrow waist, magnificent breasts and long, shapely legs. He returned his attention to her breasts, cupping them in his large palms, then bringing them to his mouth, suckling gently upon her coral nipples.

Willow stirred beneath him, the erotic sensation of his lips upon her flesh incredibly arousing. She arched her back, soaring with sweet pleasure. The feeling was erotic and delicious, and she purred her approval. She was so intent upon the wet tug of Dariq's lips upon her nipple that she momentarily lost track of his hands.

Then she felt them seeking out places that made her tingle and burn, while at the same time his mouth continued feasting at her breasts. Her nipples hardened against his tongue; she heard his breath quicken as an almost unbearable pressure built between her legs.

The heel of his palm rested lightly on the smooth pink mound at the apex of her thighs, massaging in erotic circles. When he pressed lightly on a spot low on her stomach, the sudden burst of pleasure forced a startled cry from her lips.

"What did you just do?"

Dariq grinned. "I can give you pleasure in a thousand different ways."

His hand slid between her thighs. "Your love juices are flowing."

"My what?"

He removed his dewy fingers, grasped her hand and brought it between her legs. "You are wet for me. Can you feel it? If I took you now, my cock would slide inside you on a cushion of moisture."

She pulled her hand free. It came away wet. Her face flooded with color. His hand returned to her dewy petals. "Dariq, what are you . . . oh, God . . . don't . . . Stop."

He laughed. "What did you say?"

"Don't . . . stop."

"Never." Then he created a new torment by gently probing her with his fingers.

Willow moaned. How could she bear it? She went wild beneath him when he lowered his head and kissed her

165

there, between her legs, feasting on her sensitive flesh until she wanted to scream.

He raised his head and gave her a long, poignant look. "I'm going to bring you pleasure with my mouth first."

His fingers played upon her slick flesh, parting her as his mouth returned to his banquet. His tongue was like a living flame, delving inside her, tasting, taunting, sending tiny bursts of fire through her body. She felt helpless, as if she were drowning in a whirlpool of raw sensation. And then it began: the heady rise of blood through her veins, the tremors rocking her body, the final explosion that hurled her toward oblivion. Undulating waves of rapture carried her to a distant shore; she heard a low keening and realized it was coming from her own mouth.

"This is just the beginning, beauty," Dariq murmured in a voice as tightly drawn as a bow.

He scooted upward and knelt over her, watching her expression as she spiraled down from the high place he had sent her.

When Willow opened her eyes, she caught sight of Dariq's throbbing erection. He was huge, the purple head engorged with blood. She had seen him aroused before, but never like this. Her wits scattered when he began pressing himself inside her, stretching her, pushing deeper, harder, filling her.

"You are still tight," he whispered against her mouth. She tasted herself on his lips.

"It hurts," Willow complained, shifting to accommodate his great length.

"You are still new to this. It doesn't hurt as much as it did the first time, does it?"

She looked up at him, confusion glazing her eyes. "I don't think so."

"Your tightness makes the pleasure all the sweeter," Dariq said. "Shall I stop?"

"Nay, oh, nay. It feels better now." She moved her hips, inviting Dariq to thrust deeper, harder.

"Give yourself over to me, beauty. Hold back nothing. Move with me, open to me, come with me."

The delicious friction of his sex thrusting and withdrawing inside her released a primitive instinct Willow could not suppress. Wrapping her arms and legs around him, she opened herself fully to him, raising her hips to meet his powerful strokes.

Waves of liquid fire rippled across her skin and pooled where they were joined. She dug her fingers into his shoulders as he drove her higher and higher, his muscles bunching and shifting beneath her fingertips. She felt passion, so recently spent, rebuilding, ready to burst forth again. Consuming swells of incredible sensation grew, crested, sweeping her upward into mindless bliss. She screamed his name.

Dariq felt her sheath spasm around him, heard his name on her lips and lost control. He thrust deep, held, then found his own pleasure, spewing his seed inside her. He lost all sense of time and place as he spiraled down from euphoria to the most perfect contentment he had ever known.

Dariq had always considered himself a master of sensuality. He was a hedonist who enjoyed erotic pleasure and delighted in finding new and diverse ways to please women. The concubines he'd left behind in Istanbul had vied for his attention because he always left them satisfied, giving unstintingly of himself. Beautiful women, erotic play and sexual excitement were as necessary to him as eating and breathing.

Making love to Willow had been manna for his starving soul.

Suddenly he went still, realizing what he had just done. Cursing his carelessness, he pulled out and rolled over on his back. This was the second time he had lost himself inside Willow, and the consequences could foil his well-laid plans. He prayed to both Allah and God that his seed hadn't found fertile ground.

He glanced at Willow. Her eyes were closed and her breathing erratic. Raising himself on one elbow, he kissed her eyelids.

"Did you enjoy that?"

Her eyes flew open. "Aye, it was even better than the first time."

"That first time went too fast. I hadn't had a woman in months." He stroked her breasts. "The night is still young. Give me a few minutes to restore myself, my passionate beauty, and then we will explore some of the fascinating positions available to lovers. The next time I will be more careful," he promised.

Willow's breath caught. "How can you . . ."

". . . be more careful? I won't release my seed inside you. It's simply a matter of self-control, which I seem to lack where you are concerned."

"How can you make love again so soon?"

"I am a man of enormous appetites, my sweet."

"Perhaps I should return to the harem while you rest."

His arms tightened around her. "You will remain here, in my chamber. I have yet to deal with Safiye."

"What will happen to her?"

"You do realize she planned your death, do you not?"

"Aye, how could I not? I know she deserves punishment, but I beg you, do not be overly harsh with her. She acted from jealousy."

"You want me to spare her life?"

Willow blanched. "You intend to . . . to kill her?"

Dariq shook his head. "I am not a cruel man. Killing women and children is abhorrent to me. I am not my brother."

"What are you going to do?"

"I shall put her on a ship and send her to the slave market in Algiers. If fate is kind, she will find a master who adores her. Does that meet with your approval?"

"Is there no other option? Perhaps one of your pirates would take her as his concubine. Or even wed her."

"As angry as I am with Safiye, I would never give her to a pirate. As I said before, I am not a brutal man by nature, but most pirates are. Safiye betrayed me; I can no longer bear the sight of her. Therefore, she must go."

Willow could understand Dariq's feelings. She herself wouldn't feel comfortable with Safiye anywhere near her. The other woman's jealousy had taken a deadly turn.

"Enough of Safiye," Dariq said. He leaned over her and gave her a sexually charged smile. "I do believe I am restored."

Willow swallowed—hard. While they had been talking, his sex had grown and hardened. She stared at it, marveling at his recuperative powers. Dariq left the bed, padded over to the washstand and dipped a soft cloth into a bowl of scented water. He used the cloth on himself first, then rinsed it and returned to the bed.

"Spread your legs for me, beauty, so that I can cleanse my seed from you."

Willow's legs shifted apart; he touched the cloth to her. The scent of jasmine drifted up as he washed away all traces of their recent loving. Then he replaced the cloth in the basin and returned to the bed, carrying a small vial.

"What is that?" Willow asked, though she had a good idea.

"Scented oil. I used it on you before, remember?"

How can I forget? "I remember."

"Turn on your stomach."

Willow did not protest as she flipped over on her stomach. She moaned in pleasure as he massaged fragrant oil into her skin, lavishing it over her back, her shoulders, her buttocks, dipping briefly to her more intimate parts. It felt so wondrously relaxing that she nearly fell asleep. Then he turned her onto her back and began the process again. She gasped when she felt his fingers spread the swollen lips of her sex and lave them with oil.

She arched violently as his fingers pressed inside her. The erotic scent of spices wafting up to her was intensely arousing.

"Dariq . . ." His name fell from her lips on a long sigh.

"You are ready, beauty. The scent of your love juices combined with the oil is an aphrodisiac to my senses."

She let out a tiny squeal as he lifted her and settled her on top of him.

"Take me inside you."

She opened her legs and straddled him. He grasped her bottom and slid effortlessly inside her oil-slick passage. There was no pain, only pleasure. More pleasure than she could possibly bear. He gripped her hard and bucked his hips; she rode him shamelessly, enjoying it, rushing inexorably toward the promise of ecstasy.

Even as she tasted bliss, she remembered the future Dariq intended for her, and anger at him honed her passion to a sharp edge. And when she reached that ultimate peak, anger and passion combined to create an explosion of sensation so intense she tasted heaven. She climaxed violently, tumbling into a whirlpool of incandescent bliss.

Dariq followed soon afterward, stiffening and shouting her name. She fell against the pillows, limp and exhausted.

Willow slept soundly as Dariq rose up on his elbow and watched her sleep. Desire clutched at his groin. The knowledge that he wanted her again stunned him. After taking Willow twice, he still ached for her. As sexually experienced as he was, this kind of need twisting his gut was new to him. At least the second time he had caught himself before giving Willow his seed. But, Allah, what he wouldn't have given to stay inside her!

How could he give Willow up? That unappealing thought kept him up far into the night. It was too late to renege on his offer. His plan had already been implemented. Soon Ahmed would return with Ibrahim's answer to his proposal. Dariq never doubted that Ibrahim would accept the trade he had proposed. But how would his brother react when he learned Willow wasn't the virgin he expected?

Dariq cursed beneath his breath. Why hadn't he been able to keep his hands off Willow? He knew it was more than her ethereal beauty and the color of her hair that enthralled him. There was something about Willow that defied explanation. She had more spirit than any other woman he had known, and he had known many. Her passion was stunning, and he had taken full advantage of it.

Unfortunately, he couldn't restore her virginity.

What a terrible muddle he had made of things. This business would have been pretty straightforward had he kept his distance and his hands off Willow. He felt her shiver and reached down to pull a light cover over her. Then he drew her into his arms. He wanted to make love to her again, but denied himself when she snuggled against him and let out a contented little sigh.

Sometime during the darkest part of the night Willow stirred, awakening Dariq.

"Are you all right, beauty?"

"I am thirsty."

"And I am hungry," Dariq murmured. "If I quench your thirst, will you satisfy my hunger?"

It took a moment for Willow's confused mind to grasp his meaning. "Again?"

Laughter rumbled in his chest. "And again and again."

He scooped her into his arms and eased them both from the bed.

"Where are you taking me?"

"To my private *hammam*. A bath will benefit us both."

He carried her through a door to a small room tiled in aqua and white and lit by dozens of sputtering candles whose flames were nearly extinguished. The room was redolent with incense; in the dead of night it seemed heavy and cloying. A sunken tub nearly filled the chamber. Dariq carried her down two marble steps and lowered her into the bath.

"Rest here while I fetch you something to drink."

"How do you keep the water warm?" Willow wondered as she sank down into the soothing water.

"It's piped in from the kitchen."

Willow stretched, groaning when her muscles protested. She ached in all the intimate places Dariq had spent hours exploring. She closed her eyes, enjoying the flow of water over her weary body. Dariq returned a short time later with two goblets of orange liquid. He handed one to Willow, then joined her in the bath.

"This is good—what is it?" Willow asked after her first sip.

"A mixture of fruit juices; I'm glad you like it. I promise it will quench your thirst."

He let her finish her juice before taking the goblet from her and setting it on the rim of the tub, then he reached for her. "Making love in water can be very erotic . . . and extremely satisfying."

A puff of air left Willow's throat. Everything Dariq did to her was erotic and intensely satisfying.

He began kissing her everywhere, her forehead, her cheeks, the tip of her nose, her mouth, prodding her lips open with his tongue so he could taste her fully. The tang of fruit on his tongue excited her, and she savored him as if he were fine wine.

When his lips left hers and moved down her body, she shivered and moaned his name. She adored the way her prince made her body thrum and her senses spiral out of control. Then he was inside her, the delicious pressure of his engorged sex so powerfully erotic that her hips began to buck against him. Water surged and splashed around them as their passion escalated, until it became an undulating tidal wave, laving all the sensitive places on Willow's body.

She grasped his shoulders and clung to him as his manhood surged deep, deeper, sending her higher and higher, until she reached the stars and exploded. She was still flying when she heard Dariq shout and felt warmth flood her womb.

It took several minutes to realize that Dariq hadn't pulled out in time. He was still embedded inside her, his head resting against her forehead. He lifted his head and stared at her.

"I could not help myself. I should have had Baba prepare something to render you infertile, but I never intended to touch you again after that first time."

"Permanently infertile?" Willow gasped.

"Nay, just for the time you are with me."

"Am I to be with you again?"

He sent her an endearing grin. "Aye, my innocent beauty. You will be in my bed until the day we part."

She searched his face. "Perhaps it is too late for precautions. I may have already conceived."

He frowned. "I will confer with Baba. Perhaps she knows of something that will rid you of the babe if my seed found fertile ground."

Willow recoiled in alarm. Though she didn't voice her concern, in her heart she knew she would never rid herself of Dariq's babe.

Dariq pulled out of her and lifted himself from the tub. Water sluiced from his body as he extended his hand to Willow. Her expression was thoughtful as she mounted the marble steps and allowed Dariq to dry her with a soft drying cloth. Then he dried himself and carried her back to his bed.

Willow lay stiff in his arms. How could Dariq be so heartless? Had he no morals, no conscience?

"You're angry," Dariq said as he lay down beside her. "What did I say now?"

"Murder is a sin. If I have conceived your child tonight, I will carry the babe to term despite your determination to kill it." Her voice quivered with disappointment. "I should have known you would be willing to kill your own child in order to continue your vendetta against your brother. Ibrahim might accept a woman who lacked a maidenhead, but not one carrying his brother's babe."

She turned away from him.

Dariq didn't know what to say to that. It was certainly possible that Willow had already conceived his child. He would have Baba watch closely for signs that her woman's flow had commenced. If fate turned against him, he would confront the problem when the time came, not before.

Sleep eluded him; Willow's angry words kept echoing through his brain.

Could he terminate Willow's pregnancy, even if the babe was no larger than a grain of sand and had yet to draw breath?

Dariq prayed he would never have to make that decision.

Chapter Eleven

Willow woke late the following morning. Sunshine slanting through the open windows warmed her skin, while a freshening breeze blowing in from the sea teased her senses. She stretched, moaning when her sore muscles protested. Her moan turned into a wistful smile when she recalled the erotic night she had spent in Dariq's arms.

But the pleasure they had shared did not change her predicament. Her fate rested with Dariq, and he still intended to give her to Ibrahim.

Startled, Willow realized she was still in Dariq's bed. She reached over and touched the impression where his head had lain. He must have left hours ago, for his side of the bed was cold. As if she had conjured up his image, Dariq strode through the door. She rose up on her elbow and watched him approach.

He cut an impressive figure this morning in a flowing robe and baggy white trousers stuffed into shiny black boots. The contrast of his suntanned skin against the pristine white robe made his eyes glow like silver ingots. The sight of him caused her breath to catch in her throat. Then she flushed, recalling their erotic play during the long, blissful night. Dariq knew no bounds when it came to loving; he had taught her a great deal about her body, and the pleasure she was capable of giving and receiving.

Dariq smiled at her, his intense gaze traveling over her dishabille. "You look delicious, like a rose opening its petals to the morning sun." He heaved a regretful sigh. "Unfortunately, I cannot join you in bed. Are you hungry, beauty?"

Willow couldn't recall eating since before her misadventure the day before.

"Famished."

"Mustafa is on his way with your breakfast. You had best hurry if you wish to be presentable when he arrives."

Willow looked about for something to wear.

"Your clothing will arrive soon. I have decided to give you the freedom to go wherever you desire within the seraglio, for I doubt you will try to flee again. You nearly lost your life the last time you attempted to escape.

"Therefore," he continued, "I have decided to provide you with clothing suitable for an English lady."

Willow stared at him in disbelief. "How did you acquire clothing fit for a lady?"

He crossed his arms over his chest and spread his legs in a posture of male arrogance. "I am a pirate, my lady," Dariq chuckled. "You would be surprised at the things I have taken off ships. For your information, I have trunk upon trunk of women's clothing, as well as garments suitable for a gentleman of the *ton*. You may choose gowns from the trunks I have ordered brought to you and wear them until—"

Willow didn't need to hear the rest of his sentence. "Why are you doing this?"

"You deserve a taste of freedom before joining Ibrahim's harem."

"I can dress how I want and go where I please?"

"Within reason."

"Must I wear an aba?"

"Covering your head with a scarf will suffice. Women on Lipsi dress as they please." He hesitated before saying, "I am taking you to Pirate Town today. I want you to identify the man Safiye paid to toss you into the sea. The traitorous houri refused to give me his name before she left."

He found a caftan in his wardrobe and tossed it to her. "Wear this until your clothing arrives. Mustafa will be here soon with breakfast."

Willow rose naked from the bed and tugged the caftan over her head. It dropped past her hips and settled at her feet.

Dariq watched with hungry eyes as her naked body was lost in the concealing folds. "'Tis a pity I have no time to linger."

"Did you say Safiye has left?" Willow asked, as if suddenly recalling what Dariq had said.

"Aye, she sailed with the morning tide aboard one of my ships. She is going to the slave market in Algiers."

"Oh."

Aware of Willow's tender heart, Dariq said, "Do not fret over her future, my sweet. Safiye always lands on her feet. I'm willing to bet she'll find a new master worthy of her talents."

There came a knock on the door.

"Ah, that would be Mustafa. Come in."

Mustafa entered the chamber carrying a tray laden with bowls and platters. Willow sniffed, appreciative of the delicious aromas.

Mustafa set the tray on a low table surrounded by cushions. "The trunks will arrive shortly." He sent Willow a speculative look before addressing Dariq. "Think you it is wise, my lord, to allow the lady freedom to come and go as she pleases?"

Dariq didn't take offense at Mustafa's words; he knew his friend meant no disrespect. "What harm can it do, my friend? I thought Willow would enjoy a few weeks or days—however long it takes for Ahmed to return—of freedom to dress as she wishes and go where she pleases, within reason, of course. I doubt she will be so foolish as to solicit help for another ill-advised escape attempt."

Mustafa sent Willow a lingering look of distrust before departing.

"He does not like me," Willow observed.

"You must forgive Mustafa. He is excessively protective of me and my mother. He wants to see Saliha Sultana safely delivered from harm as much as I do."

Drawn to the food, Willow plopped down on a fluffy cushion as Dariq removed the covers from various dishes and platters. She helped herself to fruit, a sweet roll dripping with honey, and a helping of hot cereal she didn't recognize.

Willow chewed thoughtfully on a piece of roll. "Mustafa sees me as an obstacle to your plans."

Dariq knew that Mustafa feared his growing attachment to Willow, but his friend also knew that Dariq had too much at stake to let his emotions run away with him. Though he had become very fond of Willow—too fond, perhaps, as Mustafa recognized—he could not stray from his original plan to save his mother's life. Turmoil darkened Dariq's eyes. How could he balance one woman's life against another when both were equally dear to him?

Where had that thought come from? Dariq wondered.

As a sexual partner, Willow was without equal, but he feared she was more to him than that. Dariq had neither the time nor energy to devote to any emotion other than hatred and revenge. His need to punish Ibrahim for the senseless deaths of his brothers and to bring his mother to safety must take precedence. He could not indulge any tender feelings he might harbor for Willow. She was here for one reason only, and it was not to fulfill his own self-ish needs. If he forgot that reason, he could lose his mother.

"Have you nothing to say?" Willow asked without looking up.

Dariq shrugged. "What can I say? Mustafa fears I am becoming obsessed with you."

She looked up, her eyes luminous. "Are you?"

Dariq swallowed . . . hard. What could he tell her? That he *was* obsessed with her? That he loved making love to her, loved teaching her about sex and the pleasures to be had in practicing what she learned? Aye, he could tell her those things, but they would not matter, for her ultimate destination was Ibrahim's bed.

"You please me," he said after a long pause. "I would keep you for myself if it were possible."

Willow set her fork down, her expression grim. "So to ease your conscience, you are allowing me a small taste of freedom. How gallant of you. I should have known better than to expect mercy from a pirate." She rose and walked away.

Dariq grasped her arm. "Where are you going?"

"To the harem, where I belong. Have the trunks delivered there when they arrive."

"You're staying here. We will eat our meals together, make love together and sleep together until you leave my protection."

181

"I prefer to be your prisoner. If you want a woman in your bed, find yourself another concubine. I thought . . . oh, how could I have been so stupid? After last night I assumed . . . I hoped . . . You are even more heartless than I thought. Let go of me!"

She twisted free of his grip and glared at him.

Dariq's mouth thinned. "You are *not* my prisoner! You are my guest."

"Guests aren't treated like chattel." She turned her back to him.

He whirled her around to face him. "Look at me and tell me you did not enjoy being in my bed. Tell me you hated what we did."

She refused to raise her eyes to him.

"Look at me, Willow." His tone brooked no argument. She lifted her chin. Their gazes met and clashed.

"Kiss me, beauty."

"I think not."

"What are you afraid of? That you might like it too well? That you will remember my hands and mouth upon your body and crave more of what we experienced last night?"

"I want naught from you but my freedom."

He sighed regretfully. "I will grant you anything but that."

The confrontation ended when servants arrived with the promised trunks.

"Choose what you will. I shall return in an hour to escort you to Pirate Town." He paused at the door. "Make use of my *hammam*, if you wish."

Her lips pressed tightly together, Willow fumed in impotent rage. She was a fool to let herself fall in love with . . . Dear God, what was she thinking? It couldn't be true! She didn't love Dariq! He was a pirate, a man without a conscience, without a heart, a man with no soul. She meant no more to him than Safiye, or any other woman. Men of his culture treated women like possessions; they bought and sold them on the open market like sides of beef.

Still angry at her inability to resist Dariq's sensual seduction, Willow rummaged through the trunks for something decent to wear. Dariq had wanted her amenable to his plans and had used seduction to render her complacent. But she wasn't complacent. Nor was she going to accept her fate without a fight.

Willow decided not to use Dariq's *hammam*. It held too many memories. She washed instead in a basin of tepid water and quickly dressed. She didn't want to be naked when Dariq returned. She never intended to be naked in his presence again.

When Dariq arrived, Willow was chastely clad in a blue gown that laced up to the neck and hugged her breasts and waist, flowing in liquid lines over her hips to the tips of her slippers.

"I see you're ready," he said, looking her over from head to toe. "Did you find a head scarf in any of those trunks?"

"I have it here," she said, extending her hand.

Dariq took the scarf from her and placed it over her head, winding the ends around her neck so that they trailed down her back.

"Now you are ready to accompany me to Pirate Town. If fortune smiles on us, we shall find the man who tried to drown you."

"Why? You care naught for me. Except as a bargaining tool, I am worthless to you."

He stopped her with a look, his eyes dark with an emotion she found difficult to interpret.

"You are only partly right, beauty. I do not know why it should be so, but I do care for you. More than I ought to. More than I have a right to. I would keep you for myself in a heartbeat but for a need greater than my own desire."

Willow regarded him in disbelief. Dariq cared for her? How easily the lie fell from his lips. He was just saying that to soothe her ruffled feelings; she knew his plans for her future remained unchanged.

Dariq realized his words made little sense, even to himself. While telling Willow he cared, he still intended to give her to Ibrahim. He had fought his desire for Willow and lost. He had made love to her when he should have avoided her. He was engaged in a fierce battle between love for his mother and his growing affection for Willow.

"Pretty words, but lies," Willow spat.

"Is this a lie?" Dariq asked, bringing her hard against him so she could feel his arousal.

Then he kissed her, deeply, greedily, attempting to prove that he cared by plying her with ardent kisses. He pulled back and searched her face for a hint of what she was feeling. Her closed expression told him she believed none of what he'd just admitted. He squared his shoulders. If he continued to harbor these maudlin sentiments, he might do something he would regret the rest of his days. His mother needed him. He couldn't be sidetracked by a blond houri who had broken through the protective walls around his heart.

"We should go," Dariq said. "Kissing you can only lead to one thing, and we haven't time for that right now. I need to find the man Safiye hired to kill you.

"We will visit the souk in Pirate Town. All but one of my fleet of ships is in port, and most of the seamen will be milling about the marketplace, selling booty and prizes they have no use for. Inform me the moment you recognize the man who tried to kill you." He sent her a sharp look. "You will recognize him, won't you?"

She shivered. "I will never forget his face."

Dariq was pleased with her answer. "It is possible the assassin is not a pirate. You will also have the opportunity to see some of the men from Lipsi Town. They often visit the souk to look over the wares. We are on good terms with the inhabitants of the island; they walk among us without fear."

He placed her arm in the crook of his elbow and escorted her through the seraglio. Willow was struck anew by the opulence of Dariq's island home. She walked upon marble floors and past columns trimmed in gold and statues that looked as if they had been wrought by famous sculptors.

Mustafa joined them at the front entrance, following close on their heels. The huge Turk rarely left Dariq's side.

Willow was surprised to see an elegant carriage and a pair of horses standing on the driveway of crushed shells.

"Wherever did you get a carriage? It seems out of place on this remote island."

Dariq's eyes twinkled. "Handsome, is it not? The carriage was in the hold of a ship we intercepted. It was meant for Ibrahim but now is mine. I purchased the pair of matched Arabians in Morocco."

Willow heard Mustafa chuckle and realized the purloined carriage was cause for merriment between the two men.

Dariq helped Willow into the carriage. She settled back against the luxurious leather seats while Dariq crowded in beside her. Mustafa leapt into the driver's box and took up the reins. It was a short ride to Pirate Town, and Willow enjoyed every minute of it. Never had she ridden in such a finely sprung carriage, and never with a prince.

Pirate Town was bustling with activity. The souk stretched the entire length of the street bordering the harbor. Dariq helped her down from the carriage and held her arm in a proprietary manner as he guided her from booth to booth.

The variety and quality of goods amazed Willow. It was obvious that pirating was a lucrative business. Dariq had been right when he'd said the residents of Lipsi Town often visited the marketplace, for she saw men, women and children in traditional Greek clothing examining the wares.

"'Tis such a fine day, and everyone seems to be out and about," Dariq said. "If you see the man we're looking for, point him out. Mustafa will handle the matter from there."

Willow nodded, her attention suddenly caught by a necklace of flawless emeralds. She reached out for it and held it up to the sun, exclaiming over the purity of the stones. Dariq snatched it from her hands and replaced it on the display board.

"Remember why we are here," he reminded her. "Walk ahead a bit while I speak to Mustafa. Do not worry, for I won't let you out of my sight."

Willow strolled at a leisurely pace, enthralled by the scents and sounds around her. Everything from rich silks and satins to precious jewels and artwork was displayed. One booth offered a variety of weaponry, around which a crowd of men had gathered.

Dariq and Mustafa rejoined her. "Have you spotted him yet?" Dariq asked. "Look closely at the men loitering near the weapons."

Willow took a closer look. Most of the men looked alike with their scruffy beards, mustaches, unkempt hair and turbans. Then she saw him. She'd never forget those eyes. He looked directly at her.

She sensed his fear as he backed away. Willow pointed to him. "There he is!" The man turned and ran.

Mustafa gave chase. Willow had never seen a man his size move so fast. Though the culprit was fleet of foot and tried to lose himself in the crowd, Mustafa soon had him cornered. He dragged the wildly protesting pirate to where Willow and Dariq stood.

The pirate fell to his knees, groveling before Dariq. "Forgive me, my lord," he wailed. "I meant your lady no harm. I was paid to take her to Greece."

"By whom, Hamid?"

"Lady Safiye, my lord."

"How much did she pay you to make sure Lady Willow did not survive the crossing?"

Hamid blanched. "You will order my death if I tell you."

"I will order your death if you do not."

Hamid must have known he was doomed whatever he did, for he started shaking uncontrollably. "I cannot betray my lady Safiye."

Dariq didn't need to be told how Safiye had induced Hamid to do her bidding, and it made him wish he hadn't let Safiye off so easily.

"Did Safiye offer her body as inducement?" Silence. "Do not deny it, for your refusal to speak condemns you. Take him away, Mustafa."

Hamid was still protesting his innocence as Mustafa dragged him away. "We are done here," Dariq said.

"Can we not remain for a while longer?" Willow pleaded. "I have never seen anything like this. Oh, look! There's a parrot. Is he not darling?" She rushed over to stroke the bird's colorful feathers.

Dariq saw no harm in allowing Willow to browse in the souk, for it was indeed a colorful place, filled with scents and sights she was unlikely to encounter again. His brother jealously guarded his women; they were allowed little freedom. On Lipsi, women were free to do as they pleased. Dariq's seraglio was the only dwelling on the island with a harem, and only Safiye had occupied it. But even Safiye had been allowed to come and go at will.

"Very well, we will stay until you have had your fill of the noise and bustle."

"What will become of Hamid?" Willow asked as she fingered a lovely piece of silk.

"Punishment among the Brotherhood is harsh when the crime is serious. He will be judged and sentenced by a tribunal consisting of myself and members of the Brotherhood."

"Perhaps the tribunal will not see what Hamid did as a crime," Willow said, moving on to examine a colorful caftan.

"There is a code among the Brotherhood. Hamid broke that code when he agreed to murder someone I hold dear. I can assure you he will not escape unscathed."

Dariq followed Willow as she stopped at a booth to examine a length of cloth. Then she moved on to a booth displaying a variety of utensils. Dariq remained a few steps behind as he spoke to the cloth vender.

Then Willow wandered back to the booth where she had seen the emerald necklace, stifling a cry when she saw it was no longer on display.

"Is something wrong?" Dariq asked.

"The emerald necklace is gone."

"Did you think it attractive?"

Willow heaved a wistful sigh. " 'Twas the most splendid

thing I have ever seen. It had to be worth a fortune. I bet it was meant for a queen, or at least a princess."

"Perhaps it was," Dariq muttered cryptically. He guided her to a stall where she had admired a scarf. He picked it up and held it out to her. "Does this scarf please you?"

"It's lovely."

" 'Tis yours," he said, paying for it with coin from his pocket.

"Thank you," Willow murmured.

"Have you seen enough? We're starting to attract attention."

"But surely no one will harm me while I am with you?"

"I would like to think not, but pirates are an unpredictable lot. One never knows what is in such a man's mind, as you learned with nearly tragic results. I hold a certain amount of control over them, but not all those who sail aboard my ships are Turks. They come from many countries and are of diverse faiths."

"Perhaps you will allow me to visit the souk another time."

"Perhaps," Dariq acknowledged. He grasped Willow's elbow and guided her through the crowd to the carriage.

"Prince Dariq!"

Dariq spun around, smiling when he saw Captain Juad. "When did you arrive, Captain?"

"Just this morning. It took longer than I expected to make the temporary repairs to my ship. When you have time, I would like to talk to you about the code your captains are required to adhere to. There is also the matter of living quarters on the island for myself and my men while my ship is undergoing the rest of its repairs."

"Mustafa will find quarters for your men. Your high rank, however, demands something more appropriate.

You may stay in my seraglio. After you gather your personal items from your ship, Mustafa will escort you to my home."

"Thank you, Prince." Juad's gaze settled on Willow. "Tell the lady 'tis good to see her well and thriving."

"Lady Willow understands and speaks Turkish now," Dariq informed him. "She is a quick learner and has mastered the rudiments of our difficult tongue."

Juad beamed at Willow. "You are indeed a treasure, my lady." He bowed gallantly. "Peace be with you, my lord Prince."

Dariq nodded and steered Willow to his carriage. He helped her inside and climbed in beside her. Mustafa was already perched on the driver's box.

"Where is Hamid?" Willow asked. "Where did Mustafa take him?"

"Do not fret, beauty. Hamid will never bother you again."

Clutching the scarf Dariq had bought her, Willow remained silent during the ride back to the seraglio. Though the gift meant a great deal to her, she would leave it behind when she left. She wanted nothing to remind her of Dariq. It would be too painful. He said he cared for her, and she wanted desperately to believe him. Unfortunately, he didn't care enough to return her to her home, or to claim her for himself.

The carriage rolled to a stop; Dariq handed Willow down and escorted her inside. But instead of sending her to the harem, he took her to his chambers.

"What am I doing here?"

"Did I not make myself clear? You are to remain with me. You may take off your head scarf now. When we are alone, you are free of restrictions and may dress as you please."

Willow unwound the scarf and tossed it aside. "Just as Safiye was free of restrictions when you were alone?"

Dariq's lips thinned. "Do not mention her name to me again. She betrayed me in a way I can never forgive. Only Allah knows how many men shared her favors while I was away."

Willow walked to the couch and sat down, folding her hands primly in her lap. She cleared her throat. "What do you suppose Ibrahim will do when he learns I am not a virgin?"

Dariq sat down beside her. "Your beauty should more than make up for your lack of maidenhead."

"And if it does not? Will he punish me? You said he was a cruel man."

"A cruel man but not a foolish one. If he is not pleased with you, he will turn a profit by selling you to one of the pashas he favors. Even without a maidenhead, you are worth a great deal."

Willow glared at him. "And that does not bother you?"

Dariq didn't reply, for there was no easy answer. Not only would it bother him, he would probably repent his action the rest of his life, just as he would regret his mother's death if he kept Willow for himself. Never had he been so torn.

"Are you hungry?" he asked, nimbly changing the subject. "We can eat in the garden—would you like that?"

He yanked on the bell pull; a servant appeared at the door almost instantly.

"Please serve our meal in the garden."

The servant nodded and left.

Dariq took Willow's hand and led her through a pair of French doors to a tiled patio surrounded by a profusion of flowers.

"How charming," Willow whispered. "I have not seen this before."

"It's my private garden. I knew you would enjoy it."

Willow glared at him. "Why should my feelings make any difference to you?"

He dragged her into his arms. "I wish I knew."

His head lowered toward hers. Willow tried to avoid his kiss, but Dariq's determination won out. He persisted until his mouth found hers and claimed it. His arms held her so tightly she could scarcely breathe. She twisted free and stepped away, her hand covering her lips. She turned her back on him, angry at herself for responding to his attempt at seduction.

She sensed him standing behind her and held her body stiff. She gasped when she felt something cool circling her neck and looked down. She spun around, her hand clasping the emerald necklace he had placed around her throat.

"*You* bought the emeralds!"

"Aye, for you. Do they please you?"

"You know they do; they are magnificent. But—"

"Hush, sweet Willow. I would give you all that you desire . . . all within my power to give."

"Will you give me freedom?"

"That, I cannot do."

She opened her mouth, hesitated, then blurted out, "Will you give me your heart?"

Dariq went very, very still, refusing to meet her gaze. "Perhaps I would, if I were free to do so."

"Say no more, Dariq. I do not believe in miracles. I cannot compete with the woman who gave you birth."

Tears came to Willow's eyes as she fingered the emeralds. Then she undid the clasp and placed them in Dariq's hand.

"I cannot accept them. I want nothing to remind me of you after you send me away."

After you send me away.

Those five words made Dariq's gut clench with unspeakable pain.

How could he let her go?

How could he not?

Chapter Twelve

Dariq stared down at the necklace as if he expected it to bite him. All he'd tried to do was please Willow. He should have known she was too proud to accept gifts from her captor.

Nevertheless, the way Willow had spurned the emeralds hurt. Was it wrong of him to want her to remember him for his kindnesses to her?

Anger took over where hurt left off. Thrusting the emeralds into his pocket, he turned on his heel and stormed off. When Dariq entered the seraglio, he barked orders to a servant standing nearby.

"Serve the lady's lunch in the garden. I will not join her today."

Mustafa appeared at Dariq's side. "Why are you angry, Prince? Your face looks like a thundercloud in a storm."

"Do not push me, Mustafa."

"Did the lady not like the emeralds? Did you give her the silk you purchased for her?"

"She spurned the emeralds, so I did not show her the silk."

Mustafa shook his head. "You have become too attached to the Lady Willow. Ahmed will return soon with Ibrahim's reply to your request for an exchange. Whether you like it or not, you must send the lady away."

"Do you not think I know that?" Dariq whispered in a voice fraught with anguish. "How am I to do something which is so reprehensible to me?"

"'Tis your duty," Mustafa replied. "There are other women, some more beautiful than Lady Willow. You will find someone to take her place."

"Leave me, Mustafa. Go fetch Captain Juad. He is waiting for you at the harbor. I invited him to stay with me while his ship is being repaired. And you will need to find quarters for his crewmen."

Dariq could tell Mustafa was worried about his state of mind. "Worry not, my friend," Dariq said reassuringly. "I will not falter. Saliha Sultana will not suffer because of my lust."

Mustafa nodded and left to do Dariq's bidding.

Still too hurt by Willow's refusal to accept his gift, Dariq did not return to his chamber the rest of that day.

Willow picked at her supper in the same desultory manner as she had pushed her lunch around her plate after Dariq had stormed off earlier in the day. She knew she had hurt him, but she couldn't bring herself to accept the necklace. Each time she looked at it she would be reminded that the emeralds were meant to salve Dariq's conscience.

Willow's thoughts ran the gamut from rage to self-pity to indignation and back to rage. She prowled Dariq's chamber. Once she even tried to leave, but was stopped at the door by a guard who barred the exit. That made her still angrier. If Dariq dared to return to his chamber, she intended to give him the sharp edge of her tongue.

Shadows filled the room as darkness covered the land. A servant arrived to light the brazier and candles. Though Willow was tired, she refused to let herself fall asleep until Dariq arrived. She sat down on the couch to wait. Exhaustion claimed her before she was prepared to accept it. Her eyelids dropped and her body slumped sideways. Before long she was sprawled across the couch, fast asleep.

Dariq spent the evening with Captain Juad and Mustafa, talking and sipping excellent brandy taken from a Turkish ship sailing out of Marseilles. Dariq rarely imbibed. The Muslim half of him avoided liquor because it was forbidden, but the Christian half allowed it, even embraced it on certain occasions. The fact didn't escape him that Willow was driving him to drink. Wanting her was a constant ache inside him, but he knew he had to adhere to reason and remember why he had taken her in the first place.

Captain Juad finished his brandy and yawned. "I believe I will seek my bed, my lord. It has been a long day, and tomorrow promises to be even longer. I am anxious to ready my ship to ply the seas in your service." He rose. "Did you mean what you said, Prince Dariq, about bringing my family to Lipsi?"

"I did indeed," Dariq said absently. "We will speak of it another day. As you said, it is late."

Juad bowed and retired to his chamber.

Mustafa lingered, his intent gaze assessing Dariq's mood. "You appear greatly disturbed, my prince."

"You are too observant, my friend."

"I know you. I can count on one hand the times you've turned to alcohol; all of them during troubled periods of your life. 'Tis the woman," he said sagely. "Perhaps you should place her in my care so you will not be tempted by her again."

Dariq's head snapped up. "Nay! I am responsible for her, not you or anyone else." He winced as if in pain. "The necessity of giving her to Ibrahim does not please me."

"You cannot back down now. Our plans have already been set into motion. You are obsessed with the houri, even though you knew from the beginning that she was not destined to be your woman. She was meant for your brother's bed, not yours. Bedding her has jeopardized our plans and placed your mother's life at risk."

"Enough!" Dariq shouted. "I do not need you to preach to me; I know where my duty lies. Go find your bed, Mustafa. We will speak again of Willow's fate when Ahmed arrives."

Mustafa bowed; his eyes were grave with knowledge that came from years of close association with Dariq.

Dariq lingered over his brandy. The talk about Willow had created a primitive need that drew his body as taut as a bowstring. Abruptly, he uncoiled himself from the couch upon which he had been reclining, picked up the half-empty bottle of brandy and strode purposefully toward his chamber.

When he felt the emeralds Willow had spurned rattling in his pocket, hurt returned with a vengeance. His steps faltered, but only for a moment. Physical need for Willow transformed his hurt, pride and anger into desperate need. Whether it was the brandy speaking or his heart he knew not, and he did not dare to delve too deeply into his emotions.

Dariq opened the door and stepped inside his chamber. Willow had left a candle burning on the table, its subdued flame a slip of gold against the blackness. His gaze went immediately to the bed. It was empty. Anger built again as he scanned the room. Then he saw her; she was sprawled on a couch, fully dressed and sleeping soundly. His loins clenched. He knew Mustafa would advise him to leave Willow untouched and seek his bed, but it did not please him to do so.

He set the brandy on the table and walked to the couch, where his lover lay sleeping. He knelt beside her and touched her lips with his. She didn't stir. He caressed her breasts, cursing the layer of cloth that prevented closer intimacy. He wanted her naked, every inch of her lush body exposed for his enjoyment. His eyes lit up when he spied the buttons marching down the front of her gown.

With trembling hands he released each button, but still she did not stir. As he lifted her to remove her gown, she awoke; her eyes were glazed with sleep and her expression fuzzy with confusion.

"Dariq? What are you doing?"

"Trying to undress you."

She pulled the edges of her bodice together. "Whatever you have in mind, forget it."

Their eyes locked. Tension drew his features taut, but then his expression swiftly relaxed into a faint smile. "Perhaps a kiss will change your mind."

Willow didn't want to kiss Dariq, for seduction would quickly follow. "Naught will change my . . . Oh—"

Dariq stopped her protest with a kiss that seemed to go on forever and ever. He was the devil's own disciple, tasting of brandy and sin. His kisses made her forget her own name. When he thrust his tongue inside her mouth, exploring more deeply, she wanted to melt into a puddle at his feet. She fought his seduction with what little remained of her resistance, but it wasn't enough.

"Don't fight this, beauty," he whispered against her lips. "I want to pleasure you until your body is sated and you scream my name, and then I will pleasure you again."

"You've been drinking!" Willow charged. "I thought Muslims were forbidden alcohol."

"Tonight I am Christian."

"You are a fraud."

"I am what I am."

Before she realized his intention, her gown was eased away, drawn over her head, fluttering to the floor. Her shift followed and then her slippers.

She reached for a coverlet; he pulled it from her fingers and tossed it aside. Pulling the threads of her dignity together, she said, "I tried to stay awake until you arrived so I could convince you to return me to the harem."

He chortled. "What makes you think I would have granted your request?"

"Since I had no intention of letting you . . ."

". . . make love to you?"

"Bed me. Bedding is not making love," she explained. "When a man and woman make love, there are supposed to be tender feelings between them."

Dariq frowned. "Do you not hold tender feelings for me?"

The chamber throbbed with silence.

He grasped the pale oval of her face between his hands and gazed deeply into her eyes. "I want to hear you say you care for me."

"Why? Even if I bared my heart to you, it would change naught. Your arrogance is appalling. Does your pride demand that every woman you bed fall in love with you?" Her lips thinned. "I . . . I like you not. Nor do I enjoy being your love slave."

Dariq's scowl should have warned her. "Love slaves must obey their masters."

Scooping her from the couch, he carried her to his bed. She watched warily as he removed the emerald necklace from his pocket and placed it on the nightstand beside a half-empty brandy bottle. Then he stripped off his clothes.

"If you consider yourself a slave, you will cater to my every desire. Spread your legs, slave, and prepare to receive your master."

Willow tried to roll off the bed, but he threw himself on top of her. She heaved against him, but he was an unmovable force determined to have his way.

"No man will ever be my master!" Willow cried. "Go away, you're drunk!"

"Drunk on your beauty and lush body. You are mine, Willow. I mastered you the first time you took me inside you."

She raised her hand to strike him, but he grasped her wrist, holding it captive above her head, subduing her with his sheer strength. Their bodies were meshed together, legs entwined, her breasts flattened against his chest. His staff was hard and heavy and massively engorged.

Suddenly the pressure on her breasts eased as he rose slightly and straddled her legs. He reached for the emeralds and held them up. They glowed intensely in the flickering candlelight. They were so stunning they stole Willow's breath. She followed the necklace with her eyes as Dariq placed it between her breasts and slowly, oh so slowly, trailed it over her nipples and down her body.

The emeralds felt cold and burning hot at the same time. The feeling was more erotic than anything she had experienced in her entire life. Then he scooted back and drew the emeralds between her legs. She lurched upward as they glided over her sensitive bud.

"Dariq, what are you doing?"

"Giving my slave pleasure." He stared down at her, where the emeralds rested in her cleft. "They don't do you justice. You are beautiful down there, all pink and moist and glowing."

He slid the necklace upward, lingering with loving attention on her stomach and breasts, and then he fastened it around her neck. "I want you wearing naught but emeralds when I make love to you."

Willow curled her fingers around the necklace. Immediately the stones seemed to glow; her hands tingled and dropped away as if burned. She had no idea what was happening, except that her body suddenly felt alive and very very, needy.

A worried frown creased her brow when Dariq reached for the brandy bottle. "You are already drunk—why do you need more?"

His silver eyes sparkled with mischief. Then, to Willow's utter shock, he upended the bottle and dribbled brandy across her breasts. The tips of her nipples tautened instantly. The erotic sensation had scarcely registered before Dariq provided another. He began lapping up the brandy with his tongue, going over and around each breast and between them, carefully avoiding her tender nipples.

Willow arched upward, offering more of herself and demanding more of him. He was a devil. He knew he was tormenting her, playing her body like a fine instrument, stealing her will to resist. And, curse him, it was working.

Then he gave her what she wanted. A low growl rumbled from his chest as he took a brandy-drenched nipple into his mouth and sucked . . . hard. When he raised his head, both nipples were throbbing and elongated.

Willow watched with bated breath as he reached for the bottle again and dribbled brandy down her torso, stopping just short of her mound. This time when he lowered his head, she knew what to expect. His tongue felt like velvet, only rougher, as he licked down her body.

"Brandy never tasted so good," he murmured as he sipped delicately from her navel and rimmed it with his tongue.

His mouth burned a fiery trail over her skin as he lapped up every drop of brandy from her breasts and stomach. When he reached for the bottle again, Willow cried, "Dariq, no!"

She might as well have been talking to the wall for all the attention he paid her. He was too intent on dribbling brandy on more intimate parts of her body. She felt her tender folds swelling, throbbing, and then his mouth was there, easing her torment while creating another. His tongue lapped and probed and thrust, until she hovered on the brink of madness. Dariq must have known when that moment arrived, for he scooted up her body and thrust his sex deep, embedding himself to the hilt.

He was so ready he could have climaxed immediately, but he clenched his teeth and persevered. Satisfying a woman had always been a large part of his pleasure, and it was even more important with Willow.

He flexed his hips and began to move, slowly, penetrating deeply, bringing tiny moans from her sweet lips. He kissed her, savoring her taste, moving his tongue in and out, duplicating the movement of his cock inside her. She was hot and tight and sweeter than anything he had ever known . . . or would ever know again.

Abruptly he reversed their positions, bringing her on top of him, forcing a deeper penetration. His hands were free now to stroke her buttocks and caress her breasts.

His breathing became harsh, grating, as his hips jerked harder, faster. Then he eased a hand between their bodies and touched the dewy pearl between her legs. Willow screamed. Dariq thrust one last time, hurtling them both over the edge.

He stayed inside her a long time, waiting for the tumultuous upheaval to subside before pulling out. When he grew soft, he lifted her off him and settled her down beside him.

Willow's voice trembled. "Do you know what you just did?"

Dariq turned toward her. "Aye, I'm not *that* drunk. I left you well sated, did I not?"

"You may have left your child inside me."

Dariq rose up, and then fell back down, his dismay apparent. "Perhaps I did that the last time we mated."

Mustafa would accuse him of deliberately sabotaging his own plans to save his mother. Perhaps his friend was right. Dariq had examined his heart and realized he wanted to keep Willow for himself.

"You will never know if I carry your child," Willow said. "I will be gone before we know if your seed found fertile ground. I hope it does not, for I have no desire to bear the child of a heartless pirate."

Her words stung sharply. "Do you think me heartless, Willow?"

I think you are the most talented lover on earth. But of course she could not say that. She had no intention of inflating Dariq's ego. She was frightened—more frightened than she had ever been before. If she went to Ibrahim already with child, the sultan would surely punish her. Did Dariq not know that? Did he not care? What kind of monster was he?

She glanced over at him; he was sleeping, his face relaxed into a smile. "Why can you not love me?" she whispered.

Dariq wasn't sleeping. He heard her whispered plea but had no answer. He prayed to Allah and then to the Christian God, prayed that he would be granted a solution to his dilemma. Choosing between Willow and his mother was a punishment worse than death.

Suddenly a thought came to him, and he mulled it over in his head. It wasn't an easy decision, but then, one's death was never pleasant to contemplate. It could work, however, because ultimately it was his death that Ibrahim wanted. Aye, he would explain his new plan to Mustafa tomorrow. Until then, he would savor every remaining moment with Willow.

Dariq left his bed the next day before Willow awoke. She remained soundly asleep while he bathed and dressed. Before he left, he covered her nakedness with a sheet and kissed her forehead.

Whatever else Willow felt for him, he didn't want her to hate him. He wanted her to think kindly of him. Perhaps, after she learned what he had done for her, she would realize how much he cared for her.

Dariq found Mustafa in the dining hall with Captain Juad. They had already eaten, and Juad was preparing to leave. Juad wished Dariq a good morning and hurried off to oversee the repairs on his ship. Dariq waved him off and seated himself across from Mustafa.

A manservant poured his tea, then placed a bowl of fruit before him. "What is your pleasure this morning, master?" the servant asked.

"This will suffice," Dariq said. "I have too much on my mind to eat. Leave us. And close the door behind you."

The servant bowed himself out and closed the door. Dariq picked at the fruit. Mustafa observed him a moment, then shook his head.

"'Tis the woman. Your involvement is more serious than I thought."

"I cannot send her away, Mustafa. Ibrahim shall never have her."

Mustafa sent Dariq an appalled look. "Are you mad? I suspected your emotions were engaged more than they should be, but I never imagined you would abandon your mother because of your obsession with a blond houri. I warned you, Prince. Did I not tell you she was trouble the moment I clapped eyes on her?"

"Save your anger for someone who will appreciate it. Don't you think I have said as much to myself? Willow is . . . not like other women. She would wither and die in Ibrahim's harem. She is a free spirit, with a will and determination few women possess."

"Once you saw her as a desirable woman, you forgot the reason she was important to us."

Dariq shrugged. "Don't you think I have argued this over and over in my mind? Don't you think I tried to tell myself that Willow's fate should not matter to me?"

"What of Saliha Sultana, my lord? Are we to let her perish? When Ibrahim learns his concubine is not forthcoming, he will respond swiftly. You of all people know the extent of Ibrahim's cruelty."

"I do know, my friend, and that is why I am offering myself to Ibrahim in Willow's stead. An exchange will still occur, but it will be me and not Willow who goes to Ibrahim. I suspect my brother will be thrilled, for my death is vital to him. Though I no longer reside within his sultanate, he still believes I threaten his power."

Mustafa made a gurgling sound in his throat. "Allah protect me from fools and men in love." He searched Dariq's face, and then he smiled. "For a moment I thought you were serious."

"I have never been more serious in my life. When Ahmed brings word from Ibrahim concerning the exchange, I plan to sail to Istanbul and place myself at Ibrahim's disposal. I am telling you this because I want you to return Willow to her father."

Mustafa uncoiled his huge frame from his chair and stood menacingly over Dariq, all six and a half feet of him, arms crossed over his massive chest. "I will not allow it. I did not save your life so you could sacrifice it. I will bind and gag you and lock you in your chamber if you attempt to do what you are proposing."

Dariq rose, going nose to nose with his friend. "You have no say in the matter. Try to stop me and I will fight you every step of the way."

"But at least you will be alive," Mustafa argued. "I made a promise to your mother, and I intend to honor it."

"At the cost of our friendship?"

"Aye, my lord Prince." He bowed and stomped off, leaving Dariq to muse that he would never have another friend like Mustafa.

Mustafa made certain Dariq had left the seraglio before visiting Willow in the prince's chamber. He knocked and identified himself, asking for an audience. Willow bade him enter.

Though she was surprised to see Mustafa without Dariq, she was curious about his visit. The huge Turk rarely spoke to her . . . didn't even seem to like her. The scowl on his face was not reassuring.

"Lady Willow, I have something of grave importance to discuss with you."

"I assumed as much," Willow replied. "Please continue."

"Has Prince Dariq informed you of his plans?"

"Do you refer to his plans to trade me for his mother? If so, aye, I have known Dariq's plans for me since I became his captive. I am intended for Ibrahim's harem."

Mustafa nodded sagely. "It is good that you know to whom you belong."

Willow's chin rose defiantly. "I belong to no man."

Mustafa shook his head, his dark eyes sad. "I do not understand why my prince is willing to sacrifice his life for you. But know you this, lady; I will not allow it."

Willow slanted him a bewildered look. "What are you talking about?"

"The prince informed me this morning that he is not going to send you to Ibrahim. He intends to sacrifice his life for you. Ibrahim will be well pleased with the trade. He fears nothing more than a coup instigated by his brother to strip him of power. A dead brother cannot challenge his power."

Willow was shocked into silence. Last night Dariq had given no indication of his intention to spare her and sacrifice himself. When had he made the decision? Why? More importantly, could she allow it?

"What do you want me to do?" Willow asked.

"Convince the prince to give up such folly. His life is too important to sacrifice, for one day Turkey may need him. Ibrahim has had no children with any of his concubines. It is a widely held belief that he is sterile. If aught should happen to him, Prince Dariq will inherit the sultanate, and he will become ruler of the great Ottoman Empire."

Willow considered everything Mustafa had told her, but nothing made sense. Dariq was a pirate. Pirates did not have a noble bone in their bodies. He said he cared for her, but by no means could that be considered a declaration of love. She knew Dariq was fond of her, but would a man sacrifice his life for a woman he was merely fond of?

"You want me to convince Dariq that his life is worth more than mine," Willow repeated.

"Aye, lady. Your life is naught compared to Prince Dariq's."

Willow bristled. "My life means something to me and my family."

Mustafa slumped, his disappointment palpable. "I thought you cared for my master, but I was mistaken."

"You are not mistaken, Mustafa. I care a great deal for Dariq. You are the one who does not care enough. If you did, you would understand that he has committed himself to a selfless act of honor and nobility."

Mustafa stiffened. "I love Prince Dariq more than my own life. I would willingly die for him. I protected him in Istanbul, and I will continue to protect him until my dying breath."

"Forgive me for having doubted you," Willow apologized. "I know how close you are to Dariq, and that he respects your opinions and values your friendship."

"Then you will help me dissuade him from his destructive course?"

"Mustafa, what are you doing here!" Dariq's voice roared from the doorway. "You had no right to divulge our private conversation to Lady Willow."

"Forgive me, master," Mustafa said, sounding not at all contrite. "I told you I would do whatever it took to prevent you from throwing your life away."

"My life is mine to do with as I please. Leave us!"

Mustafa slanted a warning glance at Willow and then departed.

"What did he say to you?" Dariq demanded.

"*Why*, Dariq? Why would you sacrifice yourself for me?"

Dariq shrugged. "Perhaps I am not as heartless as you think."

Despite his soft-spoken words, Willow sensed a deeper reason. "Is that the only motive?"

"I am better prepared to defend myself against Ibrahim than you or my mother. I do not intend to die, Willow."

One finely arched eyebrow shot upward. "Do you not? Mustafa thinks differently."

"I haven't told him everything."

"How do you expect to save yourself? From what I've heard of your brother, he will order your death the moment you step ashore in Istanbul."

"'Tis my head," Dariq drawled. "You and Mustafa are insulting my intelligence."

The words came easily to her lips, though she hadn't planned them. "I won't let you do it. I at least have a chance of surviving, while you do not. There is no guarantee you will remain alive longer than a heartbeat."

Willow couldn't let Dariq die. Mustafa was right. Ibrahim would not let his brother live once he surrendered himself.

"I know what you are thinking, but my mind is made up," Dariq said. "Naught will change it."

"You said you had a plan. What is it?"

Dariq looked away. He wished he *did* have a plan. All he knew was that he couldn't let his mother die because he cared more than he should for an English houri.

Chapter Thirteen

Dariq began making plans for his departure. He provisioned two ships, his own *Revenge* to carry him to Istanbul and another to take Willow home. Mustafa adamantly refused to help him; they butted heads constantly about Dariq's decision to sacrifice himself for a woman.

Dariq knew Mustafa would take charge of the Brotherhood once he was gone, though with great reluctance, and Captain Juad would become his lieutenant. He had already spoken to Juad about it and had received reluctant agreement. The Brotherhood would prosper regardless of who was in charge.

As for Willow, she would return to her father and live her life without him. Maybe she would wed her fiancé, or another man who caught her fancy. But until he left, she was his to make love to each night. And each night he silenced her pleas to rethink his plans with deep kisses and erotic lovemaking.

Though he hadn't given up hope, Dariq had no definite plan to escape death. He couldn't even think about how he would avoid Ibrahim's death sentence until his mother was safely aboard the *Revenge* and well on her way to Lipsi. And there was a good chance that Ibrahim would order his execution immediately.

Willow was at her wits' end. Whenever she tried to talk sense into Dariq, he refused to listen. Then he made love to her as if it were the last time, which might very well be true if he continued to tread the path to an early grave.

Willow felt certain she had a better chance of surviving Ibrahim's harem than Dariq did the sultan's prison. Ibrahim might desire her body, but he *craved* Dariq's death. She grimaced with distaste at the thought of Ibrahim's hands on her, but she was determined to do whatever it took to keep Dariq alive. Even if it meant becoming the sultan's concubine.

Willow had reached the conclusion that she loved Dariq. How could she not? Any man willing to give up his life for her was deserving of her love; her body was already his.

Dariq found Willow sitting in the garden when he came looking for her one afternoon. He sat down beside her, his expression grim. "Ahmed's ship has arrived."

Willow went still. "So soon?"

He nodded gravely. "I plan to leave on the morning tide."

"Is there naught I can do to change your mind? Send me to Ibrahim as you originally planned. I swear he will not harm me. I will charm him into making me his favorite."

Obviously, that was the wrong thing to say. A low growl rumbled from Dariq's chest. "Ibrahim will not touch you." He rose abruptly. "There is still much to be done. I shall return in time to share supper with you." His expression softened. "After, we will make love until dawn, until we must part."

Tears streamed down Willow's cheeks as she watched Dariq walk away. She had to do something, but what?

She was lost in thought when she heard the shuffle of footsteps on the flagstones. She turned her head, surprised to see Mustafa and Baba approaching.

Mustafa bowed. "Forgive us for intruding, lady. I knocked, but you did not hear."

"I already know what you have come to tell me. Ahmed's ship has returned."

Mustafa bowed his head. "I cannot let the prince go to his death. I intend to keep the promise I made to his mother."

"I agree," Willow said. "If there is any way possible, I would take his place."

Baba, who had remained silent until now, stepped forward. "There is a way, my lady, but you may not like it."

"Tell me! I will do anything to stop Dariq from throwing away his life."

"Are you willing to go to Ibrahim?"

Willow did not misunderstand. She nodded slowly. "I suggested it to Dariq, but he refused to listen. He . . . he swore that I would not become Ibrahim's concubine."

Mustafa's keen gaze dug deep into Willow's soul, as if searching for the truth. He must have found it, for he smiled, the first smile Willow had ever known from him.

"Here is my plan, my lady. Baba is skilled in the use of drugs. She will prepare a strong sedative for Prince Dariq. It will make him sleep until long after his ship has sailed for Istanbul with you aboard."

"The drug won't hurt him, will it?" Willow asked anxiously.

213

"Nay," Baba assured her. "Our master is beloved; no one here wishes him harm."

Curious, Willow asked, "How will you give Dariq a sedative without arousing his suspicion?"

"It won't be difficult," Mustafa explained. "Baba will infuse the drug into his tea. Tonight, you must refuse tea with your dinner and drink juice instead."

"What if Dariq wants juice instead of tea?"

"He won't. The prince's habits are well known to me. He will sleep deeply for many hours. Once he is deep in sleep, I will bind him to his bed. When he awakens, he will realize what has happened, but by then it will be too late to stop the *Revenge* from sailing." He sent Willow a sheepish look. "I intend for the prince to be kept bound in his bed for two days. Juad and Baba will see to his care. The *Revenge* is the swiftest ship in his fleet. Prince Dariq will not be able to overtake her."

"And I shall be on the *Revenge*," Willow said softly. "The exchange will take place as originally planned."

"Aye, my lady. But success depends upon your compliance. I will not force you aboard the *Revenge*."

"When he awakens, Dariq will be furious with you and everyone who had a hand in this."

"It cannot be helped. Saliha Sultana did not save the prince's life so he could throw it away. I will be aboard the *Revenge* when he is released, praise Allah, but I will face his wrath when I return with his mother. It is up to you, lady, to tell us whether or not you will help."

Willow shuddered. If she did not fall in with Mustafa's plan, Dariq would die. If she sailed to Istanbul, she would spend her life behind walls, bound forever by Ibrahim's will. Either way, the choice was a terrible one, but Willow did not hesitate. She had not abandoned hope that her father was searching for her and would eventually rescue her. He wasn't the kind to give up.

"Tell me what I must do."

It took but a few minutes for Mustafa to explain his plan. Then he and Baba left Willow to ponder her fate. She sat in the garden where they had left her, staring at her hands, wondering if Dariq would follow her to Istanbul after he was released. Probably not, she decided. Once his mother was returned to him, he would forget about her and what she had done for him.

Freedom might not mean a great deal in Dariq's country, but to her it meant everything. Granted, English society imposed many restrictions upon young women, but at least they weren't confined behind walls and used as sex slaves.

Lost in contemplation, Willow remained so long in the garden she didn't notice that the shadows had lengthened and the sun had sunk below the horizon. Nor did she know she wasn't alone until a pair of strong arms circled her from behind.

She smiled and leaned back against Dariq, breathing deeply. He smelled of exotic spices and a scent uniquely his.

"Our dinner will be served shortly," Dariq whispered against her ear. He extended his hand. "Come. There is plenty of time to enjoy a bath. Baba prepared a special perfume to add to the water. I think you will enjoy it."

So this is the beginning of the end, Willow thought as she placed her hand in Dariq's and let him draw her to her feet. Hand in hand they walked to the *hammam*. The small chamber was warm and humid and indolent with a flowery scent Willow didn't recognize. She sniffed appreciatively.

"Do you like the scent?" Dariq asked. "I poured it into the water."

"Very much. 'Tis intoxicating," Willow allowed.

Dariq turned her toward him, his eyes dark with desire. "I find it arousing myself. Shall I help you undress?"

Willow offered no objection as Dariq removed her clothing and then his own. He stepped back to look at her. "You have a beautiful body."

Willow smiled, her eyes taking their fill of him while he gazed at her. His legs were long and muscular; the tendons beneath his golden skin rippled with suppressed tension. "So do you."

He threw back his head and laughed. "Men's bodies are not beautiful, beauty."

"You are right, of course. I meant to say magnificent."

Smiling with a tenderness that took Willow's breath away, he led her down the steps to the water. Once she was immersed to her hips, he reached into the pot of fragrant soap sitting on the rim of the tub and scooped out a handful. His hands slid provocatively over her breasts, stomach and hips; then he turned her around to spread soap over her back and buttocks.

He surpised her when he lifted her, sat her on the lip of the tub and reached for her left foot. Raising it from the water, he soaped her foot and leg, his hand straying into the damp tunnel between her thighs. Whimpering, she arched into his caress. Then he gave the same attention to her other foot and leg. By the time he lifted her down into the water, her skin was flushed and she was trembling.

"Now it's your turn," Willow purred, dipping her fingers into the pot of soap.

Willow loved the feel of his skin beneath her fingertips; it was smooth and velvety, yet the muscles were hard beneath the surface. Every time she touched a sensitive spot, his tendons jerked in response. When she finally turned her attention to his manhood, she wasn't surprised to find him fully erect.

Holding his engorged staff between her hands, she slowly stroked up and down. She watched his face as she worked her magic on him; his head was thrown back, his teeth bared and his eyes closed. Did she look as transfixed as Dariq when he caressed her?

Abruptly Dariq's eyes flew open and he removed her hands; his silver eyes were so dark they appeared black. He slipped into the water to rinse off the soap, then scooped Willow into his arms and carried her from the *hammam*.

"I want to be inside you when I find my pleasure," he whispered hoarsely.

He dried her with a soft cloth. When he finished, she was as aroused as Dariq. Their food was waiting for them on a low table surrounded by a pile of pillows when they returned to the bedchamber. Dariq seated her and followed her down. Willow saw the teapot and tried not to think about the drug it held. How soon after he drank it would it take effect?

She wanted to have this one last night with him and could think of only one way to achieve it. She stroked his face, turning it toward her and away from the food.

"I am not hungry for food yet. I want to make love before we eat."

A slow grin spread over Dariq's face. "I have met my match. Aye, my lusty beauty, the food will keep."

He lowered her to the pillows and kissed her ravenously, all thought of food forgotten in the name of passion. He aroused her slowly, lavishing her with tender, nipping kisses, using his hands and mouth to make her body sing. She returned his ardor kiss for kiss, until he was hard as stone and they were both trembling with need. It wasn't enough.

Willow wanted more of him. She wanted to taste him as he had tasted her. Clasping his hips in her hands, she lowered her head and licked the length of his cock, from the base to the head. Then she lapped a pearly drop of dew from the engorged tip with her tongue. He reacted violently to the rasp of her tongue, arching and crying out.

She went still. "Did I hurt you?"

"Aye, you are killing me, but I love it. Don't stop."

Willow was enjoying herself far too much to quit now. She raised her head and looked into his eyes. They were narrowed into slits and watching her. She grinned at him, then slipped her lips around the head and sucked him into her mouth. His moans fell one upon another as she licked up one side of his staff and down the other. The salty sweet taste of him surprised but did not disgust her.

He grasped her head between his palms, holding her in place. "Deeper," he groaned. "Harder."

Happily Willow gave him what he wanted as her head dipped again, increasing the pressure upon his sensitive sex with her tongue and lips.

Suddenly Dariq lifted her off and away. "No more, vixen." He lay without moving several minutes, struggling to control himself. "Turn over," he panted.

She stared at him for the length of a heartbeat before obeying. Then he raised her hips and positioned himself behind her. Willow waited with bated breath for Dariq to do something . . . anything. She wiggled her hips invitingly. When he finally thrust inside her, she shoved back against him, urging him on with tiny, desperate cries.

He leaned over her, pushing in and out of her tight passage while his hands teased her nipples into hard nubs. Sweat dampened his skin, blood pooled hot and heavy in his cock. The scent of aroused female filled his nostrils as he drove himself relentlessly. He was so close to the edge, he feared he wouldn't be able to wait for her. He tried to slow down, but he was stampeding toward climax.

"Hurry, love," he pleaded. "Come with me."

Unwilling to leave her behind, he slid one hand down her stomach and gently massaged the swollen jewel nestled between her thighs with the rough pad of his thumb. Willow screamed and began to convulse.

"That's it. Come with me, sweet beauty. Soar with me."

Willow was already soaring. She felt her soul touch the moon and stars, and then she heard Dariq cry out in a voice harsh with anguish, "You are mine, Willow, mine."

Then his warm seed filled her.

For several long minutes Dariq lay panting and motionless on top of her. Then he moved away, his chest heaving as he lowered himself beside her.

"I will never give you to Ibrahim," he said fiercely. "You may already be carrying my babe."

"Is that the only reason, Dariq?" Willow asked.

Dariq stroked her face. "Nay, sweet love, but the rest is better left unsaid. We go in different directions now, you to your father and I to my . . ." His sentence fell away.

"To your death—is that what you meant to say?"

"If that is my fate, then so be it."

Rising, he lifted her into his arms and carried her back to the *hammam*. They washed quickly and returned to the bedchamber and the supper that awaited them.

Dariq poured tea into his cup and held the pot suspended above hers. "Will you have tea?"

"Juice, I think," Willow replied.

Dariq poured juice from a pitcher into her goblet. Between kisses, they fed each other morsels of chicken, lamb and beef and nibbled on tender vegetables and pieces of flatbread. Willow watched closely as Dariq drank his tea and refilled his cup. She sipped her juice, her eyes lowered as she waited for his response to the drug Baba had infused in the tea.

Willow found it difficult to maintain her composure, for she knew the outcome of this night. She became so quiet and introspective that Dariq asked, "Is something wrong? Are you feeling unwell?"

She sent him a tremulous smile. "I am fine, but I cannot eat another bite."

"Nor I," Dariq said. "The night is still young. If this is to be our last, I want to make the most of it." He held out his hand.

Willow felt like a traitor as she placed her hand in his and let him lead her to the bed. Once he awakened, would Dariq realize that she and his faithful friends had plotted against him? Would he forget about her when she was gone? Or would he follow her to Istanbul after he was freed? She hoped not, for it would be too late; she would already be ensconced in the sultan's harem with his other concubines.

Willow hoped Dariq would accept her gift of life and remember her fondly. She could do no less for him, since he was willing to die for her. The hope still existed that her father would rescue her, and that fragile hope gave her the courage she needed to see Mustafa's plan through.

"We will make love slowly this time," Dariq said, interrupting her mental musings.

As they began to make love, Willow wondered if Baba's drug had been potent enough, for he did make love to her slowly, very, very slowly. When it ended, Willow lay limp in his arms, her eyes shut, her chest heaving.

"After I rest a moment, we will make love again," Dariq murmured. His words were slurred, his eyes hazy even as he spoke.

Willow smiled at him. His eyelids fluttered as he returned her smile.

"I must be getting old," he muttered sheepishly.

She stroked his forehead. "Go to sleep, my prince. You have earned your rest." Her voice caught on a sob. "Forgive me, my love; please forgive me."

His eyes opened with difficulty. "What have you done?"

For one desperate moment Willow thought the drug wasn't going to work. But when he tried to rise up on his elbows, they collapsed beneath him.

"Forgive me," Willow repeated. "I love you."

His fingers curled around her shoulders, bringing her face close to his. The accusation in his eyes revealed the precise moment he realized what was happening to him.

"What . . . have . . . you . . . done?"

Then his hands fell away, his eyes rolled back, and he went limp.

Willow slumped back against the mattress. It was done. She was sad but not remorseful. Because of her, Dariq would live. She was frightened, however. She had no idea what to expect as one of the sultan's concubines, or what the future held for her, but she could and would pray for a miracle.

There came a discreet knock on the door. Baba cracked it open and peeked inside. "Is it done, my lady? Is the prince sleeping?"

Willow sat up in bed, holding the sheet to her breasts. "Aye, 'tis done. What happens now?"

Baba approached the bed, pulled back Dariq's eyelids and peered into his eyes. There was no visible response. "He will sleep until well after your ship has departed," Baba predicted. "I will summon Mustafa while you dress. Allah protect you, my lady."

"Please take good care of Prince Dariq," Willow whispered.

Baba departed. Willow washed, dressed in one of the gowns Dariq had given her and coiled her hair atop her head. She was ready when Mustafa came for her, but somewhat surprised to see Ali Hara with him. Had he come to bid her goodbye?

"The ship is ready to sail on the morning tide," Mustafa said after a brief glance at Dariq. "You did well, lady. I am grateful. Follow me."

Mustafa led the way out the door. Willow turned back to Dariq and pressed her lips to his. Tears streaming down her face, she hurried after Mustafa, pausing at the door for one last look at her love.

The three of them moved through the silent seraglio and into the night. A carriage awaited them in the courtyard. Mustafa climbed into the driver's box. Ali Hara handed Willow inside and followed in her wake.

"I am going with you, lady," the eunuch said.

"What? Does Mustafa know?"

"I insisted, and Mustafa agreed. My master would want me to protect you. Kamel and I will do our utmost to keep you safe."

"Who is Kamel?"

"He is Ibrahim's chief eunuch and master of the harem. We were friends before I joined Prince Dariq in exile. I suspect the reason Saliha Sultana still lives is because of the power Kamel wields."

Willow was overcome with gratitude. The knowledge that she would have someone she knew in the sultan's seraglio raised her spirits. "I thank you, Ali Hara, and welcome your company."

The *Revenge* loomed large in the harbor. The crew was preparing the ship for immediate departure when Willow,

Mustafa and Ali Hara boarded. Willow was escorted to the captain's cabin, the same one she had occupied the last time she had sailed aboard the *Revenge* as Dariq's prisoner.

Despite her sense of doing the right thing, Willow began to have second thoughts. Had she acted rashly? There were so many things that could go wrong, she began to wonder why she had let Mustafa talk her into betraying Dariq. Even though she was saving Dariq's life, she knew he would be furious. And not just with her. Mustafa and all those involved would suffer his wrath; she didn't envy them.

Exhausted after a night of no sleep, Willow walked to the bed and sat down. She glanced out the window and saw the first purple streaks of dawn. Then she felt the ship slip from her moorings and move slowly away from the harbor.

Willow's hand flew to her mouth, as if suddenly realizing where she was going and why. She ran to the door and paused with her hand on the latch. Then she turned back. It was too late for second thoughts. The deed was done. She would gladly suffer the consequences for Dariq's sake. He would live. As for herself, she would survive.

Dariq awoke slowly, surprised that the room was flooded with sunshine and painfully aware of a splitting headache. He cracked both eyes open and turned his head, battling the pain the movement caused. He was in his bed . . . alone. It took a moment of concentration to realize that something was terribly wrong.

There was somewhere he was supposed to be, but he couldn't remember where. Groaning, he attempted to lift his hand to his forehead and was annoyed when he couldn't move his arm, or any part of his body. What in damnation was the matter with him? He glanced down at himself and loosed a string of curses when he realized his arms and legs were bound to the bed posts.

"You are awake."

Dariq glanced up and saw Baba sitting in a chair beside the bed. "What in Allah's name is going on?" Suddenly the clouds in his mind parted and he recalled that he should have been aboard the *Revenge* hours ago.

"What have you done? Release me and summon Mustafa at once!"

Baba approached the bed. "I cannot do that, my lord."

"You can and you will!" Dariq thundered. "Fetch Mustafa!"

"Mustafa is not here, my lord."

A horrifying thought came hard on the heels of Baba's words. "Where is Willow?"

Baba backed away from the bed. "Gone, my lord."

Dariq pulled on the ropes. They refused to give. His head throbbed with pain and he grimaced, trying to make sense out of the nightmare into which he had awakened.

Mustafa was gone and so was Willow.

"Does your head hurt, my lord?" Baba asked. "I will fetch something to soothe it."

"Nay, I want no more of your evil brews. You drugged me," he accused. "Mustafa planned this, didn't he? Once I had succumbed to the drug, he forced Willow aboard the *Revenge*. Did you drug Willow?"

Baba shook her head, carefully keeping her distance. "Lady Willow went willingly aboard the *Revenge*. She agreed with Mustafa that your life must be spared."

"Damn you all to the darkest pit of hell! Who is in charge here?"

"Captain Juad. I will fetch him for you and mix something to ease your pain." She hurried out the door.

Fury rose to a wild crescendo inside Dariq. Mustafa had no right to countermand his orders. Heads would roll for this . . . this travesty. Willow would not have agreed to go to Ibrahim willingly, would she? Nay, she would have fought tooth and nail to remain free. Abruptly he recalled something Willow had said before he succumbed to the drug. She said she loved him and asked forgiveness.

The door opened and Captain Juad entered. "You sent for me, my lord?"

"I did," Dariq spat. "Free me."

"I cannot, my lord. Not until tomorrow."

"On whose orders?"

"Mustafa's. He could not let you go to your death, and I agreed with him. All will be well," he continued. "Mustafa will bring Saliha Sultana to you without the loss of your life."

"What about Lady Willow? Does her life mean naught to any of you?"

"Ibrahim won't harm her. She is too beautiful, and he has waited too long for her. Did Baba not inform you that she went willingly aboard the *Revenge*?"

"Aye, she told me, though it makes little difference. Why do you think I intended to exchange my life for my mother's? I could not bear the thought of Willow in Ibrahim's bed. Untie me now and perhaps I can still catch the *Revenge*. There must be at least one ship in my fleet anchored in the harbor."

"I will release you tomorrow," Juad promised, "but you should have no illusions about catching the *Revenge*. No ship afloat is swifter than your flagship. By the time you reach Istanbul, it will be too late."

"Why are you doing this? I could have sunk your ship and killed you and your crew, but I chose to let you live."

"Now I choose to let you live, my lord Prince. No

woman is worth your life, not even the lovely Lady Willow."

"If you will not free me, get out of my sight," Dariq spat from between clenched teeth.

"Very well." He sighed and turned to leave.

"Wait, Juad," Dariq bit out. "Once I am free, if you wish to keep your head on your shoulders, there had better be a ship provisioned and waiting for me."

Juad's face turned a deathly shade of green as he let himself out the door.

Dariq fumed in impotent rage, unable to think clearly for the pain in his head. He could not believe that Willow had boarded the *Revenge* willingly.

A cry left his throat when his murky mind grasped the magnitude of that knowledge. If Willow had gone willingly to Ibrahim, she must love Dariq. Loved him enough to commit herself to a life of sexual servitude to his brother.

Overwhelmed by grief, he closed his eyes so he could think more clearly. As soon as he was free, he intended to sail to Istanbul. If he failed to catch the *Revenge*, he would find another way to rescue Willow.

Dariq slept, awakening sometime later to sounds in his chamber. He turned his head toward the door, grateful to find that the ache in his head had subsided and he was able to think clearly again.

"I bring food for you, my lord," Baba said as she shuffled toward the bed. She set the tray on the nightstand and pulled up a chair. "I brought tea, too. It should refresh you. Are you still in pain?"

Dariq grimaced at the steaming cup Baba offered him and turned his head away. "I want no more of your foul concoctions."

"You must be thirsty," Baba coaxed. "I promise the tea is untainted."

"If you are lying, you will suffer."

"I do not lie, master. Please drink."

She held the cup to his lips. Dariq took a tentative sip, and then another. Then he let her feed him. He would need his strength once he was set free.

Dariq was released after the dinner hour the following day. As soon as he was free, he stormed through the seraglio in a murderous rage, fuming all the way to the harbor. Captain Juad was waiting for him.

"Has a ship been provisioned?" he asked in a voice crisp with displeasure.

"Aye, my lord Prince. You are welcome to take my ship; it has been repaired and provisioned. May Allah go with you."

It would take more than Allah, Dariq feared, to rescue Willow from Ibrahim's clutches.

Chapter Fourteen

Fair weather and cloudless days and nights followed the *Revenge* to Istanbul. The ship scudded before the wind as if it had wings. Willow would have wished for a storm if she thought it would delay the inevitable, but none appeared. Despite Ali Hara's company, Willow's mood was far from cheerful. She missed Dariq.

Dariq had been willing to die for her.

What more could a woman ask of her lover?

Willow was standing at the rail, staring morosely at the blue-green waves breaking below the ship when Ali Hara joined her.

"I share your sadness, mistress."

Willow sighed. "No one can possibly know how I feel, but thank you for your concern. Will we reach Istanbul soon?"

"Lipsi is very close to the southern coast of Turkey but a greater distance from Istanbul in the north. 'Tis at least a seven-day journey to Istanbul."

"Do you think Prince Dariq can catch the *Revenge* if he decides to follow?"

" 'Tis highly unlikely, mistress. There is no ship swifter than the *Revenge*. Mustafa hopes the prince will realize it would be futile and not attempt the journey."

"As do I," Willow whispered. If Dariq followed her to Istanbul, all their sacrifices on his behalf would be for naught. He would be seized and executed the moment he stepped ashore.

As if reading her mind, Ali Hara said, "He will not be so foolish as to enter the city once you are delivered to Ibrahim. It would be senseless, for his mother would already be aboard the *Revenge*. 'Tis likely he will encounter the *Revenge* on her return journey and reunite with his mother on the high seas."

"He will forget me," Willow murmured, turning her head so Ali Hara would not see her tears.

"I cannot know what is in my master's heart, but I do not believe he will forget you."

Willow savored those words. She feared they were all she had to hold on to for the rest of her life.

Dariq cursed the tides that were still too low to allow the newly named *Hunter* to leave the harbor. Later, he cursed the lines that fouled as the ship slipped her moorings, swearing that the gods were against him. Then he cursed the wind for not filling the sails fast enough. How could he hope to catch the *Revenge* if the wind and the tides refused to cooperate?

Dariq motioned for Ahmed to take the wheel while he helped to untangle the lines. He was grateful to have Ahmed with him. He trusted Ahmed almost as much as he trusted Mustafa. Nay, that was not true. He no longer trusted Mustafa. He didn't know whom to trust anymore. He wanted to spare Willow a terrible fate, but his friends had betrayed him.

Dariq hated to believe that Willow had not been coerced or forced aboard the *Revenge*. If she had gone willingly, it was because Mustafa had convinced her that
Dariq's life was worth the sacrifice.

I love you. Please forgive me. Those were her last words
to him. Was it true? Did she really love him? He needed
to hear her say those words again, without his brain be-
fuddled by drugs. But the wind and tide were against
him. The newly repaired *Hunter* was not capable of the
kind of speed Dariq demanded. At this rate, Willow
would be in Ibrahim's bed before Dariq reached Istanbul.

Willow was standing at her usual place at the ship's rail
when Mustafa told her they would enter the Bosporus the
following day and reach Istanbul the day after that. Thus
far the journey had been uneventful. Each day, Willow
searched the horizon for signs of a ship following in their
wake, but none appeared.

Though she had no good reason to believe Dariq cared
enough for her to try to overtake the *Revenge*, still she
feared he might attempt it—despite the fact that Mustafa
had told her no ship afloat could match the *Revenge's*
speed. Willow's fanciful heart hoped Dariq *would* catch
up with the *Revenge*, but her more practical mind prayed
he would not. It would be not only foolish but disastrous
for Dariq to enter Istanbul.

During those empty days at sea, Willow had too much
time to think about her new life. Was Ibrahim as cruel as
Dariq described him? How would she fare in a harem in-
habited by his wives and concubines? Would they be jealous of her?

Ali Hara vowed to protect her, but could he? She had
already experienced the evil machinations of a jealous

concubine. Her encounter with Safiye had taught her to trust no one.

When Willow's thoughts turned to Ibrahim, it was with a frisson of dread. If there was a way to stay out of his bed, she vowed to find it.

Two days later, the *Revenge* entered Istanbul harbor and dropped anchor a short distance from shore. Mustafa joined Willow at the rail and informed her that they would not dock at one of the long stone piers because a hasty departure might be necessary.

"I plan to row ashore tomorrow morning and seek an audience with Ibrahim," Mustafa explained. "I shall tell him the *Revenge* has arrived with its treasure. He will know to what I am referring."

Willow nodded but offered no reply. Mustafa bowed curtly and left. Willow appreciated the short reprieve, though apprehension made for a sleepless night.

Morning arrived too soon. Shortly after sunrise, Willow watched as a rowboat was lowered into the water. Mustafa, accompanied by several crewmen, scampered over the side and climbed down a rope ladder into the boat. Two men picked up the oars and rowed toward shore. Willow wondered how long she would have to wait before Mustafa returned. A long time, she hoped.

She returned to her cabin after the rowboat shoved off, wanting to be alone while she gathered her composure and found the courage within herself to face the sultan. She wasn't as brave as she pretended. Fear of the unknown was tearing her apart. Her only consolation was that her sacrifice would make it possible for Dariq and his mother to live. Nevertheless, Willow knew her knees would be shaking when she faced Ibrahim for the first time.

The day dragged on. Day turned into night without a

sign of Mustafa. Had he failed to convince the sultan to trade Saliha Sultana for Willow? Had Mustafa been imprisoned? Or worse? The suspense was killing her.

Late afternoon of the following day, Willow was lying on her bed half asleep when Ali Hara burst into the cabin.

"Mustafa has returned! He will report to you shortly."

Willow's sluggishness fell away. "Oh, Ali Hara, I am so frightened. You are the only one I can admit that to."

Ali Hara grasped her hands and squeezed. "I will be with you, mistress. I will let no one harm you."

Willow swallowed the lump growing in her throat. "Can you help me stay out of Ibrahim's bed?"

Ali Hara's dark eyes filled with compassion. "If such a thing is possible, I will do all in my limited power to make it so."

Willow dashed away a tear. "I can ask no more of you than that."

There came a brief knock on the door; Mustafa entered. His fierce expression eased as he gazed at Willow.

" 'Tis done, lady. The bargain has been struck with Ibrahim."

"He still wants me?" Willow whispered.

"Most assuredly, lady. But he wishes to see you before he releases Saliha Sultana. You are to attend him in his private chamber tonight. Ali Hara will fetch the clothing you are to wear and help you prepare for your audience. I implore you to say naught that will make Ibrahim change his mind."

Unable to find words, Willow nodded mutely.

"I will fetch your garments," Ali Hara said after Mustafa departed. "I carried them aboard before we left Lipsi. While I am gone, use the cream Baba gave you to remove your body hair. If your skin is not smooth and free of hair when you are presented to the sultan, he will be repulsed. When I return, I will fashion your hair in a becoming style."

With heavy heart, Willow did as Ali Hara instructed. It seemed ludicrous to remove hair from her body, but she did it because she didn't want to cause trouble . . . yet. She had just finished her toilette when Ali Hara arrived with the clothing she was to wear for her initial meeting with Ibrahim.

He left again to find an aba while she donned the short jeweled vest and multilayered skirts sheer enough to show the outline of her legs. A wide jeweled girdle and soft slippers completed the outfit. Once she was dressed, Willow grimaced at her image. She looked like a slave girl out of *Arabian Nights*, which indeed she would be once she entered the sultan's seraglio.

A shudder passed through her. A *sex slave*.

Ali Hara returned, placed the aba on the bed and picked up a hairbrush. "Sit, my lady, while I brush your hair. Ibrahim will not be able to resist your beauty. Your hair is like spun gold, and your skin smooth as porcelain. If you please Ibrahim, he might make you his wife."

Willow gasped in revulsion. "God help me, for He alone knows I do not aspire to that title. I would be happy if I were left to languish in the harem, ignored and unclaimed by the sultan."

"That will not happen, lady," Ali Hara averred. "No man in his right mind would ignore you once he sees you."

Disheartened, Willow allowed Ali Hara to brush her hair. Closing her eyes, she emptied her mind of everything but Dariq and their erotic nights together. She recalled how they had made love in the *hammam* and playfully fed each other morsels of food. She relived the times they had made love on the floor amid a tumble of pillows, and in his bed.

"Your hair should be worn down. It looks best tumbling past your shoulders to your waist," Ali Hara decided, setting down the brush. "I can do naught to enhance its natural beauty. You are ready, lady."

Willow swallowed hard. She would never be ready. But she had agreed to Mustafa's plan and would follow through. It wasn't as if she weren't resourceful. As long as her mind worked, she could plot and scheme, and perhaps even escape.

"Are you ready, lady?" Mustafa called through the door.

Willow's breath hissed from her throat. "Aye, I am ready."

Ali Hara helped her don the aba and opened the door. The afternoon sun was fading into a golden twilight as Willow stepped out onto the deck. Mustafa grasped her elbow and escorted her to the rail.

"Can you climb down the rope ladder to the rowboat, lady? 'Tis not a great distance. I will help you."

Willow looked down. It seemed like a great distance to her, but she would do what had to be done for Dariq's sake. Mustafa went first in order to help guide her down. Ali Hara lifted her over the rail. Willow placed her foot on the first rung and slowly descended, cursing the aba, which hindered her progress. Slowly but surely she reached the bottom, where Mustafa waited. He handed her into the rocking boat as Ali Hara nimbly scampered down after her.

Two sailors picked up the oars and rowed to shore. They reached the dock far too soon for Willow's peace of mind. The sailors held the boat steady while Mustafa and Ali Hara scrambled onto the dock and helped Willow.

"There's the sultan's carriage," Mustafa said, indicating

an elaborate equipage trimmed in gold harnessed to a pair of matched blacks. "Hurry—we mustn't keep Ibrahim waiting."

As far as Willow was concerned, the sultan could wait forever. But she had left Lipsi with the knowledge of what her fate was to be and was determined to face it with courage. Squaring her shoulders, she marched toward the carriage. A servant in black and gold livery held the door open as Mustafa handed her inside. Then Mustafa and Ali Hara climbed in beside her. The servant closed the door, and the carriage jolted forward.

What little Willow could see of the exotic city through the window was fascinating. Nothing she saw looked in any way familiar. The sounds, the sights, the mingled scents of spices and flowers were a feast for the senses. The men appeared much taller and broader than the ordinary Englishman, and the women, she noted, wore abas covering all but their faces.

"The seraglio is just ahead," Mustafa remarked.

Willow poked her head out the window as the elaborate gate opened for them. The horses clattered into the courtyard and stopped. The carriage door opened, and Willow stepped down onto a patio paved in white marble veined with gold. Marble steps led up to a pair of brass double doors trimmed in gold. Willow decided that the Sultan of Istanbul was a very wealthy man and spared no expense for his own comfort.

Mustafa guided Willow to the front entrance, where a janizary standing outside the door rapped sharply with his scimitar. The door opened immediately. Willow stepped inside, her heart pounding wildly. Then the door closed behind her. She was trapped. Would she ever see the outside world again?

"Follow me," a guard commanded. "The sultan awaits you in his private chamber."

Willow's feet refused to move until Ali Hara gently pushed her forward. She was almost too frightened to notice the opulence of the seraglio; everything seemed a blur to her. One thing she couldn't ignore, however—the wealth of gold that adorned everything she saw, from the tassels on the drapery, to the statuary, the trim on onyx tables, and the ceiling above her head.

They walked down long marble hallways, passing closed doors as well as elaborately furnished rooms open for display. She gulped back her fear when they reached the end of a long corridor and paused before a set of golden doors more elaborate than any she had seen thus far.

The doors opened.

Willow's gaze was drawn to a man seated on a chair somewhat less elaborate than a formal throne but impressive nonetheless. The sultan, for he could be no less, was resplendent in a red and gold tunic over baggy white trousers. He wore soft slippers with gold buckles on his feet, and a white turban perched atop thick black hair. Two ebony-hued children standing on either side of him waved feather fans over his head, while several armed guards stood at attention. Ibrahim gestured for Willow and her party to come forward. With Mustafa and Ali Hara all but supporting her, she approached the sultan.

Ibrahim addressed Mustafa directly. "In what language should I address the woman, Mustafa? Does she speak French?"

"I speak both French and Turkish," Willow said before Mustafa could reply.

The sultan's dark gaze settled on Willow. Ibrahim was not unhandsome, she decided, but there was a cold emptiness in his eyes that frightened her. His thick eyebrows and neat beard were dark as night, but his eyes were too bright, too cunning. He'd appeared startled when she'd addressed him without asking permission.

"What is your name, lady?"

"I am Lady Willow Foxburn, and I demand that you return me to my father."

Ibrahim's eyebrows shot up to meet his hairline. "You may demand naught of me, lady. I paid for you in hard gold coin. You are mine to do with as I please. Henceforth, you will speak only when spoken to."

"The lady is not yours until you keep your part of the bargain," Mustafa reminded him.

Ibrahim scowled. "I do not trust you, Mustafa. Were it not for you and Saliha Sultana, my brother would have met the fate I had intended for him. I wish to inspect the woman to make sure I have not been cheated. Remove your aba, lady."

There was nothing Willow could do to hide her scantily clad form from the sultan. With great reluctance, she removed her aba and dropped it to the floor. She heard the sharp intake of Ibrahim's breath and met his probing gaze without flinching, refusing to be cowed.

Silence pulsed as Ibrahim stared at her. "Ahhh," he breathed, "she is lovely. More radiant than the moon and stars." He uncoiled his long form from the chair and stalked toward her. Only then did Willow flinch.

He was as tall as Dariq but more frightening in manner, though not nearly as broad or muscular as his brother. He stopped in front of Willow and lifted a strand of her hair, winding it around his finger. When he released it, it sprang back to its original shape, as if it possessed a life of its own.

"Your hair is spun gold. I have never seen the like.

You will always wear it down for me when you come to my bed."

She blinked up at him, the picture his words conveyed too painful to contemplate.

"Your eyes," Ibrahim continued. "They are like glowing emeralds. You are indeed a treasure and well worth the price."

"Now that you have seen Lady Willow and approve, you will release Salilha Sultana," Mustafa demanded.

Ibrahim shifted his gaze from Willow to Mustafa with marked reluctance. "Not yet. Step back several paces so that I might have a private word with the lady."

Both Mustafa and Ali Hara shuffled backward toward the door. Once they were out of hearing, Ibrahim let his avid, lust-darkened eyes roam over Willow's scantily clad body.

"You were with my brother a long time, lady."

His words demanded no answer, so Willow gave none. She knew what he was implying.

His gaze grew more intense, his expression hardening. "Did he take your virginity? Did my brother have you?"

Willow knew that lying would not help her. Her missing maidenhead was tangible proof that she was no longer virginal. Looking directly into Ibrahim's eyes, she said, "Aye." A more complicated answer wasn't necessary.

Ibrahim whirled and paced to his chair. He appeared angry. His shoulders were stiff, his hands fisted at his sides. But he didn't sit down. He whipped around and strode back to Willow.

"I expected as much. I knew my brother could not resist you. Even so, he took you to defy me. If you had lied to me, I would have known it. My brother is a coward. He did not accompany you to Istanbul because he knew I would have killed him for taking what was mine."

"You would have killed him anyway," Willow shot back.

He pushed his hand into her hair, digging his fingers into her scalp. Willow gasped as pain seared through her. Reining in her anger, she blinked away tears forming in her eyes and glared up at him. "If you do not want me, return me to Prince Dariq."

Seizing her shoulders, Ibrahim snarled, "Never! You are mine. Dariq cannot have you. Think you I don't know he is planning to kill me and seize my power?"

"Dariq has no plans to seize your power," Willow argued.

Ibrahim's hands tightened hurtfully on her shoulders. She winced.

"Do not hurt her, I beg you," Ali Hara said, rushing to Willow's defense.

Ibrahim looked past Willow to Ali Hara. "Who are you to speak on behalf of my concubine?" His eyes narrowed. "I remember you now. You are Ali Hara, the eunuch who disappeared from my harem shortly after my brother ran away."

"Aye, my lord," Ali Hara admitted. "I now serve Lady Willow. I intend to remain with her, if it pleases you."

Ibrahim laughed. Willow thought it an ugly sound. "You may remain if you wish, but Kamel's word is law in the harem."

"I understand, my lord," Ali Hara replied. "I merely wish to protect the lady Willow from your concubines. There is bound to be jealousy, and you know how ugly that can get."

Ibrahim returned his hard gaze to Willow. "Are you with child?"

Willow blanched and took a step backward. "I do not know."

Ibrahim stomped his foot like a spoiled child. "I will kill my brother for despoiling you! I will not rest until his head is separated from his shoulders, nor will I take you to my bed until I have proof that you are not carrying my brother's child."

Willow almost collapsed with relief. It was the reprieve she had prayed for. She lowered her head, docile and accepting, while her mind raced ahead to the possibilities now open to her. At the most, she had a month to plan an escape. If she wished hard enough for a miracle, one might be granted to her. It would be a miracle if Ibrahim forgot she existed.

The sultan seated himself upon his throne and gestured for Ali Hara and Mustafa to approach.

"Where is my brother?" he asked. "Does he remain aboard the *Revenge* because he is too cowardly to face me?"

"Nay, my lord," Mustafa answered. "Prince Dariq is not a coward. He was . . . tied up and sent me in his stead."

"Where is his stronghold?" Ibrahim demanded. "I know he has a fleet of ships and a Brotherhood of pirates at his disposal. He has disrupted my shipping and caused me great anguish. He allows little to get through to Istanbul from other ports."

"The *Revenge* is our home, my lord. As you well know, 'tis a sturdy ship. There is naught else I can tell you."

Obviously, Ibrahim didn't like the answer. "I can deal with you in ways you will not like if you do not tell me what I wish to know."

"Prince Dariq kept his part of the bargain and expects you to keep yours," Mustafa said. "You are a great sultan. Is your word not trustworthy? An agreement is an agreement. You promised to release Saliha Sultana if my master delivered the woman to you. Prince Dariq has generously agreed to let your ships pass in peace for the period of one year. Lady Willow stands before you now, and you appear pleased with her. 'Tis time you produced

Saliha Sultana. Should you renege, word that Sultan Ibrahim's honor cannot be trusted will travel throughout the Ottoman Empire and beyond."

It was a bold speech, and Willow hoped it wouldn't cost Mustafa his head.

Ibrahim's burning gaze returned to Willow, the heat of his lust scorching her wherever it touched, and it seemed to touch everywhere. She shuddered and hugged herself, trying to hide as much of her body as she could from his vile gaze.

"Never let it be said that the great Sultan Ibrahim is without honor." His gaze shifted to a wooden screen at the left of his throne. "You may come out, Saliha Sultana."

Willow's breath caught when an older woman clad in a flowing silk caftan stepped out from behind the screen. Small of stature and delicate, with lovely gray hair and undiminished beauty despite her age, she carried herself proudly as she approached Willow.

"I am sorry, my dear," she said in English. "Had it been my choice, you would not be here. I am an old woman and have lived a full life, while you have yours before you. My son must not have been thinking clearly. You do not belong here."

Saliha Sultana's silver-gray eyes were so like her son's that Willow could have stared into them forever.

"What are you saying?" Ibrahim barked. "I do not understand your heathenish tongue."

"I was merely welcoming Lady Willow to your seraglio," Saliha said.

"Watch your back, my lady," Saliha continued in English. "There is much intrigue in the harem. Kamel will do his best to protect you. Trust him."

"Leave now with Mustafa, Saliha Sultana," Ibraham ordered. "And good riddance," he added sourly.

Mustafa grasped Saliha's elbow as if to lead her away. Willow grasped the sleeve of her caftan. "A moment, my lady," she whispered. "Please take good care of Dariq. He is . . . I . . . just keep him from harm."

Saliha's keen gaze searched Willow's face. "Oh, dear God. You love my son. How could he do this to you?"

" 'Twas my choice," Willow whispered. "I came willingly, my lady. Dariq did not send me, nor was I forced."

"We must leave, Saliha Sultana," Mustafa insisted. "I will explain everything to you once we are aboard the *Revenge*."

Her silver eyes blurred with tears, Saliha bowed her head and allowed Mustafa to lead her away.

Ali Hara stepped protectively nearer to Willow. She sent him a wobbly smile. His friendly face meant a great deal to her at this moment.

Ibrahim stood. "Fetch Kamel!" he ordered one of the guards. He returned his gaze to Willow. "Turn around, lady, slowly—very slowly."

She glanced at Ali Hara. When he nodded, she did as Ibrahim asked. She felt like a piece of meat hanging in a market stall as his hot gaze traveled over her.

"Come closer, lady."

Willow's steps dragged as she approached Ibrahim.

"Show me your breasts."

Willow's head shot up. "Nay!"

Ali Hara stepped between Ibrahim and Willow. "My lady is exhausted, my lord Sultan. It has been a long journey. You will find her willing to accommodate you after she bathes and rests. Perhaps, oh, great one, you will grant her time to become accustomed to her surroundings before you make demands of her."

Ibrahim sent Ali Hara a fearsome look. "You are too bold, Ali Hara. Are you deliberately trying to thwart me?

Since my brother has seen and touched the lady Willow, why should I not have the same privileges?"

Kamel chose that moment to make his appearance. "You sent for me, master?" The eunuch slanted Willow a reassuring smile. "Your new concubine has arrived, I see. Am I to assume Saliha Sultana has been allowed to leave?"

"Aye, she is gone, and good riddance," Ibrahim said petulantly. "I wish I could rid myself of her son as easily. Dariq is the bane of my existence. For all I know, he is gathering followers as we speak to help him wrest power from me. Turkey is a big country; 'tis impossible to have eyes everywhere."

"Dariq does not want the sultanate," Willow repeated. "He wants justice."

"Silence!" Ibrahim shouted. "Take Lady Willow away, Kamel, and teach her to speak only when spoken to. I do not like bold women. She is here to please me, not to question or judge me. Inform the mistress of the harem she has one month to prepare my new concubine for my bed. Tell Hetice I wish to be informed when Lady Willow's moon cycle begins. If I learn she is carrying my brother's child, I will present her to my stableman." He grinned evilly. "I promise she will like neither her new master nor his harsh ways."

With a wave of his hand, he dismissed Willow and the two eunuchs.

Misery rode Dariq as he stared at the rip that had appeared in one of the sails. Bad luck had plagued him since he boarded the *Hunter*. He would never reach Istanbul in time to keep Willow from Ibrahim's bed. Even after the canvas was repaired, he held little hope of his mission's success. Rage seethed within him. Heads would roll for this. Men he had trusted had deliberately foiled his plans. They had no authority to decide that his life was more important than Willow's.

For the last two years, Dariq felt he had been living on borrowed time. He should have died with his brothers when Ibrahim committed fratricide.

Even though Mustafa had been instrumental in saving his life on that day of infamy two years ago, Dariq could not forgive him nor his other so-called friends.

"Ship ahoy!" the lookout shouted from the crow's nest. "Approaching fast from the north."

"Can you make out her colors?" Dariq shouted.

"Aye. She bears your own flag, prince. 'Tis the *Revenge*."

Dariq lifted the spyglass; it took but a brief glance to recognize the *Revenge*. The spyglass lowered, and with it his spirits. His flag ship was sailing south for one reason only.

It had delivered Willow to Ibrahim and was returning to Lipsi with his mother.

Willow!

He wanted to howl her name.

Chapter Fifteen

Dariq knew Mustafa had seen the *Hunter* when he saw the *Revenge* immediately begin hauling in canvas. Dariq ordered the *Hunter's* sails furled and paced the deck as he waited for his flagship to approach. He had a few choice words for his former friend and hoped he could contain his temper long enough to say them.

When the *Revenge* eased up alongside the *Hunter*, Dariq ordered the boarding planks run out. He was the first man over the side. Mustafa was waiting for him.

"You are no longer counted among my friends!" Dariq spat. "What you did was unforgivable. You were wrong to usurp my authority. What say you, Mustafa?"

Mustafa shrugged but made no effort to defend himself. "I made a promise to your mother. Your life must be spared at all costs."

"Even if it means the sacrifice of an innocent woman to my brother's lust?"

"Aye, even then, my lord."

"I can no longer call you friend," Dariq snarled. "I will

never forgive you for convincing Willow to sacrifice her life for mine."

Mustafa did not correct Dariq. Though Willow had left willingly, he knew that was not what Dariq wanted to hear. His friend was far too willful, too angry, to listen to the voice of reason.

"I am taking the *Revenge* to Istanbul to right the wrong you and your cohorts are responsible for. You are to return to Lipsi on the *Hunter*."

"I will not leave you, master," Mustafa said defiantly.

Saliha Sultana stepped out from the shadows, revealing her presence to her son. "Do not go, Dariq—'tis too late. Mustafa is not entirely to blame. Lady Willow told me herself that she was not forced aboard the *Revenge*. She went willingly. The lady loves you, my son, and I am grateful for her devotion to you."

"Mother!" Dariq cried, opening his arms to his beloved parent.

Saliha stepped into his arms and he hugged her fiercely. Then he held her away from him and stared intently at her. "Are you well? Has Ibrahim harmed you?"

"I am well, my son. Ibrahim needed me to lure you to Istanbul so he could kill you. He fears you—fears your power as his only living brother."

"I have no interest in the sultanate, Mother. I am happy as I am. It was never my intention to seize the throne from my brother."

Saliha searched his face. "This woman, this Lady Willow—she is special to you, is she not?"

Grasping his mother's arm, he led her away. The crew was becoming too interested in their conversation. "Come, we will discuss this in private. I will deal with Mustafa later."

Once they reached the privacy of his cabin, Dariq began pacing.

"You are troubled, my son," Saliha observed.

Dariq spun on his heel, his expression fierce. "I am not troubled, I am furious. I was betrayed! Held prisoner in my own seraglio while Willow was taken from me and given to a man I cannot abide."

"You must love the lady a great deal."

"I . . . cannot explain my feelings, Mother. They are still too raw. Did Mustafa not tell you I intended to return Willow to her father and offer myself to Ibrahim instead?"

"Ibrahim seemed quite pleased with Lady Willow."

A low growl rose up from Dariq's throat. "The bastard! If he hurts her, I will kill him."

"Kamel and Ali Hara will protect her."

"Can they keep her from Ibrahim's bed?"

Saliha's silver eyes mirrored Dariq's sadness. "That is something I cannot promise."

"Willow is mine," Dariq snarled. "After I made her mine, I realized I could not part with her. The dilemma I faced was heart-wrenching. I had but two choices. Carry out my original plan to trade Willow for you, or abandon you to Ibrahim's caprices. My third and final choice was to sacrifice my own life for the two women I love and admire above all others."

"Mustafa told me you found Lady Willow aboard a Turkish ship bound for Istanbul," Saliha confided. "She was already destined for Ibrahim's harem when you took her off the ship."

"Yes, I finally had someone Ibrahim wanted enough to trade for you. And then . . ." He turned away, unable to continue.

"And then you fell in love with her and could not bear the thought of Ibrahim bedding her."

"I suppose," Dariq allowed.

"What do you intend to do?"

Dariq looked at her as if she were mad. "I am going after Willow, of course. Do I have any other choice? Willow would wither and die hidden behind the walls of a harem."

"What if Ibrahim has already taken her to his bed? Would you still want her?"

"What a silly question, Mother. I will always want Willow, regardless of what has been done to her. She is mine," he repeated fiercely.

Saliha rose and placed a hand on his arm. "You go to your death if you return to Isbanbul."

Dariq sent her a grim smile. "Not if I use stealth and cunning. I am not without resources."

Tears moistened the corners of Saliha's eyes. "I fear I will never see you again, my son."

"Pray to your God, Mother, and if He wills it, we will meet again. Meanwhile, you will sail aboard the *Hunter* to my stronghold and wait for my return. You will want for naught there."

"How do you intend to enter Istanbul without being recognized?"

"I plan to anchor in a small secluded cove south of Istanbul harbor. I have friends in a village nearby who will lend me a horse and anything else I might need. From there I will make my way to the city."

"I will pray for you, for I know you will not be dissuaded. Go find your lady, my son, and God protect you."

He kissed her cheek. "I have unfinished business to settle with Mustafa first. As long as you are praying, pray that I can hold my temper long enough to speak coherently. What I really want to do is wring his ugly neck."

"Mustafa is the best friend you have ever had," Saliha scolded. "He would give up his life for you."

"He took something from me that I value more than my life or his," Dariq shot back. Then he turned on his heel and stormed out the door.

Dariq found Mustafa leaning against the rail, staring at the *Hunter* as she rode gracefully alongside the *Revenge*.

"I am taking charge of the *Revenge*," Dariq said without preamble. "You are to accompany my mother to Lipsi aboard the *Hunter*. Stay there until I return."

Mustafa spat out a curse. "Fool! You will die. What you are attempting is impossible."

"My life is my own to do with as I please. Do not discredit my cunning, Mustafa. I intend to bring Willow and myself safely back to Lipsi."

"And if you do not return?"

Dariq stared off into space. "Then you and the Brotherhood will go on without me, and you will protect my mother until the end of her days in reparation for your betrayal."

"What I did was not betrayal. Protecting you has been and always will be my duty."

"Now you have a new duty." Dariq turned to leave.

Mustafa drew himself up to his enormous height. "I will not leave you, my prince. Where you go, I will follow. I will protect you with my life as I have always done. Others can protect your mother." He poked his chest with a thick finger. "I will stay with you."

"After what you did, how can I trust you?"

"I did naught but what your lady wanted. She wanted your death no more than I did."

"You should have denied her!" Dariq shouted. "Willow is a woman, with a woman's compassion. She sacrificed her own life to save mine."

"Ibrahim will not harm her."

"How can you say that with any certainty?"

Mustafa smiled. "My time in Istanbul was not wasted. I learned that the bulk of Ibrahim's army is fighting in Poland. The war to conquer countries in the north is not going well. The seers say defeat is inevitable, and predict the end of the great Ottoman Empire as we know it."

Dariq stroked his chin. "Interesting, but I have little faith in seers or their predictions. Besides, what does that have to do with Ibrahim's interest in Willow?"

"Think about it, Prince. Ibrahim has been meeting daily with the Grand Vizier and members of his war council, often long into the night. How much energy can he have left for his concubines?"

"If Ibrahim's army is defeated, his future will be dark," Dariq said thoughtfully. "I will consider this news when I formulate a plan to rescue Willow."

"I will see Saliha Sultana safely aboard the *Hunter* and return. If you are bent upon this disastrous course to rescue your lady, I will attempt to redeem myself for what you perceive as my betrayal."

Dariq searched Mustafa's face. Since Dariq had escaped Ibrahim's devious plan to end his life, Mustafa had never left his side, never given Dariq a moment's doubt about his loyalty. Until now. Mustafa had nearly destroyed a friendship of long standing. Grudgingly, Dariq admitted that Mustafa hadn't betrayed him; he had simply tried to protect Dariq in his own way.

"Could I refuse you even if I wanted to?" Dariq asked. "Nay," he answered his own question. "Like a dog with a bone, you will not give up. Doubtless you will find a way to follow me even if I send you away."

Crossing his arms over his burly chest, Mustafa grinned. "You will not be sorry, Prince. I will always be with you to protect your back. I know I have offended you and ask your forgiveness; I did not realize how much the woman meant to you. If we do not succeed, we will die as we have lived . . . together."

"No one will die," Dariq said fiercely. "I will fetch my mother and make her comfortable aboard the *Hunter*. Then we shall sail for Turkey."

Willow lived in fear every day she remained in the harem. She might have a month's reprieve from Ibrahim's bed, but his concubines did not welcome her. They viewed her as a rival for the sultan's affections and made her life miserable. Hetice, the harem mistress, assigned her the smallest cubicle in the vast warren of rooms that made up the harem. If not for Kamel, who maintained order with an iron fist, and Ali Hara, her self-proclaimed protector, she would have not lasted a fortnight.

One of the things that Willow learned was that poison was readily available, and that Ibrahim's favorites often died under mysterious circumstances. Of the thirty women in the harem, Willow trusted Umma the least. The fiery, dark-haired, dark-eyed beauty aspired to become Ibrahim's first wife and eyed the competition with mistrust and hatred.

Willow's blond hair set her apart from the other women, most of whom were daughters of pashas and high-ranking officials who wished to gain favor with the Ottoman ruler. Despite the sultan's numerous concubines, he had sired no children.

Ibrahim's childless state caused a great deal of turmoil within the harem. Each woman wanted to be the first to give Ibrahim the heir he desired. That woman would be elevated to the honored position of wife, a highly coveted status within the harem.

Willow was pacing her tiny room when Ali Hara arrived with a tray of food. "I tasted everything myself and watched it being prepared," the eunuch said as placed the tray on a low table. " 'Tis neither foul-tasting nor poisoned."

Willow sent him a wobbly smile. "I do not know what I would do without you, Ali Hara. My month of reprieve is nearly up. What am I to do? My link with the moon has been broken; my courses have not arrived, and you know what that means. Hetice will tell Ibrahim, and disaster will follow."

She gazed longingly out the window. "I knew before I left Lipsi that there was a chance I carried Dariq's child, but I was willing to tempt fate for Dariq's sake."

Ali Hara stroked his smooth chin. "Kamel and I have already discussed such a possibility. We've decided that one of us should cut himself and stain your clothing with blood. When you ask Hetice for cloths, she will tell Ibrahim. 'Twill gain you a few days reprieve, at least."

"I need more than a few days," Willow lamented.

"Listen carefully, lady," Ali Hara whispered as he checked the door to see if anyone was listening. "Ibrahim is upset over losing Poland. He meets long into the night with the Grand Vizier and war council. Perchance matters of state will take precedence over bedding you. But if they do not, you must go to the sultan when he sends for you."

"What?" Willow cried, aghast. "I will die if he touches me."

"You will die if you refuse him. Kamel and I will do

what we can to protect you, but no one defies Ibrahim."
He glanced at the closed door and lowered his voice until
Willow could barely hear him. "*He* has arrived."

"Who has arrived?"

"Prince Dariq."

"Oh, no! How could he be so foolish? Please tell me he
is not in Istanbul."

"Not yet, but Kamel's cousin received word that his
ship is docked in a secluded cove south of the city."

"What does he hope to gain by coming here?"

"How can you ask that question, lady? He has come
for you."

"Does he not realize that death awaits him here?"

"A man in love follows his heart, not his head."

"Love? Dariq doesn't love me. He has spoken no words
to indicate that he has such strong feelings for me."

"A man willing to sacrifice his own life for a woman
does so out of love, just as you were willing to sacrifice
yourself for love. Think about it, lady."

Willow did think about it, and Ali Hara's deduction
made sense, but she dared not pin her hopes on Dariq's
ability to rescue her from a harem guarded by armed
janizaries.

"Tell Kamel I wish to send a message to Dariq. I do not
want him risking his life on my behalf. I can endure anything as long as I know that he lives, and that his mother
is safe."

Ali Hara bowed. "I will do as you ask, lady, but my
prince will do as he wishes. Now, give me one of your
garments."

Willow chose a skirt from a chest and handed it to the
eunuch. She winced when he raised his sleeve and used
her fruit knife to cut into his flesh, smearing blood onto
the delicate cloth.

"I will inform Hetice that you need supplies for your personal care," Ali Hara said as he used a napkin to bind his arm and pulled his sleeve down to cover the minor wound.

"Thank you," Willow whispered. "I am deeply grateful for what you are doing to gain me time. I cannot bear the thought of being summoned to Ibrahim's bed." Deep in thought, she chewed on her bottom lip. "Perhaps I can develop a fever later, and who knows what else I can come up with? My greatest fear is that Dariq will not survive this rescue attempt."

"My prince is well aware of the danger," Ali Hara said in parting.

Hetice arrived a short time later with the cloths. "So," she said, eyeing Willow with suspicion, "your courses have finally arrived. Lady Umma hoped you were carrying Prince Dariq's child. My lady Umma wishes to be the first to bear Ibrahim a son."

"I want naught to do with Ibrahim," Willow said. "I would be eternally grateful if you could keep me out of his bed."

Hetice, a haughty woman of middle years, had taken charge of the harem after Saliha Sultana left, and she had her favorites. Willow was not one of them.

"You are a stupid woman," Hetice said, "Are you not aware of the power you would wield and the gifts you would receive as the mother of Ibrahim's son? To conceive Ibrahim's heir is the dearest wish of every woman in the harem."

" 'Tis not mine," Willow declared. "Leave me—I wish to be alone."

Hetice tossed a pile of cloths upon the narrow bed. "Ali Hara said you had need of these. Rest assured that I will inform Ibrahim of this new development."

"Good," Willow muttered.

Hetice stared at Willow for the span of a heartbeat, then turned on her heel and departed.

Dariq's ship lay at anchor in a secluded cove, invisible to all who did not know of its existence. Dariq had discovered the cove during his exile and had allies living in a nearby village. After disembarking, the first thing he did was to dispatch a sailor to the village to secure three horses, for himself, Mustafa and the sailor, whom he intended to send to Istanbul with a message for Kamel via his cousin Hassan.

The sailor returned with the horses, then mounted one and left immediately for Istanbul. Dariq and Mustafa left soon afterward and were welcomed by Yusuf, a horse trader and ally of Dariq's, who lived with his wife in the village.

" 'Tis a long time, my lord Prince," Yusuf said, making his obeisance. "Please enter my humble abode; Farah has prepared a meal for you and your lieutenant."

Dariq and Mustafa bent beneath the low portal and entered the two-room hut, fragrant with cooking smells. Yusuf seated Dariq with a flourish, and Farah, her face flushed with pleasure, served the well-seasoned meal of chicken, rice, dates, figs and a sticky-sweet desert that earned a flurry of compliments.

Once Farah left the room, the conversation turned serious.

"Have you heard aught of a woman with golden hair that Ibrahim has added to his harem? Her name is Willow," Dariq said.

"Aye, who has not? 'Tis said that Ibrahim hopes for an heir from her. None of his concubines has quickened with child."

Dariq swallowed a groan. The thought of Ibrahim's hands on Willow nearly brought him to his knees. He shook his head to clear it of painful thoughts and said, "Perhaps the fault lies with Ibrahim."

Yusuf grinned. "So it is said. But there are rumors that Lady Umma wishes to be the first to bear Ibrahim a son, and has taken steps to ensure that she is."

"Have you heard aught of Willow's well-being?"

"We do not get much news here, but I have heard naught to suggest she is not well. Ibrahim is much involved with other matters right now. His army is being driven from Poland, and he fears his empire is in danger of collapsing."

Dariq's relief was palpable. Perhaps Willow had escaped Ibrahim's attention.

"I need to get inside the seraglio," he said urgently.

"Why do you wish to expose yourself to danger, my lord Prince?" Yusuf asked.

"Ibrahim has my woman, and I want her back."

"The golden-haired woman belongs to you? Allah help you. What you plan involves great risk."

"I understand the risk, but it matters not. I know you are allowed to pass through the gates into the courtyard to sell and trade your horses, for I've seen you there many times in the past."

"Aye, 'tis true enough," Yusuf allowed. "What can I do to help you?"

"When do you plan another trip to the city?"

Yusuf stroked his beard. "Tomorrow or the day after. I have some prime horseflesh to sell."

"Excellent!" Dariq eyed Mustafa speculatively. "Mustafa can travel with you, for if he were seen with me, we might be recognized. I shall depart a day before you and Mustafa, and go directly to Hassan the carpet trader's stall. I will ask him to bring Kamel to me."

"What are your intentions, Prince?" Mustafa asked. "You do not plan to enter the seraglio alone, do you? 'Twould be suicide."

"I will make plans after I speak with Kamel. If there is a way to see Willow, I will find it." His chin rose defiantly. "I *will* rescue Willow, Mustafa, or die trying."

"Do not treat death so lightly, my lord, for the end result is permanent."

"I know, but give me some credit. I am not a careless man."

Mustafa snorted. "When one is in love, one tends to think irrationally."

When Dariq sent him a warning look, Mustafa quickly dropped the subject.

Dariq returned his attention to Yusuf. "Can you bring horses to Istanbul for me, Mustafa and my lady? And Mustafa and I will need clothing to disguise us as humble farmers."

The clothing that Yusuf provided Dariq and Mustafa met with their approval. Dressed in drab robes and dingy turbans, the two were unrecognizable as a prince and his lieutenant.

Dariq left the following morning after a satisfying breakfast, carrying food that Farah had prepared for him to consume along the way. Mustafa and Yusuf were to follow the next day and meet Dariq at Hassan's stall in the souk.

Dariq entered the city without being recognized and rode through the winding streets of the market, where the stalls were just closing for the day. Dariq lowered his head when a patrol of janizaries marched past him, and he remained watchful as he plodded on. Being recognized now would be disastrous.

The relentless sun was sinking and the marketplace emptying of people. Dariq sniffed appreciatively of the rich odors of spices, ripe fruit, and the pungent scent of freshly killed and drawn animals.

When Dariq bought a meat-filled pita and ate it while he wandered past stalls displaying glittering jewels, colorful silks and other merchandise arranged to catch the eye of a shopper. When he found the carpet trader's stall, he waited until Hassan's last customer wandered off.

Hassan turned to him with a smile. "How may I help you, my good man?"

" 'Tis I, Hassan—Prince Dariq."

Hassan's eyes widened, and he started to make an obeisance, until Dariq stopped him with a look.

" 'Tis dangerous for you here," Hassan whispered. "Wait for me in the back room while I close my shop. We can talk in private there. You know the way."

Dariq did indeed know the way. He had visited Hassan on those occasions when he traveled incognito to Istanbul to seek news of his mother.

A few minutes later, both men were seated at a low table, sipping tea. Hassan waited for Dariq to speak, his eyes narrowed with curiosity.

"Can you arrange a meeting with Kamel?" Dariq asked.

"Aye, my lord. I will go to the seraglio immediately and seek an audience with my cousin. Shall he meet you here?"

"Aye. I wish to know more about the conditions at the seraglio."

"I heard that Ibrahim released your mother. Several witnesses in the seraglio reported that Saliha Sultana was exchanged for a slave girl." He sighed. "I wish I could have seen her. 'Tis rumored she has hair like spun gold."

Dariq's fists tightened at his sides. "Aye, everything about Lady Willow is pure gold. And she is mine. Bring Kamel to me, Hassan; that is all I ask of you."

Hassan rose, bowed and slipped out the door.

Chapter Sixteen

Dariq waited over an hour for Kamel. The eunuch ducked into the rear of his cousin's stall and made his obeisance before the prince. With an impatient gesture, Dariq invited the harem master, whom he counted as his friend, to sit down.

"How is she?" Dariq asked without preamble.

"If you are referring to Lady Willow, she is well," Kamel replied.

"Has Ibrahim—"

"The sultan is occupied with matters of state these days. His empire is falling apart, and he meets with his advisers far into the night. He has little time for his women."

"I want Willow out of the harem before he remembers her and summons her to his bed."

"That task will not prove easy, my lord Prince. The harem is well guarded, if you recall, and the seraglio guards are loyal to Ibrahim."

"I am most desperate to see and speak to Willow. I

want her to know she is not alone, that I am nearby."

Kamel smiled. "Your lady already knows you are in Istanbul and has asked that a message be delivered to you. She said to tell you not to attempt anything foolish. She fears for your life."

"And I don't want her in Ibrahim's bed," Dariq spat from between clenched teeth. "Can you think of a way I can see Willow without being discovered?"

"What you ask will not be easy to accomplish," Kamel replied. "Lady Willow has not been welcomed by Ibrahim's concubines. Fearing poison, Ali Hara and I watch everything she eats and drinks closely. The women fear your lady will be the first to bear Ibrahim a child, and they will go to any lengths to prevent it."

"But you said Ibrahim hasn't bedded Willow."

"True, but her time will come. I can only do so much to keep her out of the sultan's bed."

Dariq's hands clenched at his sides. "We cannot let that happen."

"You must be very careful. There is a princely reward on your head."

"I would risk anything to see Willow. She needs to know that I will not abandon her. Mustafa should arrive in the city tomorrow with Yusuf, the horse trader. We will combine our efforts and come up with a plan to rescue Willow. I am not leaving the city without her. If all else fails, I will offer myself to Ibrahim in exchange for her freedom. 'Tis me he wants anyway."

"I can see you are determined in this," Kamel sighed. "You always were a stubborn man, my lord. I advise you to be patient and act prudently. These things take time to arrange."

"We have no time. We must act swiftly, before Ibrahim summons Willow to his bed."

"I will do what I can," the eunuch promised. He tapped his chin. "Your old apartment is still unoccupied. It is so remote from the main part of the seraglio that no one has claimed it."

"Aye, the remoteness was the reason I chose those rooms in the first place."

"If you can reach your chambers without being seen, I will arrange to bring Lady Willow to you by way of the secret staircase."

"Mustafa saved my life by carrying me over the rooftops, though I recall little of it," Dariq mused. "It shouldn't be difficult to return the same way during the darkest part of night."

"If all goes well, I will bring Lady Willow to you in your apartments as soon as it can be arranged."

"I am grateful for whatever you can do, Kamel. Both you and Ali Hara are welcome to return with us to Lipsi, if that is your wish."

Kamel laughed. "I always did fancy becoming a pirate. Now I must go. I will meet you here two days hence."

"I will be here."

Dariq found lodging at a cheap inn near the souk. He was so exhausted he fell asleep immediately after eating a simple supper in the common room. He returned to Hassan's stall in the souk near dusk the next day to await Mustafa. The market was just closing for the day when Hassan ushered Mustafa behind the curtain. Mustafa dropped cross-legged to the floor and gratefully accepted a cup of tea.

After he quenched his thirst, he asked, "Have you learned anything?"

"I spoke with Kamel," Dariq said "Ibrahim is concerned about his losses in Poland. Kamel said he has had scant time to devote to his concubines. For the moment,

Willow is well, but those in the harem are jealous of her. And you know what that means."

"Aye," Mustafa allowed. "Now that you know there is little you can do about Lady Willow's situation, perhaps we should leave."

Dariq bristled. "Never! Kamel is arranging a meeting between me and Willow in my old apartment. It's been unoccupied since I left."

"'Tis madness. I hope you are not overly fond of your head. Kamel is not a miracle worker; he cannot save you if you are captured."

"Naught you say will dissuade me, Mustafa."

"So be it. What do you want me to do?"

"Position yourself at the seraglio gates and keep your eyes and ears open. I've taken a room at the Inn of Seven Veils. You can contact me there if you think there is anything I should be aware of. In two days, Kamel will let me know if our plans have a chance of succeeding."

Mustafa shook his head. "What do you hope to gain by meeting in secret with Willow? No woman has ever escaped the harem. You are both doomed. 'Twould be best to let her settle into her new life while you go on with yours."

"I did not ask your opinion, Mustafa," Dariq growled. "Find Yusuf and tell him to have swift mounts ready for us."

Two days later, Kamel returned to Hassan's stall. Dariq could hardly contain his excitement as he waited for the other man to speak.

"Allah be praised," Kamel began in a hushed voice. "Ibrahim is to meet with his generals and advisers this very night. The meeting should last into the small hours. If you wish to see Lady Willow, it must be tonight. The royal astrologer has predicted an overcast sky with limited moonlight."

Dariq's heart nearly burst from his chest. "Can you sneak Willow into my old apartment?"

"Aye, everyone should be asleep when I lead her to the private staircase. Can you reach your chambers without being seen or challenged, my lord Prince?"

"Of course," Dariq said confidently. "When should I expect her?"

"At the hour of midnight I will bring your lady to you."

"Thank you, Kamel. You have done me a great service, one I will not forget."

After Kamel departed, Dariq set out to locate Mustafa and Yusuf. He found them both near the seraglio gates. Mustafa was leaning against a section of the wall, and Yusuf was haggling with a potential buyer of one of his horses.

Keeping his head down as he passed a janizary, Dariq spoke softly to Mustafa in passing. "Meet me at the Kasbah Coffeehouse in one hour."

He spoke the same words to Yusuf when he accidentally bumped into him; then he went directly to the coffeehouse and sat at a table partially obscured by shadows. Mustafa and Yusuf arrived separately one hour later.

"Everything is falling into place," Dariq said in a hushed voice. "I am to meet with Willow tonight. Kamel promised to bring her to my old apartment at midnight."

"The only way you won't be seen is by going over the rooftops," Mustafa said. "I will go with you."

"Nay, you will not. I will do this alone. After I have spoken with Willow, I will fix a time for her rescue. Then, Mustafa, you and I will assist Willow over the rooftops to where Yusuf waits with the horses. A fast escape to the

Revenge is imperative. With luck, Willow won't be missed until morning."

Mustafa remained skeptical. "Too many things can go wrong, I like it not. How do you know Ibrahim won't summon Lady Willow to his bed tonight?"

"Then I pray that Willow, Kamel and Ali Hara will thwart Ibrahim. They have been successful thus far."

"You shall have my finest horses," Yusuf vowed.

Their meeting broke up soon afterward. Dariq immediately returned to the inn to prepare for his meeting with Willow. Anticipation throbbed through him. The thought of seeing Willow again made his heart thump in his chest and his blood run hot. How would he be able to leave her after their reunion tonight? It would be like leaving a part of him behind. Invisible links had been forged between them by the intense passion they shared.

Without Willow, Dariq felt like a man with half a heart. Since she left him, he had become obsessed, vowing that once she was back where she belonged, he would never let her go. If that was love, then so be it.

Dariq prepared carefully for his trek across the rooftops. Dressed in loose dark clothing and sturdy boots, he waited until an hour before midnight to leave the inn. Unbeknownst to Dariq, Mustafa detached himself from the shadows outside the inn and followed close behind.

Dariq wended his way through the narrow streets of the deserted souk, his body tense, his senses alert. At one point, he was forced to duck into an alley to avoid a night patrol. When he reached the high walls of the seraglio, he searched until he found a place where he could grasp an overhanging roof and pull himself up.

His silhouette a dark blot against an inky sky, he leapt

from rooftop to rooftop, his steps sure and determined as he made his way to his former apartment. Nothing was going to stop him now. Willow was as essential to him as the air in his lungs and the blood flowing through his veins. She was his heart and soul.

Willow felt threatened despite Kamel's and Ali Hara's careful scrutiny of her food and drink. Things had taken an unwelcome turn today when Ibrahim had entered the harem. She could still feel his dark eyes scorching her skin as he conversed with Hetice. Willow knew they were talking about her, and realized it would be only a matter of time before he summoned her to his bed.

But it wouldn't be tonight. Ali Hara told her that Ibrahim was meeting with his advisers today and the meeting would go on far into the night.

So she was granted another day of reprieve, but then what? Perhaps she could pretend to be ill with a mysterious disease. It wouldn't be a stretch of the imagination to picture herself vomiting on Ibrahim when he attempted to bed her.

Willow tried not to show fear when Umma sidled up to her and said, "You will not live to go to him. I will be the first to bear our master an heir."

"The honor is all yours," Willow replied. "If you want my opinion, the sultan is incapable of producing children. A man with beautiful concubines at his disposal should have many heirs, yet he has none."

Though many of his subjects were of the same mind, to make such a declaration openly was tantamount to treason. Umma began to screech like a banshee, shouting "Treason, treason!"

Hetice and Kamel came running.

"What is going on here?" Hetice asked, pointing her finger at Willow. "What have you done to Lady Umma?"

"You must summon the sultan at once!" Umma cried. "The Englishwoman speaks treason against him."

"I said naught more than what is being whispered all over the souk," Willow replied.

Kamel sent Willow a warning look. "What did Lady Willow say?"

Umma repeated Willow's words. Hetice appeared shocked, but Kamel merely rolled his eyes. "Do not concern yourself with this, Hetice, for Lady Willow is right. Ibrahim's childless state is discussed in all the coffeehouses." He sent Hetice an inscrutable look. "Some say Ibrahim's concubines are being fed a drug to keep them from conceiving."

Hetice grew sullen. "Ibrahim should know of this."

Kamel sent her a stern look. "You will say naught. This is my domain, and I rule it as I see fit. No harm has been done."

The women dropped the subject, albeit reluctantly, beneath Kamel's uncompromising glare. But Willow could feel their hatred for her. She never should have spoken her mind. How was she to survive in an environment where all the women were hostile toward her? She stiffened her shoulders and firmed her resolve. She had never lacked for courage. She would survive, no matter what it took. And she hadn't entirely given up hope that her father would trace her to Istanbul and demand her release.

Of more concern was the knowledge that Dariq was in Istanbul. What madness had possessed him? What did he expect to accomplish? The harem was impenetrable and the seraglio well guarded. Kamel could only do so much for her. She hoped Kamel had given her message to Dariq and he had left the city.

Kamel disappeared later that day, so Willow did not see him again before she retired for the night. She couldn't, however, shake the feeling of anticipation—or was it dread?—that had dogged her all day. The feeling only increased when Ali Hara bade her good night that evening.

When Willow finally fell asleep, she slept hard and deep. She awoke in the dead of night, startled to hear someone call her name. She thought she was dreaming and turned over to go back to sleep. The urgency of the voice and a hand shaking her awake finally forced her to open her eyes.

"Wake up, my lady," Kamel whispered. " 'Tis time to leave."

Willow jerked awake. "Leave? Where am I going?" *Dear God, please don't let it be a summons from Ibrahim.*

"I will tell you later, there is no time now. I couldn't explain earlier, for I was called away from the seraglio. Put this on." He handed her a dark blue caftan.

"Ibrahim hasn't summoned me, has he?"

"Nay. Hurry."

Willow slipped the caftan over her night shift and slid her feet into a pair of slippers. Before she could ask more questions, Kamel was hurrying her out the door into the dark corridor.

"Kamel—"

"Shhh, do not speak. You will have answers soon."

Willow followed Kamel into the corridor and to the main room of the harem. She watched curiously as he went directly to a blank wall, felt along a piece of molding, and lo and behold, a panel opened to his touch, revealing a narrow staircase.

271

"Into the passage," Kamel urged. "Mount the stairs; I will be right behind you."

It was so dark Willow could see little beyond the end of her nose. Kamel pushed her toward the first step, and she felt her way to the top, clinging to the wall to guide her. It seemed forever before she came to a stop before another wall. Kamel pressed somewhere on the wall, and another panel slid open.

Light from a single candle danced amid the shadows of a spacious, apparently deserted chamber. At one time the rooms must have been handsome, but now they seemed sadly neglected. Willow felt the air stir as Kamel brushed past her.

"No light," he said as he extinguished the candle.

"I had to see her."

Willow froze. That voice! "Dariq! Dear God, what are you doing here? 'Tis madness."

"I will be waiting at the bottom of the staircase," Kamel said. "Send Lady Willow down one hour before dawn. If she is late, I will come for her."

The air stirred again, and Willow knew that Kamel had left. Her heart pounded with anticipation. Would Dariq be angry with her?

"Willow . . ."

Darkness prevented her from seeing him, but she felt his nearness. His scent tantalized her senses, bringing back memories that had haunted her dreams since she had left him.

"You shouldn't have come here," she whispered.

"You do not know me if you thought I would let Ibrahim have you."

She felt his breath upon her cheek, and then he touched her, a subtle caress at the nape of her neck. A shiver danced down her spine.

"I wanted you to live. Why couldn't you have accepted my gift to you?"

She felt his arms around her, his body a solid, protective wall of comfort.

"Foolish girl," Dariq chided. "You are mine. There is no way I would let you go. I'm taking you away from here. Not tonight, but as soon as my plans are in place."

"Nay, you cannot! There are guards everywhere." A heavy silence fell. "How—"

"Let me worry about how." His hands made a thorough search of her body. "I wish I could see you, but if anyone noticed light in my old apartment, it would arouse suspicion. Are you well? Kamel said you haven't been harmed, but I need to hear you say the words."

"I am fine, Dariq. Ibrahim hasn't touched me. He wanted to be sure I wasn't carrying your child before summoning me to his bed. Fortunately, his army in Poland is in disarray, and he has had no time to think of anything but war."

"I know Ibrahim better than you. Believe me, he hasn't forgotten you."

She briefly considered telling Dariq she strongly suspected she was carrying his child, but common sense told her that confiding in him would only add to his woes. If Dariq failed to free her, she didn't want him to know about his child, for if Ibrahim *did* bed her, she wanted the sultan to believe the child was his. It was the only way she could keep Dariq's babe safe.

"I will do whatever it takes to stay out of Ibrahim's bed. I will feign an illness if I have to."

"Ah, beauty, what an innocent you are. When I learned that you and Mustafa had tricked me, I was so angry, I wanted to wring your beautiful neck. Later, I was overwhelmed by a fear so great it nearly destroyed me. I doubt, however, that I can forgive Mustafa. What he did was reprehensible."

"Do not blame Mustafa. It was my wish as well as his to save your life. Why did you not accept our gift?" She clutched his shoulders, her voice desperate. "You must leave, Dariq. Return to your ship and sail away from Istanbul. Do not give your brother a second chance to end your life."

"I will not leave, beauty." He cupped her face with his hand. "I do not need light to see you. My memory serves me well."

She turned her cheek into his hand. "You are making this difficult, Dariq. The longer we linger here, the harder it will be to part."

"I am not leaving until I make love to you. I cannot bear being apart from you. Each night I dream about loving you, until my insides are crawling with need and I awake in a sweat. I want to undress you, and though I cannot see your body in this blasted darkness, I can still feel and remember how you looked the last time you lay naked in my arms."

Willow dragged in a shuddering breath. She wanted Dariq to make love to her more than anything. But someone had to be practical. "We cannot. What if—"

Dariq kissed the protest from her lips. His kisses tasted like sin and promised ecstasy. In the blink of an eye, he rid her of her caftan and shift.

He kissed a path down to her shoulder, then over the rapid rise and fall of her breasts, teasing and sucking her nipples, until she dug her fingers into his hair and whimpered with pleasure. His mouth moved lower, laving the hollow of her navel. He dropped to his knees. She trembled, buffeted by waves of raw sensation as he parted her thighs and slipped two fingers inside her. A soft moan left her lips, and her knees buckled beneath her.

Catching her up in his arms, he carried her to the bed and laid her down on the counterpane. She felt him withdraw, and when he returned, the heat of his naked skin against hers felt like heaven.

Dariq was so aroused, he feared his cock would burst. But he had never left a woman wanting and didn't intend to start with Willow, the woman he loved. Oh, aye, he freely admitted it now. Willow was the only woman for whom he would willingly sacrifice his life. If fate turned against him and he was captured this night, at least he would have these stolen moments with Willow to carry with him to his death.

"Willow, if something happens to me after I leave you tonight, I want you to know that—"

"Nothing is going to happen," Willow said, stopping his words with a kiss.

One kiss led to another, and another, until his body was raw with sensation. A thousand kisses later, he parted her thighs and found the hooded jewel that was so responsive to his slightest touch. Willow didn't disappoint him. She arched and whimpered, urging him on with words that made scant sense.

When he parted the sheltering folds to expose her center of pleasure, she choked out his name. Her inner flesh yielded to his fingertips and the moist heat of his mouth. Flames devoured her; she strained against his wicked kiss as his tongue flicked in maddening light strokes that sent unstoppable ecstasy piercing through her.

Rapture held her aloft, endless and unrestrained, then eased into eddies of trembling delight. She sensed Dariq hovering above her, his hands braced on either side of her head.

"I wish I could see your face," he whispered. "You were made for me, my love. No one is going to take you from me . . . ever. I am going to come inside you now, my love. Open for me."

Flexing his hips, he plunged deep into her welcoming heat. She sighed rapturously, her arms wrapping about him.

"I love you, Dariq," she whispered as his lips closed over hers. "I shall always love you."

Willow had no idea if he heard, for he was immersed in his own pleasure. His kisses grew frantic; his loins pumped wildly, his staff creating an intolerable friction that launched her to the stars. Had his mouth not been covering hers, she would have screamed.

Then his own climax burst, flooding her womb as he collapsed upon her sated body. He was unable to move, to think, to breathe. Ecstasy coiled deep in his gut, rendering him nearly insensate. He regained his wits slowly, then shifted himself off her, gathering her against him.

"You're trembling," he whispered after a few moments as he held her close. "I didn't hurt you, did I? It has been so long, I may have been too rough."

Willow shook her head. "You could never hurt me. It's just that I am afraid for you. After I left, I assumed you would accept my gift of life and in time forget I existed."

Their bodies were meshed so closely, he could feel her heart beating in concert with his.

"How could I possibly forget you? You said you loved me. Did you mean it?"

Her voice quivered with surprise. "You heard? I wasn't sure. Aye, I meant what I said. Only a woman in love would willingly sacrifice her freedom. I wanted you to live, Dariq." She paused, staring into his eyes. "Why did you come to Istanbul? Why would you risk your life to come for me?"

"Only a man in love would willingly surrender his life," he replied, giving her words back to her.

Willow went utterly still. "You love me?"

"Did I not just say so? You are imbedded in my heart. I need you as I need food to eat and air to breathe. I have never felt like this before. You are my heart, my soul, my life."

"You love me?" Willow repeated.

"Shall I repeat it in Turkish? Or French?"

"Nay, I understand English very well."

She glanced out the window at the approaching dawn; her arms clung desperately to him. "Our time together grows short. Perhaps you should tell me how you plan to spirit me away."

"I shall take you from this very room and carry you over the rooftops. Horses will be waiting outside the seraglio walls to carry us to my ship. Once everything is arranged to my satisfaction, I will send word to Kamel."

Dismay colored Willow's words. "Over the rooftops?"

"Fear not, my love. Both Mustafa and I are fleet of foot. We will manage just fine."

"What if something goes wrong? What if Ibrahim summons me before . . ." she gulped, unable to continue.

"Then you and Kamel must find a way to foil Ibrahim. A day or two is all I need to set my plan into motion."

"I will pray for your success," Willow murmured. "Is there time to make love again?

"Ah, sweet siren, naught would please me more."

He made love to her more slowly this time, drawing out her pleasure, stroking and caressing her with his hands, mouth and tongue. When she begged him to end it, he lifted her atop him, but when he would have entered her weeping center in one long thrust, she scooted down and grasped his staff in her hands. Then she lowered her head and ran her tongue up and down his engorged length before taking the head into her mouth and lapping his essence with her tongue.

Dariq felt paradise beckon; heaven hovered just beyond his grasp. Raw sensation pulsed through him as Willow teased and sucked him. But he wasn't made of stone, and all too soon he felt the end approaching. With a hoarse curse he raised her up, spread her legs and slowly lowered her onto his pulsating cock.

He stifled her cries with his mouth as he drove them both to a glorious, earth-shattering climax.

Chapter Seventeen

Willow slept in Dariq's arms while he watched the night sky turn to dull gray, depressingly aware of the passing time.

A step sounded on the stairs. "Prince Dariq, 'tis time," Kamel called softly through the panel. "Lady Willow must leave now."

"Just a moment more," Dariq replied.

Dariq stared down at Willow, aware that they must part for a short time, yet reluctant to wake her. Common sense prevailed, however, and he gently called her name.

Willow stirred but did not awaken. Dariq bent and kissed her lips. She smiled and opened her eyes. "Am I dreaming?"

"Nay, my love, I am here and you are in my arms. But 'tis time for you to return to the harem. Kamel awaits you."

"When will I see you again?"

"Soon, I promise. Let me help you with your shift and caftan."

He slipped both garments over her head and placed her slippers where she could slide her feet into them.

Then he quickly dressed himself and led her to the passage. Willow turned to him, her expression stricken.

"What if—?"

He stopped her words with a kiss. "Nay, do not think it. Naught will go wrong. Go now. Wait for Kamel to inform you when you are to leave."

The panel slid open; he watched her descend the stairs, his mind already whirling ahead to the day when Willow would be free to decide her future. If she wanted to return to England, he would see her safely home and pine for her the rest of his life. But if she wished to remain with him on Lipsi, he vowed to wed her and give up piracy and his vendetta against Ibrahim.

Once Willow reached the bottom of the staircase, she turned and waved. Dariq waved back, and then the panel closed. Purple streaks tinted the eastern sky as Dariq climbed onto the balcony rail and reached for the nearest rooftop. Surefooted and agile, he leapt from building to building, carefully making his way to the wall surrounding the seraglio and scrambling over. Vendors were opening their stalls in the souk as he wended his way to his room at the Inn of the Seven Veils. Unbeknownst to him, Mustafa was not far behind him.

Suddenly sensing that he was being trailed, Dariq ducked into an alley. When Mustafa walked past, Dariq stepped out to confront him.

"What are you doing?"

"Protecting your back."

Dariq gave an exasperated snort. "I did not ask for your protection."

Mustafa shrugged. "I go where you go."

Dariq glanced at the sky. "Patrols will be out soon. Find Yusuf and meet me at the coffeehouse at noon. You know which one. We must act quickly, before Ibrahim remembers Willow and summons her to his bed."

Mustafa nodded and melted into the misty dawn. Dariq continued on to the inn. Once inside his room, he fell into bed for a few hours of much-needed sleep.

Willow's return to the harem had not gone unnoticed. Umma, who had always been a light sleeper, heard voices and decided to investigate. What she saw when she cracked her door open and peeked out turned her green with jealousy. She saw Willow standing in the doorway of her chamber, looking disheveled and well loved. She was bidding Kamel goodbye. There was only one reason one of Ibrahim's concubines would be out and about at this hour of the morning. Obviously, the sultan had summoned the English houri to his bed.

Clenching her hands into fists, Umma wanted to scream her frustration. If Lady Willow bore Ibrahim a child, he would make her his wife, a position Umma had striven for from the moment she'd entered Ibrahim's harem. Unfortunately, Willow's two watchdogs had made it impossible to feed her a drug that would render her unable to conceive. Umma, the daughter of a pasha, considered herself, of all Ibrahim's concubines, the only one worthy of the title sultana.

The Englishwoman's beauty paled in comparison to her own sultry radiance, Umma thought. Aside from Willow's golden hair, there was nothing remarkable about her. A sly smile curved Umma's pouting lips. What if the lady was shorn of her crowning beauty? If she lost her hair, there would be naught about her Ibrahim would admire.

* * *

Unaware of Umma's dark thoughts, Willow bathed in the *hammam* with the other women that morning. She tried to ignore Umma's dark glances despite a strange foreboding grinding inside her. What was Umma up to? After her night of love with Dariq, Willow was too happy to let Umma ruin her mood. Soon she would be gone, no longer the object of Umma's jealousy.

What would happen then? Willow wondered. If Dariq loved her as he alleged, would he give up pirating for her? Would he be content to become a husband and father? Did he even want children? Would his vendetta against Ibrahim continue to be the driving force in his life?

Those questions and others whirled around in her head, until she despaired of ever attaining her dream of a loving relationship with Dariq. Her culture did not allow concubines and multiple wives, while his encouraged them. Willow demanded commitment and fidelity from the man she loved, but she had no idea if Dariq felt the same. The subject had never been discussed.

With love, anything was possible. Willow had to believe that.

Ali Hara approached Willow after she emerged from the *hammam* and asked for a private word. Willow invited him into her chamber.

"Is something wrong?" she asked anxiously.

"Beware," Ali Hara warned. "Umma is up to no good. Jealousy eats at her. She believes you went to Ibrahim's bed last night."

Willow stiffened. "What? How could she think that?"

"I believe, but do not know for sure, that she heard something last night and assumed you had been summoned by Ibrahim."

Willow blanched. "She may have heard Kamel and me speaking in the doorway of my chamber early this morning. I was merely bidding him goodbye and thanking him for making my night with Dariq possible. Umma could hamper Dariq's plans. What shall I do?"

"I've already alerted Kamel. We agreed to step up our vigilance until you leave with Prince Dariq. Pray Allah it is soon."

"Will you flee the city with us?" Willow asked.

"Aye—did you doubt it? Kamel also expressed a desire to leave. Once Ibrahim learns he aided Prince Dariq, his life will be forfeit despite his current position of power."

He glanced at the closed door. "I will continue to fetch your food myself so that you need not fear poison. I suggest that you remain in your chamber until we receive word from the prince."

Ali Hara bowed and departed. Willow walked to the window and stared out into the garden; several concubines strolled about, while others lounged around a small fish pond. She spied Umma and realized the woman was staring at her through the window. She immediately stepped away from Umma's hard glare.

Later, after she finished her lunch, Willow braided her hair to keep it from tangling while she slept and lay down on the bed. She had had precious little sleep the night before, and within minutes succumbed to sheer exhaustion. She neither saw nor heard Umma enter her chamber wielding a pair of sharp scissors. Nor did she feel the scissors cutting through her long braid.

Umma's triumph was short-lived. As she held up Willow's severed locks for closer inspection, Ali Hara burst into the chamber.

"By Allah's beard, lady, what have you done to my mistress?"

Willow woke with a start, suddenly aware of a commotion whirling around her. Shivers of panic skipped down her spine when she realized what had happened. Ali Hara's large hand was clasped around Umma's wrist, the one holding a sharp pair of scissors. Then Willow realized what Umma held in her other hand, and her own hand flew to her head. A scream tore from her throat.

Her hair was gone! Umma had shorn her while she slept. Naught was left but the stubby end of her braid. Coming up on her knees, she lunged at Umma. The concubine wrested free of Ali Hara, raising her hands to protect herself from Willow's fury. Ali Hara stepped in between the two women.

"Witch!" Willow screamed. "Look what you have done."

Umma smirked. "Without your hair, my master will have naught to admire about you." She held up the long tail of Willow's braid and flung it at her. "Here, take it! Perhaps Ali Hara can work a miracle."

Pivoting on her heel, she fled out the door, laughter following in her wake.

Willow held up her severed braid, tears welling in her eyes. She dared not look in the beaten-silver mirror for fear of what she would see. She must look hideous.

"You are still lovely, my lady," Ali Hara soothed. "With or without hair, your beauty is matchless."

Suddenly Kamel burst into the chamber. "What has happened? Lady Umma came running out of here as if dogs were nipping at her heels."

Willow held up her severed braid, too choked up to speak.

"Lady Umma did that?" Kamel asked.

"Aye," Ali Hara answered. "She entered the chamber while Lady Willow lay sleeping."

"Where were you when it happened? Is this how you protect your lady?"

Ali Hara hung his head. "I was gone but a moment to

relieve myself." He wrung his hands. "This should not have happened."

Suddenly Willow came to her senses. This wasn't the end of the world. Her hair would grow. It could have been much worse. Umma could have plunged the scissors into her heart.

Drying her eyes, she took a deep breath. "I am fine. 'Tis only my hair, and it will grow back. Ali Hara has been wonderful, and so have you, Kamel. Do not blame yourselves for this."

"Nevertheless, Lady Umma shall be punished," Kamel declared. "She will repent of her sins when she feels the bastinado on the soles of her feet. She will not be able to walk for days."

Willow winced. "Nay, Kamel, do not punish her. Few here like me. Punishing Umma can only make my enemies more determined. Hetice hates me, too, and sides with Umma. Pray God I will be gone soon."

"If Allah wills it, we will hear from Prince Dariq this very day," Kamel said.

"Here, take this," Willow said, thrusting her severed braid at Kamel. "I cannot bear to look at it."

Kamel cocked his head and studied her with the intensity of a connoisseur. Willow's remaining hair, deprived of its former weight, curled around her head in a riotous cap of curls. A wide smile split his dark face, revealing a perfect set of white teeth.

"You look adorable, my lady."

Willow's hands flew to her head, encountering naught but a crop of unruly curls. "You jest, Kamel, but thank you anyway."

Kamel reached for a silver mirror and held it before her. "Look for yourself, lady. Hair alone does not make a woman beautiful."

Willow glanced at her image in the mirror. At first, the shock of seeing herself without her lovely long hair brought fresh tears to her eyes. But then something happened. The longer she looked at the cap of curls, the more she realized it wasn't as bad as she had thought.

"Kamel speaks the truth," Ali Hara concurred. "Your beauty has not been diminished, lady."

Willow smiled through her tears. "Think you Prince Dariq will like it?"

"Most assuredly, lady," Ali Hara replied.

Willow remained in her chamber the rest of the day, unwilling just yet to face Ibrahim's concubines. She knew she would be ridiculed by women with long, luxuriant hair and needed time to adjust to the change in her appearance. It wasn't until after she'd broken her fast the next day that she ventured from her chamber.

Willow knew immediately that Umma had spread the tale of her daring deed, for Willow was met with titters and whispers. Holding her head high, she sat down on a couch and tried to ignore the gossiping females and their disparaging glances. To Willow's surprise, a shy young woman named Tallia sat down beside her.

" 'Tis not so bad," Tallia assured her. "Perhaps Ibrahim will be charmed."

Willow sent Tallia a warm smile. "I sincerely hope not."

" 'Twas wrong of Umma. I would fear for my life if I captured the sultan's attention," Tallia said quietly. "I have not been summoned to Ibrahim's bedchamber yet. But Hetice likes me; perhaps she will shelter me from Umma's ire."

Suddenly Tallia leapt to her feet. "Umma is looking my way, I must leave. Please forgive me." She scurried off in a whisper of skirts.

Umma ambled over to Willow and sat down beside her, her smile smug. "You are uglier than I imagined," Umma purred. "Ibrahim will lose interest as soon as he sees you."

"Then you have done me a great service," Willow shot back. "Thank you most kindly."

Umma stared at her blankly, then rose and stalked off. Willow smiled, feeling as if she had won a small battle if not the war.

Two days later, Ali Hara told Willow that Dariq had contacted Kamel through Hassan. "The time has arrived. Tonight I will take you to the prince's old apartment," Ali Hara said.

Willow's hopes soared. "Will Dariq be there?"

"Aye, but this time he will take you with him."

"Will you come with us?"

"Aye. When Ibrahim finds out I conspired with the prince, he will slay me in a most painful way."

Willow blanched. "Perhaps we should not attempt this. If the plan fails, people will suffer."

"Too late, lady. I will come for you after everyone is asleep. Wear a dark caftan."

"I will pray for success," Willow said.

They spoke together a few more minutes, unaware that Umma had overheard most of the conversation. She had grown suspicious when she saw Ali Hara entering Willow's chamber. There were far too many secret conversations going on between the harem eunuchs and Willow. Umma wanted to know what was taking place behind her back so she could protect her place in the harem.

When Ali Hara had entered Willow's chamber, Umma had followed and pressed her ear to the door. Though she hadn't heard every word, she heard enough to learn that

Prince Dariq, her master's enemy, was in Istanbul and intended to take Willow away. Umma didn't mind Willow leaving, but if she could help Ibrahim capture the pirate prince, she would earn the sultan's undying gratitude, and a great deal more.

Umma crept away before Willow and Ali Hara finished speaking.

"What about Kamel?" Willow asked. "Will he join us?"

"Aye, he too wishes to be free of Ibrahim. Kamel will leave through the gate, for his departure will raise no suspicion. He often leaves the seraglio at odd hours. Do not fret, lady, all will be well."

Willow wished she were as confident.

Willow was ready and waiting when midnight arrived. She had been too excited to rest since learning she was to leave the harem this very night. Though she anxiously looked forward to being free again, she couldn't help worrying about her future. Would Dariq be part of her future? Would he wed her and give up pirating? She hoped so, for it was the only way she would have him.

A discreet knock on the door brought Willow's thoughts to an abrupt halt. The door opened and Ali Hara stepped inside.

"'Tis time, mistress. Kamel left hours ago. Even as we speak, he waits for us with the horses."

Ali Hara walked to the secret panel. It slid open and Willow slipped through; Ali Hara followed close behind her. Willow tried to ignore her feeling of disquiet as she followed the narrow staircase to Dariq's chamber. She was so close to freedom, she could almost taste it.

* * *

Dariq jumped from the nearby rooftop onto the balcony and eased through the door to his old chambers. Mustafa followed on his heels.

"She's not here yet," Dariq whispered.

"Fear not, my prince. Ali Hara will not fail you. Your lady will arrive soon."

My lady. A smile lifted the corners of Dariq's lips. Willow *was* his lady.

The shuffle of footsteps on the stairs in the secret passage alerted Dariq, and he turned just as the panel slid open and Willow and Ali Hara stepped inside. With a cry of gladness, Willow flew into his arms. He hugged her fiercely, then released her.

"Are you ready, my love?"

Willow nodded eagerly. "Aye, the sooner the better."

Dariq turned to Mustafa. "Show Ali Hara the way. Willow and I will meet you in the alley where Yusuf and Kamel wait with the horses."

"Are we going over the rooftops?" Willow asked through quivering lips.

"Aye, love. 'Tis not as difficult as it looks. The night isn't as dark as I would like, but I wanted to get you away as quickly as possible. I couldn't wait for a moonless night."

He peered closely at her caftan. "That will never do. You'll need to move about unencumbered." He went to his wardrobe and pulled out a pair of dark trousers and a dark shirt that he had left behind. "Put these on."

"I will leave with Ali Hara now," Mustafa said. "If for some reason I do not see you following, I will come back for you."

"Nay," Dariq protested. "If something unforeseen happens, you are to continue on without us."

Mustafa and Ali Hara slipped through the door and were soon swallowed by darkness. Dariq handed Willow the trousers and shirt. He watched avidly as she pulled off the caftan and shrugged into the male clothing. When he realized the trousers wouldn't stay up without help, he grabbed a rope from a drapery and handed it to her. Only then did he notice her shorn hair. Outrage slammed through him.

"What happened to your beautiful hair?"

Willow's hand went to her cropped curls. "Umma cut it in a fit of jealousy. There is no time now for further explanation."

Dariq silently agreed. They needed to leave . . . now. He grasped her hand and led her to the balcony, but fate turned against them.

The door burst open and Ibrahim stepped into the chamber. A cadre of armed janizaries surged into the chamber behind him. Someone held a light aloft, catching Dariq and Willow in a frozen tableau of shock and despair. The look on Ibrahim's face was a twisted mask of hatred.

"How did you know?" Dariq asked as he pushed Willow behind him in a protective gesture.

Ibrahim shot Dariq a fulminating glare. "Sources faithful to me informed me of your plans."

"Umma," Willow muttered.

"Seize them!" Ibrahim ordered. "Take my dear brother to the dungeon until I can devise a death worthy of him."

First Dariq and then Willow were immediately seized. There was no escape possible.

"Wait!" Dariq cried, digging in his heels as he was being dragged away. "What are you going to do to Willow?"

Ibrahim gave Willow a disparaging sneer. "The woman

no longer interests me. She looks like a shorn sheep. I was told she deliberately cut her hair to escape my attention. Aside from that, I have decided I will not have your leavings. She will be punished, and so will Ali Hara for arranging your secret meetings."

"If you hurt Willow, I will avenge her," Dariq threatened.

"You are in no position to spout threats," Ibrahim declared. "Take him away."

Dariq fought every step of the way, until one of the janizaries grew tired of his struggling and rapped him on the head with the hilt of his scimitar.

Willow cried out and tried to go to Dariq when she saw him slump against his captors, but she was forcibly restrained.

"Only a heartless monster would kill his own flesh and blood," Willow spat.

Ibrahim pounded his chest. "I am Ibrahim, ruler of the Ottoman Empire. I do as I please. If I let my brother live, I will always be wondering when he will strike, when he will seize power from me."

"Dariq has no desire to rule. You brutally killed all your father's male children to protect yourself. Only a madman would commit such a horrendous act."

"Enough!" Ibrahim cried, slashing his hand in the air to silence Willow. "This woman offends me. Take her to the dungeon with her lover, but put them in separate cells. Let them suffer before I end their lives."

Willow's struggles were quickly subdued by her captors as she was dragged through the seraglio to a thick wooden door. A guard opened the door, and she was taken down a staircase to a dank chamber beneath the palace. A flickering torch beamed a harsh light upon an empty room with several doors leading from it.

A guard opened one of the doors and thrust her into a tiny, airless cell. The door closed; she was locked inside. It was pitch-black but for tendrils of light filtering in through vertical bars set into the upper part of the door. A quick look around revealed a straw pallet and the dim outlines of a bench and a bucket sitting in a dark corner.

"Willow—is that you?"

The voice came from the other side of an adjoining wall. She flew to the bars. "Dariq? Are you all right?"

"I am fine except for a headache. What about you?"

"I am well. What are we going to do?"

"I wish I knew." The note of defeat in his voice was so unlike Dariq that Willow nearly succumbed to her own despair.

"What about Mustafa? He must surely know that something has gone wrong."

"He knows but is powerless to help. Are you sure Umma betrayed us to Ibrahim? I felt I could trust Kamel and his cousin, but perhaps I was wrong."

"Oh, nay, Kamel is completely trustworthy. I do not know how Umma learned of our plan unless she listened at the door while Ali Hara spoke in my chamber. I wonder why she didn't just let me go. Then she would have been rid of me for good."

"She probably wanted to gain Ibrahim's good will."

The clatter of footsteps sounded on the stairs.

"Shhh," Dariq warned. "Someone is coming. Move away from the bars."

Willow moved to the bench and sat down. A face appeared at the bars. It was Ibrahim.

"Your accommodations aren't as comfortable as the ones you occupied in the harem," Ibrahim gloated. "You will wish yourself back there when you are spread beneath my stableman. If you resist, he will punish you severely."

"Let her be!" Dariq shouted from his cell.

Ibrahim crossed over to Dariq's cell. "You have no authority to tell me what to do. I am not as heartless as you seem to believe. I could have your lover tied, placed in a sack and tossed into the sea, but I did not. Sultans throughout the ages used that method to rid themselves of unfaithful wives and concubines."

Willow unsuccessfully tried to swallow her gasp.

"I have other plans for your houri. I shall gift her to my stableman. Habib is a crude fellow with a heavy hand, but she will learn not to defy him."

He laughed. "Aye, 'tis a fit punishment for a gently bred woman. But first, I shall arrange your punishment and death, brother dear. I shall sleep on it a day or two before deciding how you will die."

Still chuckling, he turned and walked away, leaving a heavy curtain of silence behind.

"Help will arrive," Willow said hopefully after Ibrahim's footsteps faded away. "Mustafa will plan a rescue."

"Pray God and Allah that he does," Dariq said fervently. "You should rest, my love."

Dariq knew Habib well, and he would rather see Willow dead than become the possession of the brutish stableman. Dariq didn't mourn his own death as much as he did Willow's cruel fate.

Mustafa and Ali Hara were aware of what was happening inside Dariq's chamber but could do little to help. They realized that rushing to Dariq's defense would probably get them all killed, so they hovered on the balcony until Dariq and Willow were dragged away.

"What shall we do?" Ali Hara hissed. "You heard Ibrahim. He's going to give my lady to a stableman and put our prince to death."

"There is naught we can do without help," Mustafa answered. I will ride immediately to the *Revenge* and bring back Prince Dariq's men."

Ali Hara shook his head. "They are so many and we are so few."

"We must first tell Kamel and Yusuf what happened," Mustafa whispered. "Perhaps Kamel knows a way into the dungeons that we do not."

Skipping from rooftop to rooftop, the two men eased over the wall and made their way to a dark alley near the seraglio, where the two men awaited with the horses.

"Where are they?" Kamel asked when he realized that Mustafa and Ali Hara were alone.

"We were betrayed," Mustafa spat.

"By whom?"

"That is what I would like to know."

"Do not glare at me like that," Kamel warned. "Think you I would betray our prince?"

"I know not what to think," Mustafa growled.

"Perhaps someone overheard our plans," suggested Ali Hara.

"Umma," Kamel speculated. "Either she or Hetice. I must return to the harem immediately."

"Is that wise?" Mustafa questioned.

"To my knowledge, my involvement in Lady Willow's foiled escape is unknown. Most likely, Ali Hara was overheard speaking with Lady Willow in her chamber. Was my name mentioned during your conversation with Lady Willow, Ali Hara?"

Ali Hara thought back over his conversation with Willow. "Aye, but perhaps the informer didn't hear or had already left. Your name was mentioned but once at the end of our conversation."

Kamel frowned. "Nevertheless, I must return. Mustafa will need someone inside the seraglio to keep him informed."

"It would help," Mustafa concurred. "But not if it places your own life in jeopardy."

Kamel laughed. "Ibrahim would not think a eunuch bold enough to take part in such a plan. Leave word with Hassan, and I will do the same. Pray Allah that we can find a way to save Prince Dariq and his lady."

Then they parted.

Chapter Eighteen

Ibrahim left the dungeon and immediately summoned Kamel. There were many unanswered question about Willow's escape that needed explaining . . . questions only Kamel could answer.

"You summoned me, master?" Kamel asked, making his obeisance before the sultan.

"How did Ali Hara arrange meetings between Lady Willow and my brother without your knowing?" Ibrahim barked. "You are supposed to know everything that takes place in the harem, yet I only heard of this plot from Lady Umma."

"There is a great deal of intrigue taking place in the harem, master," Kamel explained. "Had the Lady Umma come to me with her suspicions, I would have taken steps to stop the meetings and informed you of Prince Dariq's presence in Istanbul. But she chose to bypass my authority."

Ibrahim stared at Kamel a full minute, as if trying to discern the veracity of the eunuch's words. "You have never lied to me before, so I will accept your explanation.

I caution you, however, to exert more control. Thanks to Lady Umma, Prince Dariq is now in my dungeon. He will be executed in the city square two days hence. As for the Lady Willow, my stableman will claim her as his concubine after she watches her lover die." He waved his hand. "You are dismissed."

Kamel hurried off. He had to get word to Mustafa immediately, though he feared there was little the man could do to save the prince. He tapped his chin, a sly smile curving his lips. What if the citizens of Istanbul could be provoked into rioting against Prince Dariq's execution?

It hadn't taken long for Ibrahim to decide that Dariq should be beheaded, and he felt justified in holding a public execution. Dariq was a brigand, a pirate who had attacked his ships and disrupted shipping and naval operations. In Ibrahim's opinion, the world would be a better place without him.

The Grand Vizier, when told of Prince Dariq's fate, was swift to voice his opposition.

"My lord Sultan," Selim Pasha said, "executing your brother in public is not a wise decision. Your people hold him in great esteem."

Ibrahim fixed him with a quelling glare. "I cannot afford to let him live. His popularity empowers him."

"Precisely." Selim Pasha nodded. "He is considered a folk hero by your people for escaping your assassination plot. Holding a public execution could provoke a rebellion."

Ibrahim silenced him with a slice of his hand. "You are too soft, Selim. My people fear me too much to rise against me." He pinned Selim with a hard glare. "If you refuse to obey me, you can be replaced. If you value your life, I suggest that you make arrangements for a public execution. Have I made myself clear?"

Selim Pasha bowed to Ibrahim's wishes. "Very clear, my lord. Your brother will be beheaded according to your direction."

"Post notices," Ibrahim ordered. "A public display will affirm my authority over my subjects and make them aware of my power."

Selim Pasha bowed himself out of the chamber, leaving Ibrahim feeling highly pleased with himself. At last! He'd waited a long time to end Dariq's threat to his power. He couldn't wait to see his brother's expression when he was informed that he had but two days left to draw breath. In fact, he decided to do the honors himself.

Dariq sat glumly in the rank straw that served as his bed, wishing he could hold Willow in his arms one last time. Though he refrained from telling Willow, Dariq knew he would die soon. He had lived in the seraglio all of his life and knew of no way out of the dungeon other than the one by which they had entered; escape was virtually impossible.

At least he and Willow could communicate, but what did one say when there was no hope left? All he could do was tell her he loved her and encourage her to be brave, for she would live even if he would not.

"I hear footsteps!" Willow hissed through the bars.

Probably my executioner, Dariq thought. The footsteps stopped outside his cell. He rose lethargically and moved to the door.

"To what do I owe this visit, brother?" Dariq drawled when he recognized Ibrahim in the dim light.

"I have come to tell you that you have but two days to

repent of your sins," Ibrahim gloated. "Piracy is punishable by death. You shall die a traitor's death."

A small cry came from Willow's cell.

Dariq found the courage to laugh.

Obviously, it wasn't the response Ibrahim expected. "How can you laugh in the face of death?"

"I find it quite amusing. Even if I weren't a pirate, you would find an excuse to end my life."

"So I would, but you are an outlaw and thus made the decision easy for me. In two days, you will be taken to the city square, where you will be executed. I hope you are not too fond of your head. There is no escape this time, brother dear. You have plundered your last ship."

Turning on his heel, he stalked away.

"Do not lose hope," Willow called to Dariq. "Mustafa will bring the men from your ship."

Dariq sighed. " 'Tis over for me. There aren't enough men aboard my ship to attempt a rescue."

"The execution is to be public; perhaps your men can rescue you while a crowd is gathered to watch. There are all manner of things Mustafa can do to save your life."

"Do not get your hopes up, my love. You must accept the inevitable. I have."

"I refuse to accept defeat," Willow cried. "Neither should you."

Dariq smiled into the darkness. How dearly he loved his feisty Englishwoman. If she still harbored hope, so should he.

"You are right, my love. Where there's life, there's hope. I shall not accept defeat until the moment my head is separated from my body. Mustafa is naught if not resourceful. Perhaps God will show him a way to save us."

* * *

Willow's words proved prophetic. Early the next morning the Grand Vizier rushed into Ibrahim's bedchamber unannounced, his face pale and his robes askew.

"What is the meaning of this?" Ibrahim roared as he rolled away from Umma, his favorite concubine.

"Three English ships entered the harbor yesterday," Selim Pasha panted. "The Marquis of Bramston arrived at the seraglio with an armed escort just moments ago. He requests an audience in the name of Queen Elizabeth." He glanced pointedly at Umma.

Ibrahim shoved Umma from his bed and pointed toward the door. Umma pulled on her discarded caftan and made a hasty exit.

Ibrahim rose and pulled on a robe. "You may speak freely, Selim."

"The port master thought the ships were here to take on provisions, so he didn't bother to notify you of their arrival."

Ibrahim stroked his bearded chin. "What do you suppose the English queen wants with me?"

Selim Pasha shrugged. "There is only one way to find out, my lord. It wouldn't be wise to keep His Lordship waiting."

"Where is he now?"

"In the reception chamber, but I think a private meeting would be best. England is a powerful nation, with the most powerful navy in the world. It would not do to rile the queen or her emissary. Our troops are too far-flung at this time to invite war with England."

"Very well, I shall grant Lord Bramston an audience. Escort him to my private audience room in thirty minutes. I wish to dress and make myself presentable first."

A half hour later, groomed and dressed in royal robes, Ibrahim was waiting in his private audience room when

Selim escorted a distinguished-looking gentleman with graying hair into the chamber. The marquis carried himself with proud nobility that lent credit to his title. He bowed slightly, his sharp green eyes wary.

"As your Grand Vizier probably told you, my lord Sultan, I am the Marquis of Bramston."

"Indeed," Ibrahim replied. "We seldom see British navy ships in our harbor, my lord. Is your mission a peaceful one?"

"That depends," Bramston challenged. He paused for effect. "I am going to speak frankly, Majesty. I have come for my daughter. She was carried off my ship by pirates. It has taken many months to trace Willow, but I have good reason to believe you purchased her for your harem."

Ibrahim's eyes narrowed. "What makes you think your daughter is here?"

"I traced her to a slave market in Algiers and spoke to the slave master who sold her to your agent. I have no doubt that Willow is here, and I want her returned to me."

"Do I detect a threat in your tone, Lord Bramston?" Ibrahim asked harshly.

Bramston appeared unruffled. "Take it however you like. Just remember, two English warships besides my own *Fairwind* have their cannon trained on your city. The guns can do considerable damage should you deny my simple request."

"Your daughter never reached Istanbul," Ibrahim lied.

"My lord," Selim Pasha whispered in Ibrahim's ear. "Perhaps you should honor the marquis's request. The warships each carry forty guns. They could do considerable damage to our city, even reaching the seraglio. Our own navy has been seriously decimated by your brother, and the bulk of our army is otherwise engaged."

"Do you suppose His Lordship will be pleased when he learns his daughter currently resides in my dungeon?"

"Of a certainty he will not be happy. But the lady has not been harmed."

A sly look came over Ibrahim's face. "Perhaps we can place the blame on Prince Dariq. He did hold Lady Willow hostage and made her his whore before she reached Istanbul."

"The English do not condone fratricide."

"I did what had to be done to secure the sultanate for my own heirs," Ibrahim replied.

"Regardless, we cannot afford war with England. I believe that Lord Bramston will be so happy to get his daughter back, he will forgive your treatment of her. Perhaps the subject of her incarceration in your dungeon won't even come up until both father and daughter have left our waters."

"So be it," Ibrahim murmured.

Bramston stood at ease while Ibrahim and his Grand Vizier spoke in hushed tones. He believed the sultan had no choice but to release Willow. Bramston had the full support of Queen Elizabeth, and knew she would approve of whatever he deemed necessary to retrieve Willow.

Finally Ibrahim turned back to Bramston. "Very well, my lord, I admit I purchased your daughter for my harem, but she was never summoned to my bed."

Bramston snorted, his scorn apparent. "Bring her to me immediately."

"She will be brought to you, but not immediately. Will you accept my hospitality and join me in a light repast?"

Bramston began to sputter. "Is this a trick? If it is, I promise you will regret it."

"Nay," Ibrahim protested. "Selim Pasha will fetch Lady

Willow, but she will wish to bathe and dress herself appropriately for your reunion. You will see for yourself how well she has been treated.

"Come, my lord," he said, rising. "We shall retire to my inner chamber while Selim fetches your daughter."

Willow sat slumped on the bench, her back resting against the damp wall. A tray of congealing food sat on the table. Food did not interest her.

Tomorrow Dariq would die, and her life as she knew it would die with him. The undeniable truth of their fate sent her into deep depression.

Willow realized she had been overly optimistic to expect Mustafa and Ali Hara to be of any help. There was little they could do. Despite that knowledge, she still harbored dreams of escape.

The sound of footsteps brought Willow's desperate thoughts to a halt.

"Dariq, someone is coming! What do you suppose they want this time?"

"Probably my head," Dariq muttered.

Shock slammed through Willow. "No! Not yet. Please God, not yet."

" 'Tis Selim Pasha," Dariq said.

The Grand Vizier appeared in the outer chamber accompanied by two janizaries. He walked directly to Willow's cell, produced a key and opened the door.

"Come with me, lady."

"Where are you taking me?"

"The sultan has decided to spare you. He intends to return you to your family."

Willow found Selim's words so difficult to believe that she asked him to repeat them. She was silent a full minute after he obliged, then gave a scream of joy.

"Willow! What's happening?" Dariq called out.

"The sultan is sending me home to my family!" she cried. "We are free!"

"Nay, lady, only you are free to go. Prince Dariq's death sentence still stands."

Happiness drained from Willow, leaving her white and shaken. Why she and not Dariq?

"No, that cannot be!" she cried, storming from the cell. "I refuse to leave without Dariq."

"Willow, love, you must go. You have your whole life ahead of you in England."

"I have no life without you," Willow vowed. "This cannot be the end. I will not allow it."

She reached through the bars to Dariq. He clasped her hands and brought them to his lips. "Go and be happy, love." Then he released her and stepped back.

She clung to the bars. It took both guards to pry her loose and drag her away.

Minutes later, Willow was astounded to find herself back in the harem. Selim placed her in Kamel's care and took his leave at the door. When she saw Kamel, she burst into tears.

"Do not cry, lady," Kamel cajoled. "You are free. Rejoice in your good fortune."

"How can I rejoice when Dariq's life will end tomorrow?"

"Perhaps all is not lost," Kamel whispered.

Willow's tears ceased immediately. "What are you saying? Does Mustafa have plans to rescue Dariq?"

"I cannot say for sure, but I would not discount his cunning. He knows the prince is to be executed tomorrow in the city square. If Allah is kind, Mustafa will find a way to rescue our prince."

"Why have I been set free?"

"I know not. I was instructed to see that you are bathed and dressed appropriately. The sultan will summon you when he is ready for you." He wrinkled his nose. "Come, lady, you are in great need of a bath."

Willow followed Kamel to the *hammam*, her mind working furiously. Why was she allowed to go while Dariq still languished in the dungeon under a death sentence? What had provoked Ibrahim's change of heart where she was concerned?

"What are you doing back here?"

Willow groaned. The last person she wanted to see was Umma. "Apparently, the sultan had a change of heart," Willow replied.

"You lie! My master cannot stand the sight of you!" Umma sniffed the air and grimaced. "You smell vile."

Willow pushed Umma aside. "You would smell vile too if you had spent time in the dungeon. 'Twas your meddling that put me there."

Umma took a menacing step toward Willow, but Kamel stepped between them. "You have caused enough trouble, Lady Umma. Leave Lady Willow alone."

"Does Lady Willow's return to the harem have anything to do with the English ships in the harbor?" Umma asked.

Willow stopped in her tracks. "English ships? Are you certain?"

Umma preened for Willow's benefit. "I was with Ibrahim when he was informed of their arrival."

"Father," Willow whispered beneath her breath.

"Come along, my lady," Kamel said, grasping her arm. "You must be ready when the sultan summons you."

Willow's heart flooded with happiness. However impossible it seemed, her father had come for her, and not a moment too soon. How had he found her? Would he demand Dariq's release if she asked it of him? Would he understand that she loved Dariq and wasn't ashamed of anything that had happened between them?

Willow let Kamel undress and bathe her, still stunned by the amazing turn of events. Willow knew that her father was a favorite of the queen, and she should have anticipated that he would use their friendship to get ships and men to come to her rescue. Somehow he had traced her all the way to Ibrahim's harem.

After Willow had bathed, Hetice brought her a gown fashioned in the Western style. "Where did this come from?" Willow asked, fingering the fine material of the modest green gown. "It looks like a perfect fit."

"I was told the English emissary brought it with him," Hetice replied. "One of his escorts gave it to a palace guard, and he delivered it while you were bathing."

"You may leave," Kamel ordered Hetice. To Willow he said, "Sit down, my lady, and let me brush your hair. If the emissary is indeed your father, you will want to look your best."

"He *is* my father, Kamel. I knew in my heart he would find me." She touched her cap of cropped curls. "I hope he will recognize me."

"If the man is your father, he will recognize you," Kamel assured her.

Willow sighed. "I hope you are right. And I pray he has the authority to demand Dariq's release along with mine."

"What you ask is impossible, my lady. Ibrahim wants the prince's death, and naught your father can say will sway him." He stroked his hairless chin. "A diversion at the execution might facilitate his escape, but we cannot be sure Mustafa and Ali Hara can manage it in so a short time."

"Mustafa can and will save Dariq," Willow said with more confidence than she felt.

Kamel continued brushing Willow's hair, until Hetice arrived to say that the sultan had summoned Willow to his chamber.

"I will escort Lady Willow myself," Kamel said.

Willow's knees were shaking as Kamel escorted her from the harem. Two guards fell in behind them, which only increased her nervousness. What if the Englishman wasn't her father? That thought didn't bear considering. It had to be her own dear papa come to take her home.

The door to Ibrahim's inner chamber loomed before her. Kamel rapped. The door opened immediately. Willow hesitated a moment before crossing the threshold. Her heart nearly stopped when she saw a man rise from a chair and turn to stare at her. A cry left her lips; her father had never looked so handsome . . . or been so welcome. Tears blurred her vision.

"Papa!"

Lord Bramston and Willow started toward each other at the same time.

"Daughter!"

Willow broke into a run. Bramston stopped and held out his arms. Willow rushed into them, stifling a sob as his arms closed around her.

"You came," Willow choked out.

"Did you think I would not? It took a while to trace you here, but I refused to give up. Your mother was near despair when I told her the ship carrying you home had been attacked by pirates."

Willow drew back, staring into her father's eyes. "You told Mama?"

"Aye. I stopped at Marseilles before sailing on to Istanbul. She insisted on coming with me."

"Mama is here?"

"Not in the seraglio, of course, but waiting for us on the *Fairwind*."

"As you can see, your daughter is unharmed," Ibrahim said, interrupting their reunion.

Bramston took a long, slow look at Willow and gasped. "What happened to your beautiful hair?"

Willow's hand flew to her head. " 'Tis a long story."

Bramston waved his hand dismissively. " 'Tis not important, my dear. I want to get you aboard ship before the sultan changes his mind."

He turned to Ibrahim. "With your leave, Majesty, I will depart with my daughter."

Ibrahim sent Willow a hard glance, then waved them away. "Take her, Lord Bramston. She has caused me naught but trouble."

Bramston did not tarry as he bowed, grasped Willow's elbow and turned with her toward the door and freedom. Willow, however, had other ideas. She wasn't going anywhere without Dariq.

"No, Papa, wait!"

Startled, Bramston shot Willow a puzzled look. "What is it, Willow? Lingering in the palace is not a good idea."

"I refuse to leave without Dariq."

"Dariq? Who is Dariq? Why is he important to you?"

Ibrahim gave a nasty snort. "Your daughter is referring to Prince Dariq, my brother and Lady Willow's lover."

"What in blazes are you talking about? I thought you purchased my daughter for *your* harem. Where does your brother fit into the picture?"

"My brother is a pirate, a brigand. He currently resides in my dungeon, awaiting execution."

"Papa, please do not let them kill Dariq! I cannot bear it."

"Is what the sultan said true, Willow? Is Prince Dariq your"—he choked over the word—"lover?"

Holding her head high, Willow whispered, "I love Dariq and he loves me. Ibrahim wants to kill Dariq to protect his sultanate. Ibrahim killed all his brothers save Dariq, who escaped with the help of his mother and friends loyal to him."

The marquis shook his head. "It sounds like we have a great deal to discuss—in private. After we return to the *Fairwind*, you can explain everything."

He steered her toward the door. Willow hung back. "No, Papa, there is no time! Dariq's execution is to take place tomorrow. I refuse to leave without him."

"Try to understand, Willow. I cannot interfere in internal affairs that are none of my business, or England's," he explained.

"Dariq's mother is English. He is half English. Does that not mean anything?"

"Your prince has an English mother?"

"Aye, Papa. Please say you will help save his life. I don't want him to die."

"What are you two whispering about?" Ibrahim growled.

Willow's chin tilted stubbornly. "I demand that you release Dariq."

"You demand? *You demand?* You have no right to demand aught of me. You have your freedom; go now before I change my mind."

"Willow, please," Bramston pleaded. "We are treading on dangerous ground."

Willow gave Ibrahim a mutinous glare. "Murderer! Dariq is guilty of naught."

Ibrahim shot to his feet. "My brother has ravaged my ships, disrupted my trade routes and stolen you from me."

His face grew mottled as he pointed a finger at her. "My brother stole your maidenhead, which rightfully belonged to me. He has earned his death."

"You killed his brothers. He was merely avenging their deaths!" Willow shouted.

"My lady, calm yourself," Selim Pasha warned. "You are angering the sultan."

"Are the sultan's accusations true, daughter?" Bramston asked, ignoring both the sultan and the Grand Vizier.

"Aye, Papa, but Dariq doesn't deserve to die. Can you not do something?"

Bramston felt Willow's frustration and pain but had no authority to interfere in Turkish affairs. Had the sultan refused to release Willow, he would not have hesitated to use the ships' cannon. But effecting the release of the sultan's brother, an avowed pirate, was not within his power.

"I am sorry, my dear," he said regretfully. "I have no authority to stop the execution of the sultan's brother."

"But, Papa, did you not bring men and arms with you? The ships have guns, do they not? There must be something you can do."

"There is naught," Ibrahim roared. "Selim Pasha, take them away before I regret my generosity."

Bramston realized the situation was getting out of hand. He curled an arm around Willow's heaving shoulders and tried to lead her away. Willow dug in her heels, but it was a losing battle. Bramston was determined to take his daughter away before Ibrahim ordered them carried out bodily . . . or used violence. He wanted nothing to jeopardize Willow's release.

"Come along, dear. Your outbursts are angering the sultan. We do not want a small war on our hands."

"But, Papa, you don't understand."

"Believe me, darling, I do understand. We will discuss it aboard the *Fairwind*."

Bramston herded Willow out the door. Bramston's escort, who had been waiting in the corridor, fell in behind them.

"Our ships will need to take on water and provisions before we sail from the harbor," Bramston told the Grand Vizier.

"I will relay your message to the sultan," Selim said. "I am sure he will have no objection, since you have what you came for and intend to leave without further trouble."

Though Willow's feet moved, she had scant recollection of leaving the seraglio and walking through the narrow streets of the souk with her father and their guard. She was startled when a man sidled up beside her and grasped her shoulder. Her squawk of surprise alerted her father.

"You, there, what do you think you're doing?" Bramston challenged.

Willow looked up, ecstatic to see Ali Hara. "Ali Hara!" she cried, frantically clutching his arm. "Dariq is going to die tomorrow if we don't do something!" she said in Turkish.

"Who is this man, Willow?" Bramston asked.

"Ali Hara is Dariq's friend and mine. He tried to help me escape, but we were betrayed."

"Where can we talk?" Ali Hara whispered to Willow, obviously aware of the curious stares they were attracting. "Mustafa and I saw the English ships drop anchor in the harbor before Mustafa rode off to fetch the *Revenge*. We hoped your father was on one of the ships, and that he had come for you.

"We knew the sultan would release you when confronted by your father, rather than instigate a war. We discussed the possibility of His Lordship helping us, and made plans accordingly. We both want to save the prince, but we need outside help. Does your father speak Turkish?" Willow shook her head. "What about French?"

When Willow nodded, Ali Hara said, "I speak French, my lord."

Bramston stared at Ali Hara a long, suspenseful moment before addressing him. "Come to my ship with us. We can talk in private there. But I doubt there is anything I can do to save your prince."

Excitement pulsed through Willow. She had no idea how Ali Hara and Mustafa intended to rescue Dariq but prayed her father would agree to help. If Dariq died, her heart would die with him.

"I will meet you at the docks," Ali Hara said in a hushed voice.

Before Bramston could reply, Ali Hara lost himself in the crowed marketplace.

"Do not get your hopes up, darling," Bramston warned. "I doubt if I will be able to help, but I will hear Ali Hara out."

"Thank you, Papa. Dariq means everything to me."

They reached the docks without mishap and approached a long stone pier. A rowboat that would carry them back to their ship was waiting for them. Ali Hara appeared as if from nowhere. Bramston helped Willow into the boat, then indicated that Ali Hara should join her. Bramston and the escort followed. The boat pushed away from the pier and headed toward the *Fairwind*.

Chapter Nineteen

The first person Willow saw as she scrambled up the ladder and poked her head over the *Fairwind's* rail was her mother. Two sailors lifted her onto the deck, and then she was in her mother's arms.

"*Ma petite*, you are safe, *oui?*"

"*Oui*, Mama, I am safe," Willow choked out.

"And unharmed, *oui?*"

"I am fine, Mama." *But Dariq isn't.*

Bramston arrived on deck. "Did I not promise to bring our daughter back safely, Monique?" he said, smiling at his reunited family.

"You are a wonder, Robert, truly a wonder. I will love you forever for this."

Ali Hara's head popped up over the rail. Monique's eyes widened with fear as she clutched Willow to her bosom. "Who is that?"

"Ali Hara, Mama," Willow explained. "You have naught to fear from him. He saw that no harm came to me during the months of my captivity."

Monique breathed an audible sigh of relief. "Then I

owe him my deepest gratitude. What language does he speak?"

"He speaks French, Mama."

"What is Ali Hara doing here?" Monique asked in French.

Bramston herded them toward his cabin. "I shall explain everything, my love, once we are behind closed doors."

My *love?* Papa was calling Mama his love? And Mama was looking at Papa as if she adored him. Obviously, much had changed in Willow's absence.

Once inside the cramped cabin, Willow and Monique sat on the bed and Papa took the only chair. Ali Hara stood, apparently anxious to tell his tale and leave.

"Very well, Ali Hara," Bramston began. "Tell us how you and your friends plan to save Prince Dariq's life."

"Prince Dariq?" Monique asked. "Who is Prince Dariq, and what is he to you, *ma petite?*"

"Dariq is the man I love, Mama," Willow replied. "I will tell you about him when we are alone. Go ahead, Ali Hara. Tell us how you and Mustafa intend to rescue Dariq."

Though Willow could tell her mother was eager to question her about Dariq, Lady Bramston turned her attention to Ali Hara.

"Mustafa and I despaired of saving Prince Dariq without outside help, though we were determined to try," the eunuch explained. "Mustafa intended to fetch the *Revenge* and use the crew to attempt a rescue, though we had scant chance of succeeding.

"When Mustafa saw English ships enter the harbor, he assumed they had come for Lady Willow, and suddenly we had reason to hope. Mustafa left the city while I remained behind to seek your help. Mustafa intends to sail the *Revenge* into the harbor, arriving before dawn tomorrow.

"Executions are usually held at noon, so I expect that's when the prince will be brought through the souk to the city square. Mustafa intends to bring our men from the ships to mingle with the crowd in the city square. Even as we speak, Hassan and his friends are inciting the mob, urging them to protest the execution."

"Do you think the people will do it?" Bramston asked.

"If Mustafa and our men start a riot, the rabble will follow. The janizaries will not be able to guard the prince and deal with the rabble. While they quell the disturbance, Mustafa will spirit the prince away. Outside help will assure that our plan succeeds."

Bramston shook his head. "I cannot commit Englishmen to your daring rescue, for it is not something my queen would condone. We are not here to start a war. I brought the warships and men as a show of force to intimidate the sultan."

"Papa, please help Dariq," Willow pleaded.

Bramston ignored her. "How do you intend to get your prince back to his ship? Won't the janizaries give chase?"

"They will, and here is where we need your help. All I ask is that you send soldiers ashore to prevent the janizaries from following us after the rescue. Once Prince Dariq and his men are back aboard the *Revenge*, your soldiers can disperse."

"That is little enough to ask, Papa," Willow ventured. "You need not start a war. Perhaps the soldiers could go ashore to watch the execution and inadvertently add to the confusion while Dariq makes his escape. The janizaries won't attack English soldiers, for fear of starting a war."

"Hmmm, I did tell the Grand Vizier we needed to take on water and provisions before the ships left the harbor. I could send men ashore tomorrow morning to purchase provisions. It would not be our fault if our soldiers got in the way of the janizaries."

"Oh Papa, could you . . . would you?"

Ali Hara remained silent as he waited for Bramston's decision. Hands clasped behind his back, Bramston paced the small cabin. After a lengthy pause, he spun around and addressed the eunuch.

"Please wait outside, Ali Hara. I wish to speak with my wife and daughter before I make a decision."

Ali Hara bowed and left.

"What is it, Papa?" Willow asked. "Why do you hesitate?"

"Before I make a decision, I need to ask you a question. Do you truly love this prince of yours?"

"You love a prince?" Monique gasped.

"With all my heart, Mama," Willow replied. "I would do anything to save his life."

"A Turkish prince?"

"Half Turkish. His mother is English."

"Your prince leads a violent life," Bramston accused. "He is a pirate and unlikely to change. He is more Turkish than English by dint of his upbringing. The cultural and religious differences between his world and yours will eventually tear you apart."

"Oh, Papa—" she began in protest.

"Wait, my dear." He put up a palm. "I will help save your prince on one condition."

"And that condition is . . ."

"You will return to England with me and your mother and forget the pirate."

"Forget Dariq? Oh, Papa, what you ask is—"

"—not impossible, my dear. Difficult, perhaps, but not impossible. Your mother and I have reconciled. She has missed me as much as I missed her, and she has agreed to return to England so we can be a family again. We will help you forget this misadventure of yours.

"Think carefully, dear child, for it's the only way I will agree to help your prince. Without my help, Ali Hara and Mustafa have little hope of succeeding."

"Your father is right, darling," Monique agreed. "You have known this man but a short time, and under difficult circumstances. Trust your father to know what is best for you."

Willow blinked away her tears. Could she leave Dariq if it was the only way to save his life? Was her father right? Were their worlds too different for a union between them to succeed? Would Dariq continue his life as a pirate after his rescue? If he did, she knew there would be no lasting happiness for them. She touched her stomach. She wanted her child, but did Dariq? Would he settle down for her and their babe if she asked it of him?

"Give me your answer, Willow," Bramston said. "You know I love you and have no desire to hurt you. I do not believe a pirate can make you happy. Think carefully, for your answer could save his life."

A tremor rippled through Willow's body. "You give me little choice, Papa. I want Dariq to live, and if I have to sacrifice my happiness to make it happen, then so be it."

Bramston let his breath out slowly. "You've made a difficult choice, daughter. I applaud your courage."

Bramston opened the door and invited Ali Hara inside. "I have come to a decision, Ali Hara. Neither the warships nor the soldiers aboard the vessels will be involved in the rescue, for I have no authority to direct the queen's army in an illegal operation."

"Papa!"

"Let me finish, daughter. What I do with my own ship and men is my decision. Tomorrow morning I shall send the *Fairwind's* sailors to the city to purchase provisions. They cannot be faulted if they get caught up in the drama taking place in the city. I am sure they can create the diversion you require."

"Praise Allah," Ali Hara said. "I will give you directions to the prince's stronghold on the island of Lipsi so you can bring his lady to him."

Bramston listened while Ali Hara gave him the coordinates. He did not mention, however, that he had no intention of taking Willow to Lipsi. He planned to sail directly to England once his men were safely returned to the *Fairwind*.

"I must return to the city to help Hassan organize the uprising," Ali Hara said, bowing.

Bramston nodded. "I will arrange to have you rowed ashore. Come along, Ali Hara."

Willow sobbed quietly in her mother's arms. She didn't know how she would live without Dariq in her life. In the short time they had been together, he had become her world. Even more devastating was the thought of leaving Dariq before seeing or speaking to him.

"Do not cry, *ma petite*," Monique cooed. "Your father knows what is best for you. After your terrible ordeal, he could not let you remain with a violent pirate. What kind of future would you have with a man like that?"

"Dariq is not a violent man," Willow sobbed. "He was forced into piracy by his cruel brother. I love him, Mama."

"Would your prince be happy in England?" Monique asked.

Willow searched her heart and could not honestly say

that Dariq would be happy in England. He was a prince in Turkey, but he would be only an outsider in England. Though he would never be poor, once his past became known, he would not be accepted by the *ton*. Even though she would be with Dariq to help him adjust, he knew naught about life in Christian England or acting like a gentleman of the *ton*.

He would be miserable.

As miserable as she would be without him.

But Willow had been given no choice. She had to give up the man she loved to gain her father's help in freeing Dariq.

"Dariq and I love each other so much, Mama," Willow said on a sob.

"You will both forget each other in time," Monique predicted. "He is not of your world. You will find a man more suited to your station. Your dowry is substantial; you will have your pick of suitors."

"Dariq is the only man I will ever love. Other men pale in comparison."

Willow considered telling Monique that she was expecting Dariq's child but decided against it. Mama would tell Papa, and he might be angry enough to retract the help he'd promised Ali Hara. They would find out eventually, but not until Dariq was safely ensconced in his stronghold.

"You are young," Monique observed. "Another man will come along."

"You and Papa were separated for years. Did you fall in love with another man during the time you were apart?"

Monique had the grace to blush. "You know I did not. Our situation was different."

"I see no difference. You *are* together now, are you not?"

Monique smiled. "It seems I have fallen in love with Robert all over again. This time we shall stay together."

"I am happy for you and Papa, Mama, but that doesn't help me. I cannot leave Dariq without telling him why I must return to England. I owe him that much."

Bramston reentered the cabin. He took one look at Willow's swollen eyes and tear-stained cheeks and shook his head. "I am not the monster you think me, dear child. I cannot bear the thought of losing you to a pirate. We might never see you again."

Willow struggled to stem the flood of tears. "I know you want what's best for me, but leaving Dariq without an explanation is cruel. I made a promise to you and I won't change my mind, but I need to see Dariq before leaving him forever."

Bramston frowned. "What are you suggesting?"

"When the *Revenge* arrives tomorrow morning, have me rowed to the ship. Once I have spoken to Dariq, I will return to the *Fairwind* and sail with you to England."

Bramston gave his head a violent shake. "Absolutely not! What trickery are you planning?"

"No trickery. Surely you understand my feelings, Papa. I recall how you were when Mama left you. You felt betrayed. Give me an opportunity to explain to Dariq why we cannot be together."

Bramston sent his wife a speaking look. Monique raised her eyebrows and shrugged. "I can understand Willow's feelings. She loves the man."

"I know I coerced you into making a decision you cannot like, Willow, and I am sorry for it, but you are a lady and deserve a better life than he can give you. I cannot allow you to leave this ship."

"What if I can convince Dariq to give up piracy and live in England? Would you approve then?"

"Would a Turkish pirate be happy in England?" Bramston shot back.

"I . . . do not think so," Willow whispered. "He would not. But he deserves an explanation. Please, Papa, do not deny me this. Send me to the *Revenge* when it arrives."

"You may think me overly harsh, my dear, but I still cannot allow you time alone with your prince even if our rescue attempt succeeds. We may fail, you know."

"You will not fail," Willow said fiercely.

"Excuse me, my dear, there are arrangements to be made." He kissed his wife and daughter and left.

Willow didn't sleep that night. After writing a note for her parents and leaving it in her cabin, she spent the night on deck, watching for the *Revenge's* running lights. While she waited and watched, Willow made a plan she knew her father would neither understand nor like, but she had to do what she thought best for herself and Dariq. She still intended to keep her promise to her father, but she had to see Dariq one last time before leaving him forever.

The *Revenge* arrived with the approaching dawn. She maneuvered behind the English warships and dropped anchor. She flew no flag and was all but invisible in the misty dawn. Shortly afterward, Willow saw four rowboats from the *Fairwind* being lowered into the water. She assumed the sailors would row ashore to assist in Dariq's rescue.

Willow waited until the watch had turned away and the sailors were otherwise engaged before scampering down the ladder into one of the boats tethered to the ship. Taking up the oars, she rowed, albeit clumsily, to the *Revenge*, thanking God it was not far or she never would had made it.

Willow hoped her father would not be too angry when he found her letter. In it she explained that he should follow the *Revenge* to Lipsi, where she would board the *Fairwind* and return to England, as she had promised.

Just as her arms were about to give out, the boat bumped against the *Revenge's* hull. A sailor looked over the side, gave a shout and lowered the ladder when Willow indicated she wished to board the ship. It was a difficult climb, but she was soon pulled over the rail and welcomed aboard by Mustafa.

Dariq awoke early on the last day of his life. He tried to dwell not on death but on life . . . Willow's life. Though she was probably far from Istanbul by now, he would always remain with her in spirit if not in body. His wish for her was that she would find a good man to love, one who would love her in return.

Dariq was brought a meal that morning by a sullen guard. His last meal on this earth. His stomach rebelled, and he pushed the food aside. At mid-morning Ibrahim showed up with a woman.

"I thought you might like to know sexual gratification one last time before you are cast into hell," the sultan said. "Aziza will pleasure you in any way you desire. I am not as coldhearted as you believe, brother."

Dariq stared at the lovely woman but felt no desire. He refused to defile the memory of his love for Willow.

"Nay, thank you, brother. Take your houri and leave me in peace."

"So be it," Ibrahim said. "Rest in hell, Dariq. I will not be in attendance at your execution. You are not important enough to warrant my leaving the seraglio."

"Coward!" Dariq accused. "You fear your people will rise up against you to protest my execution." He sent Ibrahim a grim smile. "You are wise to remain behind walls, brother."

"I fear no one!" Ibrahim snarled. Dragging Aziza with him, he stormed off.

Dariq sank down on his haunches, contemplating his short life and how he would live it if he were given another chance. Then the guards came to take him away. As the guards led him through the souk, he was vaguely aware of the unruly crowd following him and wondered why the masses had turned out for his execution. Then he saw it—the chopping block and the executioner awaiting him in the square.

Dariq's pride would not allow him to show fear. His head held high, he maintained his dignity as he walked toward the executioner with firm steps. He gazed directly into the crowd, and what he saw cheered him. Many familiar faces looked back at him. He saw Hassan and friends from his former life in Istanbul. And then he spotted Mustafa and some of his crewmen. For a brief moment he knew hope, but just as quickly it died. They were too few to be of any help.

As Dariq was prodded toward the executioner, something strange occurred. English sailors seemed to be everywhere, mingling with the crowd that had come to watch his execution. Dariq watched in stunned silence as pandemonium erupted within the crowd. Angry voices became raised fists and quickly a small riot had begun. Dariq stared in utter astonishment as people began pushing through the ring of janizaries trying to hold them back.

Before he realized what was happening, the square became a solid mass of human bodies. Momentarily diverted from their prisoner, the janizaries fought to restore order. But it soon became clear that they were fighting a losing battle. The executioner staggered backward as people pushed and shoved him away from Dariq. Then

Mustafa was beside him, the men from the *Revenge* forming a protective circle around him.

"This way, Prince," Mustafa urged, edging him through a breach that had miraculously parted for them.

English sailors provided a buffer as Dariq and his men slipped through the crowd. When a hue and cry arose, Dariq realized the janizaries had noticed his disappearance, and he feared that he and his men were all doomed.

Then another miracle occurred. The English sailors regrouped and formed a formidable blockade, allowing Dariq and his men to flee unhampered. Dariq had no idea who had organized this incredible uprising, but he was exceedingly grateful.

Dariq ran through the winding streets to the docks and leapt into one of the boats tied to the pier, while his crewmen scrambled into a second boat.

"The English sailors are shielding us from the janizaries," Mustafa said.

"Where are Kamel and Ali Hara?" Dariq asked.

"There they are," Mustafa said, pointing to the two men racing along the pier.

As soon as the eunuchs reached them and found a place in the boat, they shoved off. The remaining boats followed in quick succession.

"I hope the English sailors reach their ship without loss of life," Dariq said worriedly.

"Look what is happening!" Mustafa shouted. "The crowd is forming a solid mass of bodies between the janizaries and the sailors. The janizaries cannot reach the sailors. The crowd is forming a human shield to aid our escape."

"Where is Willow?" Dariq asked anxiously.

"Aboard her father's ship," Ali Hara replied. "Your lady's father arrived with enough force behind him to convince Ibrahim to release her. When Mustafa saw the English ships in the harbor, we assumed Lady Willow's father had come for her and concocted a rescue plan. All we had to do was convince Lord Bramston to cooperate with us. While Mustafa left to fetch the *Revenge*, I approached the marquis."

"I am surprised he agreed."

"It wasn't easy," Ali Hara said, "but in the end, he agreed. I gave him directions to Lipsi so he can bring your lady to you."

Dariq thought the marquis was as likely to take Willow to Lipsi as to Timbuktu.

They reached the *Revenge* in good time. Dariq scrambled up the ladder first, and his men followed. The mood aboard ship was jubilant as the men congratulated each other. By the grace of God and Allah, Dariq was alive and none of his men had been injured. And Ali Hara and Kamel had elected to join the Brotherhood.

Soon the men and boats were aboard. "Unfurl the sails!" Dariq shouted. "The tide is turning and the wind is with us. Set a course for Lipsi."

Mustafa took over the wheel. Wind whipped the canvas, and the sails filled with air as the *Revenge* slowly picked up speed, leaving Istanbul behind. Legs braced, Dariq stood at the rail as they sailed through the Bosporus, his spyglass following the course of the *Fairwind*.

"Fear not, my lord, Lady Willow's father will bring her to you," Ali Hara said, answering Dariq's unspoken question.

Dariq wasn't so sure. Perhaps Willow wouldn't be happy living on Lipsi and had decided to return to England. He knew Willow deserved better than a pirate for a husband; it wasn't the life her family had envisioned for her. Could love breach the gap between their worlds?

Nor did living in England appeal to Dariq. He had

riches enough to keep him and Willow in luxury for the rest of their lives, in England or anywhere else she desired, but he knew intuitively that English society would not accept a reformed pirate. He was untitled and his features too foreign.

Dariq sighed deeply. The disparity in their backgrounds was one he and Willow would have to work out.

A sailor sidled up to Dariq. "Your bath awaits you in your cabin, my lord."

Dariq's dark brows shot upward. "It seems you have read my mind. Thank you, Akbad."

Akbad smirked but said nothing more as Dariq started toward his cabin. Dariq wore a puzzled expression when he noted that Akbad wasn't the only man grinning at him. Shrugging, he continued on to his cabin, deciding that his men were merely happy to see him alive.

Dariq opened the cabin door and stepped inside, eager for the promised bath. The stink of his body nauseated him. He spied the wooden tub and the steam rising above it and smiled. By the time he reached it, he had shed his clothes, flinging them hither and yon.

Then he saw her. He froze in mid-step as she stepped from the shadows at the far end of the cabin. He whispered her name and she flew into his arms, her cheeks wet with tears.

He kissed her and knew paradise again. She was here, in his arms, and he never intended to let her go.

"How—" he whispered against her lips.

"It does not matter. I wanted to be here when you arrived."

She stepped back, her gaze sliding over every inch of his body. "Are you all right?"

"As you can see, I am fine, love. I will show you just

how well I am once the stench of the dungeon is off me. While I wash, you can tell me how you got here."

Willow had no intention of ruining their reunion by telling Dariq she was leaving him, that their reunion was only temporary. She would save that for another day. Telling him now would hurt him too much, even though he would have to know before they reached Lipsi.

Dariq stepped into the tub and sank down into the water, groaning his pleasure. "I was stunned to see the English warships in the harbor," he began. "When Selim Pasha said you were being sent home, I assumed it would be on a Turkish ship. I had no idea your father had arrived in Istanbul to fetch you until Mustafa told me. How did the marquis convince Ibrahim to let you go, and how did you persuade your father to send his sailors to aid my escape?"

"I do not know what Papa told Ibrahim, but warships carrying soldiers and big guns probably convinced him. As for getting Papa to help you, I told him I loved you and would never forgive him if he refused," Willow said as she picked up the cloth and soap.

"Ali Hara and Mustafa hatched the plan to rescue you when they saw English ships in the harbor and assumed they had come for me. When Ali Hara outlined their plan to Papa, I urged him to help."

"It seems too easy," Dariq muttered. "Your father has no reason to like me. I am the man who kidnapped his daughter and took her virginity."

"You are the man I love. Lean over so I can scrub your back."

Willow didn't want to get into particulars right now. She and Dariq were together, and that was all that mattered. She wanted him so desperately that her hands shook as she ran the cloth over his back and shoulders.

When she moved around to his front, Dariq captured her hand, bringing it down between his thighs. The breath caught in her throat. His staff was hard as marble, jutting proudly upward against his stomach. Though it cost her dearly, Willow jerked her hand away.

"First your bath," she teased, keeping her voice light. If he noticed that her heart was breaking, she would have to tell him she was leaving him, and it was too soon.

Taking the cloth from her, Dariq hurried through his bath, leaving his hair for the last. Willow picked up a jar and poured clean water over his head to rinse out the soap. Then, before she realized his intention, he surged up from the tub. Dripping water on the deck, he lifted her into his arms and carried her to the bed. He set her on her feet.

Catching his enthusiasm, Willow pulled her wet bodice away from her chest. "Look what you did."

Laughing, Dariq shook his head, spraying her with water.

Willow grabbed a towel and dried his hair, but that was as far as she got. Dariq was as eager for her as she was for him. Reaching for her, he undressed her quickly, ignoring most of the tiny buttons marching down the front of her gown.

"Why must English women wear all these layers of clothing?" he muttered as he pulled the bodice down her shoulders, taking her chemise with it. Then he pushed the gown past her hips and lifted her from the pool of material at her feet. Unhampered by clothing, they tumbled into the bed.

Willow kissed his mouth, his damp throat, wanting him so badly she began to tremble, aware that each passing minute diminished their time together.

"Come inside me," Willow pleaded.

Though his eyes were narrowed with heat and raging lust, he took his sweet time arousing her. He nuzzled her breast, flicking his tongue over her nipple. "Not yet, beauty."

Willow reached up to touch his chest. His skin felt damp and hot; his muscles contracted beneath her fingertips.

Dariq groaned and gathered her against him; the hard points of her nipples teased his chest as he positioned his rigid sex at the weeping entrance to her body. Taut anticipation screamed through Willow. She had been starved for him; needed to feel him inside her. She arched up against him, begging him without words.

"Not yet," Dariq rasped raggedly. "I want to taste you first." He moved over her body, laving her skin with his tongue as he traveled downward, until he reached that tender place between her thighs.

She shuddered when she felt his fingers pressing her swollen folds open, and then his tongue touched the delicate jewel between them. Her fingers dug into his shoulders as he licked her in long, sinuous laps that made her body throb with unrelenting delight.

Willow could not stop the motion of her hips rising upward in repeated surges. His hands slid beneath her, guiding her rhythm while his tongue strummed, bathed, teased. She whimpered incoherently as sensations tumbled one after another, drawing her toward an unendurable peak.

Willow moaned out a protest when Dariq lifted his head and levered his body upward. "Please, *please* . . ."

Flexing his hips, he entered her. Willow cried out, her

yielding flesh tightening around him. As his kisses scorched her throat, her mouth, his engorged shaft delved deep inside her liquid center. He withdrew almost to the head of his shaft, then drove deep again, moving slowly and steadily in long, pleasuring strokes.

She melted around him, began to move with him, her hips meeting his in frantic urgency. She felt as if her world began and ended with Dariq. She wanted him, wanted *this*, only with him, for the rest of her life.

His mouth covered hers, muffling her cries as she shattered in his arms. Her body shook with violent spasms, the walls of her passage gripping his sex hard, convulsing around him. Dariq let out a groan and seized her hips with both hands, spending his own passion.

He collapsed against her, his heart so filled with love, he was nearly bursting with it. Somehow, he vowed, he and Willow would have a future together. Somehow they would find a place in this vast world where they could be happy together.

Willow's thoughts ran in a different direction. Despite Dariq's nearness, she was sad because she knew that today was the beginning of the end. She had given her promise to her father, and pride demanded that she keep it. It would destroy her, but the knowledge that Dariq was alive and well would see her through the difficult days, weeks and years without him. She thought about the child she carried, and smiled. She would always have a small part of Dariq to love.

Willow's secret would have to remain a secret, however. If Dariq knew she carried his child, he would fight tooth and nail to keep it and her.

Dariq stirred, rose up on his elbows and gazed into Willow's eyes. "I love you, Willow. There is plenty of time to decide where on this earth we can be happy."

Willow did not reply as he shifted off her and stretched out beside her. There was nothing she *could* say.

"I want to have children with you," he murmured against her hair. "I want to spend the rest of my life with you."

If Dariq hadn't fallen asleep so quickly after his heartfelt declaration, he would have seen the silent tears streaming down Willow's cheeks.

Chapter Twenty

The following days couldn't have been more idyllic for Willow. The weather continued warm and sunny, and her nights overflowed with passion. But undermining Willow's happiness was the knowledge that they would reach Lipsi long before she was ready to leave Dariq. She had but to look behind her to see her father's ship dogging the *Revenge*. He must have been livid when she was discovered missing and he read her note. She was surprised he hadn't brought the warships with him, but those vessels had parted ways with the *Fairwind* and set a course for England.

As Willow stood at the rail, gazing at the blue-green sea, she became aware of a dark mass hovering on the horizon. Her first sight of land sent her heart plummeting down to her feet.

"That's Lipsi in the distance," Dariq said from behind her.

She leaned back against him, taking comfort in the solid warmth of his body. His arms came around her, and he planted a kiss on top of her head.

"We are almost home, my love. I'm glad your father decided to visit. I have yet to thank him for the part he played in my rescue. I hope he will accept my hospitality for a few days before returning to England."

"Did I tell you my mother is with Papa?" Willow mentioned.

Dariq chuckled against her ear. "I've given you very little time for conversation. Have they reconciled?"

"Aye, isn't it wonderful? I knew they still loved each other, but they were both too stubborn to be the first to admit that mistakes had been made in their marriage."

"There will be no mistakes in ours, my love. Your parents are leaving you in good hands."

Willow shifted uncomfortably. Time was running out. She had to tell Dariq tonight that she was leaving him. The pain of parting came crashing down on her, and she sagged beneath its weight. Dariq's arms tightened around her.

"What's wrong? Are you ill?"

Aye, sick unto death.

"I feel fine, but the sun is a little too intense for me. Perhaps I should return to the cabin and lie down."

Dariq watched her go, dread prickling down his spine. Something was wrong. Everything had seemed fine until Lipsi appeared on the horizon. He stared thoughtfully at the English ship following in his wake. Intuition told him there was something about the ship and her passengers he should fear. Then Mustafa joined him and his attention shifted elsewhere.

Willow mentally prepared herself for the moment when she had to tell Dariq she was leaving him. No matter how difficult it would be, she intended to shoulder the blame for their parting. She prayed she could do it without breaking down. Dariq must never know how desperately she was hurting.

The afternoon waned into dusk as Willow bathed and prepared for Dariq's return. She had even asked the ship's cook to prepare something special for Dariq if supplies were available, and to bring hot water to the cabin so he could bathe.

When Dariq returned to the cabin later, he spied the tub and sent Willow a grateful smile. "You seem to know exactly what I want, beauty."

"I asked cook to prepare your favorite meal," Willow replied. "I want tonight to be special."

Dariq sent her a wary look. "Why? I thought all our nights were special."

"They are, but . . ." She could say nothing more without bursting into tears.

"Is something wrong, love?"

"I have something to tell you, but it can wait."

She helped him disrobe, but when he stepped into the tub, she turned away. She could scarcely look at him, much less touch him, knowing how terribly she was going to hurt him.

"You seem distracted," Dariq observed.

"I've been thinking about my parents," Willow replied, refusing to look him in the eye.

Dariq surged up from the tub, dried quickly and stepped into his trousers. Then he padded over to Willow on bare feet and turned her to face him. "Something *is* wrong. I sensed it earlier today. You may as well tell me, for I'll find out anyway."

Tears clogged Willow's throat as she searched Dariq's beloved face. She said the only thing she could think of to distract him. "Make love to me, Dariq. Now . . . *please*."

The desperation in Willow's voice troubled Dariq. Not

a night had passed since they'd left Istanbul that they had not made love. Sometimes they had stolen away in the middle of the day and made long, leisurely love in the afternoon heat. For some unexplained reason, Willow appeared on edge tonight.

"Please, Dariq," Willow repeated, tugging him toward the bed.

Her urgency transferred itself to Dariq, stoking his passion as he watched her remove her clothing. All his apprehension and fear were forgotten as he stripped off his trousers, pushed her backward on the bed and followed her down. He entered her quickly; she was ready for him. Her wet heat drew him inside her and closed around him.

She went wild beneath him, kissing him wherever she could reach . . . his mouth, his nose, his chin, his neck. Her hands slid down his spine to caress his buttocks as she pressed upward to meet his powerful strokes. On fire for her now, Dariq thrust deep, hard, fast, his hips pounding against hers, driving them both to a tumultuous climax.

When he was finally able to breathe, and think, he rose up on his arms and stared down at her. "What is it, Willow? Something has upset you, and I want to know what it is."

Willow choked back a sob; Dariq pulled out of her and gathered her into his arms. "Tell me what's wrong and I'll try to fix it. Seeing you unhappy is tearing me apart."

"You cannot fix this," Willow said on a sob. "No one can. 'Tis not our fate to be together. Our worlds are too different. I wouldn't be happy on Lipsi, and you would be miserable in London."

"Those aren't the only two places in the world. We can go anywhere. I can support you in style wherever you choose to live. Perhaps you would prefer France, or Italy."

Willow could not stop crying. She hurt so badly, she

was nearly sick with it. It was time to tell Dariq the truth, or as close to it as she could get.

Dragging in a shuddering breath, Willow said, "I am returning to England with Papa and Mama."

Dariq went still. So still she thought he hadn't heard.

"Did you hear what I said?"

"I heard; your words stole the breath from me." He seemed calm, too calm. "Would you care to explain?"

"We don't belong together."

Dariq's lips barely moved as he said, "Are you trying to tell me you don't love me?"

"Never that! I do love you! But sometimes love isn't enough. I want you to be happy. You would be out of place in my environment, and I would hate living on Lipsi while you pursued piracy."

"What you mean is you are ashamed of me, that I don't fit in your world," Dariq charged.

"That is *not* what I meant," Willow argued. "Papa . . ." Her words fell off. She deemed it best to keep her father out of it.

But Dariq was too astute not to catch the inflection in her voice. "What about your father? Doesn't he think I'm good enough for you?"

"Papa has naught to do with my decision," she lied.

Dariq surged from the bed and began to dress with angry, jerking motions. "I understand perfectly. Your father persuaded you to return to England because His Lordship does not want me as a son-in-law. Your parents probably have a proper husband all picked out for you; one who will overlook your past in order to get his hands on your generous portion."

Fully dressed now, he turned to confront her. "Very well, I won't beg you to stay with me. If you loved me half as much as I love you, you wouldn't leave." He yanked the door open.

Before he walked out, he said something he knew he'd regret the rest of his life. "You are not irreplaceable, you know. I will have no difficulty finding another houri to take your place in my bed."

That was the last Willow saw of Dariq until they reached Lipsi. And then she only glimpsed him from afar the day they docked. She had watched him stride down the gangplank without a backward glance. Willow had no idea what would happen next, so she sat in the cabin and waited, too sick at heart to stir. Two hours later, her father's ship dropped anchor in the cove. Shortly afterward, there came a knock on the cabin door.

Hoping it was Dariq, Willow flew to the door. Her face fell when she saw it was only Mustafa. But what did she expect, after the way she'd treated Dariq?

" 'Tis time to leave, my lady. Your father has sent a boat for you."

Willow nodded and followed the huge man to the rail. A sailor lowered a ladder for her.

" 'Tis not too late to change your mind," Mustafa said. "I do not know what happened between you and my master, but I am sure it can be fixed."

"Not this time, Mustafa. We both know Dariq wouldn't be alive today without Papa's help. Papa kept his promise to me, and so I must keep mine."

Mustafa's keen gaze pierced deep into her wounded soul. "You promised to leave Prince Dariq in return for your father's help," he guessed.

A jolt of panic surged through Willow. "Nay, that's not what happened!"

"Do not lie to me, lady, for I can see into your heart. You love the prince as much as he loves you. Tell him the truth."

"I cannot. The truth would hurt him more than my lie. Let him believe what he wants about me. Promise you will never mention this conversation to Dariq, Mustafa. He will forget me in time."

"He will never forget you," Mustafa predicted as he helped her over the railing. "But if it pleases you, I will say naught to him. You know, however, that my master is not stupid. He will figure it out in his own good time. Allah be with you, lady," he said softy as she climbed down the ladder.

Two sailors helped settle Willow into the gently rocking boat. Tears distorted her vision, but when she looked back, she swore she saw Dariq standing on the shore, watching her being slowly rowed away. She dashed away her tears for a better look, but he was gone.

Mustafa found Dariq brooding in his chamber. Saliha Sultana was with him.

"Is she safely aboard the *Fairwind?*" Dariq asked when Mustafa strode into the chamber.

"Aye, my lord."

Dariq looked out the window in time to see the *Fairwind's* sails fill with air as the ship picked up speed. "She is truly gone," he said dully. "I will never understand what happened between us. Her reason for leaving me doesn't make sense."

Mustafa exchanged a glance with Saliha Sultana and then excused himself. A few minutes later, Saliha followed. She found Mustafa waiting for her.

"What happened?" Saliha asked. "I saw love for my son in Willow's heart. Dariq told me everything that happened in Istanbul, and, like him, I can make no sense of

Willow's leaving him. I have never seen my son so bereft."

"I do not know what happened; I can only tell you what I observed. The prince and his lady seemed very happy together aboard the *Revenge* these past few days. It was Lady Willow's father, the Marquis of Bramston, and his crewmen who made Prince Dariq's rescue possible."

"I am surprised the marquis agreed to help," Saliha mused. "As I understand it, my son held Willow captive against her will. I cannot imagine an English lord agreeing to let his daughter wed a Turkish pirate."

"Think about it, my lady," Mustafa said. "If you were Lady Willow's father, how would you convince your daughter to return to England with you, knowing full well that she loves Prince Dariq?"

Saliha's brow furrowed, and then abruptly cleared. "Oh, how sad. His Lordship offered to help Dariq under the condition that Willow return to England with him. That's it—it has to be!"

"Precisely," Mustafa concurred.

"We must tell Dariq immediately."

"Nay, I think not. Once his anger passes, he will see things as we do. If we tell him now, he will pursue the *Fairwind* and launch an attack if the ship refuses to yield to him. Lives could be lost . . . perhaps his life or his lady's if the marquis engages the *Revenge* in a sea battle."

"I sense Dariq's sadness beneath his anger. We cannot let this happen, Mustafa."

"Would your son be happy in England, my lady?"

Saliha closed her eyes, her thoughts returning to her life before she became the wife of a sultan. When she opened them, her expression had brightened considerably.

"Dariq most definitely could be happy in England, Mustafa." She squared her shoulders. "I shall make it happen."

Chapter Twenty-one

London, three months later

Willow reclined in the window seat in her room, staring at the cold rain slanting against the windowpane. Shivering, she pulled her shawl closer about her rounded middle. She hadn't been warm since her arrival in London. Coldness had seeped into her soul and settled in the empty space in her heart. Numbness of mind and spirit had become her constant companion.

Monique had guessed Willow's secret before they reached England and questioned her about her condition. Willow hadn't denied her pregnancy, and of course Monique told her father. The row that transpired next had been awful. Had Dariq been within the marquis's reach, there would have been bloodshed.

Her pregnancy had renewed her father's anger at her for leaving the *Fairwind* without his permission and boarding the *Revenge*. But after he'd seen how distressed she was, he had dropped the subject and accepted her condition. He loved his daughter deeply.

The door to Willow's room creaked open. Monique walked in. "Come and have tea with your papa and me, *ma petite*. Sitting alone and brooding will do neither you nor your child any good."

Willow gazed listlessly at her mother. "Do you really care about my child, Mama?"

"Of course I do, *ma petite*. So does Robert. Please come down and join us."

"What if company drops in? I can no longer hide my pregnancy beneath full skirts."

"Your father has taken care of the gossips. The *ton* believe you were wed in France and lost your husband in a terrible accident. You are expecting your dear dead husband's child. There is no shame in that."

"It's a lie. Even the name you gave my 'dear dead husband' is a lie."

Monique shrugged. "What does it matter as long as your own name remains unsullied? After your child is born, you can go out in society again and find a man worthy of you."

"Oh, Mama," Willow sighed, "why must you make my life so difficult? I just want to be left alone. I do not want a husband. Dariq is the only man I will ever love. You and Papa have no idea how badly I hurt him."

Monique frowned. "You are wrong, Willow. Your prince hurt you more than you hurt him. Did he not hold you captive against your will?" Reluctantly, Willow nodded. "Did he not take advantage of your innocence?"

"Not exactly," Willow whispered, recalling his erotic seduction of her.

Monique hugged her daughter. "It matters not, *ma petite*. You are home with your loved ones where you belong. Your child will be as precious to us as you are. Come downstairs and have tea with us. You must eat for yourself and your babe. You are far too thin."

Willow knew her mother was right. She'd had little appetite since returning home, and she appeared pale and gaunt.

She stood and shook out her skirts. "Very well. If it will please you, I will join you and Papa."

Robert stood when Monique and Willow entered the cozy back parlor where they usually gathered informally, a delighted smile stretching his lips. He took Willow's hands and led her to a chair near the fire.

"You cannot imagine how much it pleases me to have you join us," the marquis said. "You spend too much time alone in your room. Brooding isn't healthy."

"Have you forgotten how despondent you felt after Mama left you?" Willow reminded him. "I haven't. You sat and brooded for months. I love Dariq no less than you love Mama."

"Do not mention that pirate to me," Robert said harshly. "If not for him, you wouldn't be in the condition you are in now."

Willow laced her fingers over her stomach. "I love Dariq's child and always will. Would you have let me remain with Dariq had you known I was expecting his child?"

"I'm sorry, Willow. I wouldn't have let you remain with your prince under any circumstances. I stand by my decision to save you and your child from living with a violent man. Now," he said cheerily, "about that tea. I'm famished."

A servant entered as if on cue with a tea cart weighed down with sandwiches, biscuits and tiny iced cakes. Monique poured, and offered Willow an assortment of food she had placed on a plate. Willow took the plate and nibbled on a sandwich.

They spoke of inconsequential things while they ate and drank. Willow managed to consume half the food on her plate and drink two cups of tea, which seemed to please her parents.

She really wasn't trying to be difficult; she was just desperately unhappy. She kept recalling Dariq's parting words and wondering if he had already found a woman to replace her.

Perhaps he had found more than one. What woman wouldn't find Dariq desirable? Willow prayed nightly for him, begging God to keep him safe.

Willow's thoughts were interrupted by the distant sound of the door knocker.

"I thought you told me no visitors were expected," Willow said, sending an anxious glance toward the parlor door.

Monique sent her a puzzled look. "None of my friends would venture out on a raw day like this," she replied with a shudder. "Unlike France, one never sees the sun in this dismal country."

Robert sent her a speaking look. "Oh, well, it is worth it to be with my family again," Monique quickly added.

A footman appeared in the doorway. "The Earl of Newcastle and his mother, Lady Bridgeton, and Reverend Faraday request an audience, milord."

Robert's brow furrowed. "Newcastle? I do not recognize the name. There *was* an Earl of Newcastle, but I believe he died without heirs many years ago. Show them in, Baxter, and have the tea tray refreshed."

Anxious to escape the ordeal of making small talk, Willow rose. "Please excuse me. I wish to retire to my room."

But it was too late to gracefully bow out. The earl, his

mother and the black-clad reverend waited in the doorway to be announced.

"The Earl of Newcastle, Lady Bridgeton and Reverend Faraday," Baxter intoned.

Sighing in resignation, Willow resumed her seat while her father greeted their guests.

"I am afraid you have the advantage, Lord Newcastle," Robert said. "Have we been introduced?"

"Not formally," Newcastle replied.

Willow's head snapped up. That voice! She knew it! She half rose from her chair. "Dariq?"

Robert looked from Willow to Newcastle, his bewilderment visibly apparent.

Willow took a wobbly step toward Newcastle, then another, and then her eyes rolled back and she started a slow downward spiral.

Newcastle reached her first, scooping her up moments before she reached the carpeted floor.

"What have you done to her?" Newcastle barked, his gray eyes blazing with fury.

"See here, Newcastle," Robert sputtered, "who in blazes are you?"

Lady Bridgeton stepped forward. "Please forgive us for barging in like this."

Monique rushed over to Willow, patting her cheek and murmuring in French as Newcastle laid her gently on a sofa and knelt beside her. As he had feared, seeing him in London had overwhelmed her, and he wished there had been some way to cushion the shock.

Newcastle searched Willow's face. She looked too gaunt and far too thin. His gaze traveled downward over her body, and stopped abruptly at the bulge beneath her skirts. His eyes widened and he spat out a curse. She was carrying his child! Why hadn't she told him?

"Will you please tell me what the three of you are doing here?" the marquis asked curtly.

Willow opened her eyes. Reaching up, she touched Dariq's face. "Dariq? Is it really you?"

"It is indeed, my love."

He helped her to sit up. "How . . . ? You're an earl? I do not understand."

Lady Bridgeton moved into Willow's view. "Dariq has always been an earl, my dear. He inherited my father's title. The legal end took a few weeks to clear the courts, but Dariq is now Earl of Newcastle and can take his rightful place in society."

Willow looked confused. "But Dariq is already a prince."

Dariq was still on his knees. He took Willow's hand and pressed a kiss into her palm. "A prince without a princess. Will you marry me, Willow? Will you be my countess? My life is meaningless without you."

"Now, hold on a minute," Bramston blustered. "I'm not sure you're right for my daughter."

Dariq sent him a quelling look. "Do you deny that Willow is carrying my child?"

"Well . . . er . . . of course not, but—"

"Then I am right for her," Dariq replied emphatically and turned to Willow. "Will you marry me, my love? I purchased a special license from the bishop and brought Reverend Faraday to perform the nuptials. Your parents and my mother are here, so we need not delay."

"Perhaps we should leave the young people alone for a few minutes," Lady Bridgeton suggested.

"I am not sure we should," Bramston argued.

"Of course we should, Robert," Monique argued, sending her husband a silent message. "Willow and her Dariq need to talk. Come along, Lady Bridgeton, Reverend Faraday. We shall take tea elsewhere."

Robbed of speech, Willow merely stared at Dariq. Stylishly dressed, his hair trimmed, he could easily pass as a member of the *ton*. Though his appearance had changed, his distinctive gray eyes had not. They were now regarding her with concern.

"I am sorry my arrival was delayed, my love," Dariq explained, "but it took a fortnight to set aside my hurt, gather my wits and realize why you had left me. Pain has a way of overriding common sense. It wasn't until I decided to follow you that Mother told me about the title waiting for me in England."

"You really are an earl," Willow whispered. "At first I thought it was a ploy to get around my father's objections."

"Aye, love, I really am an earl. The title is legally mine; I had but to claim it."

"No more piracy?"

"That part of my life is over."

"You intend to remain in England?"

"If you consent to be my wife, there is no other place I want to be." He spread his hand over her stomach. "Why didn't you tell me about our child? If I hadn't come to England, I never would have known." His voice held a note of censure.

"I knew that if I told you, you would never let me go. I gave Papa my solemn promise that I would return to England if he helped you escape. He knew you lived a violent life and feared for my safety. He did not learn about the baby until we were halfway to England. Are you angry with me?"

"Furious. But grateful that I gained my senses in time to bring myself to London and wed you before our babe is born."

He rose up from his knees, sat beside Willow and gathered her into his arms. He kissed her with such tenderness and love that she felt guilty for the pain she had caused him. But he was alive, and he might not have been if her father had not given his help.

"I missed you, love. Living in England will be a jarring adjustment, but I know I can do it with you at my side. Mother seems happy to be in her homeland again and is renewing acquaintances. They are helping to ease her way back into society. The scandal of her wedding a Turkish sultan has been long forgotten." He grinned. "In fact, Mother is being actively courted by society matrons eager to learn about her life in a harem."

"Saliha Sultana deserves happiness," Willow said, smiling through her tears of joy.

"Her name is Lady Ellen Bridgeton now. Saliha Sultana is a title she will never hold again, just as I exchanged the rank of prince for earl. I am now Lord Dariq Bridgeton, Earl of Newcastle. You will make an exceptional countess."

There were so many questions Willow wanted answered. "Where is Mustafa? Did he come to England with you?"

"Mustafa is still my trusted friend. He wouldn't think of letting me come to a strange land without him. You will see him again when you move to my townhouse. I also own a country estate in Kent. I visited it briefly after I arrived in England. It's being renovated even as we speak. It has a large nursery, which I'm sure you will appreciate."

"Did Ali Hara and Kamel accompany you to England?"

"They wished to remain on Lipsi and carry on my legacy of piracy under Captain Juad. The captain cannot return to Turkey as long as Ibrahim is sultan."

"I shall miss them," Willow said wistfully. She sent him a watery smile. "Though not as much as I missed you. After I returned to England, I had naught but my child to live for. The light had gone from my soul."

"I am here now, love. Just say the word and Reverend Faraday will marry us. I have the special license in my pocket. Please say yes, Willow."

Willow searched his face. "Can you truly be happy here? 'Tis not the kind of life you are accustomed to."

"How can I not be happy? I have you and my mother, and soon our child will make us a family. And I have my ship. I've renamed her *Lady Willow* in your honor. My fortune will let us live in style for the rest of our lives, and the wealth I inherited from my grandfather can be kept in trust for our children."

Willow touched his face, smiling through her tears. "I never asked you if you wanted children."

"With you, I do. For the first time in my memory, I look forward to becoming a husband and father. Until you came into my life, my needs were served by concubines."

Willow slanted him a stern look. "Once we are wed, there will be no concubines or mistresses."

Dariq's hopes soared. "Does that mean you'll accept my proposal?"

She threw her arms around his neck. "I will marry you now, today, whenever you say. I have been lost without you."

He kissed her with desperate longing; Willow felt the power of his love fill her heart and returned it with the same measure of sincerity.

"Ahem!"

Willow glanced over Dariq's shoulder at the open door. She broke off the kiss and smiled at her father. He walked into the room, followed in close order by Monique, Lady Bridgeton and Reverend Faraday.

"Have you had enough time to hash out your differences?" the marquis asked.

"We are going to get married, Papa," Willow said. "I hope you have no objections."

Dariq stood, facing the marquis squarely. "I love your daughter, my lord. She will not suffer in my care, you can depend upon it."

"And I shall make sure he keeps his word," Lady Bridgeton added.

Bramston stroked his chin. "Are you sincere about giving up piracy?"

"Absolutely. My reason for becoming a pirate is no longer valid. I have avenged my brothers' deaths many times over."

"Where do you intend to live?"

"If Willow agrees, we can split our time between my country estate in Kent and my townhouse in London. My finances are in excellent order, I can keep Willow in the manner to which she is accustomed."

"What do you think, Monique?" Bramston asked his wife.

"The earl must love Willow a great deal, to give up his former life and settle in England, Robert."

"I love Willow with all my heart. You cannot keep us apart. She carries my child—one I want very much."

"Might I say something?" the reverend interrupted.

"Of course, Reverend, have your say," Bramston allowed.

"Apparently, your daughter carries Lord Newcastle's child, would it not be expedient to encourage their marriage?"

"I am not so sure," Bramston objected. "I want my daughter to be happy, and I am not convinced Newcastle the right man for her."

"No man but Dariq can make me happy, Papa," Willow asserted. "I am going to marry him with or without your approval."

Monique cleared her throat. "Of course your papa approves, *ma petite*. Is that not so, Robert?"

Bramston stared at Dariq in silent contemplation before deigning to speak. "It seems you have won over the women in the family, Newcastle. Though I still harbor doubts, you have my consent to wed my daughter."

The reverend dug in his pocket for his Bible. "Shall we begin?"

"The wedding can wait until Willow changes into something more appropriate," Monique said.

"My son has waited this long," Lady Bridgeton replied in agreement. "I am sure he won't mind waiting a while longer."

Dariq groaned but did not contradict his mother.

One hour and fifteen minutes later, wearing a sea-green silk gown that matched her eyes, Willow walked down the stairs to join Dariq. Her golden curls had been fashioned in a becoming style atop her head and crowned by her mother's wedding veil, held in place by a diamond tiara that had belonged to her grandmother.

Dariq saw an angel walking toward him. She looked even more beautiful than she had the first time they'd crossed paths. On that fateful day, she had been ready to do battle with him, her green eyes spitting fire and defiance.

His thoughts scattered when she reached him, love shining in her expressive eyes. Soon this angelic spitfire would be his to love, cherish and protect the rest of his life.

A brief but moving ceremony united them in holy wedlock. Had anyone asked Bramston at that moment, even he would have agreed that his daughter and the pirate prince belonged together.

Bramston's staff, despite the short notice, had prepared a festive meal to celebrate the nuptials. As soon as possible after the meal, the happy couple took leave of Willow's family. Hugging her parents hard, Willow left her father's home with the man she had promised to love, honor and obey until death parted them.

Mustafa was on hand to greet them at Dariq's townhouse. His welcoming smile cheered Willow. She had missed his large, comforting presence. After introducing the servants to their new mistress, Lady Ellen excused herself and retired to her own apartment.

"I will show you around the townhouse tomorrow," Dariq said. "I cannot wait to have you to myself." Sweeping her into his arms, he took the stairs two at a time, arriving in the master suite breathless.

Willow laughed when she saw that the bed had been turned down and the bedchamber was decorated with a profusion of flowers against a background of soft candlelight. "You were pretty sure of yourself, weren't you?"

"Perhaps I was a bit optimistic. Turn around so I can unfasten your gown. You look exhausted. Perhaps you should go straight to bed."

Willow smiled at him over her shoulder. "I will go to bed if you join me. This is our wedding night."

Dariq turned her around, peeled the gown from her and lifted her out of the billowing folds. His gaze fell to her stomach; the bulge appeared more pronounced without benefit of clothing.

"I want to make love to you more than I've ever wanted anything in my life," Dariq murmured, "but I don't want to do anything to harm you or our child."

"Making love will make me extremely happy, and I'm

sure our child won't object," Willow teased. "Making love is still permissible, if my girth doesn't disgust you. Mama told me some men are squeamish about touching their wives when they are increasing."

Dariq pulled her into his arms and caressed her lovingly. "How could you disgust me when 'tis my child growing inside you? Touching you, loving you, is a pleasure I will never grow tired of."

He carried her to his bed and laid her down. Without taking his eyes from her, he tore off his clothing and joined her. As he made love to her with aching tenderness, kissing her, caressing her, arousing her, pleasuring her, Willow knew their love would survive any adversity fate placed in their path.

Their new acquaintances would know Dariq as an earl, but in her heart he would always be her dearly beloved pirate prince.

Epilogue

Three Months Later

Little Lord Phillip Robert Bridgeton was born on a cool spring day without complications at Bridgeton Manor in Kent. He was perfect in every way, especially to his doting parents. Among those eagerly awaiting the birth at Dariq's country estate were Mustafa, Lord Bramston, his wife Monique, and Lady Ellen Bridgeton.

A few days later, the *Lady Willow* sailed to Lipsi to inform those who knew and loved Dariq and Willow of the birth of Prince Dariq's son and heir, the future Earl of Newcastle.

Author's Note

While it is true that some sultans, especially those in countries that were part of the Ottoman Empire, ordered the deaths of their father's male offspring to protect their power, my story is pure fiction, as are the characters and names. There really was a Sultan Ibrahim, but he did not exist in the time period in which my story takes place.

As my readers know, I love to set my stories in exotic locations and do so as often as I can. Medievals are also a favorite of mine and I will probably write another. Many of my readers have been asking for another Western, and I just want to say I haven't abandoned them. I believe there might be another Western in my future.

My next book, however, is the result of my recent trip to Eastern Europe, where I encountered a flourishing Gypsy community. Those traveling nomads captured my imagination, and from that visit came *Gypsy Lover*, my next book. Look for it in May 2005.

I love hearing from readers. Write me at P.O. Box 3471, Holiday, FL 34690. Please enclose a self-addressed, stamped envelope for a newsletter and bookmark. Visit my website at www.conniemason.com or reach me by email at conmason@aol.com.

CONNIE MASON

The Last Rogue

All London is stunned by Lucas, Viscount Westmore's vow to give up the fair sex and exile himself to St. Ives. The infamous rake is known for his love of luxury and his way with the ladies, just as the rugged Cornish coast is known for its savagery, its fearsome gales and its smugglers.

But Luc is determined to turn away from the seduction of white thighs and perfumed flesh that had once ended in tragedy. He never guessed the stormy nights of Cornwall would bring unlooked-for danger, the thrill of the chase, and a long-legged beauty who tempts him like no other. As illicit cargo changes hands, as her flashing green eyes challenge his very masculinity, he longs for nothing so much as to lose himself in . . . *Bliss.*

BIRTHING
the ELEPHANT

BIRTHING
the ELEPHANT

The woman's go-for-it!
guide to overcoming
the big challenges
of launching a business

KARIN ABARBANEL and BRUCE FREEMAN

Ten Speed Press
PO Box 7123
Berkeley, California 94707
www.tenspeed.com

Distributed in Australia by Simon and Schuster Australia, in Canada by Ten Speed Press Canada, in New Zealand by Southern Publishers Group, in South Africa by Real Books, and in the United Kingdom and Europe by Publishers Group UK.

Cover and interior design by Toni Tajima
Interior production by Colleen Cain

Library of Congress Cataloging-in-Publication Data
Abarbanel, Karin.
  Birthing the elephant : the woman's go-for-it! guide to overcoming the big challenges of launching a business / by Karin Abarbanel and Bruce Freeman.
    p. cm.
  Summary: "A female entrepreneur's guide to navigating the psychological aspects of launching and building a business during the first 18 months"--Provided by publisher.
  Includes index.
  ISBN 978-1-58008-887-9
  1. New business enterprises--Management. 2. Women-owned business enterprises--Management. 3. Entrepreneurship. I. Freeman, Bruce. II. Title.
  HD62.5.A278 2008
  658.1'1082--dc22
                    2007039368

Printed in the United States of America
First printing, 2008

1 2 3 4 5 6 7 8 9 10 — 12 11 10 09 08

To my family, whose loving support
keeps me going and growing:
Dorothy and Albert;
David and Alex;
Stephanie, Judy, and Peter;
Joan, Luis, and Aunt Sandy.
—KARIN

To the five women I have lived with:
Joyce, Ilene, Erica, Mom, and Cuddles (the family cat).
Thank you for your love, support, and inspiration.
—BRUCE

And to all aspiring entrepreneurs:
may this book
encourage and inspire you to
follow your dreams!

✳ ✳ ✳

Life is either a daring adventure or nothing.

—HELEN KELLER

✴ Contents ✴

✳ Acknowledgments ✳

Writing this book has been exciting but challenging—and we've needed lots of help to make it happen. First, our deepest thanks go to all our experts and to the wonderful women business owners who shared their stories and hard-won wisdom with us. Their generosity and willingness to help other women succeed is inspiring—and one of the things that makes women entrepreneurs so special.

We also received invaluable guidance and advice along the way from more people than we can list here. But we would especially like to thank Bobbi Brown, founder of Bobbi Brown Cosmetics; Dr. Kim Cordingly, consultant, Job Accommodation Network (JAN)/Small Business and Self-Employment Service; Dr. Rob Gilbert, Montclair State University; Christine Serrano Glassner, regional II advocate, U.S. Small Business Administration, Office of Advocacy; Dr. Christine Horak, assistant director of research, the Center for Women's Business Research; Liz Lange, founder and president of Liz Lange Maternity; Dr. Nan Langowitz, associate professor and cofounder of the Center for Women's Leadership at Babson College; Harry Menta, public affairs specialist, U.S. Small Business Administration; Steven W. Nissen, National Capital Chapter, director of employment programs, and Arney Rosenblat, associate vice president, Public Affairs, National Multiple Sclerosis Society; Sue Tovey and Sande Foster, partners, Priority Solutions Unlimited; and Marlene Waldock, founder, Women's Empowerment Symposiums.

We would also like to express our gratitude for a great job to Alice Bryant Cubicciotti, Linda D'Amico, Joe Pinto, Rebecca Siegel, Karin Waldbrand, and Diana Layman; our agent, Grace Freedson, of Grace Freedson's Publishing Network; and our acquiring editor, Julie Bennett, our project editor, Lisa Westmoreland, and the staff of Ten Speed Press.

* Entrepreneurs and Experts *

These people generously shared their insights and advice:

Anne Afshari and **Laura Hagler,** cofounders of Exclusively RNs, an Internet-based phone counseling service for expectant mothers staffed by registered nurses

Alexandria Brown, Internet specialist and Million Dollar Marketing Coach

Bobbi Brown, founder of Bobbi Brown Cosmetics, beauty expert and adviser, and best-selling author

Roxanne Coady, founder and owner of R. J. Julia Booksellers, an award-winning independent bookstore in Madison, Connecticut

Karen Curro and **Susan Edelman,** founders and co-owners of Laugh Out Loud, a Life Is Good Genuine Neighborhood Shoppe in Montclair, New Jersey

Monica Doss, president of the Council for Entrepreneurial Development (CED) and a leading adviser to entrepreneurial businesses

Lisa Druxman, author and founder of Stroller Strides, an award-winning franchising program specializing in fitness for new mothers and infants

Ronnie Fliss, founder of Fat Murray's Doggy Treats, a company that markets healthy, fresh-baked treats via pet shops and the Internet

Dr. Rob Gilbert, author, peak performance coach, motivational speaker, and professor at Montclair State University

Dr. Edward Hallowell, author, psychiatrist, instructor at Harvard Medical School, and founder of the Hallowell Center

Crystal Johnson, president of Sienna at Home, a home fashion and decor company in Houston offering consulting, a retail store, and online services

Sharon Joseph, CEO and cofounder, with Gail Richards, of Harlem Lanes, the first U.S. bowling alley to be owned by African American women

Cathy Kerns, founder of Style Sticks, an Internet-based company that manufactures and markets customized, fashionable walking sticks

Liz Lange, founder and president of the fashion design and retailing company Liz Lange Maternity

Dr. Nan Langowitz, associate professor and cofounder of the Center for Women's Leadership at Babson College

Sarah Levy, founder and president of Sarah's Pastries & Candies, a Chicago-based retail store and company that makes gourmet chocolates and baked goods

Suzanne Lyons, cofounder of Snowfall Films, WindChill Films, and the Flash Forward Institute, a career workshop program for entertainment professionals

Gina Maschek, cofounder and owner of Beyond Blossoms, an online floral delivery service specializing in European-style bouquets

John McCarthy, stress management expert and cofounder of the Institute for Coaching

Ray Miller, stress relief and self-improvement expert, entrepreneur, and founder of Stress Relief Solutions

Brenda Newberry, chairman/CEO of the Newberry Group, an information technology consultancy, and an award-winning mentor to small businesses

Jennifer Lovitt Riggs, founder and president of Nota Bene Shoes, a company that designs and manufactures fashionable shoes for active women

Becky Rohrer, owner of the College Inn, a bed-and-breakfast in Westerville, Ohio

Patricia and **Adam Scribner,** founders of Patricia's Yarns, a Hoboken-based specialty shop offering beautiful yarns and instruction at all levels

Dr. Al Siebert, resiliency researcher, Director of the Resiliency Center, and author of *The Resiliency Advantage* and *The Survivor Personality*

Karen Spitz, president of Licensing Link Ltd., a leading Manhattan-based company in the global licensing industry

Marlene Waldock, founder of First Impressions Communications and the Because We Are Women: Celebrating Possibilities empowerment initiative

For more information on these entrepreneurs and experts, please visit www.birthingtheelephant.com.

✻ Foreword ✻

The Oxford dictionary defines an entrepreneur as "a person who undertakes or controls a business or enterprise and bears the risk of profit or loss." My definition is "someone who has the vision to create something that others want."

When I launched my cosmetics company, I didn't reinvent the wheel. I just modernized what was the standard. My lipsticks looked natural (rather than fake and garish), they felt great on the skin, and they smelled good. Similarly, my business role models have all reimagined existing products. From Apple's Steve Jobs and Virgin Group's Richard Branson to Celestial Seasonings' Mo Siegel and Starbucks' Howard Schultz, successful entrepreneurs give consumers what they want—a better, more modern product. A great idea is just the beginning. To be a successful entrepreneur, you have to be able to bridge the gap between your vision and what is feasible. Some people call this a business plan. It entails everything from figuring out how to fund your project to how to make your product, how to spread the word about your product, and, finally, how to sell your product.

Whether it's a small business or a big business you want to start, always stay true to your vision. Start small (that way you make only small mistakes). And always listen to your gut—it will never lead you astray. I hope that my story, along with the other advice in this book, empowers you and helps you bring your ideas to fruition. All my best.

Bobbi Brown

Founder, Bobbi Brown Cosmetics

✳ Introduction ✳

We've never met you, but, because you're reading this book, we know something about you that you may not have shared with anyone else—not even the people closest to you. We know that you have a dream. And not just any dream, but an enterprising, entrepreneurial one! This dream of yours may be modest—or it may be big and bold. It may be brand new or a goal that you've secretly harbored for years.

Think about it! Wouldn't it be wonderful to have a business of your own, do work you really love, and feel fulfilled? No more burnout. No more corporate politics or day-to-day indignities. No more useless meetings. No more pink slips or career plateaus. Instead, you'd have the freedom to design your own destiny and exercise greater control over your time and talent. The chance to create a product or service that you're passionate about. And the opportunity to grow, not just wiser but wealthier as well.

Sounds appealing, doesn't it? All this and more can be yours as an entrepreneur. Achieving the rewards that a small business offers *isn't* an impossible dream. Yes, it's risky and demanding: many start-ups never take flight and truly prosper. Then again, many of them do! But beating the odds isn't easy. To do it, you'll need help—and lots of it—because the biggest challenges you'll face aren't about your pocketbook or your prospects—they're about your *psyche*.

Helping you figure out how to reinvent yourself, go after what you want, and survive the emotional roller-coaster ride you'll experience in starting a new business is what this book is all about.

Birthing the Elephant is not your standard start-up guide. It won't tell you how to write a business plan or talk to your banker. Instead, it's a portable success coach. We think of it as a *What to Expect When You're Expecting* for women making the leap into entrepreneurship. It will take you step-by-step through the life cycle of a small-business launch and give you a practical road map to help you navigate the rocky emotional terrain you'll face. It will also show you smart moves to make

1

and alert you to predictable patterns and problems you'll encounter so that they won't distract, derail, or discourage you.

Launching a start-up is both exciting and intensely demanding. In fact, it's a lot like birthing an elephant! It's a huge undertaking, it takes about twenty-two months, and, if you stay with it, you'll end up with a healthy, lovable, bouncing business to call your very own!

Of course, getting there takes tremendous staying power and the right tools. Unless you can find the skill and will to tap your strengths—and manage your fears—the best business plan, the biggest bank account in town, and the savviest marketing strategy won't help you when the going gets tough. And, as the women in this book will tell you, it *will* get tough. Clients and suppliers will fail you, the phone won't ring for days, and for weeks (and even months) on end your bank balance will look more like Mother Teresa's than Madonna's.

At the same time, you'll enjoy newfound strength and confidence every time you soar over an obstacle. Surviving your start-up will put you in touch with talents you never knew you had—and inspire you to draw upon inner wellsprings of energy and creativity to boost your success. With the advice and support you'll find on every page of this book, you'll soon learn how to navigate even the choppiest of small-business seas.

We know exactly what the tough times are like. We both launched our own independent consultancies so that we could take charge of our work lives and our financial destinies. We've had fat years—and lean ones. We know what it takes to succeed and how vital it is to have a support system. That's why we've teamed up to write this book—and why the gifted women entrepreneurs you'll meet in these pages are so eager to share their own ups and downs with you.

So think of *Birthing the Elephant* as your own personal start-up survival kit. Inside, you'll find an upbeat yet practical guide to the first eighteen to twenty-four months of your venture, when the pressures of building a new work life make you most vulnerable. We've also packed your kit with quick tips at the end of each chapter to crystallize the takeaway points, and checklists to spur you to action on key start-up challenges. We've even included Resources with more helpful tools (see page 198). And throughout the book are inspiring success stories from entrepreneurs. These women are going to act as your mentors. You'll learn how they launched their businesses, how they handled obstacles and problems, what they did that worked—and didn't. They'll give you a head start on the road to success by helping you avoid the mistakes they made and inspiring you with their grit and staying power.

You'll meet Bobbi Brown, the cosmetics company founder; Lisa Druxman, a fitness pro and franchiser; Sarah Levy, a pastry chef and chocolate maker; Suzanne Lyons, an award-winning independent filmmaker; and Brenda Newberry, a high-tech entrepreneur—all of whom launched businesses in the industries where they had started their careers. You'll also meet women who catapulted themselves into entirely new fields, like Liz Lange, who never studied design yet started a breakout maternity clothing business; Ronnie Fliss, a finance exec who dove into the pet-food industry; Cathy Kerns, who left marketing for manufacturing; and Patricia Scribner, who moved from corporate life to crafts.

Armed with the insider advice these women will be sharing with you, you'll be well equipped to succeed. With their help, we'll discuss timing your move, the stages you can expect to go through, and the pitfalls you'll want to avoid. Along the way, we'll also explore the rich rewards that you'll reap as you craft a way of working that's uniquely your own—one that truly expresses your values, talents, and dreams.

"Starting your own business is really about being your own hero." That's how one woman described her personal quest for independence. After talking to many incredibly talented and resourceful entrepreneurs about their trials and triumphs, we've learned just how right she is. What bold adventurers they are! If there is one thing the world needs today, surely it is more heroic dreamers—and *doers*. Why not read on—and join them?

Your dream awaits!

Chapter 1

Design Your Destiny

Having a business isn't really about control,
but I get to design my own destiny.

—SUZANNE LYONS

You're ready to strike out on your own. Finally, you're going to do work that you love—work that reflects your personality and passions and is in harmony with your family's needs—and, oh yes, you're going to make lots of money while you're at it! It's time to run your own show. You've paid your dues. You've earned this chance, haven't you?

Come down from that castle in the air for just a minute! It's true that being your own boss offers many potential rewards. But it will also make some startling new demands on you: the need to do more with less, assume unfamiliar risks, wear many hats, and, at least for a while, give up the trappings of success. Still want in? Of course! We all do.

In making this decision, you've set an ambitious but totally achievable goal. All around you, women are reinventing themselves as entrepreneurs and transforming their personal visions into fulfilling work. Every sixty seconds, five women launch new ventures somewhere in

*Based on data from the Kauffman Entrepreneurial Index analyzed by the Center for Women's Business Research.

5

the United States. That adds up to more than seven thousand start-ups per day—and more than 2.5 million a year.* Astounding, isn't it?

What's fueling this surge in women-owned start-ups? First and foremost, there's the turbocharged Internet, which has boosted small-business owners' power and reach in amazing ways. In just a few short years, the Web has triggered a small-business explosion by creating dynamic new sales and marketing channels—and providing niche sellers with easy access to millions of niche buyers. It's also leveled the playing field by enabling small businesses to compete for profits and court customers on a 24/7 basis. One entrepreneur described the awesome experience of standing in an Internet cafe in Hong Kong, watching her website pop up—and realizing that *at that very moment* she could order her product halfway around the world from her home-business base in Orlando!

The Internet is also a vast ocean of information, with many an island of advice created especially for entrepreneurial women. Online "e-zines," networking groups, funding sources, training tools, and market data are all just a quick click away. These resources offer not just valuable facts and figures but also a sense of community: today, women-owned businesses are building support systems that are both vibrant and enormously diverse.

Stage-of-life shifts are also stoking the entrepreneurial engine. If fifty is the new forty, then there are vast numbers of women who have years of productive, high-speed living ahead of them. As they ponder fresh ideas about how to spend that time, many baby boomers who've made their mark in corporate jobs are exploring new work options more attuned to their changing self-images and aspirations. You may be one of them yourself!

All this growth creates enormous clout: today, as never before, women are attracting attention and resources from major companies who want their goodwill and, more important, their business. To woo women entrepreneurs, these companies are offering seed funding, running conferences, and showcasing the success stories of women business owners. This intense corporate interest is great news for you. All in all, there's never been a better time to launch your start-up.

Winning the Small-Business Mind Game

Despite the promising climate for entrepreneurs, the realities of small-business ownership remain as daunting as ever. According to the U.S. Small Business Administration, one-third of all new ventures won't survive their first two years and more than one-half won't survive through year four. What separates those who make it from those who don't? You might think it's money. Most people do. While that's a big factor, it's *not* the biggest one. We've spoken to top entrepreneurs and small-business experts all across the country, and most people in the trenches agree that the real key to success is *winning the small-business mind game*.

Succeeding takes more than courage and business savvy. It also takes a whole new mind-set. To survive a start-up, you need to learn how to *think and act like an entrepreneur*.

In making this move, you're not just changing your job, or changing your lifestyle, or changing careers. *You are changing your identity*. At a stroke, your office, your title, a regular paycheck, the rhythm of your workday, the deadlines, the business lunches, the built-in support system—are gone. Suddenly, you're on your own: everything begins and ends with you.

Unless you can cultivate an entrepreneurial approach, even the strongest business plan and rock-solid expertise won't be enough to ensure that your enterprise survives and thrives. And unless you can find the inner strength to rebound from the setbacks you'll meet, you'll find yourself down for the count no matter how promising your new venture is. Moments of doubt can be triggered by the loss of a client, a product disaster, or the incredible shrinking bank balance that plagues most start-ups.

How you respond to challenges like these makes all the difference to your success or failure. You can either collapse in a heap or find the staying power to land on your feet. This is the most demanding aspect of making a small business work—pushing past those times when you feel overwhelmed and everything seems to be falling apart.

Different Paths, Shared Goals

The gifted women you'll come to know in these pages all have different backgrounds and have traveled different roads in building their businesses. Yet we found four themes running through their stories:

1. *Seizing the moment:* Almost all the women we spoke with experienced a sense of urgency once they committed to launching. When the drive to strike out on their own gathered momentum, it seemed to push them forward. Something clicked, something cracked, something sprang inside them—and they simply *had* to make a move.

2. *Pursuing personal growth:* The women we interviewed expressed a strong commitment to work as a way of achieving personal fulfillment. In many cases, they had found the conventional career paths they were on to be too narrow or sluggish. When opportunities for growth didn't exist, their jobs quickly lost their luster—even if they were quite lucrative. In response, they felt compelled to challenge and stretch themselves in new ways.

3. *Balancing work and life:* Harmonizing values in their business and personal lives emerged as a key driver for many of the women we interviewed. Some of them felt drained by inflexible work situations and conflicts with family priorities. Others became disenchanted when their personal values and those of their employers proved to be seriously out of sync.

4. *Realizing a vision:* Nearly all the women we interviewed talked about building their lives around a vision. For some, this vision is clear and easily described: helping new mothers regain their fitness or creating elegant home decor. For others, clarifying their vision is an ongoing challenge—the original concept that inspired their start-up has proved to be a moving target, redefining itself as circumstances change or new markets emerge.

Finding the fulfillment that comes from achieving goals like these won't come easily; you'll have to earn it day by day. Is it worth the effort? Absolutely! Are there rewards a small business can give you that a corporate job can't? Absolutely! Running your own show offers you the power to orchestrate all aspects of your work in a way that lets you express your personal values while creating a satisfying and profitable lifestyle. Above all, women who strike out on their own want more freedom and flexibility, according to a national survey by Ladies Who Launch, a networking group that runs incubators for entrepreneurs. "Launching is good for self-esteem, creativity, and happiness," observes cofounder Beth Schoenfeldt.

A major small-business study by Intuit, a business-software developer, confirms this view. According to its findings, "American entrepreneurship will reflect a huge upswing in the number of women. The glass ceiling that has limited women's growth in traditional corporate career paths will send a rich talent pool into the small-business sector. Among them: 'mompreneurs'—mothers who start part-time, home-based businesses, often with the help of the Internet. These personal businesses will be launched by people who may not even consider themselves small-business owners."*

What else do women want? Along with freedom and flexibility, two other powerful drivers—the desire for challenge and personal achievement—emerged as the prime motivators cited by two hundred women business owners in an ongoing study conducted by Babson College's Center for Women's Leadership.**

"It's clearly about personal achievement and autonomy, which, by the way, is not all that different for men," notes Dr. Nan Langowitz, cofounder of the Center for Women's Leadership and an associate professor at Babson College, which runs the country's top-ranked program for aspiring entrepreneurs. "In many, though not all, corporate settings," adds Dr. Langowitz, "as women progress in their careers, the opportunities they see ahead of them aren't necessarily that exciting—and the trade-offs against their time and compensation may not work. So they choose to create their own businesses, their own opportunities, and their own compensation."

* Intuit Future of Small Business Report, sponsored by Intuit Inc. and authored by the Institute for the Future, 2007.
** The Top Women-Led Businesses in Massachusetts: Lessons from 2000 to 2004, sponsored by Babson College and the Commonwealth Institute.

Trading Comfort for Independence

Simply put, going into business for yourself means that you've made a decision to give up comfort for independence: you are choosing to forgo security for the ability to make decisions that put you at the center of your work life. "Starting a business is like being the general contractor of your own life," says Karen Curro, co-owner of a Life is Good store. "And, although it's a lot of work," she adds, "it's your life and you're in control versus someone else running it."

It's an empowering, but challenging trade-off. Making the shift from employee to entrepreneur is one of the toughest career—and life—changes imaginable. It affects your self-esteem, your family, your finances, your health, your retirement plans, your future, your children's futures, your hopes and dreams, your fears. Shaping an independent work life is, above all, an act of improvisation, one that takes both courage and ingenuity. Although this way of working offers enormous flexibility, it won't give you total control over your time and resources. Especially during your start-up phase, *your business controls you*—you don't control the business.

There's also an enormous "cultural" gap between working for a corporation and working for yourself. It's a lot like the difference between sleeping in a house and living in a tent. In a corporation you have all the comforts of home: people to confer with, support from other divisions, an office, perks, and a travel budget. In a small business, you're camping out: patching together new work patterns, watching your budget like a hawk, making things up as you go, pushing yourself to get the next client or make the next call.

"Are you willing to give up that beautiful four-color copy machine that automatically collates and staples?" asks Cathy Kerns, the founder of Style Sticks, when she speaks about small business. "Are you willing to give up a supply room that has anything you could ever need? Are you willing to give up the casts of thousands there to support you and cover your back at all times? Just how much are you willing to give up that you've come to love and adore about the corporate world—and take for granted? The infrastructure of a corporation is very hard to live without if you've been supported by it for a long time. So, stop and think about that copy machine!"

Along with these practical concerns, emotional challenges and worries often move front and center when you start a new business. You may experience loneliness and the feeling that you're no longer part of the business mainstream. Isolation is one of the biggest dangers that many entrepreneurs face: they have to force themselves to get out, network, be visible, and promote their ventures. Then, of course, there's the Big M: *money*. Anxiety about holding everything together financially is a major issue. If you're still a corporate employee or between jobs, then all the concerns raised here are ones that you'll need to think long and hard about. Crafting an independent, self-structured life may sound romantic, but will this path really meet your needs, both professionally and personally, not just today but six months from now? What about in five or ten years? Is this a work option that makes sense for you—one that you're prepared to commit your time and talents to?

Running a Small Business: A Yen for Yin and Yang

If there's one thing we learned from our interviews, it's that if your psyche has a cold, your business will sneeze! Time and again, your strengths and weaknesses will be exposed and tested—especially in the early days of your start-up. No one knows this better than Roxanne Coady, the founder of R. J. Julia Booksellers, an award-winning independent bookstore and a beloved landmark in Madison, Connecticut.

"When you start a small business," Roxanne observes, "you are holding up a mirror to yourself. There's nowhere to hide. If you have a problem, you can't blame it on the shareholders. You can't blame it on your boss. You can't blame it on the corporate culture. You actually have less freedom than if you had a job. But you have a lot of autonomy: you can independently make decisions that impact your work or your family life. When you have your own business, it's all about the yin and the yang, the ups and the downs. The good news is you have autonomy. The bad news is you're accountable. The good news is you've got, not freedom, but choices. And the bad news is you're going to have to live with the repercussions of your decisions."

What You'll Need to Succeed

To get your business up and running, you'll need to see yourself as the composer of your own life—someone who can orchestrate a satisfying whole out of the unexpected events, disruptions, and emotional intensity that pursuing an independent work life involves. You're going to have to be unstoppable! If you hit an obstacle, you're going to have to go over, around, under, and through it. What other inner resources will you have to tap? Here's a brief look at some of the essentials you'll need in your start-up survival kit.

PASSIONATE COMMITMENT TO YOUR BUSINESS IDEA

If the real-estate mantra is "Location, location, location," then the entrepreneurial mantra is "Passion, passion, passion!" Do what you love and love what you do: we heard this time and again from the women we interviewed. If you are lukewarm or conflicted, then think twice about taking this road. Without a deeply rooted belief in the importance of your venture and its potential for success, your business is not likely to thrive and probably won't survive.

"Having talent was important for me," observes Crystal Johnson, founder of Sienna at Home, "but the marriage of talent with passion is what has kept me going. It's passion that drives persistence. If you're passionate about something, you're just not going to give up on it. And it will not give up on you either! There have been times when I've tried to walk away from design, I really have, and it just keeps coming right at me! There have been times where there are doors closed or obstacles come up, and instead of stopping or turning or retreating, I just go around them or find a different way." Passion is the fuel that propels successful start-ups; without its power, you'll quickly lose momentum when you hit a roadblock; with it, you can overcome whatever obstacles you encounter. "In any type of entrepreneurial venture, if you're truly passionate, how can you possibly fail?" asks Dr. Rob Gilbert, a peak performance coach. "Look at what you're competing against! You know the 80-20 rule: 20 percent of employees do 80 percent of the work; 20 percent of salespeople make 80 percent of the sales. Most people aren't passionate; their heart isn't in it, they're not willing to do more than expected. Even many entrepreneurs are in business, but they're not into it—they're not totally committed. Or they may be into it for the short term, but not the long term."

COURAGE: THE STRENGTH TO MANAGE YOUR FEARS

"Courage is doing what you're afraid to do. There can be no courage unless you're scared." That's how Eddie Rickenbacker, an ace aviator in World War I, described his ability to face danger. General George Patton put it another way: "Courage is fear holding on a minute longer." You may think of entrepreneurs as bold risk-takers who carve out market niches where others fear to tread. Although there's some truth to this, courage and fear go hand in hand. Successful entrepreneurs don't overcome their fears; they learn to manage them.

Doing what you're afraid to do and holding on when you feel like letting go: that's a pretty accurate description of the kind of staying power it takes to run a business. In talking to women of all ages and backgrounds, we found that just about everyone experienced some degree of fear when they launched their venture. Going into business isn't about *not* being frightened or anxious. It's about *not letting fear stop you* from following your dream.

THE WILLINGNESS TO INVEST HUGE AMOUNTS OF TIME

The classic definition of an entrepreneur is someone who will gladly work sixteen hours a day for herself to avoid working eight hours a day for someone else. During your launch stage, the demands your business makes can seem never ending. In fact, those old days on the job may seem almost leisurely compared to your new situation. That's why loving what you do is so important, because you'll be doing *lots* of it—more than you ever dreamed!

Brenda Newberry knows all about those long hours. She vividly remembers burning the midnight oil during the early days of her IT consultancy—especially the time she committed to finishing a report right before she flew to Washington for a meeting. "It was a rainy, rainy night," she recalls. "It was three in the morning and I was getting ready to go to Kinko's because I didn't have a scanner at the time. My husband, Maurice, said, 'You can't go out at this time of night by yourself!' So he got in the car with me. And, as we were driving in the pouring rain in the dead of night, he turned to me and said, 'Would you tell me one more time why you're doing this?'"

INGENUITY IN BALANCING WORK AND FAMILY

Separating your business life from your family life will be an ongoing challenge. Turning off the business-obsessed part of your brain often proves extremely difficult. And time for yourself? That's the first thing to go. Yet it's vital that you do find the time to take care of yourself because if you don't you can easily crash and burn. The bottom line: You'll have less personal time, not more. This fact alone can place an enormous strain on your health, your family, and your friendships.

If you're a mother with young children, your time and attention will be scattered like the Lego pieces on your dining room floor. You'll quickly learn that a home-based business isn't the magic solution to the childcare dilemma that you may have been hoping for. In fact, if your venture takes off, you may be forced to seek out the very childcare services that you went into business to avoid.

A LARGE DOSE OF RESILIENCE

Resilience is a must-have on the often rocky road to small-business success. This vital asset can best be described as "bounce-back-ability"—your capacity to adapt to change, solve problems, and respond to setbacks. Resilient achievers are a "fascinating blend of long-term optimism and short-term pessimism," observes Dr. Al Siebert, who founded the Resiliency Center and speaks widely on the subject. Before making a commitment, notes Dr. Siebert, highly resilient people scope out the challenges ahead and try to anticipate everything that might go wrong; then they seek out information about how others have handled similar situations. Once armed with this information, they tap into their innate optimism and forge ahead. "High achievers are focused on feelings of accomplishment," adds Dr. Siebert. That's why they tend to set realistic "stretch" goals—ones they are most likely to achieve through their own actions and ingenuity.

A BURNING DESIRE TO SUCCEED

For some entrepreneurs, the brass ring is business growth and financial reward. They measure success in fairly traditional terms: performance and profitability. But many women business owners come to rethink their notion of success; they make a shift from valuing themselves based on their net worth to focusing on their self-worth, by paying themselves in nonmonetary ways that make them feel good about themselves, such as giving back to their communities. But success in one form or another—whether it means proving themselves in the marketplace, to their family, or to themselves—is a cherished and sought-after value.

When It's Good, It's Great!

What's it like when your venture is up and running smoothly? When the music is in tune and you're dancing to your heart's desire? Let's take a few moments to listen to what some of the women you'll be meeting have to say about the joys of working on their own.

Ronnie Fliss endured a tough corporate layoff: at age fifty-one, she found herself out of work until a friend's casual remark set her on the path to a new business. As the founder of Fat Murray's Doggy Treats, Ronnie has traded data for dough—and she couldn't be happier with her choice.

"I can remember driving those first couple of weeks with Murray, my basset hound, on the seat next to me and thinking, 'Oh my God, I can't believe it! It's two o'clock in the afternoon and I'm out!' It was extremely liberating! Corporate life is very structured and here I am, running around and doing business late at night or early in the morning. I love manufacturing. I love making something! I love the independence. I love being successful. It's having a wish and a dream and a desire and seeing it come to fruition. It's just very satisfying. But it's the independence more than anything. I'm the boss!"

Bobbi Brown began her career as a struggling freelance makeup artist who took the leap into small business with a strong vision and a fresh new product line. Today, she's at the helm of a fast-growing global cosmetics empire. But she remains true to her playful, inventive spirit and entrepreneurial roots. "What really keeps me excited," says Bobbi, "is being able to be as creative as I can possibly be and turning that creativity into something that allows me the freedom to do more—and to work with really amazing people. I'm really blessed because the people in my environment are phenomenally talented, incredibly nice, fun, fabulous people. And, to this day, when I am given something creative to do and total freedom to do what I want with it, my soul is happy."

Starting Patricia's Yarns in her hometown of Hoboken has been a "whirlwind" for Patricia Scribner and her husband, Adam, a middle-school teacher and enthusiastic partner in her enterprise. "Making the transition was challenging," says Patricia, "but it's your health, it's your life, it's an investment in your future." "Everything has to be achieved with great sacrifice," adds Adam. "But what we've gained has been fantastic! We've made ourselves part of the fabric of our town—it's just a wonderful lifestyle."

Becky Rohrer's decision to transform a half-renovated real-estate disaster into the College Inn was a leap of faith that has opened the door to a whole new life and exposed her son to wonderful, talented people. "I'm happy in a way that most of the people I know are not," says Becky, "because I actually have the gift of waking up and doing what I want to do the way I want to do it and with the customers I want to have. I get to pick all that! How many people are that lucky? Hardly anyone. I think the inn has made me the person I was meant to be in order to raise my son with the right attitude and sense of self. I have this little laughing voice inside my head that says, 'This is what you're supposed to do. You're happy doing this.' And I am!"

Liz Lange started her business on a shoestring. There were times when she had no customers and didn't know if she would make it. To survive, she did everything from designing to waiting on customers to packing FedEx boxes. Yet there was a romance to her early start-up days that Liz recalls fondly. "I always think of starting a business now like a marriage. It's harder than you can ever imagine, so if you're not passionate about it, it's never going to work! I am madly, madly, madly in love with the idea of Liz Lange Maternity—what it is and what it could be, and I have been from the beginning. That's what sustained me and kept me going through what was a very, very difficult time. I feel like I am the luckiest person in the world because I get to do something I absolutely love as my business. I get up excited every day! I feel that anything is possible, and, if I have an idea for something new, I have the opportunity to make it happen. It's a dream come true."

For Ronnie Fliss, launching a business has given her freedom. For Bobbi Brown, it's given her the chance to nurture her creativity and build a wonderful team. For Patricia Scribner, launching has led to a soul-satisfying lifestyle. For Becky Rohrer, becoming an innkeeper has exposed both her and her son to wonderful new people and experiences. And for Liz Lange, doing work that she loves makes her feel lucky and blessed.

Each of these women, in her own way, has discovered new strength and joy in pursuing her own venture. What about you? As you meet these and other bold, enterprising women in coming chapters and learn their stories, look closely at why and how they made their moves—and the choices they've made. Can you see a glimpse of your own dream reflected in theirs?

Quick Tips ⇨

Quick Tips

Do what you love—and what you're good at.
Passion fuels small-business success. Commit to an idea that you absolutely love and can't wait to tell people about. Enthusiasm is contagious—catch it and share it!

Know what you're getting into.
Be clear eyed about what to expect. You have to be unstoppable! You'll face difficult trade-offs and decisions. Learn before you leap—and you'll be ready to launch.

Assess your yen for yin and yang!
A start-up is intense. The highs are higher and the lows are lower than they are with a regular job. Check your emotional pulse: are you ready for the roller-coaster ride?

Be prepared to invest huge amounts of time.
You'll have to feed your business constantly! Your start-up will consume countless hours. But since you love what you're doing, you won't be counting!

Reframe your notion of success.
The brass ring isn't just money. Flexibility is also a form of success. So is fulfillment. Decide what success means to you—and what you *really* want from your launch.

Embrace the joys of entrepreneurship.
Keep your eye on the prize! Your start-up is more than just an idea for a product or service. It's about creativity, balance, happiness, fulfillment—and financial independence.

Chapter 2

Real Stories behind Real Start-Ups

If there are no doors open, then go find a window!
Don't take no for an answer.

—BOBBI BROWN

We've all heard those tales about the girl who sees a Broadway show, finds stardust in her pocket on the way home, and knows in that instant that she's destined to be an actress. But most of us aren't so focused. Our work histories are often more the product of circumstances and chance—and it may take time for our callings to ripen and command our attention. Interestingly, the same holds true for starting a small business. For every woman who satisfies the image of the classic entrepreneur—a bold, risk-embracing, convention-bucking innovator with a burning idea—there are at least two or three others whose drive to launch their own ventures takes longer to surface.

We call these women "emerging entrepreneurs" because it takes a while for them to settle on a start-up concept. Emerging entrepreneurs aren't born, they're made—or, rather, they create themselves. The ideas for their businesses don't spring into life full blown, like Athena from the head of Zeus. For these women—and you may be one of them—the initial decision to start a business may be more reactive than proactive. Circumstances or events rather than a clearly defined, compelling start-up concept may be the catalysts that trigger a move into entrepreneurship.

So, if your confidence in your ability to make it as a business owner seems a little shaky right now—or if you have a strong desire to be your own boss but aren't sure exactly what you want to do—take heart! There are many paths through the entrepreneurial gate—and not all of them are straight and narrow. To give you a better idea of just how varied those paths can be, let's take a close look at the stories and decision-making processes of six women who launched their start-ups at different stages of their work lives.

Bobbi Brown: A Passion for Color, Creativity, and Caring

Bobbi Brown has appeared on *Oprah*, *Martha Stewart at Home*, and *The Today Show*, as well as on the E! and Style channels—and she has been featured in countless top fashion and women's magazines. She's traveled the world, first as an in-demand freelance makeup artist and, more recently, as the woman who engineered one of the most successful cosmetic launches in decades. But in her heart she remains an entrepreneur.

Today, her line of natural-looking, easy-to-use cosmetics imprinted with the elegant Bobbi Brown logo stretches halfway around the world, from the United States and Canada to Japan and Australia. Some four hundred stores in twenty countries carry her line, which she is constantly refining, with the support of her parent company, Estée Lauder. But, as Bobbi tells the story, her road to success was anything but smooth.

Like so many entrepreneurs, her creativity expressed itself early in nontraditional ways. "I couldn't paint or draw a horse to save my life," she recalls, "but I loved crafts and anything visual. I used to make necklaces and beads and boxes. I even remember making perfumes when I was a kid. In seventh grade, my friends and I had a store in the basement where we made jewelry. I don't think anyone ever went down there and bought anything, but we *did* have a store. That's when I felt most happy and creative and open."

After a few false starts, Bobbi landed at Emerson College, a communications school in Boston filled with energetic, creative people, many of them in the performing arts. It was there that "I really found myself," Bobbi comments. She did makeup for the school's theater productions, TV programs, and her friends; she made drama students look bloody or old—and her dorm mates look gorgeous. After graduating, Bobbi spent a year in Boston waitressing and building her portfolio. But Boston isn't a glamour town, so she headed to New York, with a little money and "a lot of naiveté." Her dad helped out by paying the rent for a few months while she searched for freelance work.

With no contacts and no experience, finding work wasn't easy. Bobbi opened the Yellow Pages and began canvassing modeling agencies and fashion magazines. A cold call to a friendly agent netted some great advice and Bobbi landed her first assignment with *Glamour* magazine. However, the life of a freelance makeup artist proved to be anything *but* glamorous: Bobbi was constantly pounding the pavement looking for work. It took her seven years to get a cover and a major spread in *Vogue*. During this period, she married, moved to New Jersey, and struggled to put her husband through law school. She also became pregnant with the first of her three sons.

As a new mother with a family, Bobbi felt at odds with the fashion industry lifestyle and began thinking about what else she could do. While on a shoot, a chance conversation with a chemist set Bobbi on the path to entrepreneurship. She had an idea for a lipstick that wasn't greasy or dry and actually looked natural. The chemist made a sample for her, and then a few more. "I loved them," Bobbi says, "and told him, 'I think I can sell these!'" With a line of ten lipsticks, Bobbi began running a small business from her home in New Jersey. When a friend at *Glamour* wrote about the line, the phone started ringing.

Not long after, Bobbi was at a party and happened to meet a cosmetics buyer who worked for Bergdorf Goodman, a stylish Manhattan department store. This was the break Bobbi had been waiting for, and she was ready. Impressed by the lipstick's fresh, appealing color palette, the buyer agreed to carry the line. "It was my passion for what I was doing that came through," Bobbi observes. "I really believed in it and was eager to talk about it. People felt my excitement and saw that it was a great product and something new. I didn't know what marketing was, and I didn't know what PR was, but I guess that's what I was doing—marketing and PR!"

Bobbi began working with a full lab on product development, and she launched Bobbi Brown Essentials at Bergdorf Goodman. It was a promising but stressful time. Bobbi had a new baby, her husband was still in school, and keeping it all going was a financial struggle. They took their life savings—about $5,000—and poured it into her dream. The business took off instantly. "We thought we'd sell a hundred lipsticks in the first month," Bobbi recalls, "but we sold a hundred in the first day! There was a big buzz. People were buying and it was really exciting. Every time we needed more lipstick, my husband would get in the car with a shopping bag full, drive to Bergdorf's, knock on the door, and deliver them."

Within a year, Bobbi had opened a tiny office in Manhattan with one employee. To make ends meet, she continued to work as a freelance makeup artist on magazine shoots. It was slow going and there were plenty of ups and downs: caps that didn't fit and a huge order of broken lipsticks that was shipped to stores, to name a few. Each time, Bobbi remembers thinking, "Oh my God, it's over!" But she kept on going, fueled by her vision of easy-to-apply makeup with a fresh, natural look.

Ultimately, the company launched in Neiman Marcus, and then in Henri Bendel. When the company moved into Canada and then Japan, business exploded. About five years after Bobbi's initial launch, Estée Lauder knocked on the door. With the goal of expanding globally, Bobbi sold her firm and began working with her parent company to build what is now Bobbi Brown Cosmetics into a worldwide brand.

As an entrepreneur, Bobbi is committed to constantly reinventing herself and creating innovative new products, all while managing a big company—a challenging proposition. Today, in addition to running her firm, she works closely with Dress for Success, a nonprofit group that provides clothes and job-finding support to disadvantaged women. Bobbi also mentors cosmetology students at the Jane Addams Vocational High School in the South Bronx. Whether she's talking to young teenagers at Jane Addams or to college students, Bobbi stresses the importance of persistence. "Starting a business is really hard work," she says. "It takes everything you have. You have to take chances and things don't always work out, but you just keep going."

Lisa Druxman: A New Family Inspires a New Business

A "mompreneur" with a flair for marketing, Lisa has parlayed her love of fitness into a thriving national franchising enterprise. Before she launched her venture, Stroller Strides, Lisa spent about twelve years working in the fitness industry; by the time she was pregnant with her first baby, she was the general manager of a high-end health club. Though a salaried employee, Lisa always brought a strong dose of independence and creativity to her job. At one point, she designed a weight management program called L.E.A.N. (Learn Eating Awareness and Nutrition), which became a popular offering at exclusive health clubs. She also consulted at well-known spas, including The Golden Door.

It was the birth of her son that ignited Lisa's inner entrepreneur. Since her family is based in San Diego, where living costs are high, managing on one income wasn't an option for Lisa. But as her maternity leave flew by, returning to full-time work grew less and less appealing. While weighing her options, Lisa did what came naturally to her: she created a daily fitness routine that allowed her to get a good workout with her baby boy. It was a great hour of bonding and fun for them both.

One day, as Lisa tells the story, "A lightbulb literally went off over my head and I said to myself, 'You know, this could be a business!' I realized that women always want to lose weight and get in shape after having a baby, but that they wouldn't want to drop off their children somewhere to do it. I also realized that most new moms would also enjoy connecting with each other because they often feel isolated.

"Then I thought, 'Wouldn't it be great to put together a workout that new mothers could do along with their babies?' I came up with the whole idea and even the name for my business—Stroller Strides—in one hour. At the time, I had no vision of it becoming a national company. I really just thought I would start a class, make a bit of extra money, and have a chance to be with my son. I didn't even think the idea was going to replace my having to go back to work."

Lisa launched her venture by posting handmade flyers in her neighborhood and attracted four women to her first class. A local TV station, intrigued by the idea of new moms toning up with their tots, aired a show about it. When dozens of moms contacted Lisa for more information, Stroller Strides was off and running. In just twelve months, it spread from one to twelve locations—and had attracted one thousand new moms. A natural marketer, Lisa built the business without expensive advertising (see chapter 8, page 168).

Lisa's "lightbulb" launch has continued to gain speed. In response to a constant stream of queries, this bold, creative entrepreneur began a franchising program. Today, some twenty-five thousand women participate in Stroller Strides in more than six hundred locales worldwide—including forty-four states, British Columbia, and Japan. And the numbers keep climbing. Lisa now presides over a multimillion-dollar enterprise and continues to find new ways to share her fitness vision—most recently, as the author of *Lean Mommy*. With its family-friendly environment, it's not surprising that Stroller Strides is one of *Working Mother*'s top twenty-five companies to work for. It has also been ranked as one of the fifty fastest-growing franchises in the country by *Entrepreneur* magazine.

Ronnie Fliss: From Stressful Layoff to Successful Launch

It was a nightmare scenario. After her company went through a traumatic series of three takeovers in four years, Ronnie Fliss, a vice president of data management at a financial services firm, was forced to let half of her department go. Years later, Ronnie can still recall seeing the names of her friends and coworkers being erased on a blackboard as "expendable" employees. Then, without warning, the ax fell a second time—and Ronnie was laid off as well. A veteran of thirty years in corporate America, at fifty-one, Ronnie suddenly found herself without a job.

In middle age, in middle management, and a woman, Ronnie faced a "triple whammy" job loss. Although her husband was very supportive and she was financially secure, Ronnie found her layoff tough to handle. With IT jobs being outsourced left and right, she couldn't even find consulting work. "The experience of losing my job, then looking for six months and not finding anything, was very demoralizing," she recalls. There were a few bright spots in this bleak situation, however. Job stress had triggered a mysterious illness, and once her job disappeared, so did her symptoms. With the help of her family and Murray, her beloved basset hound, she began to regain her health. At this point, an idea walked in her door.

A friend dropped by her house for coffee and, out of the blue, he said, "You love to bake and you love your dogs. Why don't you make gourmet dog biscuits?" Maybe it was Murray, lounging nearby, who inspired the question. Wherever it came from, Ronnie's response was immediate: "Oh, that sounds like a good idea!" She explains, "I felt low, and I needed to do something that would make me feel good." Ronnie went on the Internet, found some recipes, baked a couple of items, and sold them to local pet stores with the help of Murray, her four-legged marketing rep. The more she baked, the better Ronnie felt—and Fat Murray's Doggy Treats was born.

Before she totally committed to the business, Ronnie drew on her training in data intelligence and spent close to six months carefully researching the pet-food industry. What she found was encouraging. At the time, it was a roughly $7 billion industry. Fueled by doggie daycare, dog-friendly hotels, and baby boomers with lots of discretionary income, the industry was experiencing explosive growth. In choosing to manufacture only wholesome, sugar-free treats, Ronnie caught the "organic" wave as well.

There have been lots of rocky moments: a recipe glitch, the loss of a big customer, hectic bouts of seasonal baking, and endless runs to

Costco for supplies. Not to mention the time that Barney, Murray's little brother, managed to drag a newly opened fifty-pound bag of flour across the floor and dump it all over himself, Murray, and the entire kitchen!

But there's been plenty of fun and satisfaction, too. Ronnie has had enthusiastic support from her family, from a professor and mentor at Fairleigh Dickinson University, and from her banker, who arranged a line of credit to jump-start her launch. Fat Murray's Doggy Treats couldn't be more different from Ronnie's old job. "Massaging data—that had always been my field," says Ronnie. "But for this, I had my hands in dough. I was actually manufacturing—making something tangible—and I love it! What I'm doing now really fulfills something in me. It's a feel-good business."

Cathy Kerns: Managing a Business and MS with Style—and Strength

Cathy Kerns spent her entire corporate career—more than twenty-five years in all—in advertising, marketing, and public relations. As an executive with Hyatt Hotels Southeast, she traveled the world promoting Orlando, Florida, as a convention destination. Later, as vice president of corporate public relations for the Rank Organisation, a British company that owned more than 150 theme restaurants, Cathy helped make the Hard Rock Café into a mega brand.

The fast-paced hospitality industry is demanding. This proved doubly true for Cathy, who was dealt a tough blow in mid-career when she was suddenly diagnosed with multiple sclerosis (MS). The symptoms were devastating. During her late thirties, Cathy began losing the sight in her left eye and strength in her left hand. Soon after, she developed double vision and balance problems as well, and began walking with a cane.

Her boss was very supportive. Cathy kept working full-time and even assisted at a major White House event. But a change of management brought a change of attitude; her new boss was uncomfortable around Cathy's disability. Faced with this reality, she chose to leave her job. Seeking her next career move, she invested in a gourmet gift shop, which she eventually sold. Then, in classic entrepreneurial style, she took a personal challenge and transformed it into an income-producing opportunity. Cathy came up with an innovative concept: a walking-stick design with interchangeable colors, allowing users to match their canes to their clothing. In a single stroke, she transformed an everyday necessity into a fashion accessory. Cathy designed a sample and began stepping out with it.

When Joan Rivers saw it at a party and practically ran away with it, Cathy knew she was onto something. She created a customized version for Rivers and started searching for a manufacturer to transform her vision into a reality. After some intensive research, she launched Kerns Able Enterprises and began making customized Lucite canes under the trademarked name Style Stick. Today, she has a thriving business and an enthusiastic, incredibly loyal customer base. A small group of local artisans hand-glue petals on flower stems in more than eighty colors, which can easily be inserted into a lightweight but sturdy Lucite cane. Thousands of Cathy's cheerful canes are waltzing around the country, and her customers love the idea of being mobile and "mod" at the same time. Ladies going on summer cruises, for example, send Cathy swatches of the outfits they plan to wear and she creates matching interchangeable flower stems for them.

A customized product and niche market make Style Stick an ideal online business. Cathy advertises primarily on Google and runs the company comfortably from her home in Orlando. Small-business ownership and Internet marketing give Cathy the flexibility she needs to generate income, handle her MS, and provide a satisfying service.

"Working at home has been a godsend," says Cathy, "because extreme heat really intensifies MS. The fatigue that results is also horrifying. There are some days when people with MS can't lift their heads off their pillows. My office takes up about half of my downstairs; I've put twin beds in, so I can lie down right in my workspace. This gives me the ability to better control my lifestyle while building my business." With five million people using walking canes and an exploding baby boomer market, Cathy's business appears to be poised for growth. In addition to her work, Cathy is active in her community and serves on a regional board of directors for Canine Companions for Independence. She also sits on the Regional Chair's Advisory Council for the National Multiple Sclerosis Society (NMSS), a nonprofit organization that supports vital research and provides counseling, advocacy, education, and employment services.

Reflecting on her growing business, Cathy observes, "When you work for a large corporation, you keep getting hit over the head about the bottom line, the bottom line. Well, this isn't ever going to be a bottom-line producer in the traditional sense. But if I don't become a millionaire, who cares? I have over four thousand sticks walking around and I know for a fact that 150 percent of my customers love my products. And you can't have any more successful a business than that."

Increasingly, people facing physical challenges like Cathy's are launching enterprises for the most entrepreneurial of reasons: they want to work for themselves, have an idea for a product or service, and want to make more money. In addition, self-employment offers them much-needed flexibility (see Resources, page 198). "People with MS and other disabilities find small business attractive because it can offer them the opportunity to better control their work environment and hours," notes Steve Nissen, director of employment programs for the National Multiple Sclerosis Society. "They can work when they have the energy to do so and around the symptoms they experience."

Becky Rohrer: Burnout Fuels a Life-Changing Move

As she describes it, Becky Rohrer had the job from hell: a tyrannical boss, a sixty-hour workweek, nonstop deadlines, and a staff who viewed her as irritable and demanding. Becky comanaged a $70 million residential construction portfolio, overseeing large-scale projects, directing a staff of forty, and working with banks and investors. Saddled with huge work responsibilities, married to a man with three children from a previous marriage—and a new mother herself—Becky was coming apart at the seams. She was very good at her job, but it was physically—and emotionally—killing her.

"I lost myself," Becky recalls. "I never slept. I smoked. My eating habits were terrible. I was a complete stress ball all the time. It was horrible. I would go to meet someone and my cell phone would ring, my pager would be going off, and I would get annoyed. People thought that I was rude and inconsiderate, but I was doing what I had to do to get the job done. It gives me chills just to think about it—I am such a different person now."

Finding the courage to create the kind of life she wanted for herself and her son, Jared, has been a challenging journey for Becky. She took the first step when she quit her job. The day it happened, Becky simply snapped. She took her keys, her cell phone, and her pager, dropped them on her boss's desk, and said, "You know what? I'm done. I'm leaving." And then she did exactly that. Becky took refuge at home, cared for her baby, and didn't answer the phone for three weeks. It took almost twelve months before she felt the stress from the last six years of work drain away.

Even so, it was a tough time emotionally. In addition to her lost income, Becky's marriage was failing. She now faced the loss of her stepchildren, she had a baby to support, and she didn't really even have a home.

Realizing that she needed a new place to live, Becky asked a local realtor in nearby Westerville, Ohio, to show her around the town. On one trip, she spotted a diamond in the rough, which she snapped up and lovingly transformed into The College Inn. Today, it is admiringly described as an "1870s Victorian Italianate house." But when she first saw it, this now-stately B&B was far from a vision of beauty. Says Becky, "It was a completely annihilated brick house—abandoned, gutted, with no roof, no windows, and bats flying around."

Unfazed by its sad condition, Becky walked inside; instantly, her real-estate expertise kicked in. She knew exactly what the house needed and how to get it done. Situated on the campus of Otterbein College, her alma mater, the house had been partially renovated for use as an inn. As she wandered through its rooms, it seemed as much in need of care as she was. As she restored it, Becky knew she would be healing herself as well.

At the time, she didn't even know what a bed-and-breakfast was. She went to the library and read whatever she could find. Support was in short supply. "Everyone told me I was an absolute nut," Becky recalls. "They said it was a disaster. But from the moment I walked in, I started dreaming about the house. I could see each room completely done. I knew what color the walls were painted, what lights it had, what furniture was in it." Becky put a budget together, found an architect, secured a bank loan, and The College Inn—and a whole new life—were born.

A cosmetic designer, a fitness pro turned franchiser, a pet-food entrepreneur, a cane maker, an innkeeper: at first glance, these stories seem to have little in common except a start-up. In fact, each of the women profiled seems to have experienced a different trigger event that pushed her off the employee track and into her own business. But there's more to these start-up decisions than meets the eye. Look a little deeper, and you'll see that, in almost every instance, it was actually a *convergence of factors* that propelled each woman's move.

Take Ronnie Fliss. In her case, it wasn't a layoff alone that led her to launch Fat Murray's Doggy Treats. Behind her decision were several dispiriting takeovers, a stress-related illness, and a tough IT market— all of which were counterbalanced by the chance to enter a "feel-good" business and take control of her work destiny. Lisa Druxman's light-bulb moment was sparked by the need to help her family financially, job constraints, and her intuitive belief that new mothers wanted to connect.

Like so many other major decisions in life, launching a start-up is frequently fueled by a volatile mix of desire, destiny, and dissatisfaction. Ultimately, it's not one big thing that seems to drive women to the entrepreneurial edge—though one event, like a layoff, usually pushes them over it. Still more revealing is the fact that many of the women we interviewed *weren't even considering launching businesses* when the idea that sparked their start-up came their way. They fall squarely into the "emerging entrepreneurs" category described earlier.

Their early careers offer little or no evidence of entrepreneurial fever. Instead, their paths are winding and filled with detours.

For these women, discovering what they want to do is more the product of intention and desire than the result of a clear-cut direction—at least initially. Their start-up ideas tend to percolate over time or present themselves serendipitously, or through happenstance. More often than not, the idea they eventually choose to run with seems to find them—not the other way around. That's exactly what happened to designer Liz Lange.

Liz Lange: Emerging Entrepreneur Extraordinaire

Today, the founder and president of Liz Lange Maternity is widely admired as a retail pioneer. Drawing on her ingenuity and intuition, she invented a new design niche: stylish clothing for expectant mothers. She's dressed everyone from Cindy Crawford to Kelly Ripa and Gwyneth Paltrow during their pregnancies—and her collections can be found not just in her signature boutiques but also in fifteen hundred Target stores in forty-seven states.

A great entrepreneurial success story? Absolutely! But no one is more surprised than Liz herself at the unexpected direction that her creativity took. She describes herself as an "accidental entrepreneur" who "stumbled" upon her business. "I'm not one of those people who grew up with a burning knowledge of what I was going to do," she observes. "I was always driven in terms of being a good student. But majoring in comparative literature at Brown, I certainly wasn't thinking I'd have a career as an entrepreneur."

In fact, nothing seemed farther from her mind. After college, Liz took a job at *Vogue* magazine as a writer. Though she loved fashion as a "consumer and shopper," she didn't know anything about the industry as a business. She enjoyed *Vogue*, but she didn't feel that it was her passion or calling. She began pursuing a PhD in psychology, but realized she'd made a mistake and took a publishing job. Recalling her lack of focus, Liz notes, "As you can see, this wasn't at all a case of 'Oh this success is going to be so obvious!'"

Then fate came calling. Liz met Stephen DiGeronimo, a struggling clothing designer with a small Manhattan studio. "I just fell in love with what he was doing," Liz muses. "I just wanted to be part of it. He had no money, and so basically I begged him to take me on as an unpaid intern." At twenty-five, she found herself part of a tiny design team. Liz married and so did her friends; some soon found themselves pregnant.

"They would come into our showroom, as they had before, and squeeze themselves into our dresses," recalls Liz. Her friends' response led to an "Aha!" moment: she realized they wanted clothing that made them feel stylish and sexy during their pregnancies. "I did have a very very specific idea," notes Liz, "but it was an idea that came to me—it wasn't anything I spent time researching."

"I didn't really want to be an entrepreneur," Liz notes. "I had a Geronimo maternity line all planned out in my mind. I proposed it to my boss, who said what everyone else basically said: 'I don't get this.'" But, as Liz puts it, "I couldn't get the idea out of my head! I think that's one thing that all entrepreneurs share in common. I didn't have this burning desire to start my own business, it was just that I felt the idea was right and it really grabbed me. It kept me up at night. I had a note-book by my bed and started sketching things.

"I finally realized that if I didn't go with my idea and then saw something like it in the marketplace later, I just wouldn't be able to live with myself. So I left Geronimo, not by choice, but very, very trepida-ciously, feeling completely unqualified. I hadn't studied design, I hadn't really been in the world of retail, and I had no business background."

Experienced retailers warned Liz that the maternity business wasn't viable and that she'd have to be prepared to sell the clothes herself. "So even opening up my own stores was not my original plan. I had to do it out of necessity," she observes. Instead of giving up, she said to herself, "I can't let some retail store get between me and my customer. If I can get my clothes to the right women, they'll get it."

"But it required an enormous amount of belief and willfulness—and blocking out all that negative noise," Liz comments. "Looking back, it's amazing to me that anything ever gets done because there are so many naysayers out there and it seems as if there's such an aversion to any sort of change or newness. It really took me much longer to get this product out than it should have; I spent a lot of time in a state of paralyzed inertia because of all the negative feedback.

"Oh my gosh, it was discouraging! I spent so much time thinking to myself, 'If this were a good idea, someone much smarter than I am would already be doing it. It must be a bad idea.' And I think that if I had had a better business background, I probably wouldn't have begun my company. I think you almost need a certain amount of ignorance if you want to start your own business."

An optimist by nature, Liz believed that if she could get the clothing right it would sell naturally by word of mouth. "That was a big part of my original vision," she notes. She started on a shoestring budget with no money for advertising. Operating from a tiny, windowless studio, she began creating made-to-order clothing because she couldn't afford an inventory.

She focused on designing an innovative product and didn't get caught up in what she did or didn't know about business or retailing. She decided she could figure it out as she went along. She also realized that the key to attracting customers wasn't buying advertising that she couldn't afford, but building her visibility by dressing high-profile celebrities during their pregnancies. Her instincts were on target: once Cindy Crawford and other stars wearing her clothes began singing her praises, her business exploded.

Liz Lange's story is so inspiring precisely because, as she points out herself, she showed no strong entrepreneurial bent early in her career and had no burning desire to launch her own business. But when the right idea came along, she recognized it, embraced it, protected it, and decided that she simply couldn't *not* run with it. Once she committed to making her vision a reality, her inner entrepreneur emerged.

Frontline Advice to Jump-Start Your Launch

With the smorgasbord of inspiring start-up stories given here, we're sure that you'll find your own longings echoed within one of them. The driver in some of these launches was a negative situation: a layoff or stressful job. In other cases, there was a positive pull toward entrepreneurship: a passion or an idea whose timing seemed right. As you think about these launch scenarios in light of your own circumstances and desires, keep the following frontline advice in mind.

INTENTION CREATES OPPORTUNITY

Some people are lucky: Lisa Druxman's lightbulb idea triggered her move. If your start-up idea is crystal clear and your path seems well marked, then you should focus on mobilizing the resources you need to support your launch, just as Lisa did. But if you find yourself in the "emerging entrepreneur" club, then you'll need to channel your energy toward identifying ideas that excite you and then narrow your options. Remember, launching a business isn't always about *getting* a great idea—it's often about *recognizing* a great idea when it comes your way. Sometimes that idea seizes your imagination; sometimes it simmers, then bubbles to the surface; sometimes it sneaks up on you.

Moving forward with intention is key. Put yourself firmly on the path to commitment by exploring any and all ideas landing on your mental doorstep that seem to hold business promise. For opportunity to find you, you have to meet it halfway: you have to be at the right place in the right time doing the right thing. If an idea grabs your attention and imagination, then run with it for a while and learn all you can about what's involved in making it a business reality.

DON'T LET NEGATIVE FEEDBACK DERAIL YOUR DREAM!

Whatever your idea is, there will be naysayers who'll do their best to discourage you. Becky Rohrer encountered them and so did Liz Lange. As you identify or flesh out your start-up idea, don't let your enthusiasm be dampened by other people's insecurities and fear of change.

Your own self-doubt is enough to handle! If you start absorbing others' anxieties, you could give up on a promising concept prematurely. This *doesn't* mean ignoring real risks or drawbacks; it simply means putting them on the back burner early on so that they won't distract you.

ADOPTING A "BRAINS FOR BUCKS" MENTALITY IS A SMART INVESTMENT

As you scan the stories we've shared here, you'll begin to see a strong thread running through them: a "brains for bucks" attitude. The message: launching a small business successfully means unleashing your creativity in service to your dream by finding better, faster, and cheaper ways of doing what you need to get done (for more on this, see chapter 3).

REMEMBER, YOU DON'T NEED TO KNOW EVERYTHING

That's a relief, isn't it? According to an old and comforting Estonian proverb, "the work itself will teach you." It's the kind of saying that you might just want to pin to a bulletin board so you can see it every day, alongside your "brains for bucks" mantra! If you make the decision to take the leap, it's likely that you won't be fully prepared—especially if you're launching in a field that's totally new to you.

As we'll see in chapter 5, when Karen Curro and Susan Edelman were racing to open their Laugh Out Loud store to catch the holiday season, their list of must-do tasks that they didn't have a clue about was a mile long: it included everything from using a cash register to ordering socks in the right sizes. But Karen and Susan had a goal, so they forged ahead. Their attitude was simple: *we'll figure it out or find it out.*

Liz Lange had a very a clear vision of *what* she wanted to do, but only in the broadest sense did she know *how* it would work: she figured she would get her clothes to the right customers and her market would evolve organically. She didn't even have a business plan. And, though she had doubts about her ability to pull it off, *she never doubted the idea itself*—and this rock-solid belief pulled her through. She kept moving toward her vision and gave her attention to creating solutions, not to her self-doubt.

So relax! Accept the fact that you're probably going to feel like you're treading water for a while and you'll save yourself from a sea of stress! Knowing that you don't know everything—and that it's perfectly OK—will help defuse that paper tiger, self-doubt. Deciding that you can figure out or find out whatever you need to know is tremendously liberating. It lets you focus on creative problem solving instead of unproductive hand wringing.

As Dr. Rob Gilbert, a peak performance coach, points out, "Everybody is blessed with more potential than they'll ever need. You have all the ability you need to succeed already inside you. What you are lacking is strategies. But, when most people do poorly, they say, 'Oh, I'm not cut out for this.' No! You're not using the right strategies. So, number one, if you believe in your abilities, number two, you have the right strategies, and number three, you put them into action—and you get out of your head and ignore the little voice that says, 'but, maybe, impossible'—then you're going to get results.

"If you get good results, then keep doing what you're doing. If the results you get aren't working, then change strategies. 'I can't do it, period' is failure. 'I can't do it . . . yet' is delayed success. All you need is a new strategy. You can always get more motivated, you can always find another way, you can always find a mentor, a teacher, a coach, a new technique."

Quick Tips

Carve out your own path to the start-up gate.
Some start-up ideas percolate. Some need to be coaxed. Launching isn't always about getting a great idea—often it's about recognizing one. So get yourself out there!

Let your "emerging entrepreneur" flex its muscles.
Clarifying your vision takes time. Shift from reactive to proactive. Keep moving in the direction of your desire. Commit to creating an independent work life!

Help opportunity find you.
Intention creates opportunity. Put yourself on the path to launching. Explore any and all promising ideas. Meet opportunity halfway so it can find you!

Just say no! to naysayers.
Don't let others derail your dream! Deflect their fears and insecurities. Focus first on benefits and potential, and then assess risks before you move ahead.

Decide to figure it out or find it out.
No launch is problem free. Forge ahead anyway! Make "I'll figure it out or find it out" your motto. Shift your focus from self-doubt to finding solutions.

Think and act like an entrepreneur.
Go over, under, around, and through obstacles. Believe in yourself! You have all the ability you need—just work to find the right strategy. Get excited, get help, get going!

Chapter 3

Substitute Brains for Bucks

When you don't have money, you get creative.

—LISA DRUXMAN

Wherever you are on the money anxiety meter, how you handle it will affect every other stage of the launch cycle. Our goal here is to help you cultivate the best possible attitude about the many-headed money monster. We want to give you the tools you need to cut it down to size so that it won't stand in the way of your start-up.

Let's start by examining two different ways of looking at money: from the outside and from the inside.

While we were in the middle of writing this chapter, a friend called and lamented, "Everyone I know hates their job, just like I do! We're all dying to make a big change. But we're afraid to take the leap because we're terrified about giving up our paychecks." *Terrified!* That was the word she used—not scared or anxious or stressed. That's how money, or the lack of it, often looks from the *outside*: really, really scary.

Now, here's the "insider" view of money. During an interview with Anne Afshari and Laura Hagler about Exclusively RNs, their advisory service for expectant mothers, Laura said, "The way we launched is actually very short and simple. We required the first office that used our service to pay for just about everything. We used our personal cell phones to handle calls. The only money that came out of our pockets was the money we paid our attorney to do our incorporation, our LLC setup, and articles of operation." Then Anne chimed in: "This is the funny part. We both invested a whopping $250 to start our business!"

A shoestring start-up budget and a savvy money-saving strategy based on building up-front costs into their first customer's contract. That's how money looks from the *inside*, when you're committed and in full launch mode. Out of necessity, you become incredibly resourceful and figure out ways to substitute creativity for cash. Yes, the money issue is scary and often stressful—and it never really goes away. But it's manageable. Other launchers have handled it, and you can, too. Like them, you'll find that the very act of taking the leap opens up amazing wellsprings of ingenuity on the financial front. So relax, breathe deeply, whisper "brains for bucks" three times . . . and read on! In this chapter, we're going to show you how to accomplish the following:

- Begin managing money like an entrepreneur.

- Give up your "paycheck player" mentality.

- Cultivate a "brains for bucks" attitude toward spending.

- Leverage your dollars so they work harder and smarter.

The Big "M": A Real Hot Button

If you're like most aspiring female entrepreneurs, then money isn't the key driver behind your decision to start your own business. Your quest for control over your own destiny, flexibility, and personal fulfillment is likely to be as important to you as money, if not more important, especially during the start-up phase of your business. Yes, you hope and intend to earn more money on your own than you would as an employee, but passion, not pay, is driving your move. This sounds great, but, in reality, for better or worse, money is going to be a dominant theme during your start-up.

In fact, as an entrepreneur, your emotional relationship with money is likely to be more intense and powerful than it ever was when you were an employee. Recognizing this, redefining your relationship with money, and managing old, unhelpful financial habits so that they don't sabotage you will be among the hardest—and most liberating— entrepreneurial challenges you'll face. As you begin to come to grips with money early in your start-up, here are some of the ways you're likely to feel.

VULNERABLE AND OUT OF STEP WITH EVERYONE ELSE

"With money in your pocket, you are wise, and you are beautiful, and you sing well, too." In many ways, this old saying is surprisingly fresh and apt. It captures the feelings of comfort, power, and success that our society associates with money. As a new entrepreneur, however, you are marching to the beat of a different drummer and voluntarily emptying your pockets to invest in yourself and your new venture. Your vision of financial success is a dream deferred. You are trading steady pay for potential: the future earning power that your fledgling enterprise offers.

At times, this is going to make you feel vulnerable and worried about your family's security and well-being. While people around you may be enjoying steady incomes and building retirement funds, you're going to fall behind financially, perhaps even way behind, at least for a while. There's no way of knowing how long you'll remain in this financial limbo; but, if there's one thing entrepreneurs agree on, it's that launching a new business always takes more time and money than you imagine, no matter how carefully you plan and try to hedge your risks.

Yes, people may be patting you on the back, telling you to "go for it!"—and wishing they had the guts to do what you're doing. At the same time, they may feel secretly relieved not to be saddled with all the financial problems you'll be facing—and content to remain a "pay-check player" with a steady income. Their choice is very different from yours. It's important for you to recognize this and maintain those long-term friendships while also seeking out like-minded new business owners who really understand what you're going through and why you're doing it.

FOCUSED ON YOUR FINANCIAL SURVIVAL

Whatever your money-management strengths and weaknesses are, they'll be intensified when you launch your venture. And whatever amount of money you start with, you're probably going to feel that it's not enough and that you'd have a better chance of beating the odds if your bank balance were larger. Not surprisingly, your dollar power— or lack of it—is going to be on your mind *a lot*: finding it, making it, spending it, wasting it, wanting it. You're going to be focusing on it more than you ever did in your corporate life, and it will make you anxious. Sometimes very anxious.

Start-up funding is a hot button for women entrepreneurs for a good reason: it's often hard to come by. So much so that finding capital consistently ranks as the top priority for National Association of Women Business Owners (NAWBO) members, according to the association's surveys. Fortunately, this situation is improving. There are more funding options available than ever before. Microlenders, the SBA, and even venture-capital "angels" are tailoring their funding strategies to meet the start-up needs of women. Microlenders, for example, offer modest loans, fast-track applications, and mentoring support. Consider Count Me In, a not-for-profit online microlender that uses a "women-friendly" qualifying system for loans of $500 to $10,000. (For more funders, see Resources, page 198.)

Although programs like these are enormously helpful, the demand for start-up dollars continues to outstrip supply. As a result, bootstrapping—not bank borrowing or venture capital—will be your most likely path to success.

This means that you'll probably find yourself tapping into your personal assets and/or borrowing money from your family—and perhaps even friends—to finance your dreams. This can easily make you feel financially overextended and anxious about paying back everyone who's helped you. That's the bad news. Ironically, it's the good news as well. Why? Mainly because, as we'll see, lack of outside funding will force you to think and act creatively on the financial front. Not only will this be a huge confidence booster for you, but it will also unleash your ingenuity in other areas.

A fortunate few find themselves taking the plunge with a comfortable financial cushion. But for many of the women we spoke with, it was a major anxiety producer. Confronting money issues is tough: persistent shortfalls can easily trigger fears about making ends meet, paying employees, covering health care costs, and a host of other concerns. Here's how Becky Rohrer candidly describes her feelings as she was transforming an abandoned house into The College Inn—and attempting to rebuild her life as well:

"The first few months were very stressful for me. I cried a lot. I had left my house with my son—and was going through a not very pleasant divorce. Of course, I felt fearful and anxious. I would say to myself, 'Oh my God, I've risked everything on this. I don't have any savings left. I've run my credit cards to the max buying furniture and bed linens.' To go into JC Penney and spend $900 on sheets and towels is a very frightening experience! I was thinking, 'I don't know if I can pay these bills next month, but I have this stuff to start, so I have to keep doing this. I just kept driving forward and saying, 'OK, I'm afraid. It's OK to be afraid and I'm moving on.' You have to be prepared to go through this if you're going to have your own business."

Feelings like these aren't uncommon—and, as Becky did, you're going to have to find ways to feel the fear and do it anyway in order to make your start-up work. It can be a rocky road, but, with the help of seasoned entrepreneurs, you'll find that the path to success is better marked and easier to follow than you might think. Eventually, you'll make a shift from "net worth to self-worth" that will empower you to see money as a tool rather than a reward—and to wield it as you never have before.

Learning to Manage Money Like an Entrepreneur

The ultimate goal for any entrepreneur is to view money as a wealth-building tool. When money is viewed in this way, you can risk it to achieve bigger aims, to shape and forge not just an at-home career but a company with substantial earning power. Only when you can treat money as a neutral mechanism can you leverage it to expand your business—out of the basement and into new markets, new product lines, and higher-profit activities. But, as we'll see, getting there will require some fundamental shifts.

Just as we found that women passed through different emotional stages on the road to building their businesses, we also found that they passed through what seemed to be four stages in their relationship to money. As their businesses started, evolved, and matured, so did the way they handled their finances. During the start-up stage, not surprisingly, money was viewed mainly as a source of anxiety. As women grew more attuned to the ebb and flow of their businesses, they became more relaxed and secure about their ability to generate the money they needed. To get a better handle on these stages, let's take an in-depth look at how they unfold over time.

STAGE ONE: MONEY AS AN EMOTIONAL SCORECARD

In this stage, net worth and self-worth are intertwined: money is closely tied to self-esteem and seen as an indicator of success and self-worth. It's also an emotionally charged issue. The financial sacrifices made during the launch stage—surrendering a steady paycheck, benefits, and insurance—often trigger fear and self-doubt about regaining lost ground.

To compensate, some women may push themselves to the edge in order to beat the odds. They seem unwilling or unable to accept the two- to three-year break-even cycle that characterizes most small-business start-ups. The result may be financial self-sabotage: they set themselves up for failure by overspending or setting unrealistic growth targets. During this stage, the feast-or-famine work pattern most start-ups experience—and the cash flow problems it creates—can have a direct impact on your emotional well-being and self-esteem. Your mood swings will be closely tied to a day-to-day financial scorecard—you'll tend to feel anxious and down when money isn't flowing in and upbeat when a check finally arrives. In the work world, the accepted standard of success is financial earning power. Breaking the link between your emotions and your bank balance won't be easy, because your paycheck days have conditioned you to respond in this way.

STAGE TWO: MONEY AS THE ENEMY

During this stage, your business is needy and cash hungry: the more money you feed it, the more it wants. You can find yourself spending scarce dollars on things you never dreamed you'd need. As you struggle to stay afloat, you can find yourself growing more anxious about how to make ends meet. However large your launch nest egg, you'll find it shrinking by the minute. In fact, the larger it is, the faster it may seem to disappear. You may find yourself borrowing more money than you ever intended from family and friends just to stay afloat. To survive, you may be forced to rob Peter to pay Paul and juggle your dollars in a way that's totally foreign to you.

Though you once grandly envisioned the money you'd be making in your new venture as your ticket to a more rewarding lifestyle, it's become the enemy—a barrier to your business goals. It's the problem, not the solution. Like a dark and forbidding mountain, it's in your way. If only you had more money, you could afford a more professional image, buy better equipment, have a real office instead of a closet, buy a better wardrobe, be able to hire help so that you could spend time strategizing rather than doing the books. The list of money-related woes goes on and on.

What's happening? You're feeling fragile, so you're letting money control you instead of the other way around. You've given money power over your emotions and now you're going to have to wrestle with it in order to regain what you've given away. Money has become a kind of emotional scapegoat; not having it can be used to explain away or justify some of the fears and self-doubt you're feeling as you let go of the past and struggle to create a new future.

The danger here is that lack of money will immobilize rather than energize you. When this happens, not having enough money can become an excuse for inaction. You can use it as a reason to avoid doing the tough things you have to do to survive but feel anxious about, like drumming up new business or negotiating better terms with suppliers.

Using lack of money as an excuse can also prevent you from confronting the very real fears that you have about failure—and success.

How do you handle this stage? As a first step, you have to depersonalize money by recognizing that it isn't the enemy. Just as money won't solve all your problems, it isn't the *source* of all those problems either. Some of them, yes. But all of them, no. Next, you have to look beyond your lack of money and the stress that it's triggered to see what's really going on. Is lack of money just an excuse for not dealing with other, deeper fears you may have about your ability to succeed at your business or provide for your family? And finally, you need to defuse money as an emotional trigger by focusing on solutions, taking action, and adopting a "brains for bucks" approach.

STAGE THREE: MONEY AS PROTECTION

By this stage, you've weathered some pretty serious financial storms and managed to stay afloat, so you're feeling more comfortable, not just with the entrepreneurial life but with your own personal style as a business owner. Your confidence is growing and your business is finding its rhythm. You've begun to separate from your start-up emotionally: your personal identity and professional image, so closely intertwined in the two earlier stages, are now beginning to decouple themselves. One of the most positive aspects of this process is that having and spending money becomes less an issue of survival and more a by-product of success.

After being in business for a while, you begin to see money as a means of protecting yourself. Appreciating the protective nature of money is a major step toward thinking about it rationally rather than purely emotionally. During this stage, you'll make exciting progress in renegotiating your relationship with money. As you learn to manage cash flow more effectively, the balance subtly shifts—money is no longer your enemy, but your friend. You also see its role clearly: just as money isn't the root of all your problems, it isn't the solution to all of them either.

Money can insulate you, give you a cushion, and buy you time. It can also give you more control over the work you do by enabling you to say yes to some projects and no to others. At the same time, money can't buy you emotional freedom or prevent you from making mistakes. It can allow your business to grow, but the decisions you make about how and when that growth should take place will dictate whether or not you expand successfully.

STAGE FOUR: MONEY AS A TOOL

When you reach this stage, you've really earned your entrepreneurial wings! Your attitude toward money will be very different from what it was when you first launched your business. Money is no longer emotionally charged for you: you'll see it simply as a vehicle for enacting your business decisions. At this stage, money has become transactional and fluid. You view it objectively as fuel for moving your business in the direction you want it to go, not as a measure of your personal or professional success.

By now, you've begun to use it as a tool to maximize your resources—negotiate a contract, build a relationship, market your services, create a product. You'll also have a more realistic understanding of the true meaning of money as independence. Money can give you financial freedom to work when and where you want to, give you access to new and exciting talent and projects, and allow you to grow your business from within rather than relying on outside funding sources. Let's take a closer look at this money-as-a-tool entrepreneurial style.

As part of a major ad campaign, a business owner commissioned an expensive photographic shoot. When the photos arrived, she wasn't happy with them. Early in her business, she noted, she would have been very upset and emotional about the results. She would have blamed herself for choosing the wrong person for the job and focused on her lack of judgment. When this incident occurred, however, she was further along the learning curve: she had been in business for a while and was no stranger to the problems that can arise when using freelance talent. Her experience had also given her a more businesslike relationship with money.

So, instead of letting her emotions cloud her judgment, she found herself zeroing in on the steps she needed to take to fix the problem and get the artwork she wanted. She quickly saw that she had three options, each with a different price tag. She could have the photographer reshoot the photos for her at cost, she could hire someone else to do the job over, or she could contact a stock photo house. When she first started her business, this entrepreneur recalled, she would never have been able to think in such a clearheaded, unemotional way about a project bottleneck. But, by the time it happened, she was well equipped to handle it with cool professionalism.

When you reach this stage, you too will see more clearly what money can and can't accomplish from a business perspective. You'll understand its value as a shield against some of the slings and arrows your business may suffer, but you'll also have a healthy grasp of its limitations. You'll view money as a kind of valuable but invisible employee. You'll be free to let it do its job while you do yours. You'll know that money plays a powerful and important role in your business, but it's a passive rather than an active one. *You* are the piper who calls the tune, and money does the dancing.

Giving Up a Paycheck Mentality

Viewing money as a tool requires you to give up the traditional "paycheck player" mentality of a jobholder. This can be very challenging. Separating money from your emotions and seeing it as an instrument is critical to successfully making the mental shift from employee to entrepreneur. How do you get there from here? The answer lies in understanding your money management style and the potential impact of financial patterns that you've acquired over the years. The first step in identifying your money style is to ask yourself: How have I handled money in the past? What mistakes have I made? What are my weaknesses when it comes to money?

Consciously, you may see yourself as well prepared to take risks and jump into entrepreneurship. But old, subconscious patterns die hard. Since this is such a crucial issue, we asked Dr. Edward Hallowell, a psychiatrist who's researched the emotional aspects of money, to take an in-depth look at its impact during the start-up process.

"Stress, insecurity, the drive for freedom—all these emotional factors can play themselves out along financial lines," explains Dr. Hallowell. "Look at your emotional responses to money and your money style—the way you handle it. This is where most people stumble: they don't take the emotional aspect of their money style into account. They focus all their energy on 'the numbers,' on graphs and spreadsheets, without any awareness of their psychological attitude. For example, some people tend to overspend. They throw money at problems as a way of solving them. At the other extreme, some people are just naturally afraid to take a risk. They are tight with money and may have a problem spending enough to make the investment their business requires."

Both overspending and underspending are psychological problems, not financial problems, according to Dr. Hallowell. By learning to understand the behavior patterns that money can trigger in you, especially when you're under stress, you have a much better chance of preventing your old spending habits from sabotaging your start-up. The key to handling these emotional hot buttons is to demystify your feelings about money, so that you can get them out on the table and deal with them. This means taking an honest look at your attitudes toward your competence at handling financial issues, such as budgeting or purchasing big-ticket items like computer equipment. As a woman, you should also be especially alert to two major financial traps during your transition from employee to entrepreneur: ambivalence about achieving independence and avoidance of money issues.

"Without knowing it," Dr. Hallowell notes, "some women feel guilty about the idea of being financially independent. They may be afraid that it will affect their ability to find or stay in a relationship. At an even deeper level, they may feel that they are violating a fundamental taboo, that making money will put them in a place they shouldn't be. When this happens, they can hurt their chances of success by behaving in ways that make them look as if they are afraid, as if they don't deserve to have a business, or as if they are guilty. As a result, they may have a hard time negotiating their fees or take on a partner they don't need or share a business they don't really want to share."

Another money pitfall for women to be aware of during their start-up phase is avoidance: not wanting to deal with finances or feeling that they are somehow inadequate when it comes to money management. This is the feeling that causes a woman to think, "I'm good at business, but I can't handle the financial end of things." Women who have this attitude can endanger their financial security by becoming over-dependent on their accountants or financial advisers. Or, they may end up using money as an excuse for failing, for demonstrating that they don't actually have what it takes to start a business and succeed at it—instead of realizing that the financial problems they're facing are just a natural part of any start-up situation.

What's the bottom line here? "Earning" the right to succeed. There's an emotional undercurrent to your business decisions that flows from deeply ingrained attitudes around making and spending money. It's important to be aware of this so that you can recognize old money patterns and habits when they surface during the intense, emotionally charged start-up phase. Understanding your money mind-set and your emotional behavior around money isn't easy—but it's crucial. Once you know what you're up against, you can offset these tendencies so you can manage your money proactively and productively.

The Creativity-Cash Connection

By operating on modest budgets, most women-owned ventures keep their overhead low, are not dependent on bank credit, don't give away huge chunks of their equity to investors, and run tight fiscal ships. Taking this approach often pushes businesses in new and profitable directions. It forces owners to market innovatively, to be alert to new opportunities, to seek out new money-saving technology, and to forge helpful alliances.

This pattern of slow-paced, strategic growth was evident in our interviews with women business owners. Most of these women had launched their ventures by using savings, taking on modest credit lines, moonlighting, and going the F & F route: borrowing from family and friends. In fact, many of them ran their businesses for the first six to twelve months—or even longer—with virtually no major outside funding. Even if you feel secure about your start-up stash, every dollar that you save by adopting a "brains for bucks" mentality is a dollar you'll have on hand for a rainy day. And, as one of our entrepreneurs, Crystal Johnson, puts it, "There *will* be rainy days."

Let's take a look at how two entrepreneurs in two very different businesses used brainpower versus dollar power to help finance and nurture their start-ups.

PATRICIA'S YARNS: STARTING SMART, STAYING SMALL

Cozy, colorful, and cultured, Patricia's Yarns is a retail shop in Hoboken, a fast-growing community just minutes away from Manhattan. Patricia Scribner opened the store after a four-year stint in financial services, and from the start it was a family affair. Her husband, Adam, a dedicated middle-school science teacher, is a full partner in the enterprise, both creatively and financially. He scoured Hoboken for an affordable, high-traffic rental space and spent an intense summer vacation renovating it. Patricia's dad, a retired accountant who had launched three businesses, not only donated financial advice but also built sleek wooden shelves to house the store's cheerful rainbow of luxurious wools.

From the moment that Patricia quit her job, she and Adam saved everything they could to finance their venture. Parents from both sides of the family invested small amounts. "For months, we didn't spend a penny," recalls Patricia. "We didn't go out or do anything. We bought Carlo Rossi wine in a jug and borrowed movies from the library."

Early on, the young couple made a decision to ignore industry conventions and shape a business model tailored to their modest budget, lifestyle goals, and financial comfort level. Pros at a trade show cautioned that Patricia would need from $50,000 to $100,000 in start-up funds and at least 1000 square feet of space. But Patricia's Yarns was successfully launched in about 350 square feet and on a budget of about $30,000. "It was money that we scrimped and saved to put together," says Adam. Their strategy was simple: "Keep overhead low, keep inventory low, and be in the best possible location."

This single-minded focus on keeping costs down ignited their ingenuity. Patricia tapped free advice from retired executives at SCORE and free legal counsel from the SBA. She registered her business online for $125 to save attorney fees. Resisting pressure from sales reps, she ordered a small, select inventory of yarns and supplies. She and Adam "recycled" an apron sign and laminated it at an office-supply store for

$6. To give her store a warm, inviting feeling, Patricia bartered with an artist friend, trading free knitting lessons for colorful original water-color paintings. Instead of spending crucial dollars on advertising, Adam contacted major newspapers and successfully pitched stories to them, generating priceless free publicity.

The "start small" strategy that Patricia's Yarns adopted quickly paid off. Soon after it opened, the store more than recouped its overhead costs, and during its first year of operations, Patricia and Adam poured their profits back into the business. By the time they celebrated its second anniversary, Patricia's Yarns was thriving, with an ever-changing inventory, loyal customers, and a fully attended class schedule. Its smart start-up and healthy bottom line recently enabled Patricia and Adam to move their enterprise to a bigger space in a prime location.

NOTA BENE: A STRONG VISION AND STRATEGIC GROWTH

The leap from management consultant to shoe manufacturer was a huge one for Jennifer Lovitt Riggs, and she made it in classic consulting style: strategically. Though the idea to design stylish shoes for career women first hit her after a blister-producing walk to a business meeting, Jennifer didn't pursue it for two years. Ultimately, a new baby and excitement about her shoe concept led to a life-changing detour from her intended career path, and Nota Bene was born.

Dipping into the modest savings that she and her husband had put away, Jennifer mapped out a three-year launch strategy built around a series of milestones, each with a dollar figure attached to it. Having reached the stage where she would need to outlay money on a regular basis, Jennifer began approaching F & F. A moderate infusion of cash from her family fueled the next stage of growth, motivating her to keep moving forward in pursuit of her dream.

Jennifer's family also provided critical technical support. Her husband, Todd, an MBA and former consultant himself, acted as her sounding board and bookkeeper; her brother-in-law, an orthopedic surgeon, helped her with design concepts and technical issues around manufacturing stylish shoes that stressed both comfort and a healthy fit. Her stepfather, a retired engineer, built her website and runs her warehouse—and her sister and mother help out on the sales and marketing front.

As a new mother with a baby as well as a business to nurture, Jennifer quickly realized that she needed to stay focused and in control. While she was pressured by suppliers to move faster, she decided to build Nota Bene at a rate that worked for her not just financially, but emotionally as well. "Other people weren't paying the bills, this wasn't their dream, and they weren't taking responsibility for it," points out Jennifer. "It was very important for me to stick with my plan and do things at my own pace."

Early on, she remembers seeing money pour out and thinking, "Am I spending my child's college tuition? Is this my vacation house that's gone forever?" Whenever she felt anxious, revisiting her business plan and seeing the progress that she'd made helped allay her fears. "If I was too far away from the numbers and a reality check, getting back to them helped, because I was always imagining things were worse than they actually were."

Nurturing Nota Bene at her own pace has proven advantageous on a number of fronts, says Jennifer. It enabled her product to find its niche and build a solid market foothold among influential women across the country. Letting her business find its own rhythm also allowed her to make important midcourse corrections. "Never waste a good mistake," she advises. Her business plan has proven surprisingly accurate: three years into her launch Nota Bene became self-supporting, and less than a year later Jennifer began exploring options for her next growth phase.

Beyond Bootstrapping: Manage Your Money Carefully!

Ironically, sometimes the biggest financial challenge you can face is not having too little money, but having too much. When this happens, it can throw your business rhythm off and make it hard to regain your balance financially. That's what happened to the cofounders of Beyond Blossoms. Like Patricia's Yarns and Nota Bene, Beyond Blossoms started out with a modest investment. But when the budding company refocused its strategy, moving from a home-based enterprise to an Internet-based business, the ante was upped considerably.

Gina Maschek's online enterprise started out as a student project called "Flower Power," which she created for a course at Babson College, the country's leading business school for entrepreneurs. After receiving their MBAs, Gina and a classmate, Josh Grossman, decided to give the idea—providing floral arrangements to corporations in the Boston area—a chance to grow. Christening their venture "Beyond Blossoms," they each kicked in $4,000; to cut costs, they worked from their garages without pay and bought fresh flowers daily. After a few months it became clear that their original concept was too limited.

Undaunted, Gina and Josh began investigating online delivery—the flower industry's fastest-growing segment. Ultimately, they commissioned a unique box design for their arrangements and decided to shift their business online. By this time, the two partners had applied for an SBA loan and been refused. When they found a bank willing to give them a $20,000 loan, Josh's mother helped out by stepping in with collateral.

The costs of gearing up an online business—especially the sophisticated e-commerce website required—quickly ate into their loan dollars. The team's box designer came to the rescue by connecting them with a major flower wholesaler-distributor. After months of negotiating, he invested $200,000 in Beyond Blossoms in return for a sizeable equity position. Buoyed by what seemed to be buckets of cash, Gina and Josh went on a spending spree that was anything but strategic! For more than a year, the two hadn't paid themselves a penny. Now, though they gave themselves only modest salaries, they began overspending in other critical areas, especially marketing. "When we got that big chunk of money, we thought, 'Oh, we have full pockets now, nothing can go wrong,'" Gina recalls, amused at their naiveté. Looking back at this stage of her venture, Gina laughs as she cites a classic case study from business school in which a start-up launched in the heady days of the dot-com era received several rounds of venture capital. "This company got huge funding," Gina observes. "And the more money the founders raised per round, the more poorly they spent it.

After several years, you could see that with less funding, they made better decisions.

"Even though we had read these case studies, we made the same mistakes! You just think that $200,000 is so much money that $2,000 here or $5,000 there doesn't really matter. From the beginning, we should have done what real companies do—set up a marketing budget and a budget for operations. We didn't! We just jumped in and said, 'OK, we have this money, let's try this, let's try that.' It was very unco-ordinated, very unprofessional. We were misled by all this money in our bank account." Despite this precarious phase, Beyond Blossoms' online strategy has led to a steady climb in profits. When Gina's part-ner left the company for personal reasons, she decided to continue building it and began a search for second-round financing.

Leveraging Your Start-Up Dollars

As Beyond Blossoms' cautionary tale demonstrates, a modest bank balance not only compels you to get more bang for each and every buck you spend, it also ensures that any financial mistakes you make will have a high price tag and aren't likely to be repeated! That's why learning to manage money like an entrepreneur is so critical. As you fine-tune your money style, there are plenty of practical steps you can take to make your money work harder for you and to reduce your emo-tional vulnerability when it comes to financing.

To help you make better, smarter decisions on this front, we asked the entrepreneurs interviewed for this chapter to share their ideas (see also chapter 9, page 184). Drawing on their frontline experience, they offer plenty of hard-won advice for managing your start-up funds with maximum impact.

Patricia and Adam Scribner, who launched Patricia's Yarns, offer this advice:

- *Figure out your financial comfort zone and stay within it:* At the very start, Patricia and Adam mapped out a business plan and bud-get that they felt comfortable with and made a decision to work within it. They launched successfully with a budget that was far lower than industry experts told them they would need. But, by being resourceful and persistent, they beat the odds. "Figure out a financial framework that you feel comfortable with and then stick with it," advises Adam.

- *Create a financial safety net or buffer zone:* Building a cushion can be a major help in managing the risks associated with your start-up. Unexpected things will always come up—and being financially prepared for them is a real stress reliever. With untapped funds to fall back on, you don't have to rely on other people to bail you out during tough times.

- *Be creative in how you spend your money:* You can always upgrade, but you can't downgrade. Figure out how to create the image you want within your budget. You don't have to spend a fortune to project a tasteful, polished image. Be resourceful: with some hunting, for example, you can find a used cash register for $40 instead of spending $750 for a new one.

- *Don't be a pushover:* Don't do anything you don't want to do, just because someone pressures you to. For example, don't let an outside supplier, eager to make a sale, persuade you to take on too much debt or assume more risk than you feel equipped to handle.

- *Be sure you have health benefits:* Since Adam is a teacher, Patricia is covered by his health policy, which was an important comfort factor in launching their business. It may take some financial stretching and work on your part to find an organization that offers decent coverage, but it's worth it, believes Patricia. People with small businesses who don't have benefits can find themselves in a "nightmare," she warns, because they literally can't afford to get sick.

- *Stay in touch with your original vision:* When new ideas crop up, they can be very seductive, but it's important to remember why you went into business in the first place. It may be tempting to grow a lot bigger or go into franchising, for example, but the main reason you started your business may have been to create a certain lifestyle for yourself—one that may become impossible to enjoy if you expand in certain directions. More is not necessarily better: ultimately, upping the ante may not be as satisfying as staying true to your founding concept.

Jennifer Lovitt Riggs of Nota Bene offers the following wisdom:

- **Stay streamlined:** "It's amazing what you can do with a laptop, a home office, and through being resourceful," says Jennifer. "You don't have to have a marketing firm on retainer and you don't have to have an ad every month. You can have a professional start-up without spending a fortune."

- **Focus on core value in marketing your product or service:** It's important, says Jennifer, to stay with what's central to your business concept and communicate that core idea. A phrase she used often during her launch was, "It's just about the shoes!" "Certainly, packaging was important," Jennifer notes. "But focusing on our core value added—that was the most important thing. And that isn't as expensive as all the other things that people might encourage you to do."

- **Create milestones for your business:** Setting milestones and then attaching budget figures to them has proven very helpful to Jennifer. "My family always says that you can eat an elephant one bite at a time," she observes. "It really helped me to say, 'OK, I just have to work on this next bite and then I can make a decision about the rest.' If I had looked at the whole picture at every stage, it might have been too much to handle."

- **Be creative—it's a confidence builder:** When you're creative, you're putting more of yourself and your vision into your business. That can be "very unifying and really boost your confidence," observes Jennifer. It can also help you pace your business's growth in a way that works best for you. This allows you to make course corrections and apply lessons learned.

Finally, Gina Maschek of Beyond Blossoms suggests the following:

- *Have several financing options:* If at all possible, line up several funding options before negotiating for major financing, so that you have some real bargaining power. Giving yourself choices gives you flexibility; without them, you may be forced to accept tougher terms than you want in order to get the money you need.

- *Don't outsource prematurely:* Hiring other people to do work that you can do yourself too early can be a real cash drain, warns Maschek. When you're really still a start-up—even if you have a couple of hundred thousand dollars in the bank, as Beyond Blossoms did—"take the guerilla marketing approach," advises Gina. Wait to outsource until you can hire really seasoned professionals who will do a first-rate job without breaking the bank.

- *Do your homework before you engage anyone:* Just because you're a start-up doesn't mean it's a good idea to turn to another start-up for support in key areas. Instead, do your homework: make sure that the people you hire for critical jobs like website development are really experienced and can deliver what they say they can, on budget and on time. Look for people with strong track records and talk to references. Make sure they know what they're doing and can give you accurate estimates—otherwise you can end up missing crucial deadlines or overspending to fix costly mistakes. Watch your money carefully! Don't make the classic mistake that Beyond Blossoms did, cautions Maschek, and overspend when an infusion of cash beefs up your bank account. Stay focused and in control. Create budgets for key functions like marketing and operations—and stick to them!

Easing Your Financial Transition

As we've seen, figuring our how to manage money like an entrepreneur is an ongoing process—and a challenging one. It's just about guaranteed that you'll make plenty of mistakes along the way—they're all part of the learning curve. Talking about your financial concerns is one very important way to work them out and defuse the tensions that money problems can create. It can also help you spot dangerous financial patterns that might short-circuit your success. Thinking through different options for financing your business and handling your money can make you feel more confident and in control.

"'Never worry alone'—that's the best advice I ever received from one of my teachers," observes Dr. Hallowell. "Having someone to bounce your worries off of can help you find ways to handle them. Sit down with a consultant, for example, and worry with that person; use your concerns constructively. Look at the worst-case financial scenario and come up with a game plan for it. It's also very important to have someone whom you trust and who will listen to prevent you from getting out of line financially. It can be a spouse, a partner, or an associate. If there is one practical strategy I would advise more than any other, it would be this: find a trusted adviser and listen to what they tell you."

In the end, most of us find the money to do the things we really want to do. If we don't, then it's probably lack of desire or drive, not lack of dollars, that is holding us back. As we've seen, if you have a business idea that you're passionate about, a shoestring budget can actually be an asset. It can compel you to be more focused, more resourceful, more creative, and more attuned to a growth strategy that evolves slowly but organically. All in all, a winning combination!

more brains for bucks

To spark your own creative juices, here are a few more money-saving ideas:

Lisa Druxman: When Lisa first launched Stroller Strides, she bartered with some of her new clients, trading workout sessions for legal services with one of the moms who attended her classes, for example. Unfazed by her lack of ad dollars, Lisa also gained priceless exposure by pitching newsworthy stories about her business to the media.

Brenda Newberry: During her launch, Brenda kept costs down by using the local Denny's as her "satellite office." She also designed her own business stationery and learned how to upgrade her complex phone system herself, without having to hire a technician.

Becky Rohrer: While restoring her inn, Becky recruited her mother as a temporary chef and her dad as a landscaper.

Crystal Johnson: While building Sienna at Home, Crystal saved thousands of dollars by learning how to design and manage her company's website. She also designs her own advertising.

Karen Curro and **Susan Edelman:** When they needed help stocking their shelves for the opening of their Laugh Out Loud store, Karen and Susan turned to two friends, Chris, who was a visual designer, and Ray, who worked at a major department store and gave them a crash course in merchandising.

Sarah Levy: While starting her business, Sarah bartered with a top-notch photography firm, creating gift baskets for its clients in return for lush, eye-catching photos of her chocolates and baked goods that gave her venture a polished, professional image. She also delivered a pizza to a radio show host at six in the morning in return for free airtime to promote her new business!

Quick Tips ⇨

Quick Tips

Manage money—don't let it manage you!
Manage money like an entrepreneur! Treat it as an invisible employee, not an emotional barometer. Wield it as a decision-making tool to achieve your business goals.

Let go of your paycheck mentality.
View money as a neutral instrument, not a reward. Identify your emotional hot buttons around finances. Ask trusted allies to monitor your spending patterns.

Cultivate a "brains for bucks" mind-set.
Don't spend money you don't have! Think creativity instead of cash. Make thrifty ingenuity a habit—the benefits will astound you!

Leverage your start-up dollars.
Bet on smart money—put it to work! Stay strong! Don't let vendors or experts push you beyond your budget and comfort zone. Figure out your distinctive value-added feature and build on it.

Avoid overspending.
Act like a start-up—do it yourself! Adopt a "guerilla marketing" strategy. Vet vendors carefully. Create budgets for key functions—and stick to them. Plan for a "rainy day."

Separate your self-worth from your net worth.
Reevaluate your concept of "making it." Decouple your feelings of self-worth from your earning power. Enjoy the nonmonetary rewards that your start-up offers.

☑ Use this checklist to clarify, in your own mind, which challenges and action steps apply to you.

BRAINS FOR BUCKS ACTION STEPS

What is my money management style? Under financial pressure do I tend to

- ☐ Overspend to relieve my anxiety?
- ☐ Underspend out of fear?
- ☐ Set unrealistic goals to "prove" myself?
- ☐ Overrely on "experts" to help me?
- ☐ Use inaction as a way to avoid risk?
- ☐ Become unfocused and unproductive?

I plan to substitute brains for bucks by

- ☐ Generating my own publicity.
- ☐ Keeping overhead low.
- ☐ Bartering creatively and consistently.
- ☐ Seeking out money-saving technology.
- ☐ Mining the Internet as a marketing tool.
- ☐ Leveraging vendor relationships.

I will remind myself to

- ☐ Concentrate on results, not image.
- ☐ Create satisfying, attainable milestones.
- ☐ Resist sales pressure to buy excess inventory.
- ☐ Focus on core value, not bells and whistles.
- ☐ Stay in touch with my business vision.
- ☐ Treat money as a tool, not a success index.
- ☐ Pay myself in nonmonetary ways, such as _____ _____

Chapter 4

Take the Leap

You have to believe in yourself—and have the strength to pursue what you really want.

—RONNIE FLISS

If you find yourself thinking seriously of turning your life upside down by starting your own venture, then the number one question you're probably struggling with is "How do I know when I'm ready to take the leap?" You may be trying to decide whether to launch now or wait—until you save more money, the economy picks up, or you feel better prepared. We'd love to be able to tell you, "Here's a 'Test Your Entrepreneurial IQ' quiz. If you score 60 points or above, then you've got what it takes to make your business dream come true."

However, no such easy methods for gauging entrepreneurial readiness emerged from our interviews. Timing, like life itself, is a very personal affair. The responses about timing that surfaced were too individual and complex to be reduced to a one-size-fits-all formula. Among the women we spoke with, we found different degrees of emotional energy, frustration, family and financial pressures—and, above all, different dreams and desires. But there's good news as well: we also identified ten start-up "triggers" that may act as useful guidelines as you wrestle with that all-important question: To leap or not to leap?

Ten Telltale Signs to Watch For

As we saw in chapter 2, it's rarely just one factor that triggers a move. With this in mind, we're going to take an in-depth look at ten triggers that surfaced during our interviews. Not surprisingly, several of these may strike a chord with you. Think of them as emotional signposts alerting you to pay closer attention to your inner voice. Their message: "Warning! You Are Entering the Land of Entrepreneurial Longing. Proceed at Your Own Risk!"

1. ***Your personal values are out of sync with those of the corporate world:*** Take a long, honest look at your attitude toward remaining in a corporate setting. As you think about continuing to work in a corporate or institutional environment, what's your immediate response? Is the idea energizing or draining? How do you see your future unfolding? Are your personal values in harmony or at odds with the demands and rewards of corporate life? What are your expectations about the success this career path offers? Would another title or more money make a difference? Are you asking too much—or too little?

   As you reevaluate, you may find yourself wishing for a work environment that's more in tune with your personal values. It's precisely this desire that compelled Sarah Levy to launch Sarah's Pastries & Candies. "I've worked at different restaurants where the atmosphere was very stressful," says Sarah, "and I wanted to have a place where I could dictate the tone and mood. I really wanted to create a comfortable environment where people would enjoy coming to work. One day, Rafael, who runs my kitchen, said to me, 'We always look forward to your coming—it always brightens our day! We feel so much more relaxed—everything's so much better when you're here.' To hear him say that was huge for me. For the store's first anniversary, everyone took me out to a really nice dinner to celebrate. This tells me that they're happy—and that's very rewarding. It's really like creating a family."

2. ***Your "learning curve" flattens:*** When your learning curve flattens, it's easy to feel stymied and stuck. Not only can your job seem like

it's no longer a source of growth, but it can actually seem to be an obstacle to your professional development. When this happens, the desire to learn more and achieve more on the job can quickly fade away. If you can't reenergize your approach to your responsibilities, then you may need to consider not just a job change or industry shift, but a major transition to a whole new way of working.

When her firm, Warner Entertainment, decided to consolidate its licensing operations in California, Karen Spitz found herself resisting the move from her Manhattan-based office. A highly regarded industry pro, Karen had handled the licensing of both the *Superman* and *Batman* film franchises, among others, and her small team generated well over half of all the revenues of her company's licensing program. With her company moving in a new direction, Karen realized that the change had nothing new to offer her and decided to set up her own licensing firm. Building on her network of contacts, Karen's company, Licensing Link Ltd., has managed to thrive and innovate in a highly competitive industry. Looking back, Karen feels she made the right move at the right time.

3. *You find yourself beyond burnout:* Work long enough at a demanding job and you're likely to experience some form of career burnout. You may find yourself feeling unusually fatigued and unable to summon up enthusiasm for the projects you have to tackle. In many cases, the antidote may simply be to reshape your job. Sometimes more radical steps are called for: changing companies, for example, or changing industries. But, like many women, you may have reached a point where none of these approaches proves adequate.

As we saw in chapter 2, Becky Rohrer's decision to quit her job was the result of a deep-seated frustration with her life choices that was both mirrored in and intensified by her work situation. "I didn't like the person my work was making me become," Becky recalls. "I was afraid of not doing a good enough job. I was afraid of losing my job. I was afraid that I wasn't hiring the right people—I was afraid of everything—and this was not a way to live."

Most of us know when things are in balance—and we're feeling good about our work and our lives. We also know when we feel unsatisfied and overwhelmed. Are you simply overtired and overreacting to your job? How do the people who know you best and care most about you—your friends and family—view your situation? What are some of the signs that you may have moved beyond burnout and need to seriously reassess both your health and your future as a corporate employee? While everyone reacts differently, some obvious symptoms are trouble sleeping, inertia, and lack of concentration. Other signs may be fatigue and even depression. Any of these problems can affect your well-being as well as your productivity.

4. **You find yourself thinking about a great idea—constantly:** Here's the would-be entrepreneur's classic malady: you're obsessed with an idea for a product or service to the point where it begins to interfere with your work and your personal life. If this happens, it's time to rejoice—not panic—because your launch decision is being made for you. This is exactly how Liz Lange's entrepreneurial voyage began. After seeing her pregnant friends attempt to pour themselves into snug designer dresses, she began to obsess about her idea of stylish maternity wear. She thought about it night and day. Eventually, she found herself propelled forward.

    If you find yourself totally immersed in your idea, then resisting the inevitable will only intensify your discontent with things as they are. So start mapping out a game plan for making your move—in your own time and on your own terms. Taking action and moving in the direction of your dream will turn your frustration and obsession into turbocharged entrepreneurial fuel.

5. **You've been fired or laid off, your job is at risk—or you've just had enough:** Every month, tens of thousands of corporate jobs disappear across America. Over the course of their lives, most employees can expect to weather at least five or six employment changes or career switches. If you've been downsized or your job is at risk, then self-employment may be an option that you are seriously

exploring. Or a sudden change in your job or work environment may spur a move. That's what happened to Patricia Scribner.

Patricia and Adam Scribner had talked on and off for more than a year about starting a business that Patricia could run. Adam loved his work as a middle-school teacher, but Patricia no longer enjoyed her job at a major financial services firm. Her department had been reorganized and her small team of colleagues dismantled. As the work piled on, Patricia's situation took a nosedive—and so did her normally upbeat disposition. When Adam or her parents called her at work, they could hear the unhappiness in her voice. She began having migraines and living for the weekend.

The couple agreed that the time was right for Patricia to find work that she really cared about. She enjoyed crafts and zeroed in on the idea of opening a yarn shop in their hometown. Armed with a business plan, enthusiastic family support, and lots of elbow grease, Patricia and Adam went from concept to launch in a matter of months—creating a cozy, inviting store that's become their "second living room."

"When Trish started to do well," Adam observed, "a lot of our friends began questioning their own jobs and where they were headed. One person left a job in finance where he had been very successful for many years and went into real estate—something he had always wanted to do. It was as if watching Trish spurred and inspired people to make some changes or test the waters."

6. ***Your career and family priorities are undergoing a life-changing shift:*** The existence of the term "mompreneurs" indicates just how powerful a force working mothers have become in fueling the start-up engine in the United States. It also expresses in a nutshell the continuing challenge that women face in balancing work and family needs. In our interviews, women talked with fervor about their search for flexibility as a key driver in their start-up scenarios.

Anne Afshari and Laura Hagler are prime examples: commitment to their families was a major motivator in their decision to launch their Colorado Springs–based company, Exclusively RNs. The two OB-GYN nurses went through nursing school together, and between them they have six children ranging in age from teenagers to toddlers. While Anne and Laura enjoyed their action-packed jobs as members of OB-GYN delivery teams, they both worked long hours away from home.

After a chance conversation with an overworked doctor, Anne realized that she and Laura could use their nursing expertise to offer a valuable time-saving service to physicians—and Exclusively RNs, their telephone advisory service for expectant mothers, was born. Today, with the help of affordable advanced technology in the form of Virtual PBX's Web-hosted private exchange service, Anne and Laura have expanded far beyond their home base of Colorado Springs. They've built a staff of specially trained nurses in Colorado, Arizona, Florida, Texas, and North Carolina—and plan to continue to expand their enterprise. Giving other skilled nurses a family-friendly and flexible work option is one of the biggest rewards of their business.

"We were finding that because we were working full-time we were missing out on a lot of our children's lives," explains Anne. "We were having a difficult time juggling both a professional career outside the home and our personal family lives. With our home-based business, we can be around when our kids go to school and get back, help them with their homework, and take them to their activities. Meeting our families' needs has always been our driving force and one of the motivating factors for us to be successful."

7. *Lack of opportunity is constraining your growth:* Catalyst, an organization that tracks work trends for women, predicts that it will take at least another fifty years before the glass ceiling really cracks and women attain true equality in senior positions in corporate America. Given this outlook, it's not surprising that many women are choosing to leave corporate jobs to run their own shows. Though entrepreneurs can increase their net worth more quickly than corporate employees, the deal-breaking issue isn't always earning power. Often it's about advancement, ethics, work-life balance, or simply work satisfaction.

Brenda Newberry's decision to launch her own information technology (IT) firm was motivated in part by a lack of corporate opportunity. When Brenda began her St. Louis–based company, she had one employee and a bootstrap budget of $1,000; to help make ends meet, she contracted herself out to clients. Today, she runs an IT powerhouse: the Newberry Group is approaching $25 million in annual revenues and ranks among Inc. 500's "Fastest Growing Private Businesses." A tireless mentor to new entrepreneurs, in 2005, Brenda was chosen by the SBA as Missouri's Small Business Person of the Year.

Brenda's pre-entrepreneurial career is equally impressive. After spending six years in the Air Force and earning a master's degree, Brenda went to work for McDonnell Douglas. Five years later, she joined a leading financial services company, where she advanced from systems programmer to vice president of a stand-alone business unit for which she had profit and loss responsibilities.

In some ways, this was a dream job. Brenda attended customer conferences at major resorts and traveled to Brussels, Paris, and even Bogotá. But, despite her prestige and perks, Brenda felt isolated. As a vice president in the mid-1990s, she saw that there weren't any women of color above her, and the future didn't seem promising. In her view, her employer was also "becoming more political than performance driven," and she felt that her ethical standards were being compromised. Experiencing a midlife crisis, an ethical dilemma, and the glass ceiling all at once—Brenda decided to quit her job.

Seeing the uncertain economy and Brenda's daughter headed for college, some people thought she was making a huge mistake. After undergoing numerous interviews for executive-level positions, Brenda realized that, as an African American and a woman, she would constantly have to prove herself in the corporate world. Then a business associate suggested that she use her background to start her own company. After a few months of job searching and soul-searching, Brenda launched what is now one of St. Louis's most successful women-owned enterprises.

8. ***You find yourself fantasizing about starting your own business:***
Just about all of us toy with the idea of leaving our jobs and striking out on our own. Whatever form such fantasies take, they often
act as stress relievers. Sometimes, however, our dreams take firmer
root in our hearts than we expect. And, as happened to Roxanne
Coady, a combination of circumstances can unexpectedly bring a
dream center stage.

"I was very, very happy in many ways at my firm," comments
Roxanne about her position with a leading tax accounting company. "I was made national tax director, which was a big deal. I was
young and no woman had held the job before. I had a great sense
of accomplishment about it. I was very well treated, which is why
my leaving came as such a surprise."

What induced Roxanne to give up a satisfying, high-paying job
where she was well respected and given every opportunity? One of
the main reasons was her acute awareness that " . . . many women
are, by nature, outsiders in the business world. I'm collegial. I like
open communications. I was not very good at internal politics. And
these qualities are not necessarily best suited for a happy day in
the corporate world. All these things percolated," says Roxanne,
"and led me to ask, 'What would be the perfect environment for
me?' That got me thinking about my own business. What it was
about was never an issue: it would always be about books."

Roxanne's passion for reading led to her dream of opening a
bookstore where people could gather, connect, meet authors, and
talk about ideas. Propelled by the twin engines of desire and cir-
cumstance, she gave six months' notice and embarked on a literary
adventure tour, visiting bookstores all over the world. Ultimately,
she bought and renovated a building in Madison, Connecticut—
and, happily, became pregnant at the same time. Two months
after opening her bookstore, Roxanne gave birth to a son. Named
for her grandmother, R. J. Julia Booksellers is a nationally known
independent bookstore—and Roxanne is admired as an innovator
in a demanding, intensely competitive industry.

9. ***You find yourself moonlighting in response to an inner drive:*** Moonlighting for fun and profit is something many of us have experimented with during our work lives. But when you reach a point where you derive far more psychic and emotional satisfaction from moonlighting than from your day job, then it may be time to reevaluate your situation. Sometimes moonlighting can be so much more rewarding and remunerative than a nine-to-five position that it becomes the basis for your start-up. Making this decision when you have only one or two clients can be risky business, however, since their demand for your services might be short lived.

If you are tempted to chuck your day job in favor of your moonlighting enterprise, proceed carefully! There's a big difference between moonlighting while having the security of a regular paycheck and trying to transform a part-time venture into a full-time business. You and your family may be far better off if you keep your day job and build your sideline business slowly until you're confident that it can provide adequate support. This is exactly how Anne Afshari and Laura Hagler started Exclusively RNs.

With no business background, but an office of doctors urging them on, Anne and Laura put together a formal proposal and set up their company; within three months, they were fielding calls. "For quite a while after we had started wearing our business-owner hats, we both continued to work clinically," says Laura. "So our new company was another job we were doing, another plate we were spinning. And, because we have families and kids, we had to do it all." Ultimately, the two budding entrepreneurs left their jobs so they could focus full-time on building their enterprise.

10. ***You realize that you would rather lead than manage:*** Lots of ink has been spilled about the difference between managers and leaders. For women in demanding corporate careers, the distinction is critical: being pigeonholed as a competent manager or singled out as a potential leader can make a big difference in the way your company views your contributions and career path. Gaining leadership skills within corporations can be challenging for women, mainly because they often lead differently from men. They tend to favor

relationship building, open communications, and inclusive operating structures. Launching their own ventures enables them to give full rein to their leadership skills and discover untapped talents.

Warren Bennis, a management expert, has described successful leadership as "fully becoming yourself." As you look at your own future within the corporate world, how likely—or unlikely—is it that you will receive the resources, training, and ever-widening responsibility you need in order to strengthen your leadership skills and fully become yourself? Equally important, do you feel a powerful drive at this stage in your work life to make the leap from manager to leader, from employee to entrepreneur?

Assessing Your Assets

As you think about timing your launch, adding up all the invaluable work assets that you've developed to date can act as a powerful motivator and confidence booster. Though your career so far may have had its limitations, it's also given you priceless lessons along with invaluable skills and experience. In making the move from employee to entrepreneur, you're *not* starting all over again; your previous career provides a treasure trove of strengths and contacts that you can build on.

Yes, you are refashioning your professional image, but the identity you're creating is firmly rooted in your past experience and success. Now, at last, you have the chance to run your own show and showcase what you know. As you review the transferable assets you've developed on the job, you'll find they fall into the following six categories:

1. ***The industry knowledge you've absorbed:*** Not surprisingly, this particular resource is going to be most directly useful if the business you're launching is in the same field as your corporate career. You're in the best possible position in starting your venture, since you can mine virtually every nook and cranny of the corporate mountain you've climbed for precious nuggets of expertise, information, and support.

2. ***The business planning experience and self-discipline you've gained:***
   As an employee, it's more than likely that you've been primarily
   or partially responsible for overseeing projects, managing a staff
   and/or teams, meeting deadlines, handling budgets, producing
   deliverables, monitoring performance, and/or measuring results.
   All these are valuable business skills that you can now utilize on
   your own behalf.

   When Jennifer Lovitt Riggs made the leap from management
   consulting to women's shoe manufacturing, she took full advantage of the strategic planning, project management, and budgeting expertise she had acquired at Booz Allen Hamilton, a global
   consulting firm, to help her map out a launch strategy for her new
   enterprise. She conducted market research, created a business
   plan, identified product development and financial milestones,
   and completed a feasibility study—all things she had learned while
   working as an employee.

3. ***The managerial/functional skills you've acquired:*** In your years as
   a jobholder, you've added any number of managerial and/or func-
   tional skills to your business quiver that you can use to take aim
   at your newfound entrepreneurial goals. You may have learned to
   oversee multifaceted projects, run teams, conduct surveys, build a
   public relations network, write brochures, mount online ad cam-
   paigns, organize special events, analyze market data, and monitor
   industry trends. The list of on-the-job skills you've mastered that
   can be put to use in your launch is virtually endless.

   Ronnie Fliss spent almost thirty years as an IT executive specializing in business intelligence. Mining data may seem a far cry
   from baking gourmet dog biscuits, but when Ronnie decided to
   explore the gourmet pet-food industry, she used her sharply honed
   research skills to analyze its growth potential, evaluate the competitive landscape, and identify a promising market niche.

4. ***The professionalism you've developed:*** You've handled stressful
   deadlines, managed difficult clients, orchestrated complex projects, successfully completed tough negotiations, and brought
   grace, skill, and efficiency to the tasks you've been assigned. In the

course of doing all this, you've probably developed a high degree of confidence in your capabilities, experience, and business judgment. In short, you're a "pro," with all the positive attributes that this level of achievement implies.

The polish, judgment, and grace under fire that you've demonstrated in your work life will be invaluable to the new enterprise you're planning. Though the ways in which you express these attributes may change as you become attuned to your new lifestyle or the conventions of the new field you may be entering, it's the aura of professionalism you bring to your new venture that counts.

5. *The contacts and networks you've fostered:* Since you have probably been in the workforce for some time, one of your prime transferable assets is the constellation of contacts that you've developed. Like the spokes of a wheel, these contacts radiate out in many directions. They may include team members and other colleagues, industry and professional groups, suppliers, and even your counterparts at competing organizations.

   Many of these contacts may continue to prove helpful, even if you're making a 180-degree shift into another industry in your new venture. Attracting clients, finding the right people to help build your website, getting sound advice on your business plan, locating reliable suppliers—all these activities will require generous support, sound advice, and solid referrals. So save that Rolodex—you're definitely going to need it!

6. *The insights on work styles you've gathered:* One of the biggest assets you bring to your start-up is your exposure to different management styles and work environments—and your insights regarding what works and what doesn't. Reflect even briefly on the boss you admired most and the one who made your life miserable and you'll see how much you've learned. You know the types: the nurturing mentor and the nit-picking tyrant. As the star of your own show, you have the freedom not only to surround yourself with the kind of people you want to build a future with but also to manage and mentor them in a way that reflects your personal style and values. In our interviews, we found that the opportunity

to create a professional yet flexible and friendly work environment was a powerful motivator for many women.

An impressive list of assets, isn't it? Add them all together and you have a dynamic platform from which you can make the leap into entrepreneurship. And that's not the half of it! Consider all the other strengths you're bringing to this new stage of your work life—the ones that can't be described so easily. Your problem-solving talents, for example. Or your restless curiosity and innovative flair. Or your sensitivity to elusive industry trends. Or your uncanny ability to tackle a hydra-headed project and keep everyone on task. No doubt about it: you have a lot going for you!

Whatever the unique mix of abilities that have enriched your employers to date, you now have a tantalizing opportunity to push those abilities to the next level in service to your own growth, mission, and earning power. They're yours to draw on and they'll kick in naturally as needed. You'll have plenty of opportunities—more than you bargained for—to add to your strengths as you wrestle with your start-up.

Taking Your Entrepreneurial Temperature

Even after assessing your assets and reviewing the ten signs we've described, deciding whether or not you've caught the start-up bug isn't always easy. Neither is separating feelings of frustration about your work from the events or circumstances that may have triggered them. Then there's the push-pull dilemma: yes, factors within corporate life may be pushing you out the door, but how strong an entrepreneurial pull are you feeling? What are the biggest barriers you see to making the move? How much emotional and financial support can you really count on from your family, friends, and contacts? As you think through these questions, keep in mind the following practical advice from women who were once exactly where you are now.

LISTEN TO YOUR INTERNAL CLOCK

Intuition and a strong sense of timing are critical to successfully launching a new venture. One or more of the ten triggers or signs identified earlier may have really hit home for you. But, though any of these factors may contribute to your decision to pursue an independent work life, they shouldn't be the ultimate drivers of that decision. Instead, it's your own inner clock and personal readiness that you should be paying most attention to.

Get that right and you have a good shot at surviving even exceptionally challenging business conditions. If your internal sense of timing is off and you aren't emotionally equipped to handle the demands of a start-up, however, then a tough external environment can throw you off balance. So internal momentum, not external drivers, should be your touchstone when it comes to timing.

ARM YOURSELF WITH INFORMATION

During our interviews, many different women offered the same advice: Do your homework. Research your market. Talk to people. Learn everything you can about entrepreneurship, finance, pricing, and marketing. Ask questions. Don't be afraid to reach out for help if you don't know something.

When you are starting a business, inner momentum is all-important—but it needs to be bolstered by solid research and practical action steps. The more you know, the better your chances of success—and the surer you'll become about precisely when and how to orchestrate your move. You can also use much of the data you gather as the basis for building a business plan, formal or informal.

Your information-gathering process can build your confidence, fill major skill gaps, and help you zero in on a winning start-up idea, if you haven't identified it already. To find the one idea that sparks your imagination, you may have to work through your share of also-rans. Eventually, one idea picks you and the others will fall by the wayside. But unless you're willing to go through an informed winnowing process and make some mistakes, you may not recognize the right idea when it finally comes your way.

EASE ON DOWN THE ROAD

While some people take the leap without hesitation, others find it less stressful if they create a transitional period and ease their way into entrepreneurship. Launching your venture doesn't have to be an either-or situation, at least initially. You don't have to quit your job in order to start your business—you can juggle both for a while by planning a gradual move.

Moonlighting is the most obvious transitional route, and it can be a smart strategy, both economically and emotionally. Although it's physically and mentally demanding, it can enable you to test-market your product or service, build your skills, cultivate a clientele, and strengthen your financial position. Overlapping your job and your venture gives you stability—it buys you time and the peace of mind to plan your move. It also allows you to hang on to your medical and other benefits for a while, which can help you gather enough savings and support to fuel your start-up.

There are also other steps that you can take to phase into business ownership. You can create a "freedom fund," for instance, and set aside part of every paycheck to finance your venture. If you're in a two-paycheck situation, then you and your partner might decide to live on one salary for a while and "invest" the other in your dream. Jennifer Lovitt Riggs and her husband, for example, had always operated this way—living on one paycheck and saving the other. So when Jennifer chose to launch Nota Bene, a company that manufactures stylish, comfortable shoes for active women, her family was already well accustomed to managing on a one-income budget. This eased her launch considerably.

Another way to transition into your start-up may be to line up one or more "anchor" clients that can provide a base of support for your new business. With some thoughtful planning and extra work, you can also leverage your time and talents as a volunteer or unpaid intern in order to learn the ins and outs of your new field as a way of building a bridge to your entrepreneurial dream. Then there's the partnership route: teaming up with another businessperson who has a track record of creating an operating structure in which both you and your partner devote a specified amount of time to engineering your start-up.

In launching their Laugh Out Loud store, for example, Karen Curro and Susan Edelman set things up so that Susan devotes about 75 percent of her time managing the store while Karen is employed full-time elsewhere and works with Susan during off hours and weekends.

"Jump—and the Net Will Appear"

That's how one gifted and seasoned entrepreneur described her philosophy on taking the plunge. Women's networking groups, training seminars, mentoring programs, and financing sources are growing both in numbers and sophistication (see "Scoping Out Start-Up Options," page 78). It makes great business sense to take advantage of these programs, in order to give yourself a firm footing before you make your move.

At some point, however, you're going to have to move beyond training, thinking, and talking—*and actually take the leap!* You can always use more money, more marketing savvy, more support, more courage. You're going to have to learn to be comfortable being uncomfortable and adopt what Dr. Rob Gilbert calls the "ready, FIRE, aim" approach—and go for it, even though you don't feel totally prepared and in control. In short, you're going to have to dive in, make mistakes, adjust your strategy, and keep driving forward.

"The smartest move I made was just getting out there," says Ronnie Fliss of her Fat Murray's Doggy Treats start-up. "Not sitting in my house, but getting out there and doing the legwork. Talking to people, doing events. It's not easy to create a situation for yourself. It's much easier working nine to five and letting somebody else worry about everything. To really do it, you have to take charge, go out, and make it happen."

scoping out start-up options

Here's a small sampling of what's available in the way of workshops, mentoring, and ongoing support. (For contact information and more help, see Resources, page 198.)

The U.S. Small Business Administration's (SBA) Office of Women's Business Ownership: This agency's website provides practical tools for women of all economic backgrounds, ages, and business interests—including business plan advice, marketing counsel through its SCORE program, and funding information. Via this site, you can also access the SBA's Women Business Center Program, which offers local assistance in all fifty states.

Ladies Who Launch: This organization offers a range of forums for aspiring entrepreneurs to connect with each other, share products and services, exchange ideas, and network. Its incubator program, available in forty-five cities around the country, consists of an intensive workshop and ongoing forums.

Powerful You!: This national membership organization has local chapters across the country, which offer events, teleseminars, and strategies to help women develop their leadership skills and grow their businesses.

VocationVacations: A company created to help career switchers and potential entrepreneurs "test-drive" their dreams, it offers one- to three-day immersions in some 150 different areas of work. It connects people with more than two hundred mentors in thirty-five states.

The Mompreneur Center: Hosted by Entrepreneur.com, this site features monthly columns and advice from successful mothers in business.

Job Accommodation Network: Sponsored by the Office of Disability Employment of the U.S. Department of Labor, this nationally available resource provides information, consulting, and referral services. Counselors will work with individuals to identify local, state, and federal resources to support them in their pursuit of small-business opportunities.

Quick Tips

Listen to your internal clock.
Focus on your personal readiness, not external drivers. Let inner momentum fuel your start-up. It will drive your success and boost your staying power!

Add up your assets.
Build a launch platform! Amaze yourself! Take an inventory of all the skills, experience, and contacts you bring to your start-up. Inspiring, aren't they?

Do your homework!
Bolster inner drive with data. Conduct research. Talk to people. Learn about finance and marketing. Become Internet savvy. The more you know, the better your timing will be.

Mobilize the support you'll need.
Find people who share your excitement. Network to strengthen your entrepreneurial "muscles." Join workshops, online support groups, and incubators. Connect with like-minded launchers!

Ease your way into entrepreneurship.
Gradual shifts to launch mode can ease stress and promote success. Create a "freedom fund" to cushion your start-up. Find anchor clients to help support your launch.

Test-drive your dream.
Find creative ways to take a trial run. Volunteer. Find mentors and tap their know-how. Join trade groups. Get comfortable with being uncomfortable!

Birthing
Your Elephant:
The Four Stages
of Success

The next four chapters chart, stage by stage, the events and emotional terrain you can expect to go through during the first eighteen to twenty-four months of your business start-up. The chart opposite offers a handy road map to the opportunities and obstacles you'll encounter during this crucial make-or-break launch period, when every decision seems daunting and every mistake looms large. By using the step-by-step guide that follows, you'll stay strong, focused, and on track!

✳ ✳ ✳

YOUR EMOTIONAL ROAD MAP TO START-UP SUCCESS

STAGE 1: START YOUR START-UP

What You'll Feel
- Exhilaration
- Loneliness
- Stretched to the limit
- Intensely focused

Key Success Strategies
- Choose a launch strategy
- Anchor yourself
- Set boundaries
- Make your first 100 days count

STAGE 2: RUN YOUR OWN SHOW

What You'll Feel
- A sense of loss
- Image anxiety
- Mixed internal signals
- Renewed commitment

Key Success Strategies
- Find a compelling vision
- Create a mission statement
- Manage your emotions
- Build an internal power base

STAGE 3: FROM BREAKDOWN TO BREAKTHROUGH

What You'll Feel
- Performance anxiety
- Self-doubt
- Fall-apart jitters
- Determined

Key Success Strategies
- Use fantasy to defuse tension
- Find a secret motivator
- Resist the "I quit!" impulse
- Build your resiliency muscle

STAGE 4: FIND YOUR BUSINESS RHYTHM

What You'll Feel
- Been there, done that blues
- Pedal-to-the-metal fatigue
- Financially challenged
- More confident

Key Success Strategies
- Let your market find you
- Use downtime productively
- Push promotion to the next level
- Make renewal a priority

Chapter 5

Stage 1: Start Your Start-Up

We just went ahead and did it. We said,
'We'll figure it out as we go along.'

—KAREN CURRO

Congratulations are in order! You've done your prep work—your prelaunch Lamaze training—and now you're ready to deliver your dream! It will take some time and careful planning to make it all happen, but you're committed to taking control of your talent and earning power. Your inner entrepreneur is waiting, eager to be released! You just need to combine your creativity and skills with the right strategy to get started—and, as we'll see, there are several promising ones to choose from. Yes, there will be rocky moments ahead, but you can overcome them, just as Suzanne Lyons did when she started the Flash Forward Institute and first began offering workshops.

"There was this little pain in my heart," says Suzanne. "I kept asking myself, did I do the right thing? Did I make the right decision? Why did I leave the safety and comfort of friends and family and the constant paycheck for the unknown? Was I being crazy? I remember feeling fear looking over the cliff, but jumping was pretty easy. I think that when you're standing looking over the cliff—that's when the emotional ride happens. But the minute you jump, you realize, if I'm jumping, then I'm more than capable of this. And the more you jump, the better it is!"

Like Suzanne, you're going to find that once you've jumped, you're "more than capable" of doing what you have to do to make your enterprise a reality. And, each time you jump out of your comfort zone, your self-image expands: the more capable you realize you are, the stronger and more confident you become. Right now, you need to stay action-oriented and on task: the decisions you make will send signals to both the marketplace and those around you about exactly how focused and committed you are. During this stage, your major goals will be to do the following:

- Select a start-up strategy you're comfortable with.

- Make your first one hundred days as productive as possible.

- Anchor yourself with a new operating structure.

- Enlist your family and friends for support.

What You Can Expect to Feel

As you make the transition from one way of working to another, you'll be faced with a raft of unfamiliar concerns—things you never had to worry about as an employee. You may also experience the sensation of standing with one foot in the past and the other in an unpredictable future. To help you anticipate what lies ahead, let's explore some of the feelings that you're likely to undergo during this phase of your new venture.

EXHILARATION

Free at last! During this heady phase, you may feel more relieved at finally launching than worried about surviving on your own. You may feel surprisingly confident about your ability to handle what lies ahead. You're filled with energy, ready to take on whatever comes your way. You're not at the top of the mountain yet, but it feels just great to finally lace up those hiking boots and start climbing!

Feedback from your friends is likely to be very positive; they're all telling you to go for it and offering you lots of advice. Hopefully, support from your family will be equally strong: your husband or partner, siblings, kids, and everyone else may be rooting for you and cheering you on. They really have no clue about the demands your new venture will make on you—and them!—but they're assuring you that they'll back you up, whatever it takes.

With all this enthusiasm bubbling up around you, it's easy to see your business taking flight: now that you're free to be yourself and make your mark, the sky's the limit! In fact, you may be so excited with your new situation that you radiate a sense of self-confidence that's positively magnetic. People may wonder where this side of your personality has been hiding all this time. Without a doubt, this is the honeymoon phase of your venture. Bask in its glow for as long as you can!

LONELINESS

Needless to say, all honeymoons come to an end. As the days turn into weeks, no matter how committed you are to making a move, your anxieties about the future are likely to surface. Your initial enthusiasm may start to seem naive and misguided. During this critical time, your feelings of isolation can be intense—especially if you're flying solo. Your old structure—the familiar round of emails, meetings, lunches, coffee breaks, and project deadlines that defined your day—is gone. Until you put a new work pattern in place, it's easy to feel adrift.

Becky Rohrer describes the "disconnected" feeling she had after leaving her job to renovate an abandoned house and turn it into a bed-and-breakfast: "I found it hard not being the boss of someone. I was so used to directing people that when I started the College Inn, I'd tell myself, 'OK, you vacuum,' and I'd answer, 'OK, I'll vacuum,' because I was the only one in the room! It was hard to figure out how I was going to get everything done without help. So I'd order myself to do things and then I'd do them. I really needed to structure my time. It was difficult to learn to work alone: suddenly, there was no one but me. It was a big adjustment."

STRETCHED TO THE LIMIT

Practically speaking, you'll be working long and crazy hours and your personal life will be virtually nonexistent for weeks and even months. This may mean turning down dinner with friends because you're on a tight budget, which is what Patricia and Adam Scribner found themselves doing when launching Patricia's Yarns. It can also mean facing your family's frustration as you frantically rush to meet a deadline, real or self-imposed. Or telling your husband that you won't be able to spend much time with him after work anymore, at least for a while. In fact, "after work" is a meaningless phrase for most entrepreneurs during their start-up phase, since virtually very waking hour is devoted to nurturing their new businesses. At a time when family support is critical, the adjustments required can be very stressful for everyone.

CONCERNED ABOUT FINANCES

The risks you've assumed because you no longer have a consistent source of income can hit you like a ton of bricks. It's easy to begin dwelling on what you've given up: the steady paycheck, the insurance, the vacations, and all the little extras that make life fun. Even seasoned moonlighters, accustomed to the ups and downs of project work, often find it shocking to realize how cash hungry a full-fledged start-up is.

During the first weeks and months of your new working life, you'll watch your costs climb relentlessly upward. There's a price tag attached to everything—every piece of computer software, every phase of setting up a website, every new phone line. Watching whatever money you have to work with melt away before your eyes can be scary, even if your short-term financial picture is strong.

Many people just starting out think long run: we're going to sell this much, and it's going to be a fantastic success, and there will be pots of gold when you reach the end. But, in the meantime, you need enough to cover both your business and day-to-day personal expenses. Ask yourself, what do you need to invest up front, how are you going to get paid, what are your ongoing costs going to be, and how are you going to pay for everything until cash starts flowing in instead of out? When it comes to cash management, avoidance is one of the biggest dangers you'll face. The sooner you get a handle on your business and personal expenses, the more prepared you'll be to create a strategy for meeting them. If you find it hard to set up a basic system for managing your cash flow, then find someone who can help you as quickly as possible.

INTENSELY FOCUSED

One of the most powerful signs you'll receive that you're on the right track is the zestful intensity you'll feel as you focus single-mindedly on surviving your first months on your own. The capacity for work that you discover within yourself as you push past your fatigue and fears may surprise not only you but also the people who know you. It can empower you to perform small miracles, survive setbacks that once might have devastated you, and win the help of total strangers with just a call or an email.

Success Strategies

You may have the greatest idea since Internet dating and a business strategy for wooing markets from Texas to Tokyo. Whatever your ultimate game plan is, right now you're in survival mode and your goal will be to make the first stage of your venture as productive as possible. In these first few months, you may experience emotional flare-ups, but in general they'll take a backseat because you're so driven and focused on action. As you begin to transform your business concept into reality, here is frontline advice for maximizing the impact of your launch.

LET YOUR PASSION SHINE THROUGH—BUT CONSERVE YOUR ENERGY!

In launching her Life is Good retail store with her partner, Karen Curro, Susan Edelman's newfound commitment exerted a powerful influence: "Be passionate about your idea because that's what will guide you and get you through—and that's what people feed off of and get excited about. If you really believe in what you're doing and can express this, people will sense it in you. And that will work to your advantage in business settings—whether it's for financing, leasing a space, or the hundreds of things you have to do. This is the first time in my life that I'm 100 percent passionate about what I'm doing: it makes a big difference."

Enthusiasm is infectious! It rubs off on other people, draws them into your launch orbit, and inspires them to want to help you succeed. Bobbi Brown's genuine excitement about her new line of lipsticks was so intense that she sold a buyer on her product without even realizing that she was marketing it! Liz Lange's passionate belief helped her convince celebrity moms-to-be to try out her clothing when she was a total unknown. Lisa Druxman's dedication to fitness for new mothers turned her into a publicity dynamo with the persuasive power to pitch a steady stream of news story ideas that generated priceless exposure in the media.

The message: Don't hide your light under a bushel! Let your enthusiasm shine through and it will catch fire in others—and win their support and resources. Share your vision of what you want to accomplish and why it matters. Then let people know what you need help with. Let your enthusiasm fuel your efforts on the marketing front as well, just as Bobbi Brown, Liz Lange, and Lisa Druxman did. It can be the engine that drives the contacts you'll make, the exposure you'll win, and the alliances you'll forge. However, keep in mind that talking about starting a venture is one thing, getting on with it is another. Don't fritter away your energy rhapsodizing about your business during long, rambling phone calls or leisurely lunches. Stay focused on making it happen.

SET BOUNDARIES IN TIME AND SPACE

Setting boundaries in the early days of your start-up is one of the best ways to stay grounded. Let people know about your new setup: customers, clients, family members, and friends all need to know what your work hours are. Resist the temptation to answer your home phone while you're working. After a while, people will get the message and adjust. Create a transition for yourself to separate your workday from the rest of your life: take a walk, do an exercise routine, or take your dog for a daily stroll—something that signals that you've shifted from work time to personal time.

ANCHOR YOURSELF WITH A NEW OPERATING STRUCTURE

Time is yours to use or misuse now as never before; it's easy to procrastinate and waste it when you're the only boss around. More than money, time is the most valuable commodity you have, so learn to value it and spend it well. Beware of time wasters! Poor organization, misplaced perfectionism, unfocused networking, and unnecessary meetings can all fritter away your hours and days—and deflect your energy from client service, new-business development, and marketing. Actions have consequences. Manage your time strategically, with an eye on both your mission and your bottom line.

Planning daily and weekly routines to ensure that you make the most of your time is key to survival during this stage. It can be a smart move to investigate time-saving software that's designed by companies like Intuit for small businesses. There are electronic calendars and tickler files, business proposal packages, lead-tracking systems, and marketing support tools that can increase your efficiency. Of course, some of these have hefty price tags, so initially you may have to be highly selective about what you invest in.

Finding the work pattern that's best for you—given the nature of your business, your optimal schedule, and your start-up dynamics—is one of the instant benefits of working on your own. It can give you the flexibility you need while allowing you to organize projects around your periods of peak performance. After years in a highly regimented environment, however, it's often a major challenge to design a new work routine that encourages you to use your time most productively.

There are a number of approaches to choose from, including the tried and true. One entrepreneur we know has opted for basically the same operating timetable he followed as an employee. He's at his desk by 8:30, takes a one-hour break for lunch and a quick romp with his dog, gets back to his desk, and stays there until five or six in the evening. At this point, he usually calls it a day, unless he has a massive project or major deadline to meet.

Choosing to break out of the nine-to-five mold may be a more appealing option. But doing it without setting yourself totally adrift demands ingenuity and discipline. Settling on the right framework may take time—and trial and error. Some entrepreneurs, for example, find that they're most productive when they adopt a "work/play" mode. This work pattern is based on intense periods of planning and task-driven concentration followed by time off to reenergize. After refueling during your downtime, you shift back again to the project at hand, extending your workday into the evening if necessary.

Whatever approach you adopt, creating a work structure to anchor your day, and also your week, is essential. For example, one consultant created a highly efficient, personalized strategy: to keep herself focused, she decided to maintain the same workflow from week to week. She usually sets aside one day a week, typically Monday, for the business of running her business—billing, filing, correspondence, and so on. Tuesdays, Wednesdays, and Thursdays are devoted to client work—planning and research, meetings, setting up systems. Friday is usually spent following up new business leads and mapping out the coming week. If her weekly workload is especially heavy, she'll devote Monday afternoon and Friday morning to servicing her clients, leaving Monday morning and Friday afternoon for administration.

This weekly work pattern may give you some ideas you can adapt to your own situation—or it may not strike a chord with you at all. What's important is that the operating structure outlined above evolved naturally. When Ronnie Fliss started Fat Murray's Doggy Treats, the dynamics of her business called for a different, but equally consistent, way of working.

"I was pretty structured during my launch," Ronnie comments. "At first, I was baking on my own three days a week. Then I found a woman who was a fabulous baker and wanted to get into the business. She would come two nights a week and we would start baking at six in the evening. As things started to grow, I had her come in during the day. I would get the batter and dough ready for her in the morning, and I started taking time during the day to make calls and handle other parts of the business. At night, I did packing and shipping. So we created a structure and the work formed itself into a schedule."

ASSESS TASKS BY QUALITY RESULTS, NOT TIME EXPENDED

While forward motion is important, it's also easy to mistake motion for actual progress. Your time will be at a premium, even more so than in a nine-to-five job, largely because you'll be doing all of the little things that people on your staff at work used to do—emailing, filing, returning phone calls, whatever. Don't let these low-priority tasks be the ones you spend the lion's share of your time on. This doesn't mean bringing in a horde of employees you can't afford. Instead, look for other small-business owners who may want to trade their expertise for yours, a concept called "clustering." Or bite the bullet and pay an outside person to do your books, computer graphics, or whatever else you're spinning your wheels trying to complete.

CHOOSE YOUR LAUNCH STRATEGY CAREFULLY

How you launch your start-up is as important as what start-up you launch. Your strategy determines the pace of your move as well as the practical and financial challenges you'll be dealing with. During our interviews, we identified three basic start-up approaches that many new business owners use: the phase-in model, the moonlighting model, and the full-throttle model. Each approach offers different advantages—and will make different demands on you, emotionally and economically. To highlight these distinctions, let's look at the three models in action.

The Phase-In Model: Sarah's Pastries & Candies

Sarah Levy loves chocolate and baking—and always has. As a teenager, instead of hitting the beach, she spent her summer vacations working in bakeries and restaurant kitchens. Once she had her degree from Northwestern in hand, she plunged into a six-month immersion course at the French Pastry School in her hometown of Chicago. Then Sarah caught small-business fever: she left her part-time restaurant job as a pastry chef and set up shop temporarily in her family's kitchen so that she could create her own recipes for gourmet chocolates, with mouthwatering names like Chocolate Delights and Coconut Almond Crunch.

At first, Sarah worked alone, which wasn't easy for the bubbly twenty-three-year-old. Some days, she tuned in to the *Ellen DeGeneres Show* to keep her company or talked to her friends on a headset while she was baking. "Oh, my God," she remembers telling herself at one point, "I need to sell some chocolates so I can hire someone to work with me, because I am driving myself crazy!"

Sarah survived her solo stint and officially launched her business, Sarah's Pastries & Candies, while still baking in her mother's kitchen. In all, she spent about eighteen months working there. This approach minimized both the financial demands of her start-up and her stress level and enabled Sarah to pour her limited funds—and unlimited energy—into product development. In her first months, she incorporated her business, fine-tuned her recipes with the help of a volunteer panel of chefs, and began to market her treats. To cut costs, she had a high school senior who was a friend of her sister's design her first website. With two part-time helpers handling the baking, Sarah began "a lot of knocking on doors," making the rounds of local gourmet markets with samples in tow. It was a tough sales climate.

Eventually, a cold call to the midwestern manager of Whole Foods, followed by long months of emails and persistence, paid off. Whole Foods began selling her chocolate creations regionally; soon, she was servicing forty wholesale customers. A year later, after a five-month search for the right location, a major renovation, and countless eighteen-hour days, Sarah opened a bright, cheerful store on Oak Street, Chicago's equivalent to Rodeo Drive.

What compels a young woman in her twenties to work nonstop for weeks at a time, give up sleep and her social life, and assume responsibility for the salaries and well-being of more than a dozen employees? "When I'm on my way to work," says Sarah, "it's still shocking and exciting to realize that I'm driving to my own store! I'm busy eleven or twelve hours a day, but time flies by because I love what I do!" Today, Sarah has a booming retail, wholesale, and Internet-based business.

The Moonlighting Model: Sienna at Home

Crystal Johnson had a satisfying, lucrative job in the high-tech industry. As a human resources consultant with a global software developer, she helped major companies plan self-service employee benefit systems. She traveled extensively, honed her communication skills, built a great reputation, and had a promising career with a $100,000 annual salary.

Although Crystal's job was secure, her company was going through a period of intense product change at a time when she was facing a major shift in her own life as well. She was expecting her first child and didn't want to travel as much as she had in the past. After four years at her firm, she also felt the need for a new challenge and found herself asking, "OK, what am I going to do now?" As soon as she asked the question, she knew the answer: interior design.

Amid her intense work and travel schedule, Crystal had discovered a hidden talent: creating warm, distinctive decors. Her newfound passion first surfaced when she got a chance to decorate her new home, and her designs won rave reviews from friends and family. Next, over a two-week vacation, Crystal tackled her first official design project: decorating a townhouse for a friend. Buoyed by the results, she tested the waters on a more ambitious scale at the Texas Home & Garden Show. When her furnishings sold out at this major event, Crystal knew she'd found her niche.

"Something kept pulling me to get to another level and do something else," she explains. "I just hit upon my design talent. It wasn't anything I planned. I just got the spark. I was taken aback by it. I always thought of myself as a person who was not creative—that's the irony in this. I would tell people, 'Oh, I'm not creative, that's not me'—and that is so not true! I get inspiration from the trees outside, from the smallest, most minute things."

As her passion for design grew, consulting lost its allure. Crystal began having serious discussions with her husband about leaving her job. She now had a new baby and was still traveling—and the two didn't mix well. Determined to make a major life change, Crystal carefully planned her new venture, Sienna at Home. She moonlighted for almost a year—researching the design field, sharpening her technology skills, getting her decorating license, and building start-up capital. Before she left her company, Crystal also carefully tested the market for her design concepts in her hometown of Houston.

About a month after her successful debut at the Texas Home & Garden Show, Crystal handed in her resignation. Today, after several years of nonstop work, Crystal has created a lifestyle that gives her the flexibility she needs as a mother with young children—and the freedom to pursue work that she loves. With annual revenues of over $500,000, a large showroom, and a growing design consultancy, Crystal also plans to build a national "footprint" via the Internet.

The Full-Throttle Model:
A Life Is Good Genuine Neighborhood Shoppe

Over the years, Karen Curro and Susan Edelman had talked about starting a small business in their hometown of Montclair, New Jersey. They looked into creating a health club, but rents were high and the up-front capital required was steep. They also considered opening a Kids 'N' Clay franchise, but the location and timing were never right. So they stayed put: Karen working as a global sales manager for an outsourcing company and Susan as the CEO of a family-owned business. Then Susan's company was forced to close due to changing economic conditions. It was a difficult process, and ultimately she lost both a family legacy and work that she valued and enjoyed.

But miraculously, marvels Susan, a situation that was "tragic and devastating turned into an opportunity." She was freed up, both economically and emotionally, to explore other work options. While vacationing in Maine, Susan and Karen walked into a Life Is Good store—and stepped into their future. They fell in love with the company's philosophy, and with the idea of opening a Life Is Good Genuine Neighborhood Shoppe in their hometown.

Launched by two brothers who once sold T-shirts out of the trunk of a battered car, the Life Is Good line of colorful clothing and lifestyle products includes everything from leisure wear to caps, mugs, and bags emblazoned with upbeat sayings and playful images. Susan and Karen were attracted to the spirit of fun and charitable giving behind the fast-growing, customer-friendly enterprise: community-based philanthropy and support for children's organizations are integral to the Life Is Good business model.

As Susan puts it, "The company has an energy to it that's very positive and very much the way we feel and what we want to project. Life Is Good made the work transition easier for me, because it was not just about getting involved in a clothing line, but in a whole philosophy of giving back to the community, of brightening people's day, of being optimistic. At first, I struggled with pulling together a resume and going on interviews. Then I saw the store in Maine and I said, 'Wait! This is it! This is what I want to do.' It just felt right."

Karen and Susan returned home and quickly shifted into "let's make it happen" mode. They found a small, but ideally located, space for their store on Valley Road, the main street in Montclair—and launched intense negotiations with the owner. They wanted to seize the moment and have a fall opening so they could take full advantage of the holiday season. They signed a lease and jumped into a high-speed renovation. Within six weeks, their store, Laugh Out Loud, was open for business, and cheerful Life Is Good T-shirts, caps, mugs, slacks, and sweaters lined the shelves in a rainbow of colors.

"It just moved very quickly," Karen says. "We didn't know what the heck we were doing!" she adds with a laugh. "At one point, I said, 'Susan, have you ever used a register?' She said no. I said, 'Me, neither!' The education we got in using Visa, American Express, and MasterCard alone was mind-boggling! We had no idea how to do anything! But we just went ahead and did it. We said, 'It's not brain surgery. We'll figure it out as we go along.'"

WEIGH YOUR LAUNCH OPTIONS

Sarah's Pastries & Candies, Sienna at Home, and Laugh Out Loud are all very different businesses, and each of their owners pursued a different launch path. Yet today they are all thriving. Not only can these start-up strategies be used separately—they can even be combined. To start Exclusively RNs, for example, Anne Afshari and Laura Hagler adopted the full-throttle model, going from concept to launch in three months. But to allow for time to build the business, they moonlighted for about a year. They gave up their full-time jobs only when they felt confident that Exclusively RNs was strong enough to begin supporting both of them.

Each of the three models we described has a different launch rhythm. The staged approach that Sarah Levy adopted—in her case, first finding wholesale clients and then shifting into retail—works well only if it's driven by self-imposed deadlines and energetic marketing. Even though this kind of low-overhead start-up keeps the financial wolf away from the door for a while, it's still critical that any business launched using this approach exhibit its viability and momentum fairly early in the game.

In the moonlighting model, the pressures involved aren't usually about money; they're about time, stamina, and family support during a long and intense transition. Working a day job, running a home, and launching a business all at once is definitely a recipe for rapid burnout, as Anne and Laura learned when pushing forward with Exclusively RNs. Jump-starting their business in response to an eager client had clear benefits, but it meant that the two partners were working literally day and night for about a year.

The full-throttle model has the advantages of momentum and a "climb on board" appeal that can really mobilize other people. However, it's physically, financially, and emotionally demanding. It requires tremendous stamina, a secure funding platform, and a flexible, strong-minded decision-making style, along with the ability to respond quickly and proactively to unexpected problems and delays. In this model, sacrificing sound business planning to speed is always a danger.

In some cases, your choice of a model will be totally within your control; in others, external factors may play a key role in your choice. For Anne and Laura of Exclusively RNs, the key launch driver was an eager client; for Karen and Susan of Laugh Out Loud, an upcoming holiday season. As you think through which of these models might work best for you, be sure to examine each one from every angle: its financial requirements, business tempo, and the physical and emotional demands it's likely to make on you.

Get up-to-date, realistic start-up scenario information. Talk to seasoned small-business owners and professionals like those in the SBA's SCORE program to get an accurate picture of what each type of start-up involves. Once you've decided on the approach that will work best for you, given your business goals and family needs, scope out the key elements of your start-up budget—and then double it! To be on the safe side, you may want to double the amount of time you expect to invest as well. As Adam Scribner pointed out, during a start-up, the business you're launching "is this living, breathing thing that you have to feed constantly."

USE A BUSINESS PLAN TO STAY FOCUSED

A business plan is a road map: it lays out the path you'll take to launch your business and sets milestones so you can measure progress against your goals. Since you can easily find detailed guidelines for designing a plan elsewhere, we're not going to cover them here. Instead, we will look at why crafting a business plan—even an informal one—can be an asset when you are making the psychological leap from employee to entrepreneur. Creating a plan, even an informal one, can bolster your resolve, build confidence in your launch strategy, and help you view your business concept from a customer or client perspective.

"We did a business plan mainly to keep us focused," says Patricia Scribner of the plan that she and her husband, Adam, developed to launch Patricia's Yarns. "You need a structure, you need a basis for going forward, you need to look at the pitfalls—it can't be all roses," she adds. "We gave it to friends, who critiqued it, and I went to the SCORE office in Newark. They looked at my plan and said, 'You're going to be fine.'" Ultimately, Patricia and Adam presented their proposal to their families; to finance their venture, they relied on small loans from their families, personal savings, and a credit line. Even though the plan wasn't used for outside financing, as Patricia noted, it "gave us structure, a focus, and objectivity."

As Patricia and Adam Scribner found, developing a business plan can help you take charge of this new phase of your work life. Apart from its economic impact, a plan can be a powerful communications tool for expressing both your vision and your strategy for achieving it. Equally important, using your plan as a touchstone can help you keep your eye on your long-term goals. It also provides a framework for the financial demands you'll face, which can help you plan your cash flow needs—and manage your money anxieties more effectively. Putting your goals, resources, and financial projections on paper has another benefit: it can help you identify your core assets and resource gaps.

Not surprisingly, many people view writing a business plan as a daunting task: they see it as a roadblock rather than a road map. That's probably why so many new business owners don't put together a plan before launching their enterprises; they simply dive in. But a business plan doesn't have to be set in stone; it can be a living document—one that you can easily adapt as your goals evolve. It's also a way to demonstrate that you have the skills, resources, and drive to translate your vision into a viable, profitable enterprise. When you start thinking of your plan as a responsive, creative tool, you'll find that writing it is a much more enjoyable and satisfying experience. A plan that's seen as a dynamic work in progress can be clarifying and inspiring—not just for you but for everyone around you. It can be a powerful partner in your efforts to help people you depend on—from employees to suppliers—better understand your business. You can get even more mileage out of it by using it as a motivational tool.

MAKE YOUR FIRST ONE HUNDRED DAYS COUNT!

According to a Chinese proverb, "The beginning and the end reach out their hands to each other." How true this is! You are making a fresh start and entering an exciting new phase of your work life. Make the most of this precious time, and you'll be setting the stage for success; let it slip through your fingers, and you'll lose valuable momentum. So whether you're officially launching in January or July, make a "new-business resolution" and resolve to stay totally focused on your course of action for your first one hundred days, however stormy the seas prove to be. You'll be amazed at the strength this simple, but powerful, decision will give you.

Approach the early days of your venture with an open mind and without any preconceived notions about the image you should present, how things should work, or what your financial outlook should be. After all, you're new to the entrepreneurial life. Keep in mind that most successful change occurs incrementally: big changes are made up of small ones. So don't try to do everything you want to do at once—

you might end up scattering your energies, getting bogged down in details, and losing sight of the big picture. Instead, ask yourself where you want to be by the end of your first three months and then set some priorities.

As part of your new-business resolution, choose three—or at most, five—key goals you want to accomplish in the first months of your launch and drive toward them every day. Keep them realistic and doable within your time frame and budget. Ultimately, each goal may have long to-do lists, but stay focused on the endgame—don't lose sight of what you really intend to achieve. Be clear on *why* you want to achieve each goal, so you'll stay motivated. Finally, break each goal down into specific daily tasks—think through *how* you can achieve each goal you've set, so you can map out a plan of action. Put both your goals and plan on paper, so you'll feel committed. And don't forget to reward yourself when you make real progress! Treat yourself to a nice lunch, take your whole family out for a celebratory dinner, or make an appointment for a restorative massage. Provide yourself with whatever launch perks you need to make yourself feel appreciated and attended to. Taking time to luxuriate in your successes—even the small ones—is a great way to stay energized and excited about the work you're doing.

If you keep yourself organized and goal oriented, you'll be amazed at what you can accomplish in the first three months of your start-up. To show you exactly what we mean, here's a glimpse of the intense round of activities that several of the entrepreneurs we spoke with completed in their first one hundred days.

Anne Afshari and Laura Hagler of Exclusively RNs

With no formal business training, these two enterprising nurses turned to the Internet and off-the-shelf guides to find out how to prepare a proposal and business plan. Anne and Laura made their first client pitch in mid-November 2002; by the end of November, they had written their first proposal, chosen a name, decided how to set up their business legally, and sorted out basic accounting issues. Their basic business concept was elegantly simple, but logistically challenging: they planned to set up a phone-based advisory service for expectant mothers that doctors could subscribe to as a way to relieve their workload.

While handling the business side of their start-up, Laura and Anne also created an operating structure. This meant designing detailed protocols for fielding calls, researching standards of care, anticipating medical complications, and creating a documentation system. By January 1, 2003, Exclusively RNs was officially launched with its first client on board—and Anne and Laura's beepers were busy! From the first night, they saw huge potential and invested countless hours to get their venture off to a solid start.

"Even though we knew we were working extremely hard," recalls Laura, "we didn't recognize or at least we didn't verbalize how much time we were putting in. We were working at home late at night, early in the mornings, and when the children were taking naps. This was one of the biggest things we were unaware of: the time commitment involved. We were working one hundred hours a week between our full-time jobs and building our business."

Brenda Newberry of the Newberry Group

Once she committed to launching her own company, this experienced high-tech pro jumped in with both feet, creating a home office in the upper story of her house and searching for information technology (IT) consulting projects. Brenda attended any "start your own business" seminars she could find, wrote a business plan, and made the round of banks looking for financing. The terms they offered didn't make sense for a start-up, so she and her husband loaned the company its first $1,000 so she could buy a fax machine, copier, and other basic equipment. A first project came in and Brenda hired her first consultant; she ended up borrowing $10,000 from herself to make payroll for the first two months.

Brenda was teaching an IT course at an Air Force base and would arrive by 7:30 A.M., finish her class at 9:00, go home and write proposals until 3:00 or 4:00 in the morning, then drive to the Air Force base by 7:30 and start all over again. During her early days, there were plenty of cold calls and disappointments. There were also many nights when she fell asleep in her office upstairs. "My husband would come up at 3:00 in the morning and say, 'Are you coming to bed?' Instead, I would work some more."

Karen Curro and Susan Edelman of Laugh Out Loud

For these two novice retailers, the first few months of their launch were "fueled with adrenaline," recalls Susan. "We had some moments of panic where we asked, 'What are we doing?' but those were few and far between. We were running so fast, we had no time to feel anything." Adds Karen: "Everyone told us we couldn't go from inception to completion in the short time we had. We signed our lease on September 19, started working on the build-out on October 1, put our first inventory order in on October 19, and opened on November 11. It was an insane process!"

Susan adds: "At the same time we were doing the build-out, we needed to set up our point of sale (POS) system, merchant services, and corporate accounts. So we divided and conquered. I held on to the POS portion and business end and Karen did the build-out. On each of our to-do lists, there were literally hundreds of things to go through." To give you a better idea of exactly what's involved in a high-speed start-up like this, we asked Karen to share an actual to-do list from her computer files (opposite page).

What's most impressive about Karen's list is the fact that she had to figure out exactly what she needed and how to get it done without any real experience in planning a space renovation! To launch their Laugh Out Loud store, she and Susan simply adopted a "learn as you go" strategy. While Karen's drive and can-do attitude came naturally, she also drew on her strong sales experience to make contacts, find vendors, and keep everyone on task. The message here is one that any new business owner can benefit from: get organized, stay focused, and set realistic targets. These steps will help make your first one hundred days rewarding and productive.

Karen Curro's Life Is Good To-Do List

- ☐ Lease Agreement
- ☐ Life Is Good contract: Attorney review
- ☐ Change the locks
- ☐ Put a steel door on in the back
- ☐ Pick name of the store
- ☐ Send name to Brian to make the sign
- ☐ LLC Corporate Documents/Fed ID: (Susan)
- ☐ Need phone lines: Phone lines and data lines ASAP
- ☐ Banking relationship: Need to go to two local banks and get % point and service info
- ☐ Signage: Application for Certificate of Appropriateness (apply for signage ASAP)
  - Get a quote and get someone to put the design together with pictures of how it will look on the storefront.
  - Doesn't look good for it to be hanging sideways . . . so we may need to put it next to or over the awning and then put the Life is Good sign above the awning with a light.
  - Sign cannot be more than the total square footage of the storefront
- ☐ Contractors: Get quotes: Michael's men are $200 per day per man; electrician will also get a quote.
  - Need to build out registers
  - Shelves
  - Paint
- ☐ Awning needs to be 2 1/4 feet and 4-foot projection no less than 7 feet above the sidewalk.
  - Letters can be a maximum of 6 inches.
  - Only 20% of the windows can be covered with signage

- The hearing for all applicants is October 18th—someone needs to be present.
- ☐ Inspection of property: J. B. Home Inspection
  - Spoke with Joe and he was going to follow up. He was going to look at the inspection he did for the entire building and determine what we needed to focus on. We may also need to look at the smoke detector and the smoke alarm to make certain it is up to code. This may need to be done by code enforcement in Montclair.
- ☐ Electrical: Ralph Smith. He needs to take a look at the store inside to confirm. I gave him the general layout and what we would want him to do.
  - Track lighting and hanging lights over the register and the middle of the table in the store. Will also need to get some low lights.
  - We need to pick out lighting.
- ☐ POS system: We need to get in touch with the individual below or any suggestions from Ray.
  - Dave L is the listed QuickBooks Pro Advisor
- ☐ Hardwood Floors: I looked online and found some deals, but Gina got a good deal from Garden State Flooring. Need to contact them and/or go to Home Depot or some other discount flooring source. Need wood flooring for over 800 sq feet. Pricing $6–$8 per sq ft.
- ☐ Inventory: Need to sit down with Paul and decide on the opening inventory; also need to get his suggestions on shelves and displays based on our space.

ENLIST SUPPORT FROM FAMILY AND FRIENDS

During this start-up phase, organize a cheerleading squad for yourself: a small band of like-minded people—ideally, new business owners like you—who will bolster your confidence and brainstorm ideas with you. This doesn't mean, of course, that you don't need help from lawyers, accountants, and other professionals. What we're talking about here is mobilizing emotional as well as practical support you can count on.

Coincidentally, when Liz Lange began her company, Liz Lange Maternity, two of her closest friends from her college days at Brown University were launching at the same time. The three of them would meet on a regular basis to talk about their businesses and support each other. One friend, Jacquie Tractenberg, started a successful publicity firm and eventually became Liz's publicist. The other friend, Jonathan Adler, is well known in the pottery and furniture fields and has built a thriving retail and licensing enterprise. To this day, Liz and Jonathan still meet once a week to talk about their work.

Involving family members in your business in any form can be a blessing or a burden—a source of strength, or one more problem you have to deal with. So, from the beginning, you'll need to set the ground rules for their contribution to your venture. Decide what kind of help you want from each family member, and let everyone know, tactfully but clearly, how he or she can support you. This holds true for friends as well. Assigning specific tasks to members of your "backroom" team can be a useful strategy. It lets you set some limits while giving the people around you a way to participate. If your sister is an ace marketer, for example, then put her to work checking out online options for designing a brochure. If your aunt is a media maven, then ask her to be on the alert for useful ideas and trends.

Remember, though, that your family's first and more important job is to help keep you motivated and support your can-do spirit. You may or may not want family members to influence key start-up decisions, so keep their contributions limited but productive. And, as appealing as the idea may seem, give very careful thought to bringing family members, however well meaning and skilled, into your fledgling enterprise on a more formal basis.

It's also important at this stage to be sure your family is fully briefed on how your business will affect your personal life—and theirs. This is especially crucial if you have children and plan to work at home. Starting a business is tough enough without facing complaints about why meals aren't as good as they used to be or why the house isn't as neat as it once was.

BEWARE OF OLD SPENDING PATTERNS

If money is tight, you can easily fall into one of two traps. You can micromanage to the point where you're worried about every penny instead of focusing on planning, client service, and other launch imperatives. Or you can go to the other extreme and downplay your financial problems. You may also respond to financial anxiety by clinging to old spending patterns. In your paycheck days, for instance, you may have used "retail therapy" to ease your feelings of job dissatisfaction by treating yourself to something special—a new bag or an expensive scarf. In your new life as an entrepreneur, you're going to have to find less costly ways to calm your anxieties.

Adjusting your lifestyle and reining in your personal spending in response to your start-up's fragile finances can take a while. But failing to give up old patterns can easily sabotage your new business. Overspending on equipment, hiring help you can't afford instead of doing most things yourself, and making image-driven expenditures, such as renting a pricey office or investing in an overly complex website, are all potential budget busters. Each of these mistakes can put your business at risk. As we noted in chapter 3, knowing the emotional triggers that influence your spending is an important step toward keeping this problem under control. Finding a trusted ally who can keep an eye on your spending patterns and alert you when they shift into the danger zone can be extremely helpful.

CELEBRATE YOUR FIRST ONE HUNDRED DAYS

Transitions are never easy, but you've begun working through a major one. If you've survived the first hundred days of your new life, then you deserve a badge of honor! You've set some ambitious goals for yourself and persevered in order to make them happen! When you hit the one-hundred-day milestone, let yourself go. Celebrate! Be amazed at your stick-to-itiveness! Then, when the confetti settles, take stock of what you've learned.

Make a clear-eyed assessment of exactly what appeals to you and what doesn't about the new work life that you're shaping for yourself. What do you really love about it? Is it the freedom to work at your own pace? The flexibility your new life gives you and your family? The satisfaction you get from putting yourself on the line? Then look at the flip side. What do you avoid doing and wish you could pay someone else to do for you, even though you can't afford to right now? Identifying less-than-satisfying tasks that you'd love to hand off to someone else can be a real motivator and help push you to the next level of business productivity.

Once you've created a balance sheet of the joys and burdens of being your own boss, take a deep breath. As you move into the next stage of your start-up, you're entering exciting but dangerous territory. What you've learned so far will be useful, and you'll be adding many unfamiliar tasks to your start-up agenda. However, just knowing that you're moving in the right direction will help you handle the road ahead with self-assurance. You're on your way!

Quick Tips ⇨

Quick Tips

Enthusiasm is infectious—share it!
Zeal is the fuel that drives your start-up engine. Keep your tank full!
It ignites admiration and inspires people to help you. It's your best ad
and your most powerful marketing tool!

Choose the start-up model that's right for you.
Slow start, moonlighting or full throttle: how you start is as important
as what you start. Factor in family, fears, and finances.

Anchor yourself—or you'll go adrift.
Time is your currency—spend it wisely! Find an operating structure
that works for you—and fine-tune it. Stay flexible, yet focused.

Make your first one hundred days work for you!
Hit the ground running. Focus on action, not angst! Set clear goals and
keep driving forward, all day, every day. Take risks, be relentless!

Avoid old spending patterns.
Spending money as a stress reliever is dangerous—don't do it! Avoid
budget busters like image-boosting expenditures. Keep your personal
budget lean.

Mobilize family and friends.
Create a cheerleading squad to boost your spirits. Enlist family
support—it's crucial! Assign family members specific, but limited,
tasks.

This to-do list will help you plan the tasks during Stage 1.

STAGE 1 ACTION STEPS

☐ Set up my business work space.

☐ Decide on a daily operating structure.

☐ Scope out my start-up budget, then double it!

☐ Choose the launch model that meets my needs.

____ Phase-in   ____ Moonlighting

____ Full-throttle   ____ Hybrid

☐ Choose three to five major launch goals for my first one hundred days.

1. _____   4. _____

2. _____   5. _____

3. _____

☐ Assign family/friends specific tasks.

☐ Use clustering and bartering to fill gaps.

☐ Select three skills I have to offer:

1. _____

2. _____

3. _____

☐ Select three skills I need to acquire:

1. _____

2. _____

3. _____

☐ Enlist support team to meet with weekly.

Chapter 6

Stage 2: Run Your Own Show

There's always a way to get around everything—
if you don't panic and just figure it out.

—SUSAN EDELMAN

Action-packed: that's probably the best way to describe your first three months. Like many entrepreneurs, you'll find that being in launch mode puts you in overdrive, and, just as Susan Edelman did, you may have found yourself running on adrenaline. As you move into this stage of your start-up, your frenetic pace is likely to slow down. In the best-case scenario, you'll have established a business rhythm for yourself that feels comfortable. In the worst-case situation, after the intense "honeymoon" phase of your launch, you can hit a real lull—and feel lacking in the drive you need to keep pushing forward. This can be a natural response to the last couple of months of nonstop activity—and it's not unusual.

Whether you crash-land or glide gently into this stage, you're in for an exciting, but bumpy, ride! In the first few months of your start-up, your emotions may not have been at center stage most of the time precisely because you were so driven and action oriented. Now that this high-intensity period is over, you may suddenly find yourself confronting the fallout of making a major life transition. This can test your belief in both your start-up and your staying power. Stay the course and you'll begin to change in exciting ways as you reshape your business identity and hone your leadership skills. To keep your start-up on track, your focus should be on the following:

- Embracing your role as an entrepreneur.

- Shifting into leadership mode.

- Formulating a vision for your business.

- Handling your emotional ups and downs.

What You Can Expect to Feel

Your new start-up isn't news anymore: the novelty of your launch may be wearing off, both for you and the people around you. As an employee, you may have cheerfully juggled many projects, but being self-employed can tax your resources in very different ways. Here's what you may find yourself coping with.

A SENSE OF LOSS

Whether or not you recognize it consciously, unresolved issues and emotional baggage from your days as an employee may still be affecting you even months after your move. Given the web of associations and feelings that you've woven around your work over the years, it's not surprising that releasing the past and reshaping your professional identity can prove to be more demanding than you might expect. A fortunate few never have a moment's regret or sadness about letting go of their corporate life—or being let go by their companies. As one woman put it, "You mean I no longer have to stuff myself into pantyhose every day? YES!"

But most people don't weather a major transition like making the move from employee to entrepreneur quickly or easily. Instead, they find it disorienting: feelings of being uprooted, a sense of unexplained ennui, or even depression isn't uncommon. In the case of a firing or a layoff due to downsizing or outsourcing, you may find that it takes you weeks or even months to absorb what happened, accept your sense of loss, and identify your transferable assets. If this emotional process of releasing your old corporate identity overlaps with your start-up, it can be very challenging to stay focused.

IMAGE ANXIETY

As you reshape your work life, you may find yourself in the midst of a minor—or major—identity crisis. After all, if you no longer have a title, a "real" office to go to every day, or a clearly defined project to work on, then it can be hard to get a handle on your professional persona. This raises lots of touchy questions: Where do you fit into the scheme of things in the business world? Apart from your family and friends, who really cares about this huge step you've just taken in your life? How should you plan your time? What's most important—and what can you put on hold?

There's also another, deeper form of image anxiety that you may find yourself grappling with. A fundamental life change like making the move from employee to entrepreneur can open up a Pandora's box of feelings by forcing you to confront old self-images and limitations that you may have ignored for years. These may be self-imposed or they may reflect deeply ingrained attitudes held by your family, teachers, or other influential people in your life. A decision to reinvent yourself by starting a new business can force you to do battle with these old, but still powerful, images of the kind of person you are, what work you should be doing, how much money you should make, and how successful you should be. When this happens, fear, anxiety, and even anger can surface.

Feeling anxious about all these issues can lead you to overspend on your image as a way to bolster your confidence and make your business feel bigger than it is. Yes, you want to put your best foot forward, but don't cut it off! Start out with only the basics; keep everything simple. Remember, clients and customers want services and products; *they're focused on delivery.* They don't really care about whether or not your office is stylish or your computer has the latest bells and whistles. Professionalism depends on the results you produce, not on how or where you make them happen.

MIXED INTERNAL SIGNALS

The next few months of your start-up can be especially demanding because you can find yourself buffeted by contradictory feelings. You may be encouraged because you've survived your first three months; but, at the same time, you can find yourself battling serious concerns about your skills and abilities. You may have started your venture with a bang, but, as things wind down, fear about lack of work can undermine your sense of accomplishment. You may have burned through your email lists in an energetic quest to renew contacts and create new ones. But, instead of equipping you to take further action, all this prospecting can create insecurity about your ability to successfully promote your new business.

Pushed and pulled, you may find yourself wavering between fear and optimism: you now know enough to realize just how much you *don't* know about what you want to do. Concerns like these can make you feel at war with both yourself and your new business goals. What's really happening here? The answer can be summed up in three words: *you're testing yourself.* And perhaps you're also being tested, in a way, by the new circumstances you've created. In the first three months, you dipped your toe into entrepreneurial waters. Now you're being forced to face up to some of your shortcomings and fears, real or imagined: Are you managing your time well or letting it slip through your fingers? Are you mobilizing yourself to find new business or just treading water? Can you acquire the new skills you need to survive? Can you handle the financial strain? These are some of the questions that are likely to crop up during this time of testing. What's really at issue, however, is not simply your business ability, but your *emotional stamina.* What you're really asking yourself is this: Do I want this enough to make it work, whatever it takes? Am I willing to accept rejection and disappointments? Can I keep myself motivated?

RENEWED COMMITMENT TO YOUR VENTURE

You may have moments, and even days, when you think about giving up. But these will pass. While the coming months may test your patience and energy, there's nothing you'll face during this time that you can't handle. Why? Because during this stage, you'll discover a precious gift that will sustain and uplift you: a sense of deepening commitment in your venture and the values it expresses.

When this happens, you'll find that you've crossed an imaginary line. There are no signposts to guide you, yet it is a major milestone in the brief life of your new business, because crossing it means that you have truly become emotionally invested and identified with your fledgling enterprise. You've moved beyond thinking "This idea could really work," to saying "I want to make this happen and I will do whatever it takes to succeed." In this moment, you've taken a huge step toward assuming the mantle of the entrepreneur.

As your emotional investment in your venture pushes through to a new level, your decisions take on a new urgency. You no longer just *think* you can create the business you've envisioned—you *need* to make it happen. You've raised your stake in your business's success or failure. Making it happen has become a test not just of your ability and experience but also of your self-esteem: *you have become your business, and your business has become you.*

Success Strategies

You're definitely still in a survival situation, but the pace and some of the pressures you're now facing have changed. While the intense activity that fueled your first three months may have slackened, your emotional investment has intensified. As you approach the midpoint of your first year in business, we think you'll find the following advice extremely helpful in stabilizing yourself.

FINISH THE EMOTIONAL BUSINESS OF LEAVING

Few people associate the idea of grieving with work. Most of us link grief with illness, losing a loved one, or an intensely personal emotional crisis like divorce. But, if you think about it, coping with a job loss, changing careers, and giving up corporate life in pursuit of an entrepreneurial dream are all highly stressful events. And each involves loss. What are you grieving for? For friends who are no longer part of the fabric of your day. For familiar routines. For the paycheck that gave you stability and security. For the old self you've left behind. For the identity that you may have painstakingly cultivated but must now reinvent.

Recognizing the cycle of emotions you can expect to pass through can help you weather this emotional watershed. Sadness, nostalgia, and a sense of loss; abandonment and, in some cases, anger; acceptance; integration; and renewal—these are the classic phases of the grieving process. As your intense feelings subside, you are likely to experience a growing acceptance of your losses, your vulnerability, and the anxiety your move is causing. Once this happens, you'll begin to integrate your old skills and beliefs with your evolving goals and enjoy a newfound sense of wholeness. Ultimately, you'll experience renewal as you embrace the change you're making—and tap into your inner reserves of energy and optimism.

Unfortunately, there are no shortcuts to this process! To experience renewal, you must pass through the previous stages. That's why it's so important for you to accept your need to grieve and release the past as both inevitable and natural. It may also help to remember that thousands of other successful entrepreneurs before you have endured and survived this cycle. You can increase your chances of success if you finish the emotional business of leaving your old life behind by following the advice below.

Sorting Out Your Job-Related Feelings

There are some very specific reasons why you've decided to strike out on your own—and identifying these clearly is essential to making a new start. Writing down the reasons for your leap into entrepreneurship can help you clarify your intentions. On the flip side, it's also important to openly state your regrets about leaving your old work life. Whether it's your lost job status, your team, and/or a career path that meant a lot to you—get your views out and on paper, so that you can deal with them. Unless you acknowledge your feelings of loss, you run the risk of having these unresolved issues unexpectedly surface and distract you later on, especially when you're under stress.

Analyzing Your Work History

Do a quick, but objective, inventory of both the strengths and weaknesses you exhibited as an employee. This will help you avoid carrying over outworn, unproductive patterns into your new venture. Even more important, it will remind you of those all-important skills and approaches that you want to develop as you move forward. It will also help reinforce the positive drivers behind your move.

Creating a Ritual of Completion

A ritual of release can be a satisfying and empowering way to say goodbye to residual aspects of your job life—and to signal to yourself that you're making a fresh start in a whole new direction. When college students graduate, for instance, they flip the tassels of their caps from one side to the other to signify the rite of passage that they've undergone. Why not borrow a leaf from their book and create a ceremony for yourself? It can be as simple as taking all those personnel manuals you've been hanging on to and throwing them away—or, better yet, tossing an old pile of unneeded files into a friend's fireplace while you and she make a toast to your future success.

REMEMBER THAT A MAJOR LIFE CHANGE IS AN ONGOING PROCESS

Reshaping your business identity is extremely rewarding. It will enhance your confidence in your abilities, encourage you to build your negotiating and networking skills, and expand your self-image. But reaping these benefits isn't an overnight process: it's going to take work to change the way you think and how you operate. Suzanne Lyons's move from employee to independent filmmaker, for example, was a journey that took her from Nova Scotia to Los Angeles, and to a deeper understanding of her natural talents and strengths.

As a university student in Canada, Suzanne had her "career path all planned out. I always thought I was going to be in the corporate world where I'd have a steady paycheck. When I began working, I said to myself, 'This is the company I'll be with for thirty years and then retire from.' Loyalty and safety were probably ingrained in me, even though there was a little bug in my brain the whole time saying 'No, no, girl! Get out there!'"

Initially, Suzanne ignored this voice and went to work for the Atlantic Television System (ATS). A few years later, she was asked to help develop ATS's satellite network in Nova Scotia. She scored a coup soon after, becoming the first female vice president of marketing and promotions—and one of the first female senior executives in Canadian broadcasting. But it was tough sledding.

"On my very first day as a vice president," Suzanne recalls, "my boss called me up to his office and said, 'Suzanne, I just want you to know one thing. You're a woman, therefore you're stupid and you belong in the kitchen—and I will do everything in my power to put you there.'" Determined to survive this hostile attitude, Suzanne began taking courses. During long months of "job hell," she designed her own workshops to teach other women what she'd learned. "That's how I knew I had an entrepreneurial streak," Suzanne comments. "The minute I learned something helpful, I'd say to myself, 'Wow, I could put that in a workshop so that other women won't have to go through what I've gone through.'"

Eventually, Suzanne won the admiration and respect of her peers. When she and her husband relocated to Los Angeles, Suzanne began heeding her inner entrepreneur and decided to produce independent films. She also wanted to use her hard-won marketing knowledge to teach people in the entertainment industry how to promote themselves. So Suzanne teamed up with a partner, Heidi Wahl, to found the Flash Forward Institute, a workshop for entertainment professionals. Later, she partnered with Kate Robbins to launch Snowfall Films and WindChill Films. Together, they've won several awards and worked with talented performers like Naomi Watts, Jon Lovitz, and Alfred Molina.

Though she's faced many ups and downs in her entrepreneurial life, Suzanne is happy with the path she's taken: "I don't have any regrets when it comes to my career. I think jumping was the best thing for me. My best asset is knowing my weaknesses. I'm awake to them and work around them by finding people who are better at certain things than

I am, so that those weaknesses don't sabotage the entire operation. You've got to get out there and make it happen.

"The more powerful we are, the stronger the example we set for others. As an entrepreneur, people are looking up to you and asking how you did what you did, and how they can do it, too. I think I'm a natural-born teacher. I'm really good at simplifying everything that I've learned the hard way. That's part of why I like being an entrepreneur: I get to take what I've learned and turn it into something that I can teach and give back and contribute."

As Suzanne's exodus from employee to independent filmmaker shows, learning to be an entrepreneur is as much an inner journey as it is an outer one. It's as much about discovering your strengths and managing your weaknesses as it is about making a product or offering a service. Being willing to constantly move out of your comfort zone— and jump again and again. Empowering yourself, setting an example for others, and sharing what you've learned. Getting out there and making things happen. All these actions contribute to your role as an entrepreneur—and a leader.

CLARIFY YOUR VISION

Spend any length of time with a true entrepreneur and you'll find yourself talking to a doer with a dream—in short, someone with a *vision*. Visions come in all shapes and sizes—and are woven from many impulses. A vision can spring from a sense of mission. A strong sense of personal ethics and integrity. An idea for a product or service that you feel impelled to bring into the world. A desire to put your values into action in the workplace. Although any of these objectives is worthwhile, it's *having* a vision that really counts.

As an entrepreneur, your vision is more than just a pie-in-the-sky dream about doing it all and having it all. It's a touchstone that helps you stay focused and an emotional yardstick that helps you measure how far you've progressed and whether you're headed in the right direction. It can also be a lifeline when things get tough, especially during the weeks or even months when there are no tangible results to show for all the time and effort you've invested. A vision has to have real firepower: it has to keep you warm and motivated on those long nights when you're worried about making ends meet.

As Crystal Johnson, the founder of Sienna at Home, puts it, "You're going to get to a place where other people question your vision. It could be people close to you, or strangers. There are going to be times when you are the only person who believes in you, so if you don't have that and if you look to someone else to validate it for you, then you will quit. Because everyone can't see what you see and you can't convince everyone of what your vision is. There are going to be times when you're going to be challenged. It can be by your spouse, your parents, or by the bank. I can't say it enough: you have to have that belief in yourself."

That's why, during this stage, it's important that you begin to clarify your vision for your new business. The sense of purpose and forward motion provided by clarifying your vision will be critical in helping you summon up the energy and enthusiasm to stay in the game, especially when you face tough problems or sudden setbacks. Discovering the true nature of the vision that lies at the heart of your business venture is a challenge that's worth grappling with. As you begin this process, the following guidelines should prove helpful.

Keep Your Vision Personal—and Real

A vision must be personal; it must embody a heartfelt desire. It must also be in harmony with your values—something you really need to achieve to feel fulfilled, not something you *think* you should want. To sustain you emotionally, a vision has to be a positive rather than a negative emotional driver. It also has to be ambitious enough to propel you forward. Keeping your vision intact in the real world of deadlines and dollars isn't easy: it takes a strong sense of inner purpose. That's why it should be something that you are prepared to stand by even if that means turning away work or losing clients.

In Brenda Newberry's case, this is exactly what happened: "We actually ended up walking away from a $2 million a year contract because I felt that things weren't being done the way they should be on the client side," says Brenda. "That spoke volumes to my team with respect to our corporate culture. It's one of the hardest things I've ever had to do and in hindsight I'd do it again, because it was the right thing to do. You have to be working for something greater than yourself. It's not about you; it's about the people we're serving. That's what I tell my team. And if you're doing it in the right way for the right reasons, then you'll get past the obstacles. Without this frame of reference, when you hit the peaks and valleys, you'd say, 'Forget about this. It's too hard.'

"Part of our mission is building careers and enhancing the lives of both our customers and our people," adds Brenda. "I like it when I get a note from a client that says, 'Because of your team's successful work and my recommendations, I was promoted'—that's a great feeling! And when I see people in my company able to buy homes or put their kids through college and know that they're comfortable and at peace—that's what I mean when I say I'm working for something greater."

Brenda's vision for her fast-growing IT company is a blend of high-tech excellence and high-touch concern for the people she works with and for. It springs from her strong faith-based sense of service, her focus on performance, and her personal ethics. Her mission, as she envisions it, is to enrich the lives of both her customers and her employees—and give back to her community.

Create a Mission Statement

"If there's a big enough why, you can always find the how," comments Rob Gilbert. Creating a mission statement that captures your vision—and writing it down in a sentence or paragraph—can be enormously empowering and energizing. It can act as a kind of emotional umbrella for your budding enterprise and help solidify your self-image as an entrepreneur. Now that your venture has been up and running for a while, you've gained invaluable experience and perspective. You're in an ideal position to identify what you plan to accomplish through your business. When writing the statement, concentrate on the big picture: your values, your beliefs, and what you really want to achieve. Once your ideas and insights begin to jell, capture them in a rough draft and then live with them for a while. Don't worry about the wording or specifics, just focus on getting down on paper what you want to do as fully as you can. When you feel reasonably happy with your first effort, hang it up where you can easily see it while you're working. Leave it there for a couple of weeks without changing or judging it. Then gather your new thoughts and revise it until it really reflects the direction you want to take. Keep it on hand as a touchstone for your planning.

A mission statement can support this stage of your venture in several ways. First, it will help you stay focused and screen out extraneous activities that might distract you from doing what you need to do to keep your fledgling business alive. Second, it will make it easier to balance your priorities and schedule your time. It can help you decide what to say yes to—and what to say no to—based on the vision you've committed to and are moving toward. It can also be a great source of inspiration when you question your sanity and feel tempted to pull out the want ads!

A statement that reflects your business vision can be very simple and direct. In fact, the simpler it is, the more powerful it can be. Consider how straightforward this trademarked statement capturing Lisa Druxman's vision for her enterprise is: "Stroller Strides helps moms make STRIDES in fitness, in motherhood and in life."

Supporting this statement is a description of Stroller Strides' values:

- We will help moms achieve their ultimate potential, both physically and emotionally.

- We will offer support and education for moms.

- We will inspire moms to reach optimal health and well-being.

- We will inspire children to emulate their moms and make fitness a part of their lives.

What a wonderful statement of vision and values! What better way to keep yourself motivated—and motivate everyone around you—than to create a statement like this to bring your own vision to life. Taking a simple, but powerful step like this will pay wonderful dividends as you begin to communicate your goals more broadly and market your enterprise.

BUILD AN INTERNAL POWER BASE

During your career as an employee, you most likely honed your work skills by managing projects, meeting budgets, and solving problems. As an entrepreneur, you'll be performing many of these same tasks, but with one huge difference: *you're running the show*. At a stroke, your professional identity will shift from that of a follower-manager to a leader-entrepreneur. Your success depends on creating a strong internal power base for yourself—one that's grounded in your professional abilities and willingness to be accountable for your decisions.

As a manager, for example, you may have been part of an organization with a history, culture, resources, and identity that you shared and drew power from. Right now, you are probably an organization of one or two. You have no business history, except for your collective accomplishments. You also have no culture to draw on for sustenance as part of your power base; you're creating it as you go. Your resources are personal, not institutional.

As a manager-employee, you may have played the role of facilitator. As a leader-generator, your primary role and responsibility is that of creator and new-business generator. You don't just react to goals or projects imposed on you by others, you initiate and shape them yourself. Coming up with fresh ideas and new approaches will be vital to your survival. Equally important, you must induce others to believe in what you're doing and add their energy to yours.

As a manager, you knew that imposing order and keeping things under control were critical. As a leader-entrepreneur, you're realizing that shaking things up and quickly jettisoning unworkable approaches are essential. At times, you'll have to throw things off balance, force action, and put serious pressure on yourself and others. You'll have to learn to live with a degree of chaos and expand your tolerance for uncertainty. You'll have to handle unforeseen crises, cash flow problems, and, often, a feast-or-famine work pattern that can strain your resources.

In short, when you were an employee, your status and authority flowed from an external power base outside yourself; you borrowed it from the organization you worked for. As an entrepreneur just starting a new business, you generate and sustain your power base internally. It is rooted in your personal ability to build on past experience, to innovate, and to inspire confidence in your capabilities, drive, and delivery.

TO BECOME AN ENTREPRENEUR, BEGIN ACTING LIKE ONE!

As you move ahead with your venture, it's vital that you accept your emerging identity as an independent business owner. How, exactly, do you do this? In a nutshell, you need to begin to view yourself differently. In addition, your actions and the way you communicate with the rest of the world have to reflect this new image of yourself. The key to doing this is simple, but it's not easy: *you become an entrepreneur by acting like one*—by making decisions not as the employee you were but as the independent take-charge business owner you want to become. Here's how peak performance coach Rob Gilbert describes the process:

"I'd say that the three most powerful words in the English language are: *act as if*. Actions change attitudes, motions change emotions, and movements change moods. You might not be able to change your thoughts and you might not be able to change your feelings, but you can definitely change your actions. Your behavior doesn't have to equal your feelings. Your actions can change your feelings; your actions can change your thoughts. You can act differently than you feel."

As an entrepreneur, you need to think differently about your abilities, your resources, and your time. This involves a shift in your mind-set on a number of fronts: First and foremost, it means realizing that you can mobilize and creatively recast your corporate skills to build a business of your own. Second, you need to accept fully that your business is now your livelihood and that you must put structures in place to anchor and solidify your new self-image. Third, this new mind-set requires that you manage your time proactively—and constantly reevaluate your work and resources: is it more valuable for you to be doing X right now, or Y? Finally, thinking like an entrepreneur means accepting the pivotal importance of marketing vigorously and constantly—and reaching out for information and support in order to gather the resources you need to succeed. All these actions will come into play as you begin to form a new image of yourself. Building an inner core of security and strength will depend to a large degree on how willing you are to let go of limiting ideas you may have developed about what you can and cannot do. To succeed as an entrepreneur, you'll need to trade comfort for growth: you're going to have to push past the boundaries of your existing self-image by projecting a bigger, more flexible view of yourself, what you have to offer, and what you are capable of doing.

MAKE YOUR BEGINNER'S STATUS WORK FOR YOU

There's a Zen concept called *shoshin*, or "beginner's mind," which can be a powerful tool in building your business and your image of yourself as an entrepreneur. As one Zen master describes *shoshin*, "In the beginner's mind, there are many possibilities; in the expert's mind, there are few." As a budding entrepreneur, you are free to explore, to experiment, and to challenge. Your mind is open and unencumbered by preconceived notions about how things should work.

If you take this idea to heart, then you can use your lack of experience to powerful advantage. You can use your beginner's status to open doors and gather vital information: instead of being overwhelmed by the industry insiders or experts that you encounter, simply soak up whatever they share with you. Your buck-the-system attitude and eagerness to learn can also prove enormously appealing to seasoned pros, who may agree to mentor you or put you in touch with valuable contacts. If you use your "new kid on the block" status to question conventional wisdom, take a fresh look at what works and what doesn't, and frame innovative solutions, then your hunger and curiosity will prove to be huge benefits.

TRANSFORM PASSION INTO PERFORMANCE

Emotionalism is both an asset and a liability in a business context. Conveying the passion, intensity, and commitment that you bring to your new venture will be vital to your success. But if you allow your emotions to overwhelm your objectivity or cloud your judgment and decisions, you'll enter dangerous waters.

Turning your passion into performance requires that you think strategically about your business and avoid letting your personal feelings dictate your business relationships. It also requires that you master the way you respond emotionally to business situations on a day-to-day basis. For example, spending too much time taking your emotional temperature and talking about how you feel about your immediate business problems can make you seem less than professional and not in full control of your time and your resources. Of course, it's important to share your fears and concerns, but not with everyone you talk to—and not all the time. Your feelings may often have to play the role of silent partner when it comes to running your start-up. Acknowledge your inner emotional state, but don't let it prevent you from doing what you need to do to foster relationships and build your business.

"Balancing head and heart," as she describes it, has been a consistent theme for Roxanne Coady. When she first opened R. J. Julia Booksellers, it was "all about heart," recalls Roxanne. "I wanted to do the right thing for the customer and my employees. When I worked in the accounting field, it was all about head. Because I went into a business that I was passionate about, I went too much in the direction of heart. I used too much money; I would actually have been better off if I hadn't had enough—I think I would have made some better decisions. I let things happen that I shouldn't have let happen. I didn't let people go. I paid bonuses because they were working hard, even though they weren't showing good results."

When money got tight, Roxanne pulled in the reins and refocused herself. She realized that if her bookstore was to survive, she needed to fully utilize her financial background and put in place business concepts that were normal operating procedure in most enterprises. "I needed to analyze data in a kind of heartless way to determine what was working and what wasn't, what I could afford to do and what I couldn't. I went back to using all the data I knew how to use to run my business and make decisions. It didn't matter how I felt about things. I had to reconcile head and heart."

To get her business back on a sound financial footing, Roxanne instituted cash flow spreadsheets, budgets, job descriptions, and employee evaluations. Roxanne's more tough-minded approach paid off. In an industry where profit margins are historically low and most bookstores are not operated using traditional business concepts, R. J. Julia survived and thrived. Ultimately, it received *Publishers Weekly*'s Bookseller of the Year honor.

MANAGE YOUR EMOTIONS BY TAKING ACTION

Managing your emotions is pivotal to making the leap from employee to entrepreneur. To make this transition, you're going to have to be comfortable with being uncomfortable. You're going to have to make tough demands on yourself and meet intense deadlines. You're going to have to do things that you don't feel like doing at times when you really don't feel like doing them.

As a peak performance coach, Rob Gilbert is an expert on helping people push past self-imposed barriers so they can get to the next level, whether they're in sports, sales, or small business. Here's his advice on dealing with negative feelings so that they don't prevent you from doing what you have to do:

"Your thoughts determine what you *want*. Your actions determine what you *get*. So *can* you do what you have to do? Of course you can. *Will* you do it? That's the big question. What makes you cross the bridge from can to will? How come you can't pull the trigger? The gatekeeper is your feelings: I don't feel like writing that report. I don't feel like making those calls today. But our feelings aren't facts—they're just temporary."

So, how do you enlist your feelings so they help rather than hinder you? You do it through actions—and by using the "Fifteen-Minute Rule." "Make your calls or write your report for fifteen minutes," advises Rob Gilbert. "And then, fifteen minutes after you've started, renegotiate and see if you still want to do it. And you know what you'll find? In almost every case, you'll have broken down a lot of the resistance and built enough momentum to want to keep going. It's the start that stops most people. So even though you don't feel like it, push yourself through the starting gate—and you'll be off and running."

You're Not Only in the Business You're In— You're Also in Marketing!

Like it or not, there's lots of truth to this statement. You must constantly reach out to the clients and customers you're interested in. Your goal? To create top-of-mind awareness so that you'll be the first person people think of when they need a product or service. Don't look to just the classic methods—advertising, direct mail, splashy brochures. Marketing takes other forms, too—telephone solicitation, news releases, special events, referral cards—and, of course, the endless Internet!

Getting the word out about the benefits that your business offers is absolutely essential to your survival. The key lies in developing a marketing approach that plays to your strengths and puts you squarely in the path of new opportunities to build and expand your business. That's why cultivating a marketing mentality is integral to your entrepreneurial mind-set. Learn to communicate creatively and consistently—and you can be every bit as successful in your chosen market niche as the corporate giants are.

Building awareness about your background and your business may be a real stretch for you. If so, then you're part of a big club. Some newly minted entrepreneurs find that they have a real flair for promoting their businesses and enjoy it tremendously. But these star marketers are probably the exception. Many new business owners find themselves swimming upstream when it comes to marketing and can only bring themselves to do it in fits and starts—usually when business threatens to dry up. Some entrepreneurs are so stressed by this role that they ignore it, hoping that their product or service will magically find its market niche. Don't be one of them!

We know it's tough. Most likely, in your experience, marketing or sales has always been someone else's department. As a result, the communications tools you're most familiar with are resumes, memos, reports, internal meetings, and industry conferences. The marketing kits, brochures, press releases, pitch letters, cold calls, and media outreach that are the stock-in-trade of the small business owner are probably all foreign territory to you. And, while you may be an old hand at email and surfing the Net, you may be less familiar with online marketing, an aspect of the Web that you'll need to master in building your business.

While marketing may seem mysterious, it's a skill like any other. If you're willing to recognize the critical role that marketing plays and work at mastering some basic techniques, then you should be able to fine-tune your skills with impressive results and a minimum of anxiety. This is an area where there is lots of help available—through online courses, SCORE and SBA workshops, books, newsletters, and associations. Marketing is also an area where finding a mentor can be a highly efficient way to get up to speed quickly.

A widely recognized expert in online information marketing who's made the move from employee to entrepreneur herself, Alexandria (Ali) Brown knows exactly how vital a proactive communications strategy is to a strong start-up. After working for several years at a small ad agency, Ali struck out on her own as a freelance marketer, but without great initial success. In fact, her own launch was anything but auspicious! She was living in a "little shoebox apartment" in New York City and racing from one networking meeting to another in search of work; the results were disheartening. At one point, she had less than $20.00 left on her only usable credit card and seriously considered calling her mom and asking if she could move back home.

Breakthroughs are often born out of breakdowns. At a really low moment in her self-employed life, Ali tried a new approach: she began communicating with potential clients via email, offering marketing tips as a way to reconnect with people whose business cards she'd gathered. She met with instant success: within six months, she began attracting major corporate clients like New York Times Digital and Dun & Bradstreet. The "e-zine" (an online newsletter) she ultimately created positioned her as an expert in her field, and she began building her expertise in a niche enjoying explosive growth: online marketing.

Today, Ali has a seven-figure income, enjoys a solid reputation as the "E-zine Queen," and runs a thriving virtual business out of her beach house in California. Since adopting a market focus is so critical to your success as an entrepreneur, we asked Ali to provide some basic off- and online marketing advice. Whether your launch is built around a product or service, her practical suggestions and perspective on communicating as a business owner should prove valuable.

"The worst thing you can do," warns Ali in recalling her own rocky launch, "is to run your business out of a place of desperation. Then you're going to give off vibes of being very needy—and people don't want to work with needy people—they want to work with successful businesses. So, even if you feel desperate, keep your chin up and your game face on: say everything's wonderful and business is great!"

Once Ali began freelancing, she was doing exactly what she had done on her job and felt comfortable doing: copywriting and developing ads for clients. "This is what I see a lot of women—and men—doing, too," says Ali, "leaving their jobs to start their own business doing the thing they're good at. The problem is, you're not actually in the business of doing that thing. You're actually in the business of *marketing the thing you do*. The marketing is more important than the mastery."

When Ali first began working for herself, she made a classic mistake that she now cautions her clients about: she spent a lot of money putting together a huge, beautiful website, with a flash intro and a spinning logo. "My mother loved it," Ali laughs. "It was so impressive! But it did nothing to make me money or build my email list." With this in mind, here's what she tells her own clients who are ready to go on the Internet:

1. *Put up a one- to two-page website:* Keep it very simple and basic. Offer a free report or free newsletter on your specialty: planning for financial success, for example. Your offering can be a simple question-and-answer series or timely "tips" that you offer on a weekly basis or a single article on a high-impact issue. This will encourage people using the Internet to sign up to receive your insights and advice on a regular basis. For a sample of a one-page website that's an effective list builder, you might want to visit Ali's site at e-zine.com and see how it's set up.

2. *Use your website to build an email list:* Instead of, or along with, marketing one-on-one through personal meetings, use the Internet to build an email list of people who are interested in your

services. You can do this by creating reports or a simple e-zine (an online newsletter)—and then publicizing them via the Internet. By having people sign up for your newsletter or report, you can build a database of email addresses that you can repeatedly market to online. This list can be a major asset when you're promoting your business—and much more valuable than spending huge amounts on a website with lots of bells and whistles.

3. *Use niche marketing to grow your business:* On your website and in all your marketing copy, be very clear about who you are and who you help. Let's say you're in financial planning—you might position yourself as a "financial coach for single moms," suggests Ali. Once you've zeroed in on your target market and your niche, your marketing becomes much easier: you can figure out what websites single moms visit and what associations or networks they belong to—and then make connections with those networks in order to reach your target audiences.

4. *Use your email list to build relationships:* Through your free e-zine or reports, you can showcase your insights and expertise to your email list of potential clients. As you offer them new insights on a regular basis, they are more and more likely to think of you when they have an immediate need for help from someone in your specialty. To build rapport, make it a point to share a little personal information about yourself, your activities, and even your family in your e-zine. "People buy from people they know, like, and trust," points out Ali. "If someone has found your website, they are very valuable to you. They're there because they are interested in your topic. If you don't get them on your email list, it's as if they're showing up at your store and your door is locked!"

Soliciting for business is one of the most difficult demands of a business start-up. It means putting yourself in a position to be rejected, sometimes over and over again. This is where motivation and persistence come into play. Always remember, there are millions of people in this country; in any given city and even in small towns, hundreds of businesses are represented. All you need is a piece of what's out there!

Professionalism: More Important Than Ever

At times, you may find yourself slipping back into old patterns of behavior or feeling besieged as you attempt to master several new skills at once. You will also find that your whole approach to relationship building takes on new urgency and reveals new sensitivities. During these moments, you may feel extremely vulnerable, even fragile. That's to be expected.

Reshaping your identity is an ongoing process; it may take many months or even years before you feel that you're really on the road to the new life you're reaching for. Talk to other business owners who've moved beyond the start-up stage of their ventures and benefit from what they learned during their transition. But, most important, accept responsibility for the demands that redefining and expanding your business image will make on you. You may be starting on a shoestring, but you must never let that affect your professionalism when it comes to dealing with clients and customers.

So be absolutely sure to deliver on every commitment you make. Reputation is everything for a small business, especially a start-up. If you want to generate business at a high level, then service is one of the biggest assets you'll be selling. So think twice before you overpromise and underdeliver. Many start-ups, especially in service businesses, have to overcome client concerns about not being there when they're needed. That's why it's doubly important that you communicate honestly and deliver everything you commit to. Surpassing expectations is even better!

Service is what your clients say it is. You're not the boss; your client is—at least early on, when building your client base is most critical. Yes, you decide when to start working and when to stop, how much effort to devote to major projects and how much to put toward new client acquisitions. At the same time, your clients' needs will drive your day and determine your priorities. The key here is avoiding the tendency to overservice a handful of clients at the expense of your new business development and marketing. Sacrificing your business needs to short-term client demands will be a losing proposition for everyone involved.

So, if you promise to get back to someone with a price quote or delivery data, be sure to get it done. If you can't take on a project, then go the extra mile by finding a supplier who can. Never misrepresent your resources or fudge your track record. Build on your strengths; don't try to disguise your limitations. When you hold yourself to a high standard of professionalism, you'll find that you stretch and grow to inhabit your new self-image comfortably and confidently.

Quick Tips

Say YES to no more tight panty hose!
Focus on a fresh start. Take the best and leave the rest. Release the past and move on. Old job-related baggage can weigh you down—refuse it or lose it!

Balance head and heart.
Run your business like a business! Treat your emotions as a silent partner. Don't let them cloud your judgment. Keep your hard-core management skills on tap.

Act as if: a powerful success strategy.
Actions change attitudes! Becoming changes behavior! Make decisions like the entrepreneur you want to be. Frame a new image of yourself. Move toward it—and it will move toward you!

Be a doer with a dream.
Your vision is a lifeline in tough times. It will keep you moving—and motivated! Successful business owners reach for something bigger than they are.

Create a mission statement to help focus your efforts.
Use it as a touchstone and an emotional umbrella. Keep it simple—it will pack more punch! Look at it often—and live it every day.

Marketing trumps mastery!
Mastering your new business is important. But ignore marketing and you won't have a business to master! Exploit off- and online resources—leave no tool untried!

☑ This to-do list will help you plan key tasks during Stage 2.

STAGE 2 ACTION STEPS

☐ Create a mission statement.

☐ Focus on delivering results, not image.

☐ Take advantage of my "beginner's mind" to do the following:

_____ Open doors in a new industry.

_____ Build my contact base.

_____ Challenge conventional wisdom.

☐ Use the "fifteen-minute rule" to overcome resistance.

☐ Select three key projects I really need to complete:

1. _____

2. _____

3. _____

☐ Boost my marketing IQ with extra training:

_____ Contact SBA/SCORE.

_____ Take special courses/workshops.

_____ Find a marketing mentor/coach.

_____ Explore the Internet.

_____ Assess my website for impact—keep it simple!

☐ Tap the tools in this book's "Resources" section.

Chapter 7

Stage 3: Turn Breakdowns into Breakthroughs

Unexpected things are going to happen.
Keep learning and keep going.

—SARAH LEVY

Your first months of entrepreneurial life probably have been exciting, confusing, hectic, and more than a little bit surprising. If you've used your time well, then you've taken some important steps to anchor yourself, both professionally and emotionally. So far, you've managed to survive without the infrastructure of your employee days—in fact, you should be well on your way to fine-tuning a satisfying operating structure that's tailored to your preferred work style.

Right now, your personal life may be on the lean side, but the days are certainly flying by and more interesting than ever. You'd have plenty to talk about at a cocktail party if only you had time to go to one! All things considered, you're beginning to think that you might just be out of the start-up danger zone. The sense of freedom is really intoxicating. There's no way you can go back to being a nine-to-fiver now—or ever. You really *are* hooked.

Then *wham!* You're knocked flat. Even if you started out with a pretty solid financial base or a couple of anchor clients, as you head into the second half of your first year, alarm bells may start ringing. Yes, the project that launched your start-up has been going well, but it's winding down now and you've been too busy giving 200 percent to your client work to drum up new business. Yes, the research for the new product you want to produce has been very encouraging; there seems to be a definite market for it. But you're past the R&D phase, and to develop a prototype you're going to have to come up with some serious money. Where will you find it? Yes, you fantasized endlessly about what it would be like to be your own boss and call all the shots. But now that you're knee-deep into your start-up, you've run into a huge roadblock that you didn't anticipate.

What's going on? In a nutshell, *your fragile, fledgling start-up is colliding with reality*. Life is pouring cold water on your dream and your psyche is shivering.

You've become the entrepreneurial risk-taker that so many magazine articles wax eloquent about—and it's proving to be a risky proposition. Suddenly, you find yourself facing a seemingly enormous chasm: the gap between the idea of *running* your own business and the day-to-day reality of actually *doing* it.

As reality sinks in, some aspects of the self-employed life that you may have brushed aside early on may begin to trouble you: the demands on your personal life, the financial worries, the time required, the rejection, the overwhelming feeling of having to do everything and never being able to do enough. During this stage, it will be essential to overcome the obstacles that reality will throw your way while staying focused and pushing forward. Your goals in the next six months will be to accomplish the following:

- Hang tough during your fall-apart stage.

- Manage your self-doubt and fears.

- Pace yourself and stay motivated.

- Strengthen your resiliency muscle.

What You Can Expect to Feel

Building a business from scratch can begin to feel like pushing a boulder uphill. You may find that your time management skills aren't as strong as they should be. Or, you may have a stellar contact base, but your follow-through may be weak. Whatever your apparent shortcomings, they'll loom large in your eyes during this stage. Yet, despite the inevitable problems you'll encounter, if you stay calm and action oriented, this can prove to be an exciting time of personal and business growth—we promise! As you move ahead, here are some of the concerns you're likely to experience.

PERFORMANCE ANXIETY

Your anxiety about how well you're doing may take a quantum leap. Without a paycheck, boss, or promotion, how do you measure your progress or lack of it? The need to produce tangible results—or to sustain them at an unrealistic level—can put you under tremendous pressure. This is especially true if you launched with a big project, a hot idea, or a strong initial market response. Everyone, including yourself, expects you to keep up the pace—even though you may have simply reached a natural plateau. You know the stats about small businesses needing from one to three years or more to break even and show a profit—but somehow you expected (or were expected) to beat the odds virtually overnight.

When business doesn't come in, but the bills start piling up, you may feel compelled to rethink your game plan, sell beyond your comfort level, or take on any kind of project, just to survive. At this point, you may also begin to feel that those in your personal support system—namely, your friends and family—really don't understand what you're going through and how hard it all is. You may be feeling besieged, underappreciated—and even abandoned.

Emotionally, you're in for a pound while the people who should be investing most heavily in you seem to be in for a penny. Your husband, for example, who pledged his enthusiastic support during your venture's honeymoon days, may now feel ambivalent. He may begin to resent the amount of time your new business demands or the pressure he feels to make more money because you're not contributing much, if any. In short, your cheerleading squad seems to be packing up while you're still out on the field—and it's starting to rain!

SELF-DOUBT

How do I know if I'm doing the right thing? How do I trust myself and my vision? When self-doubt hits, you may find yourself second-guessing or waffling about even the simplest decisions and trying to keep your options open by procrastinating or turning to other people for advice. You may begin replaying old situations in which you failed to reach a goal you had set for yourself or think back to other times in your life when you took a big risk and suffered the consequences.

Self-doubt can also lead you to dwell on the issue of timing—maybe you should have waited until the economy picked up, you put away more money, or your personal life was in better shape. If you start thinking this way, your response may be to retreat—to begin hedging your bets; instead of a full-out drive to build your business, you may adopt a test-the-waters stance toward your new venture. You may even be tempted to put out some feelers in the job market, just in case things don't work out the way you've planned. More often than not, however, this approach backfires. Instead of relieving your anxieties, exploring job options at this stage will simply make you feel confused and fragmented.

FALL-APART PHASE JITTERS

The general anxiety you're feeling may be intensified by the fact that you've reached a critical juncture in your venture's infancy: *the fall-apart phase*. Look closely and you'll probably recognize the signs from your job-holding days. If you were in public relations, for example, it was the day of reckoning when you submitted a painstakingly prepared media campaign, only to have your client complain that you weren't listening and your concept was totally off base. If you were a product designer, it was the moment you discovered that the initial specs you were given had changed drastically and you had to take your entire project back to the drawing board. You get the picture.

Frustration, thy name is *fall-apart!* Just when your project seems to be coming together, something hits you from left field, everything disintegrates, and you have to pick up the pieces and find a fresh way to reassemble them. This phase seems to be a natural part of the life cycle of many major undertakings that involve significant time, creativity, and psychic energy. When you're self-employed and your new business goes through this kind of upheaval, the stakes are likely to be much higher for you than they were in your job-holding days: you may have invested heavily, despite tight dollars and a tight time frame, up until this point—and your whole livelihood may appear to be threatened as all your hard work seems to crumble before your eyes.

This is definitely one of the defining moments of your launch; it often separates the winners from the losers in the start-up survival sweepstakes. You may feel discouraged, but, as we'll see, you simply have to pick up the pieces—and fight to regain your balance and sense of control. The payoff for persevering: whatever emerges from the fall-apart stage is often better and stronger. Just remember Dolly Parton's words to the wise—something to the tune of "Winners never quit and quitters never win!"

DETERMINATION

In the midst of all this turmoil, pressure to prove yourself, and self-doubt, there's a part of you that's knowing—and growing. Over the past six months, you've already faced your fair share of problems—and, somehow, you've managed to muddle through them—and keep going. In fact, you may have surprised yourself more than once with your "brains for bucks" ideas or the elegant solutions you came up with in tough client situations. You've seen a glimpse of your power as an independent problem solver, unfettered by convention and other people's agendas. These moments—when you're in "flow" and there's an organic, harmonious feel to what you're doing—are seductive and satisfying enough to fuel your will to keep going.

Success Strategies

Finding balance in the face of distraction: that's the key to success over the next six months. You are going to have to find new ways to motivate yourself and to mobilize all your inner resources to push through moments of fear and panic. And you're going to have to find the stamina and creativity to get through your own personal fall-apart phase. As the next months unfold, use the following practical strategies for handling those tough, demanding times that will test your mettle.

RUN YOUR MARATHON LIKE A SPRINT

One of the keys to staying motivated is to keep yourself energized and alert. Running a business isn't a sprint, it's a marathon: you have to summon up real staying power, both physical and mental. But if you want to be successful, advises Rob Gilbert, "you have to run a marathon like a sprint. You have to go hard and stop. Go hard and stop. Run. Rest. Run. Rest."

What does all this mean, practically speaking? It may mean working sixty or ninety minutes and then taking a break, before starting again. This pattern of working intensely and then giving yourself a chance to recoup your energy is one that major athletes use when they're in training. It helps keep you focused and on task during those times when you're working, and it lets you slow down in between so you can recharge.

This work mode can be especially helpful when you're under intense pressure. Relaxing instead of tensing up enables you to deal with the challenges at hand with maximum creativity.

There's a variation of this run-rest approach you can use to energize your day-to-day activities. When your vision or long-term goal seems really far away, shift to an immediate goal and use it to drive you toward your long-term goal. During those times, when your immediate goal seems boring, connect with your long-term goal and use it to spur you on to tackle the task at hand. Using your long-term goal to push you to complete your short-term projects—and your short-term goal to help bridge the gap between where you are and where you want to be—can be a powerful way to keep yourself moving forward even when tough circumstances collide with your dream.

OVERCOME THE "I QUIT!" IMPULSE

When you find yourself hitting the fall-apart phase in the early months of your new venture, it helps immeasurably to remember that it's a temporary situation and a predictable phase of the launch process. In addition, you need to mobilize a practical defensive strategy to address and get through this inevitable phase quickly and forcefully. Whatever form your personal fall-apart phase takes, you'll recognize it when it happens. It won't be a garden-variety problem that crops up—it will be something that seems overwhelming and appears to put your whole enterprise at risk. It's the equivalent of a runner hitting the wall during a race: you'll feel like you're totally out of energy, emotionally and creatively.

Ronnie Fliss of Fat Murray's Doggy Treats knows exactly how that feels. A former IT executive, she had absolutely no professional experience as a baker. At first she started baking with meat, but, after a few weeks, the results "looked like a science experiment," says Ronnie. She worked through her initial recipe snafus but hit her fall-apart phase when a serious product development issue cropped up.

"We had a problem in the beginning with mold," Ronnie recalls. "After a couple of weeks on the shelf, because of moisture in the product, it would turn moldy. Also my product wasn't packaged properly, so there were breakage problems. I lost some wonderful customers as a result. I had a small chain of stores in New England, but I've never been able to get in there again; it's one of my biggest regrets. Once you lose a customer, it's hard to get them back."

Even though Ronnie had once worked for Nabisco, she'd never gotten near the ovens! The mold problem surfaced just as she was beginning to get traction with her organic gourmet pet-food sales. But Ronnie was down, not out. Though her initial product problems cost her valued customers, Ronnie moved quickly to find a workable solution. Drawing on her strong research skills and contacts, she located a food chemist who came up with a new recipe formulation that solved the mold and breakage difficulties she was experiencing—and she was back on track.

Ronnie also received much-needed encouragement during this period from both her family and Dr. Ethne Swartz, her professor and mentor at Fairleigh Dickinson University. "You need somebody behind you to keep pushing you and to say, 'Keep going, keep going!' when you hit these rough patches," she comments.

Sarah Levy's fall-apart phase also came early in her launch. She had started Sarah's Pastries & Candies in March 2004 and was using her mother's kitchen as her base of operations.

After a lot of knocking on doors and visits to small gourmet shops around Chicago, Sarah finally found a company that agreed to buy her chocolates and put them on its dessert carts. Excited and hopeful, Sarah geared up for her first big order. At one point, she had turned out so many trays of chocolates that she began stacking them up in her brother's old room! Unfortunately, the company ended up carrying her chocolates only minimally. The owner wouldn't let Sarah offer samples as an incentive and then said that her chocolates weren't selling and cancelled the order.

At the time, it was a near-disastrous outcome for the eager twenty-three-year-old entrepreneur. Sarah had really banked on this initial order; suddenly it fell through and she was back to square one. Disheartened, Sarah began to question whether she could really make her business work. "When I had an account fall through and no one was buying my chocolates, I said, 'OK, I'm going to give myself until December. And if I don't get some accounts, I have to start making some income, so I'll have to get a job.' I definitely said to myself, 'This might not be working, so let me give myself a deadline,' which was really sad, but I realized I couldn't be making chocolates that nobody was buying."

Fortunately, Sarah had avoided making the common start-up mistake of putting all her eggs in one basket. While pursuing the customer she eventually lost, she was also persistently wooing Whole Foods. Instead of caving in after her customer suddenly bailed out, Sarah pushed forward with her email and phone campaign to convince the regional manager of the Whole Foods chain that she could handle its account. She also did everything in her power to make it happen: to satisfy the chain's rigorous requirements, Sarah found additional suppliers and new ingredients. Her persistence paid off. Just two months before her "get a job" deadline, she landed the Whole Foods account and cheerfully committed to servicing its stores throughout the Midwest—an ambitious undertaking for an untried start-up.

With a huge customer on board, Sarah's credibility soared. She quickly lined up other wholesale accounts around Chicago—and Sarah's Pastries & Candies was off and running. Reflecting on her launch, Sarah comments: "It's important to really trust your instincts and not be discouraged, because in the beginning things will be coming at you left and right—and it will feel overwhelming. But just know that, with time, it gets so much better and more manageable."

When Suzanne Lyons and Heidi Wahl launched the Flash Forward Institute to train actors in personal marketing, their fall-apart experience was sparked by a business model flaw. Suzanne temped for a few months while Flash Forward was getting off the ground, but when its first course attracted 120 people, she quit her temp job. Then, enrollment took a nosedive: their next course attracted only 32 registrants—barely enough to pay operating expenses. It was a huge wake-up call for the two newly minted entrepreneurs.

"We actually made a profit on the first course, but then where did everybody go?" Susan remembers asking. "This was supposed to be easy! I wasn't trained to handle this part of being an entrepreneur—those times when your business only makes enough money in a quarter to pay your expenses. When we had only 32 registrants for one course and 18 for another, Heidi and I realized, 'Oh my God, we need to generate something more to make this business work.' What this forced us to do was to become more creative."

Instead of giving up on their idea when they hit a major roadblock, Suzanne and Heidi tapped into their ingenuity. Realizing that their business model was too narrow, they brainstormed ways to expand it in order to reach a broader market. They quickly created some advanced courses with higher price tags for more seasoned professionals and designed follow-up programs for alumni who had taken their basic course. "We said, 'Let's look at ways to offer other courses that will bring in more profit and, at the same time, push the envelope for both of us to create some amazing programs,'" Suzanne notes.

In addition to expanding their market, Suzanne and Heidi adopted two other strategies to manage the ebb and flow of their business with a minimum of stress. First, they created what Suzanne calls an "existence system"—a visual display that allowed them to track their course enrollments in real time. This planning tool showed them the progress they were making in reaching their enrollment goals so they could adjust their marketing strategy as needed.

"You want to be a cause, not an effect in life," observes Suzanne. "And in order to be a cause, you need to create existence systems to let you know that life is not a mystery—it's available to you just the way you design it. If we weren't getting the enrollments we needed at any particular point, then we needed to make more calls or lower our goal or bring in a partner or brainstorm about what was missing. Until you have a system in place, it's like going down a road without knowing where it's leading. As an entrepreneur, being accountable for where you are at any given moment is critical."

Along with designing a goal-setting tool, the two partners created an emotional "safety net" for themselves by getting outside help. "The minute I formed my own company, I got a coach," notes Suzanne. "If there were any meltdowns along the way, if we had 20 registrations and we needed 30 in the next two weeks, we'd meet with our coach. In our courses, we asked everyone to get a coach and that's what we did ourselves. Anytime we were in a position that could have created intense stress or when we smelled the fact that we were close to the breakdown stage, we would call our coach and tell her we were way off our goal on this or that. Then we'd set up a brainstorming session and work through our situation until we had some sort of breakthrough."

In this case, the coach's role wasn't to contribute creatively, but to help defuse crises by being a sounding board and, as Suzanne describes it, by "lessening any emotional mess that we might have gotten ourselves into. Instead of heading in the wrong direction, we used a coach as a backstop to reorient ourselves and get into a positive mode. There were times we didn't even know we were in breakdown: we had our heads in a hole in the ground. But the more you catch yourself, the better you get at it."

Tough Out Your Fall-Apart Stage

Each of the intrepid entrepreneurs whose stories we've recounted here found different ways to battle through a major meltdown and come out on the other side. Somehow, some way, they managed to survive the "I quit!" feelings that washed over them when their new-business hopes and dreams seemed to be crumbling before their very eyes. If you find yourself in a similar position, consider the following practical advice for crossing this challenging emotional Delaware.

DON'T PANIC

When you're in the middle of a fall-apart scenario, whatever the circumstances, it's important to stay as calm and focused as you can. Getting into a downward spiral about the difficulty you're facing is never helpful—it just forces you to expend needed energy talking yourself back out of a negative mind-set. As we mentioned earlier, the fall-apart phase is a natural and even predictable part of the development of creative endeavors like yours. It's not something that's necessarily the result of anything you did or didn't do; it's simply a rite of passage that you need to complete to continue in your start-up life cycle. So don't waste any more time than you have to beating yourself up because you couldn't avoid it or didn't see it coming. Instead, adjust to your new reality as quickly as you can and shift from a wheel-spinning worry mode into a problem-solving groove.

As Rob Gilbert puts it, "Oprah once said, 'If you have a pulse, you have a problem.' When it comes to problems, you have to get fascinated with them, not frustrated. If you get frustrated, the game is over. So get fascinated, even if you have to fake it!" The more you relax and become intrigued by whatever problem you're facing, the more quickly you'll begin brainstorming possible solutions, and the more inventive those solutions will be. Opt for playfulness instead of panic and your problem-solving skills will become sharper and more accessible (see "Strengthen Your Resiliency Muscle," page 151).

DON'T RETREAT—PUSH FORWARD

When you hit a major roadblock, you generally have one of two choices: you can retreat, nurse your wounds, and spend your time asking "Why me?"—or you can propel yourself forward. Instead of putting your head "in a hole in the ground," as Suzanne Lyons described it, redouble your efforts, intensify your activity level, and push forward and outward in search of a solution.

Taking that approach, Ronnie Fliss located a food chemist who could solve her mold dilemma. Sarah Levy didn't hide in her mom's kitchen; she sucked up her disappointment and persisted with her program of emails and product adjustments to gain a contract that was far bigger and more prestigious than the one she'd lost. And Suzanne Lyons and her partner, Heidi, didn't throw up their hands and say, "This whole training program of ours is a loser." Instead, they asked themselves, "How can we get more creative about making this idea of ours work?" and they came up with a strategy to tweak their business model, broaden their market, and boost profitability.

CORRECT YOUR COURSE QUICKLY

If you do find yourself facing a major meltdown, it's very important that you promptly assess your situation as objectively as you can, mobilize support for yourself, and take action. In circumstances like these, the longer you wait, the worse things get: your money gets tighter, your stress level rises, your self-doubt mushrooms. So allow yourself the luxury of a little moaning and groaning—and then get on with the job at hand: generating creative options to salvage what you can and strategize your way back on track.

As Suzanne Lyons points out, knowing exactly where your business is at any given point and taking ownership of your situation is part of what it means to be an entrepreneur. That's one good reason why developing a tracking system of some type, just as Suzanne and Heidi did, is such a powerful idea. It allows you to see those "breakdown" moments in advance. If you're not blindsided, you'll have more time to explore all your potential options. But whether you see the fall-apart stage coming or it takes you by storm, your best bet is to tackle your situation swiftly and vigorously. The longer you let it slide, the harder it will be to recover and reorient yourself.

CALL IN THE TROOPS

You're in business *for* yourself, but you don't have to be in business *by* yourself. When you hit a serious roadblock, it can feel overwhelming and isolating. You can easily feel as if the harsh hand of fate has singled you out. As in most situations, this "poor me" attitude won't get you very far. It's also not really accurate. All around you, there are fledgling business owners going through trials by fire that are every bit as taxing and discouraging as yours is. The ones who'll get through with the least amount of psychic wear and tear are those who reach out for advice and support.

This much-needed help comes in many forms: it can be an expert with the knowledge to tweak a product design problem, or a contact who gives you a solid lead for a promising new customer, or the advice of a seasoned industry pro who's faced the same kind of tough market climate that you've encountered—and figured out a way to survive it. "Very few of us have to reinvent the wheel," comments Suzanne Lyons. "That's the nice thing about this planet: there's probably someone out there who's done something you're about to do before you. I'm all for mentors and coaches. There are six billion people on this planet—and hell, I'll take everybody's advice!"

CREATE A BRAINSTORMING GAME PLAN

When you run into a fall-apart situation, it's important that you shift from being reactive to being proactive. One way to do this is to come up with a brainstorming strategy that you can call into action as soon as you realize that things have gone awry. Suzanne Lyons and her partner structured ad hoc sessions using a coach whose main role wasn't to act as an idea generator but as a facilitator. You can follow their lead or take a different approach and create a "brain trust"—a small, supportive team (preferably drawn from a variety of industries) that you can call upon to help you generate solutions during a serious crunch period. Another strategy might be to hire a consultant for a day to assess your fall-apart situation with complete objectivity and then help you map out the most viable options and potential results. Whatever route you take, it's a smart idea to put a meltdown strategy in place early in your start-up, so that you can mobilize it quickly when needed.

MAKE STRESS REDUCTION A PRIORITY

We all know how physically and emotionally demanding a major project breakdown can be. It can sap your energy and block your creativity, which makes it doubly difficult to generate useful ideas or make smart decisions. That's why it's vital that you do everything you can to defuse the stress and tension that a fall-apart situation can trigger. One of the key functions that Suzanne Lyons's coach performed when the Flash Forward Institute started was to help Suzanne and Heidi relieve stress and defuse emotional anxiety so that they could shift into a positive, solution-seeking mode.

FIND YOUR SECRET MOTIVATOR

One of the keys to tapping into your staying power is to find your own personal "secret motivator"—the tool or technique that gives you emotional strength to keep on going when you feel like giving up. Some people find that reading the right material does more to boost their morale than anything else. When they read inspiring stories or a great how-to guide, it sparks something inside them. Suddenly, they get a new idea or see a whole new path. For others, journal writing is a source of inspiration and stress relief. Self-help tapes are another good way to stay upbeat and hopeful, according to many entrepreneurs. Visualization and affirmations are two additional self-motivators that some new business owners find helpful.

MANAGE YOUR FEARS

The single biggest obstacle most people face when starting a business is an emotional barrier, not a professional one: it's fear of the unknown. It's this fear that keeps most women—and men as well—from "going for it" and taking control of their work lives by launching and building something of their own. This same fear can also sabotage your early launch efforts. By fear of the unknown, we don't mean external circumstances, such as fear of a market slide or competitive move; we're referring to something deeper and more personal.

What we're talking about here is a fear of unknown elements within yourself—of whether you have what it takes to make your new enterprise work. Even if you've enjoyed tremendous success in the past, you may still be concerned about letting yourself and your family down. In short, your biggest fear may be not that you lack experience or skill or contacts—but that you lack endurance. Like a short-distance runner, you may be great at creating lots of energy and enthusiasm at the start of a project. But you may secretly or even openly question whether you have the staying power to really go the distance. When you hit a major roadblock, like a fall-apart situation, this fear can really kick in. If you find yourself responding in this way, it's important to stabilize yourself so you don't lose valuable momentum.

Feeling Fearful Is Healthy—and Creativity Boosting!

Whatever form your fear takes—fear of losing a client, of suffering financially, or of not knowing enough—it's not only natural, it's also rational. Just about everyone experiences some degree of fear during his or her launch; it comes with the territory. As you remind yourself of this, and of other situations you've mastered, you'll be taking a big step in managing the anxieties that are par for the course in any major undertaking.

Here's how Becky Rohrer candidly describes her feelings as she was restoring her bed-and-breakfast—and attempting to rebuild her life as well: "The first days of my venture made me feel very anxious, but I just kept driving forward and saying, 'OK, I'm afraid. It's OK to be afraid, and I'm moving on.' You have to be prepared to go through this if you're going to have your own business."

Take action, keep moving forward, "feel the fear and do it anyway"—this is the approach that Becky took. You have to be willing to live with your fear and say, "OK, I'll see where this takes me. Maybe there's something valuable down this road." As you push ahead despite your fears, you'll often find that they dissipate on their own. "False Evidence Appearing Real"—that's how Rob Gilbert describes the kind of self-generated anxiety that we can all sink into without any concrete proof that what we fear is real. For example, he points out, "We might think that more powerful people are going to reject us or not listen to us. I've found, however, that in the pyramid of success, the people who are most willing to help you are those at the top—not the people in the middle, because they're still striving."

There's also an upside to fear: it can be enlivening and energizing. When you're getting started, what keeps you moving a lot of the time is fear. It can drive you to get up, get out, and do what you have to do to survive. It can also stretch you in unexpected, business-expanding ways. In fact, fear can be a powerful teacher if you can keep it from overwhelming your sense of discovery. This is an ongoing challenge, because, like a guest who overstays its welcome, fear never really leaves. Even after more than a decade in business, Brenda Newberry still finds herself getting anxious.

"Running a business is wonderful. I love it and I would do it again, but it's not perfect—it's not without fear. But that's what makes it exciting, too. Even when my first employee came on board, I thought, 'What if I can't make payroll?' I get anxious and fearful now—and I get energized. When we reached one hundred employees, I realized that I was responsible for at least three hundred people, because everyone had a husband or wife and children. I think if you lose your fear or passion or the ability to get anxious, then you become complacent and lose your edge."

Make Your Fear Work for You

How do you begin to get a handle on your fears so that you can make them work for you, instead of against you? The first step is to simply acknowledge the fact that fear of the unknown—especially within yourself—is a perfectly acceptable response, even though it may ultimately turn out to be unfounded. Second, be honest with yourself about what you're feeling and don't let your concerns about appearing foolish or inexperienced get in the way of finding the support you need.

Giving your fear a name and an "address" can also help. So identify your own personal Mount Everest: pinpoint the inner lack or weakness that you think is your toughest adversary—the one that looms in front of you like a massive mountain. Are you afraid that you're not experienced enough, that you're not really a risk-taker, or that you know too little about marketing?

What's the biggest nut you have to crack? Whatever it is, get it out in the open. Once you've identified the nature of your fear, you can begin to cut it down to size by using it to pinpoint skills you need to strengthen or information gaps you need to fill. On the other hand, if your fear remains vague and diffuse, it will simply undermine your confidence and drain your energy.

Getting up and out every day is also a fear buster. If you've ever had a serious case of the blues or seen someone go through a depression, then you know how easy it is to give in to feelings of helplessness and malaise. If your fear has that kind of effect on you, you may begin to retreat into yourself. If you find yourself letting the four walls of your office close in on you, sleeping late, and letting yourself go, then it's imperative that you act quickly to counter your fear response.

As a first step, see if sticking to a nine-to-five schedule helps get you back on track. Get yourself dressed and ready for action in a way that makes you feel professional and productive. Taking a more casual attitude toward clothing is fine, but don't let yourself go too far down that road. You wouldn't go to a job in your nightgown—don't do it if you're working at home, either. If a client phones while you're still in your bathrobe, you'll find yourself feeling unsettled and unprofessional. This will only fuel your anxiety. When you feel physically well put together, you feel more focused and alert—it's that simple.

It's also important not to continually isolate yourself, especially if you're working at home alone all or most of the time. Make it a point to get yourself out every day or at least several times a week. Have breakfast at a favorite diner. Take a real, honest-to-goodness lunch break—or, better yet, make a date once a week to get together with a friend or small group you feel comfortable with—and share your feelings and concerns with them. A reality check may be all you need to cut those pesky private fears of yours down to size.

USE FANTASY TO DEFUSE TENSION

If you're feeling overwhelmed, force yourself to take time to indulge in a mental minivacation. Daydreaming—setting yourself adrift in a sea of desire with no real goal in sight—may not seem like an especially useful activity to you now, but it is. In fact, giving free rein to the playful, wishful side of your imagination can be one of the keys to success in launching your start-up. Why? The emotional release that daydreaming offers can also be a lifesaver: it can lift you above the pressures you face on a daily basis and renew your will and passion to succeed.

Having a fantasy isn't the same as having a vision. A vision for your business involves goals and a mission. But fantasizing about it sets you on an open-ended voyage of discovery. You have no goal to confine you, no limits to your imagined success, no shore to head for. You're setting yourself free to go where your imagination takes you and to expand your horizons. Yes, you're doing this with a purpose: to energize yourself and unleash your creative powers. But there's no goal in mind to inhibit you.

Becky Rohrer knows all about using fantasy to keep a dream alive when days are long—and times are tough. When she first began transforming a gutted, roofless home into the College Inn, a stately bed-and-breakfast, she had a clear vision of what she wanted each room to look like. But when she needed to determine how she would actually run the inn and what she'd be doing all day, she let her imagination take full flight.

"My fantasy," she laughs, "was that I'd be in my pretty little outfits, entertaining guests, serving them cheese and crackers and wine on a little silver tray. I had this other image of myself in a cute little apron and a frilly blouse, my flowerpots looking all beautiful, sweeping the front porch as the mailman came by, and cheerfully calling out, 'Good morning!' It never happened! I'm up there in my shorts and my garden boots with my power blower! I'm lucky if I get a shower!"

Some fantasies can come true—and are meant to. Others are simply meant to inspire and energize. Yet, however fanciful it is, fantasizing can be a powerful tool for igniting the desire that leads to purposeful action. If you are in the throes of launching a business, then don't hold back! Take a blue-sky approach to your venture. Daydream about it with abandon. Set aside the *hows*—the production aspect of your venture—and set yourself adrift in a sea of desire. Dream boldly—the bigger, the better! Just a brief note of caution: make fantasy your friend, but don't get too carried away! Don't use fantasizing as a way of avoiding tasks you don't want to do or as an excuse to overspend.

STRENGTHEN YOUR RESILIENCY MUSCLE

As the ups and downs of this stage prove over and over again, small-business success requires resilience—and lots of it! In fact, the attributes of the resilient personality and the traits of successful small-business owners are virtually identical, according to Dr. Al Siebert, a small-business owner himself. Here's what he's found out about you:

"You're self-reliant. You've learned from experience to count on yourself rather than others. When there's a setback, you see it as temporary but surmountable. You have a complex, paradoxical inner nature. You're both creative and well organized. Relaxed and tense. Optimistic and pessimistic. Calm and emotional. Task oriented and people oriented. Serious and playful."

These are just a handful of the unique mix of qualities that small-business owners display. Combining emotional survival skills with business savvy enables them to weather the choppiest of economic seas—and they often emerge even stronger as a result of the setbacks they've overcome. That's why resiliency is such a powerful inner resource for you as an entrepreneur—and one that you'll want to develop as fully as possible.

Handling Setbacks and Managing Crises

As your start-up moves through the next few months—and beyond—you're going to face a barrage of difficulties: tough decisions, erratic market shifts, employees who suddenly quit, clients who cancel orders, industry slowdowns and shake-ups. And, predictably, the shock waves they'll create for you are far more intense than they would be for a large corporation. You may be lean and mean, but you're also less insulated from the slings and arrows of the business world.

How you respond is key: positive emotions increase your mental agility and problem-solving skills while negative emotions weaken them. That's why resilient people deal with crisis situations so well, notes Dr. Siebert: "Instead of getting all embroiled in their emotions, they focus outwardly on making the right things happen. They avoid lots of anger or fear and quickly shift into a strategizing mode. They size up a situation through rapid questioning: What's my new reality? What needs to be done right now? What's the easiest, most efficient solution? What's the hidden benefit I can extract from this situation? What about longer term?" Above all, they meet obstacles with optimism: they expect, somehow, some way, to deal with the problem successfully.

Solving Problems Creatively

Resilient people are creative: playfulness, curiosity, and a sense of humor are part of their response to obstacles. They discover a path out of their troubles by using three different types of problem solving. First, there's the left-brain, analytical, rational form of strategic thinking that follows a step-by-step approach. Then there's the creative, right-brain response, which leads to off-the-wall solutions that seem to defy logic but often work. Finally, there's a third kind of fast, nonverbal problem solving that leads to simple, practical solutions.

Cultivating each of these problem-solving approaches is vital for you in your role as entrepreneur. If your problem-solving skills are weak, then you are more likely to react like a victim and blame external circumstances when something goes wrong. This stops you from mobilizing your inner resources and focusing outwardly on the challenge at hand. A victim reaction also makes you more vulnerable to fear, which can prevent you from taking quick, decisive action.

Acting Resiliently to Create Resiliency

Just as success breeds success, so resiliency creates resiliency: we become resilient by acting in resilient ways, and then reinforcing this behavior. We come to see ourselves as optimistic solution seekers who can handle ambiguity and thorny problems. Instead of giving in to anxiety, we reach out—asking questions, generating ideas, getting feedback, and pushing forward. And, as we exhibit a more resilient response in one situation, we strengthen our resiliency muscles, so that, the next time around, taking this approach will seem easier and more natural.

MINE THE DAZZLING OPPORTUNITIES THIS STAGE OFFERS

We've spent a lot of time talking about breakdowns, meltdowns, and the fall-apart phase. But where's the breakthrough that we mentioned in the title of this chapter? Good question! As Rob Gilbert puts it, a "breakdown is really a setup for a breakthrough." And that's exactly the message we want to deliver here. Embedded within the difficulties you may have faced during this stage are any number of precious, business-building gifts, tangible and invisible, that you can take with you as you push forward into the next stage of your start-up life cycle.

First, whatever obstacles you've faced in the last six months or so, one thing's for sure: they've definitely blasted you out of your comfort zone! And that's where the real growth is. You've been stretched six ways to Sunday, and if you're still with us it means that your dream is still alive—maybe a bit battered, but still kicking. To get to where you are at this moment, you've definitely had to push past barriers, both external and internal. That means you've flexed your resiliency muscles—which will only make you stronger.

Second, you've been given the opportunity to view failure in a whole new way—not as a defeat, but as feedback—and an invitation to do some course correction. No matter what your personal fall-apart phase or major problem in this stage turned out to be, it has revealed some fundamental weakness or flaw in your start-up strategy. Receiving this feedback early in your new-business cycle is incredibly valuable, because you can trace its root cause fairly easily—and then work to eliminate it before too much harm has been done.

Just imagine if Ronnie Fliss had built up a huge national customer base for her gourmet pet treats—and *then* her mold and breakage problems had surfaced! She would have faced a far bigger problem than she actually did: instead of losing a few valued customers, she might have lost dozens; her start-up's credibility and reputation for quality would have been seriously damaged—perhaps even destroyed. But, because her fall-apart situation revealed a serious product weakness early on, and she nipped it in the bud, the fallout was relatively minimal.

Finally, as we noted earlier, there's another hidden gift in virtually every fall-apart situation that almost seems to defy logic. When whatever you've labored to build seems to shatter into pieces *and* you find the inner strength to pick them up and start again, the end product invariably proves to be better and stronger. The whole process seems mysteriously designed to catapult you to another level of innovation and quality. Perhaps Napoleon Hill said it best: "Effort only fully releases its reward after a person refuses to quit."

That certainly proved to be true for Suzanne Lyons and Heidi Wahl during their Flash Forward launch: when their basic course offering proved too limited to sustain their business, their brainstorming sessions forced them to think outside of the box. Ultimately, this led Suzanne and Heidi to design breakthrough courses that pushed the envelope—both in their own growth as entrepreneurs and in the people they were training.

All in all, the breakthrough side of the balance sheet looks surprisingly strong, doesn't it? The assets we've described here will serve you in good stead as you move into the next stage of your start-up cycle. And so will the determination you've shown. You've proven that you believe in your business enough to learn how to tough out your most demanding challenges yet. You've gone the distance: you're not a sprinter after all!

Quick Tips

Resist the "I quit!" impulse!
The fall-apart stage is a rite of passage in business ownership. You can't cure it, so endure it! Hang tough—and you can tough it out. The results may astound you!

Manage your fears—or they'll manage you!
Fear isn't fickle—it hits everyone. It's also energizing—and a creativity booster! Be bigger than your fear and you'll cut it down to size. Find your Mount Everest—and start climbing!

Blue-sky yourself out of stress.
Fantasy is a powerful stress reliever. Indulge yourself! Expand your horizons. Live your dream before doing it!

Get up and out every day.
Let fear in the door, but don't let it stay. Dress for success—even at home! Oust yourself from your office. Mingle!

Build your resiliency muscle.
Upbeat emotions boost agility. Shift into strategy mode quickly. Be playful, be curious, and laugh out loud!

Unwrap your presents.
Mine your meltdown! Accept the hidden gifts this stage offers you. See failure as feedback. Learn and grow. Enjoy your endurance!

This to-do list will help you plan suggested tasks during Stage 3.

STAGE 3 ACTION STEPS

☐ Identify my fall-apart situation.

☐ What is my fall-apart survival strategy?

___ Mobilizing a small "brain trust."

___ Using a coach as a catalyst.

___ Finding a consultant to generate options.

☐ Brainstorm problem-solving scenarios.

Come up with three to six possible solutions:

1. _____   4. _____

2. _____   5. _____

3. _____   6. _____

☐ Reach out for advice and support.

Come up with three people to call for ideas and resources:

1. _____

2. _____

3. _____

☐ Find my secret motivator:

___ Books ___ Tapes ___ Affirmations

☐ Pinpoint my "Mount Everest"—my biggest skill gap.

Come up with four ways to tackle it:

1. _____

2. _____

3. _____

4. _____

Chapter 8

Stage 4: Find Your Business Rhythm

It's absolutely true that the market finds you.
And it's not usually what you expected.

—BECKY ROHRER

You've come a long way! To reach this stage, you've met the challenges and problems you've faced with enormous flexibility and staying power. You've also probably never worked harder in your life! What's driving you on? The quest for freedom: the field you've plowed is your own. It's a great feeling, isn't it? The seeds you've planted may not be bearing fruit yet, but they will, *as long as you sustain your momentum.* You're still in survival and total action mode: finding time to plan is a tricky proposition. Sometimes, all your energy is spent just getting from one day to the next. Making ends meet may still be a priority, but you are definitely much farther along the learning curve.

You'll also find that your business has a rhythm and a life of its own that you couldn't have predicted when you launched. And, as we'll see, during this stage, your market will find you and begin to redefine your business for you—often in surprising ways. This redefining process is one you'll encounter throughout your venture's life cycle. When it occurs during this stage, your major challenge will be to recognize what's happening and take advantage of it to push your business in new and more promising directions. Over the next twelve months, your major goals will be to do the following:

- Gain a better sense of your business's rhythm.

- Let your market reveal itself to you.

- Take advantage of mentoring and build new alliances.

- Create a renewal strategy to prevent burnout.

What You Can Expect to Feel

Now more than ever, you feel there's no turning back. Sometimes, it seems as if you've been running your own business—or it's been running you—forever. You're still working crazy hours, but you may be rewarding yourself by taking advantage of the flexibility that being your own boss gives you. In fact, time may be one of the major ways you're paying yourself right now. As you move forward, a number of concerns are likely to surface. Here are some of the feelings you may be dealing with.

BEEN THERE, DONE THAT BLUES

> **EAT. SLEEP. WORK.**
> **EAT. SLEEP. WORK.**
> **EAT. SLEEP. WORK.**

This may describe your daily grind exactly. So where's all the fun you're supposed to be having? Where's all the glamour, the glitz? Oprah publishes her own magazine and appears on every issue looking gorgeous and totally together. Sarah Jessica Parker has found life after *Sex and the City* selling her own perfume in a belle-of-the-ball pink organdy dress. And what are you doing?

You're crouched on the floor of your garage stuffing envelopes. Or scanning your bank statement for the tenth time, trying to figure out why your balance is hugging zero. Or checking your emails every five minutes, waiting for that green-light message from a client you've been wooing for weeks. You've taken the plunge and put yourself on the line. You've given up vacations and expensive lunches and a dozen other indulgences, large and small. Now you're longing to feel entrepreneurial with a capital E.

Forget the profits, you want the perks! You're still in the "before" stage of launching your business and you're seriously wondering when the "after"—the rags-to-riches success story phase—will finally arrive. Will anyone ever interview you about your start-up for *Entrepreneur* or the *New York Times* or even the *Gizmo Gazette*? Will you ever be big enough to move out of the garage or the basement, so that you can see daylight like everyone else?

PEDAL-TO-THE-METAL FATIGUE

You'd like to take it easy and coast a bit. But right now, your only option is to fuel your business's growth by stepping on the gas. And so you do. However, it's easy to push yourself into the red zone, especially if you're a one-woman band. Unless you pay attention to reenergizing yourself, the strains of your start-up can really catch up with you and put you on the defensive, physically and emotionally. When this happens, your can-do attitude, stamina, and business judgment may suffer. Taking care of business also means taking care of yourself. As we'll see, building time into your day and week for renewal is especially important in this stage.

As your business consumes more and more of your time, the toll it takes on your personal life can intensify. The irony of this can hit you like a ton of bricks. One of your key goals in launching may be to bring the personal and professional sides of your life into better balance. Yet right now, just the opposite seems to be happening. Your family and friends may believe, perhaps with good reason, that your business is taking the best of you—and may begin to feel neglected and shortchanged.

FINANCIAL ANXIETY

If you've been zealous about your effort to generate new business from day one, then you should continue seeing results. On the other hand, if you've let your new-business prospecting take a backseat, then you may find yourself forced to scramble for funds just to keep going. Most aspiring entrepreneurs manage to pull together enough reserve funds to survive at least the first six or seven months. Somewhere toward the end of the first year, severance pay, savings, and perhaps even family support begin to drain away. If you've poured your entire nest egg—or most of it—into your start-up but have little to show for your efforts so far, then financial anxiety can rear its unwelcome head again.

MORE CONFIDENCE

Like every other stage, this one has a silver lining. As you enter the next twelve months of your new venture's life cycle, the groundwork you've laid during your launch days is beginning to pay off. Despite the ups and downs that you've encountered, you're likely to feel more confident about your chances of survival and success. There are solid reasons for this growing belief in your abilities. In the past twelve months, you've gained a gold mine of new experience. Enthusiasm combined with your newfound expertise is a powerful combination!

During this stage, you are also likely to become more and more adept at applying your new and existing repertoire of skills to your venture. You've learned a lot, not just about your business, but about yourself. You may also have a clearer picture of both your strengths and your weaknesses. Your shortcomings may be cause for concern, but they also offer the incentive for improvement. After all, if you can just get past the survival stage, you'll be in a position to attract other people's skills to complement yours.

Success Strategies

Despite the pressures you face, you and your business are beginning to blossom and grow together. This is a time of tremendous opportunity and choice. The decisions you make about direction, markets, product development, size, and structure will be more demanding and require a higher degree of sophistication. Once again, you've upped the ante. Here's frontline advice on handling the pressures you'll face and staying your course:

BE YOUR OWN BEST RESOURCE

Being your own best resource means that you, and you alone, are the ultimate expert when it comes to planning and running your business. Yes, you may continue to need help from lawyers, accountants, and mentors. But their role in your start-up is to help you stay on course—*not* to determine that course for you. As we'll see, giving your power away by relying too much on experts is one of the biggest traps you can fall into (see chapter 9, page 190). Though you may feel uncertain about your next steps at any given point, you are never totally lost and without direction. Either you have the answers within you or you have the ability to reach out and find what you need.

This means that you must do inner work as well as outer work—and listen to yourself. It means having the courage to ask yourself, "What decisions am I about to make for the wrong reasons? Because I've bought into someone else's image of what an "entrepreneur" is? Because I'm desperate for money to keep myself afloat? Because I'm trying to prove myself—to myself, my family, my friends, or even my old boss?" And finally, it means stepping out of action mode long enough to quiet your mind so that you can tap into your intuition—a must for any successful entrepreneur.

LET YOUR MARKET FIND YOU

As you move through this stage, your business will begin to find its market and the market will begin to find your business. This process is a natural, organic one and it's really a very positive development, although it may throw you off balance initially. When this happens, your job—and it's not always an easy one!—is to let your enterprise evolve, rather than trying to push it in the direction that you *think* it should be moving. To get a better handle on how this process unfolds, let's look at how three women let the market tell them what it wanted.

Unexpected Target Customers

When Becky Rohrer opened the College Inn, she thought she knew all about who her customers were going to be. After all, she had a real-estate background and she'd used all the traditional tools of the trade to research her market and identify the most promising avenues to reach them. "I had targeted my audience as being sixty-plus years of age, semiretired or retired with expendable income of a certain dollar amount. I also expected that they would find me through print advertising—which was pretty reasonable, because when I first started people weren't really using the Internet. But just a year later, a guy who opened a bed-and-breakfast fifteen miles away called and said, 'So where are you advertising online?' And I answered, 'Oh, I'm not, because those aren't my clients: retired people don't use the Internet.' And he answered, 'You're kidding me! I went on the Internet three months ago with a website and increased my business by 200 percent in the first week!' That got my attention! It took me another six months before I set up a website for the College Inn, but, once I did, my business increased 100 percent a month from that point on."

The primary market that Becky envisioned when she launched—retirees—was way off base. Instead, her core market turned out to be at her doorstep: Internet-savvy college students coming to see Otterbein College (the campus on which Becky's inn is located) and parents who visit during the year. Today, as baby boomers retire and begin traveling more, they, too, are now knocking on her door. The Web has been huge for Becky's business. She has people booking a year in advance and it's allowed her to reach customers overseas—a market segment she never dreamed she'd be attracting.

Making a shift so that Becky's market could find her took both flexibility and a huge dose of courage. "I resigned myself to change," she recalls. "I resigned myself to the fact that I didn't have all the answers, that sometimes things were going to be different than what I wanted them to be, that change had to occur, and that it had to be OK. I had this special plan about what I wanted the B&B to be—how I wanted to interact with people and the price I wanted to charge. And right away, in the first year, it wasn't happening. It took on a life of its own and, had I not been willing to change who I thought my guests were going to be and to work with and embrace the change, I would not have survived."

Emerging Customer Expectations

When Patricia Scribner started Patricia's Yarns, she and her husband went through a major belt-tightening phase. As we saw in chapter 3, they adopted a "brains for bucks" mentality early on and kept their costs lower than industry norms—all of which contributed to a strong, successful launch. But they soon found that they had projected their cost-cutting attitude onto their customers. "We had to learn about our clientele," Patricia notes. "We had no idea that our clients would spend what they spend. That was something we were wrong on. We were looking at our clients as though they were us—but they're not! You have to put yourself in a different mind-set."

Patricia and Adam made a start-up mistake that's not all that unusual: they assumed that because they and their customers shared key demographics, they also had identical purchasing habits. Instead, they learned that the customers visiting their Hoboken store weren't nearly as price sensitive as they expected them to be. They often shopped in New York City, were used to Manhattan prices, and were more than willing to pay premium prices at a local store. As Patricia's knowledge of her customers grew, she also became more attuned to their needs. She put her newfound expertise into play in her inventory planning, the accessory items she stocked, and the classes she offered. Knowing what her customers want has been critical in attracting a loyal clientele for Patricia's Yarns.

Matching Products to Market Demand

When Ronnie Fliss first began Fat Murray's Doggy Treats, she had no idea how seasonal the business she was entering would prove to be. In her first year, when she hit several slow periods, she didn't know why the slowdowns were happening, and she often felt down during a lull. But she continued to stick with it and learn more about the business she'd entered: by talking constantly to store owners, she began to get a better handle on pet owners' buying patterns.

In response to frontline market feedback, she turned her standard eight-inch "bone" made of sugar-free applesauce and oatmeal into a gift item by writing "Happy Birthday" on it. Then her baker came up with the creative idea of inserting little candleholders in the bones—and sales surged. Since many customers view their dogs as family members, Ronnie realized, the festive birthday bones had great market appeal.

As Ronnie continued to listen to her market, she gained a better sense of its rhythm and seasonal nature—and responded by developing products geared toward the most popular retail holidays: Christmas, Halloween, and Valentine's Day. Today, she has a growing line of gift items targeted to each of the prime dog owner buying occasions. To pick up the slack in the summer, Ronnie markets heavily to beach and resort areas from New Jersey through New England. To extend her market reach still further, she has also begun to sell her products over the Internet.

By now, you probably have an idea of some of the ways a business can be reshaped by market demand. So what about your start-up? Did you think you were going to be doing one thing and find that you're actually doing something different? Have you found that one market isn't responding while another seems very promising? Have you broadened your vision of your business in order to give yourself more options for survival or expansion? Are there markets within markets that seem to be a great match for your products or services? Have you pinpointed any market trends that your company can respond to by adjusting its direction rather than totally changing course?

Asking these kinds of questions can be immensely fruitful as your venture evolves and you learn more about your industry and its potential customers. At its simplest, the redefining process we've described may lead you to adjust ideas about your true core market, refocus your product or promotional strategy, or rethink your views on exactly what business you're really in. The bottom line? Finding the flexibility and objectivity to let your business gravitate toward its natural markets or target audiences is key to growth during this stage.

RELY ON MENTORS FOR FAST-TRACK ADVICE

Mentors can be lifesavers, stress relievers, and business boosters. They can help you find shortcuts and avoid costly detours on the road to success. Find and cherish them! Let them help you fast-forward up the learning curve and bypass costly mistakes. Having a professor as a mentor has given Ronnie Fliss a boost when she's hit rough patches. Liz Lange has turned to a variety of mentors as her business has grown—and she now enjoys encouraging other women who dream of starting their own ventures. Brenda Newberry found that joining a small group of business owners who mentored each other was a real asset during her launch.

For some start-ups, mentors not only serve as business advisers but offer emotional support as well. That's certainly true of the mentoring relationships that Sharon Joseph and her aunt and cofounder, Gail Richards, have developed in their launch of Harlem Lanes. Along the way, they've made history as the country's first African American women to own a bowling alley. Helping their community is vital to the business model that Sharon and Gail developed. Today, their thriving venture, located in a former vaudeville palace, provides jobs for forty-five to fifty people—many of them local residents. But getting those bowling balls rolling hasn't been easy!

During her start-up, Sharon has repeatedly turned to mentors for help. Her informal team of advisers and "cheerleaders," as she calls them, is rooted in the strong relationships that she forged while working for two years at Booz Allen Hamilton, the global consulting firm—and as an MBA student at Columbia Business School. Even though she decided to forgo a corporate career in favor of entrepreneurship, Sharon has been able to leverage not just her on-the-job experience but also her job and school contacts creatively and consistently.

After intense research using analytical skills Sharon had honed at Booz Allen Hamilton as a consultant, she and her aunt determined that a bowling alley would be a much-needed community asset for Harlem. When she shared her vision with Booz Allen Hamilton senior partners Reggie van Lee and Gerry Adolph, her former colleagues not only encouraged her dream but helped make it a reality by offering advice and contacts. So did Sara Moose, the administrative manager of the consulting firm's New York Women's Network.

Reggie went a step further and recommended Sharon for the Urban Enterprise Institute (UEI), a local technical assistance group for start-ups. Ultimately, the UEI mobilized a team of Booz Allen experts to help Harlem Lanes get off the ground. "It was like having the firm do a consulting project for us, only it was pro bono," Sharon notes. She also turned to a professor at Columbia and to other business-school members, who advised her on financing and business structure.

"It took me three to four years to get the project launched," says Sharon, "so it was really helpful having people encourage me to stick with it and not give up—and when certain doors were closed, to help me open new ones. When you're a small business, there are so many different skill sets that you don't necessarily have, so finding mentors is really important. First, for emotional support—it's good to have outside cheerleaders urging you on—and second, as a sounding board for strategy and operations-related questions."

For Sharon, mentoring isn't just about asking for help, it's "really more about building long-term relationships. Once they help you, people want to know how the project is going; having some kind of mechanism for staying in touch is a way of saying thank you. It also makes it a lot easier if something really big occurs and you need their help. You want people to have a vested interest—and often that happens because of the mentoring relationship. It's also important to find ways to give back—to be a giver as well as a receiver. I try to ask my mentors how they're doing and if there's anything I can do to be helpful to them."

FORGE CREATIVE ALLIANCES

Along with mentoring relationships, there are other creative ways to forge alliances that will help you move your business to the next level. During this stage, you'll benefit tremendously from building a more sophisticated support team. Often this means seeking out talented professionals in a range of industries who can provide reality checks on a regular basis.

"It's very rare that an entrepreneur has all of the knowledge and capability needed to run a business successfully," observes Nan Langowitz, director and cofounder of the Center for Women's Leadership and an associate professor at Babson College. "So one of the keys is figuring out the pieces you really know well; maybe it's the vertical niche that you're positioning your business in, maybe it's customer relationships. Then you need to figure out what you *don't know* and how to fill those gaps. Some entrepreneurs are hungry for knowledge and learn how to do all these other things. Others bring in a partner or find trusted advisers they can work with—and they'll probably make some mistakes along the way, but that's OK. Mapping out what you know and what other pieces have to happen to create the value chain to get to your customer and get to cash flow is really critical."

You can set up a "kitchen cabinet," for example—an informal group of professionals whose judgment you trust and who are willing to meet with you from time to time. You might ask your accountant and attorney to join—or even a friendly banker. You can use this forum to fine-tune your business plan, and you can mine it as a source of ideas about marketing, new business, and financing. One business owner organized a loose group of people in different fields who enjoy each other's company—and she taps their expertise by inviting them to dinner for creative brainstorming sessions, which she structures around an agenda that she sends out in advance.

Finding a partner who's not a partner—who'll team up with you temporarily to fill a need—is another approach you can use. Joining forces with other small-business owners—and bartering among yourselves to fill skill gaps—can be a real budget and stress reliever.

Once your business achieves critical mass, you may want to set up a formal advisory board to monitor your company's progress and strategy. This more structured approach is one that Brenda Newberry adopted after she'd been in business for several years. The benefits have been so great that Brenda believes that this type of support system can work well even earlier in the start-up cycle.

PUSH YOUR PROMOTION TO THE NEXT LEVEL

Keep your marketing program proactive—and consistent! The real key to success is slow and steady progress: it's likely that many of the things you try during this stage will fail. But if you keep experimenting, making mistakes, and then adjusting, you'll eventually hit on an approach that really works. For most small businesses moving into their second year, the most valuable tools tend to be word of mouth, Internet promotion, and publicity exposure, rather than paid advertising. In the early days of Stroller Strides, Lisa Druxman did her own marketing and PR. "The thing that grew our company more than anything and got us the most attention was media publicity. And we got that because we didn't have funds to advertise—back then, $400 for an ad seemed like a million to us! We realized we needed to spread the word, so I would find as many ways as I could to create stories—whether it was doing special events that were tied to a charity or doing something for the community. Then I would approach every single newspaper and radio and TV station. I wouldn't just send a press release, but I would call the producer and say, 'I've got a great story for you. I think it's something you're really going to want to cover.' And we got *amazing* coverage.

"I was very aggressive and proactive. I would contact the producers at every single local news station and give them five story ideas. I was surprised to see they were *looking* for story ideas from the outside. And I'm incredibly accommodating and flexible; a reporter can call me at six in the morning if someone drops out of her show and she knows I will be there in half an hour.

"When people ask me for advice, I always tell them that the press isn't going to write a story on your business, they're going to write a story on something that's newsworthy. So you have to find a way to make your business newsworthy and visually exciting. Now that we can afford to buy ads, we realize that advertising is not a way to get customers—not in our business. It really is TV and magazine exposure more than anything that gets us credibility."

Like Lisa, if you make a strong commitment to expand your repertoire of professional skills to include marketing, you'll find that, as with everything else, practice makes perfect. You may also find that you come to really enjoy this aspect of business building because of the opportunity it gives you to share your vision and stay close to your customers.

KEEP EVOLVING YOUR BUSINESS MODEL

You can have the best business plan in the world, but at some point it's going to change. The business environment or market changes, the technology changes, or there's a hurricane. The key is to remain flexible and responsive, so that when there's a shift in the wind, you can sail with it. Your decisions now will be more demanding and far reaching. Your business may have grown bigger and faster than you expected, for example, and you'll need to manage that growth effectively. Many small businesses actually fail due to early success: their operating structures can't keep up with the demand they've created. You can also find yourself facing overhead "creep," where your basic expenses can begin to spiral out of control (see chapter 9, page 184).

Another major roadblock is one you've seen before: often, it's when you start growing your business during this stage that everything seems to fall apart yet again. Brenda Newberry has experienced this firsthand as chairman and CEO of the Newberry Group, an information technology and systems consulting company. A seasoned entrepreneur who's built a multimillion-dollar high-tech business, she knows this cycle. "That's the moment you find yourself asking, 'What business am I really in?' If you push past that, it comes together," she says. "When things don't work out as planned, you have to either change or stop. It's an indication that you need to reevaluate and make some modifications. This is often driven by the market, customers, or technical advances.

"These junctures almost always coincide with the growth surges of a business—at two years, five, eight to ten, and then again at fifteen years. If you survive the first two years, you know it's probably real. By the fifth year, you have to decide how you're going to grow. What are you about? What are your core competencies based on your industry? Now you're really real. Then you're looking at how to grow the business in eight to ten years, and you have to decide how to accomplish it—acquire, get acquired, financing, lines of credit. We were about $19 million in 2006. To get to $50 million will take some real ingenuity."

Crystal Johnson sees these moments of intense change as challenging, but positive. "These are growth situations—and they happen in cycles. As you hit different levels, you always experience the bottom falling out. What's happening is that you're being propelled to think of ways to move in the next direction. The bigger you get, the more people you're involved with, the more exposure you receive, the more this happens. Expect problems, but don't fold and retreat—see them as growth opportunities."

Crystal is constantly pushing the boundaries of her interior design business, Sienna at Home, and looks at large companies for inspiration. While she doesn't have their deep pockets, she believes that "if you strategize and plan and adopt the same thought process, you will eventually be on that level. This is my leap of faith. Sienna has three different businesses: design consulting, retail, and the Internet. Instead of enlarging our physical footprint, I want to have a national presence: I want to increase our revenues without increasing our overhead. My next step is to take our Web base to another level—and I want a catalog."

Crystal's ultimate goal is to expand her clientele and manage her growth through the Internet. Instead of opening more stores, as some people would do, she is giving Sienna a virtual national presence. This will allow her to achieve more balance—by building her business in a way that allows her to remain close to home and focus more attention on her family.

Another way to push your business model to a new level is to find business owners who are far more successful than you are and gain exposure to their ideas and techniques. "Mastermind with people at the level you want to be at," advises Ali Brown. "When you get a powerful group of minds together, the ideas that come out of conversations are just phenomenal." So find a group you can meet with on a regular basis—and keep raising the bar and getting advice from each other and supporting each other. You can do this on the phone or you can join a structured mastermind group.

MAKE YOUR DOWNTIME WORK FOR YOU

Keeping productivity high will be a priority during this stage. This can be challenging if the service you offer is largely client driven or if your business is seasonal. You can find yourself in the classic feast-or-famine situation where you juggle several assignments for intense periods of time and then experience droughts when business seems to dry up. As we saw earlier, a big facet of letting the market find you is accepting and figuring out how to work with—and not against—the natural rhythm of your business.

How can you use slow periods to greatest advantage? One way is to view such periods not as downtime but as creative time in which to explore new ideas, fully integrate the gains you've made, and reenergize yourself for the next wave of activity. You can use these periods to reassess and fine-tune your business strategy. You can seek out new information that may spark a new idea or direction. Investigating new marketing options is another great way to stay focused on growth: you can gather new market data or map out a way to repackage your services and create a new product line.

In-between periods also offer a perfect opportunity to solicit feedback on your performance. You can follow up every major assignment or project you work on with an evaluation form asking your clients to identify both the benefits received from your work and any bottlenecks they encountered. These can serve as the basis for recommendations when you're in new-business development mode.

Other ways to make your downtime more rewarding can include taking a business-related workshop to improve specific skills or targeted networking. Building your credentials is another great investment. Some entrepreneurs use time between projects to write articles about hot issues in their fields, for example, and submit them to industry publications. To make these quiet periods profitable, plan your creative downtime as carefully as you do your work projects. If you don't, then precious hours and even days can slip away without any real progress being made. You can also find yourself unprepared when your workload suddenly spikes.

MAKE RENEWAL A PRIORITY

When you're in business, finding time for yourself is almost impossible; your private time is the first thing to go. This can easily put you in a personal deficit situation. Regaining your emotional balance is something you can and must do every day, wherever you are. This doesn't mean you have to go off to a mountaintop somewhere. It simply means finding time for yourself in an environment that is soothing and sustaining for you: it can be a room in your house or a corner in your office. How do you find time to reenergize yourself, emotionally and creatively? You *make* the time.

"When we're stressed out, we're just reacting—and that's not a good way to run a business," observes Ray Miller, the founder of Stress Relief Solutions. "Trying to do everything, instead of focusing on your strengths, creates frustration and stress and actually causes a lot of people to quit. You can get more done in one hour of focused time doing something that you're really good at than in five hours of unfocused time. And when you're away from your business, really be away or it will consume your whole life—and ruin your relationships."

Like new-business development or marketing, a renewal strategy has to be built into your start-up game plan, advises Ray. One key is to give yourself the private time you need to relax, get in touch with your intuition, and reward yourself in ways that have nothing to do with work. Lack of balance is destructive. To focus on business to the complete exclusion of other interests is to become narrow in both mind and spirit. Read books and magazines that carry you far afield from your daily routines and demands. Socialize with your friends. Go to the movies. Don't feel guilty because you spend a night or two watching TV. If you have an absolutely compelling desire to do something other than work, it may be nature's way of telling you to relax. (For stress-relieving tips, see "Relax and Recharge!" page 174.)

Exercising is one tool that the women we interviewed mentioned as a great antidote to stress and a way to build stamina. Meditation is another tool that many women use to free themselves from daily tension and connect with their inner resources. Listening to tapes or music are two other popular relaxation techniques. Humor is another great source of renewal and stress relief. Think of a sitcom that your day reminds you of, or watch funny, uplifting movies that remind you of how rewarding life can be. Have lunch once in a while with a friend who can really tickle your funny bone. Do whatever it takes to stay on the sunny side of the street—especially when you hit a tough patch.

And, for many of the women we spoke with, giving back to their communities by volunteering or by supporting other aspiring entrepreneurs is a very rewarding way to recharge, both emotionally and spiritually. Whatever path you take, giving yourself the gifts of time, love, and laughter is one of the smartest, most productive business decisions you can make.

NURTURE YOUR PRIVATE LIFE

During this stage, when you are faced with bigger decisions and more committed than ever, it's tempting to keep your personal life on the back burner, where it may have been for quite a while. Don't give into this feeling! In fact, at this stage, you should be doing the opposite—and reawakening and reaffirming your personal relationships. Your family and friends are vital to your well-being. There's no need to sacrifice your personal life to your business. Far from it! A full personal life will enrich and enliven your venture; the lack of one will diminish it. So recommit yourself to the idea of setting boundaries. Otherwise you'll find yourself facing an endless horizon of work—and you will quickly burn out.

As Becky Rohrer says, "Women need to create balance for themselves. You have to juggle so much. You have all those balls in the air and you can't let any of them drop because they're all crucially important. But at some point, you have to put your hands down at your sides, let the balls fall down, and go, 'Wait a minute, these aren't weighted the right way. I need to really look at what's happening to me and how I can find some balance so I can be a better juggler.'"

Yes, you want your business to grow and prosper: it's an important part of who you are and who you hope to become. But achieving business success and personal fulfillment shouldn't be a win-lose proposition. Make the issue of balance a priority and you'll find a way to achieve it, at least most of the time. Let yourself be pushed too far and too fast from those you love, and all the business success in the world won't fill your empty nights. Remember, you're not just building a business, you're also creating a life strategy—one that satisfies both your need for fulfilling work *and* your need to feel happy and whole.

relax and recharge!

Stress and burnout can sap your energy and enthusiasm. Here's some expert advice on keeping yourself relaxed and at peak creativity.

John McCarthy, peak performance coach and stress management expert, suggests the following:

- Avoid tunnel vision. Spending every minute of every day on your business can drain your passion for it. So fill up your tank and nourish yourself by doing activities in the creative, affective realm.

- Take a yoga class. Yoga is relaxing and strengthening. It helps center you, slows the world down, and stretches your body—and your mind.

- Mix it up. When exercising, go for cross training. Use different muscles, interact with different people, and have varied fitness goals.

- Give yourself gifts at regular intervals. Build rewards into your work schedule as mini-motivators. Treat yourself to a new book, a jazz CD, a Broadway play—whatever makes you feel enriched and special.

- Get involved in group activities. Helping out in a youth group or in your church replenishes your spirit and exposes you to different people and situations.

- If you can see it, you can be it! Visualize yourself running your company happily and successfully in the office of your dreams!

Ray Miller, stress relief and self-improvement expert, suggests these activities:

- Do deep breathing. Take a few moments several times a day to breathe from your diaphragm. Inhaling more air more slowly is very energizing.

- Take regular computer breaks. Just five minutes a few times a day can be helpful. Get up, move around, or take a quick walk outside.

- Give yourself an aromatherapy boost. You can have a diffuser in your office and fill it with lavender oil to relax or peppermint to invigorate yourself.

- Schedule regular exercise sessions. Exercise and a healthy diet are incredibly important for building stamina and relieving stress. Pencil exercise into your work plan.

- Keep your hobbies going. Even though you're working intensely, don't neglect pursuits that give you pleasure like playing music or gardening.

- Watch your self-talk. We can talk ourselves into or out of anything! Don't let that tape in your head keep running—it's exhausting! Get instant perspective by consistently connecting with other business owners.

- Do guided meditations. When you're relaxed, ideas start flowing. Take ten to fifteen minutes each morning and night to close your eyes and go to your favorite beach or mountain. It's a great tension reliever!

Quick Tips ⇨

Quick Tips

Meet and greet your markets!
Don't push your business—let the market pull you in the right direction. Find your business rhythm, and then put on your dancing shoes!

Be a giver as well as a taker.
Mentors are supporters and stress relievers. Let them boost you up the learning curve. Cherish them as advisers and cheerleaders.

Mind your marketing.
Push the envelope! Make mistakes, adjust, and adopt promising tools. Be aggressive and proactive. Get the word out!

Bust your business model!
Don't cling to an old model—change it! The bigger you get, the more often the bottom falls out! See problems as invitations for growth.

Downtime equals creative time.
Use business lulls as springboards for growth, and investigate new areas. Energize, investigate, integrate!

Nurture your personal life.
Make renewal part of your start-up strategy. Refill your emotional well every day. Reward yourself and rejoice in your progress!

☑ This to-do list will help you plan suggested tasks during Stage 4.

STAGE 4 ACTION STEPS

☐ Help my market find me:

_____ Identify new market niches.

_____ Broaden my business vision.

_____ Pinpoint promising trends.

_____ Refocus my promotional strategy.

☐ Use mentors for fast-track support.

☐ Forge creative alliances in the following ways:

_____ A "kitchen cabinet" to advise me.

_____ Temporary "partnerships" to fill skill gaps.

_____ Formal advisory board to oversee strategy.

_____ "Mastermind" group to push me to the next level.

☐ Continue to make promotion a priority.

☐ Use my downtime productively:

_____ Investigate new marketing options.

_____ Solicit feedback from clients.

_____ Take a skill-building workshop.

_____ Write credibility-building articles.

☐ Create a renewal strategy to prevent burnout.

Chapter 9

Avoid the Ten Biggest Pitfalls

When you see an opportunity running in front of you, you'd better take action!

—MARLENE WALDOCK

Throughout this book, the women we've interviewed have generously given you their best advice on how to succeed. Here they're going to tell you how *not to fail*.

When we asked entrepreneurs about the pitfalls they encountered as they built their businesses, they were eager to talk about the mistakes they had made along the way—and the ones they avoided. They all recognize how easy it is to fall into these traps and how depleting it can be—financially and emotionally—to have to climb your way out. Bypassing *any one* of these pitfalls will increase your chances of success exponentially.

Some of the advice here is from women just starting out and some comes from women who've been running their businesses for more than five years or even a decade. Even if they're not in the same field as you are, they are intimately familiar with the challenges of the start-up cycle, the make-or-break decisions, the growing pains, and how wonderful it feels when that first big, fat contract finally comes through. (*Yes!*)

These time-tested entrepreneurs know where you're heading, so let them guide you around the potholes and obstacles in your way. Think of this chapter as the road map to where you *don't* want to go. Especially in the early days of your launch, steering clear of these pitfalls can mean the difference between success and failure.

PITFALL #1:
Romanticizing Being Your Own Boss

As you plan your big move, it's natural to project forward and imagine the best-case scenario of striking out on your own. Sometimes it's that very vision that provides the fuel, the impetus, you need to take the leap. One big—no, huge!—daydream many entrepreneurs have, especially if they work in large companies, is about how wonderful it will be to be their own boss. Now you're finally out from under that tough taskmaster who's been squeezing your budgets and riding your back for the past several years. Freedom at last! Well, not exactly.

"When I first started, people would ask, 'Well, how does it feel to be your own boss?'" recalls Brenda Newberry. "And, to this day, that's not the case. Actually, you have *more* bosses because you have your customers, your employees, your attorney, your accountant, your bank—many, many people who are counting on you to do the right thing and who hold you accountable. So if you look at all this as your responsibility, you really do have more than one boss.

"I think women in particular romanticize being an entrepreneur. Yes, you do have more flexibility, but that flexibility comes with some trade-offs and choices," adds Brenda. "I can't expect my team to be totally dedicated to my business if I come in at ten and leave at two. Would I like to do that? Absolutely, but it's not going to happen! It's like kids—people watch what you do, not what you say. So romanticizing is a risk."

Having too rosy a picture of being your own boss can set you up for disappointment and failure. The benefits are many and enormously appealing, but, like all good things in life, there is a price tag attached to them. In particular, many women tend to have unrealistic views about the family-like work environment that they hope to create.

Small-business owners who were unhappy in their previous work situations often vow to make life easier for their own employees. This is a worthwhile goal, but it's one that's almost impossible to realize. Getting too caught up in your employees' lives and personal problems takes valuable energy away from your business. Be careful not to become a mother hen or a confessor—that's not your role!

It's also important to be realistic about the benefits you can offer. Put together the best package you can, because you want to attract good people. But be careful not to jeopardize the financial health of your new enterprise for the sake of putting someone on salary and not commission, for example, if a commission makes more financial sense for you. Offering people nonmonetary perks like flexible work schedules, a dinner or two, or even theater tickets to say thanks for a job well done goes a long way toward creating a pleasant work environment.

PITFALL #2:
Not Getting the Right Help Early

You've probably heard the expression "It takes a village to raise a child." It also takes a village to run a business. To get your venture off the ground and sustain it through thick and thin, you need people you can rely on, whether you have a simple question or a looming crisis.

"Who's on your team is critical," says Nan Langowitz of Babson College, "whether they're your employees or part of your virtual team of accountants, bankers, lawyers, and vendors. You really have to think about this carefully and get it right. People get burned a lot from having bad teammates. And, if there's proprietary knowledge involved, you absolutely need a lawyer. If you've invented something new, you need to get that protected in some way."

Many of the women business owners we spoke with agreed that finding a good attorney should be one of your first moves. "There have been times when we tried to skimp, when we thought that we just couldn't afford it," says Lisa Druxman, who started Stroller Strides.

"Don't skimp when it comes time for legal advice because it can bite you later. And it's better to pay for the *right* advice. We learned that lesson when we've had to redo things because they weren't done right the first time."

Becky Rohrer, who runs the College Inn, learned the value of getting accurate advice the hard way. "I think the biggest pitfall is getting erroneous or incomplete information," she says. "For years I lived in fear because someone told me that the fire department had to inspect my place because I had people sleeping here. I put so much worry into it. You multiply that by five, six, or eight erroneous things people tell you and you burden yourself with all these worries that you don't need to have. You need to have a good tax adviser, a good financial planner, a group of people you have confidence in, too. In my case, I found people who were willing to barter a few nights' stay in exchange for their services."

As you inventory the people who can offer you seasoned advice and support, don't forget vendors. They can be invaluable in helping you get your "sea legs" either in a new industry or even in the same field where you were a jobholder. Maintaining good relationships with vendors can help you launch successfully; if they believe your business has promise, some vendors will even work to ensure the timely delivery of materials you may not have the cash to pay for upfront. Vendors can also be a great source of client referrals. And if a project is appealing, they even may be willing to help underwrite it financially in order to tap a new market or generate a new revenue stream. So be sure to see the vendors you work with as a valued part of your expert start-up team.

PITFALL #3:
Not Understanding How to Network

At different stages in your venture's business cycle, it's almost inevitable that you're going to feel isolated and alone, especially if you've just left the corporate world. These are the moments when you'll think back with longing about that support structure—read: safety net!—

you left behind. Now, you've got to create that structure for yourself, so you can regain a sense of connection and build an emotional support system that will get you through the tough days. You need someone you can call and say, 'Oh my God, I don't know why I'm doing this!'" Targeted, effective networking can help fill in many of those gaps.

When Marlene Waldock, founder of First Impression Communications, first moved from Atlanta to New Jersey in the mid-1990s, she didn't know anyone. The Internet wasn't a factor back then, so it wasn't easy to find a women's group to get involved with. Someone eventually connected her to the New Jersey Association of Women Business Owners and the rest is, as they say, history. "I joined NJAWBO early that year and by September I was on the board. I stayed in a leadership position for ten years, part of the time as president. It was a means of getting connected."

A skilled relationship builder, Marlene believes that many people don't understand that networking is a *mutually beneficial* tool. "A network is how things connect. Whether it's an electrical network or a computer network, you're connecting one thing to another. The idea is to figure out how to connect yourself and others beneficially. It isn't about just getting other people's business. *That isn't networking. That's selling.* Networking is saying, 'What do I want to have happen here? What is my ultimate goal? And who, in the general sense, would be able to help me?' Then you start going to meetings with a purpose in mind.

"For example, financial planners and estate attorneys have a natural connection to each other. They can work off each other. Someone who's doing estate planning really needs to have a financial planner involved, and a financial planner will often help you find an attorney to do estate planning for you. So it's not about, Let me sell something to you. It's about, How can we work in tandem to help each other? The best networker gives first before she ever tries to receive anything. It's the theory of reciprocity—if you give something to someone, then she or he will be more inclined to want to give you something back."

Start building your circle of influence and your network, as Marlene Waldock advises. When you meet someone, decide how you can work together for mutually beneficial results—and then figure out how you can connect your networking partner to someone else in your circle, so that eventually everyone is connected to someone else—and, together, you're building a chain of support and contacts. "You want people who are of like minds and will work well with each other," notes Marlene. "You can call upon them when you need something and they can call upon you. And you can have several different circles of influence."

PITFALL #4:
Running Yourself Ragged

Even in the best of circumstances, it's tough to pace yourself, especially when you've got a to-do list that's a mile long. So you keep barreling through, trying to get everything done. Then you wake up the next day and start all over again. It's exhausting. You can quickly find yourself running on empty.

Sarah Levy began Sarah's Pastries & Candies as a wholesale business. For her, the big push came when she expanded into retail. "There was a lot of stress at the launch of the store," she recalls. "I was working literally sixteen to eighteen hours a day, seven days a week. We were open from 8 in the morning to 9 every evening during the week, then 8 in the morning to 11 at night on Friday and Saturday. My stomach was in knots. I must have lost ten pounds! I was eating tons, but I was literally on my feet for sixteen to eighteen hours, seven days a week. If my friends wanted to see me, they had to come to the store. I didn't go out to dinner or do anything but work and sleep. Now I have much more manageable hours."

Once Sarah found her business's rhythm, she decided to close the shop for one day a week. "It wasn't very popular with my dad, who was my investor. But I needed one day to just relax. It makes the biggest difference. It's important to step back and see the bigger picture sometimes."

When Crystal Johnson started Sienna at Home, she had no formal (or informal!) training as an interior decorator. Her on-the-job training resulted in a whirlwind of activity that didn't stop for breakfast. "Once I committed to my business full-time, I would literally go to bed when the sun came up. I'd be on my computer from eight or nine at night until morning, researching and networking because I had to go through a learning phase to set up my business. I've learned to delegate. I've had to set boundaries."

If you drive yourself to exhaustion for months at a time, you're going to crash and burn, warns Lisa Druxman of Stroller Strides. "If you're really going to be the leader of a company, you have to be well enough to lead. And you can only do that if you take care of yourself. So you have to exercise, eat well—this is the fitness professional in me speaking!"

PITFALL #5:
Spending Money for the Wrong Reasons

Many people try to re-create the safe and comforting office environment they enjoyed in corporate life, only on a smaller, more intimate, and more manageable scale. Of all the traps that you can fall into, being overly self-conscious and sensitive about your business image is probably the biggest and the most serious. It can lead you to overspend, overpromise, and oversell yourself.

Doing this can be extremely costly not only in dollars and overhead but in the anxiety and stress it creates. It can impel you to move your workplace out of your home and into rented office space before you can really afford to, to buy costly equipment so that you can present a first-class image to the marketplace, and to hire other people to do the draggy, time-consuming jobs you don't want to do so that you can focus on what you do best (translation: what you're most comfortable doing).

Ronnie Fliss managed to avoid this trap. Four years after starting Fat Murray's Doggy Treats, she is still baking dog treats in her home kitchen. When she gets really big orders, a baker across town lets her use his ovens, but she had hoped that by now she would have had her own factory. "I think one of the biggest pitfalls is starting out very grandiose and investing a lot of money without really having the experience behind it. I was very conservative. You get into trouble with all the expenses that come with running a very large business without having the foundation to support it."

Though she now runs a thriving IT consulting company with more than 140 employees, Brenda Newberry also still watches her costs, just as she did when she first launched. To hold down expenses, she, too, worked out of her home for the first few years. "My first employee, who's still with us, remembers meeting me at my remote office— Denny's! I would go to customers' offices to meet them, but I would meet job candidates at Denny's and that's still the case. The restaurant was always open and you didn't have to buy a whole meal. If it wasn't lunch- or dinnertime, you could buy just a soda or a cup of coffee.

"You have to learn to do whatever needs to get done," she says. "Sometimes I ask people who are considering entrepreneurship, 'If you walk up to a printer and you see a message that a drum needs changing, what do you do?' And if they say, 'I go find somebody else to fix it or go report it to someone,' I tell them, 'You may not be ready to be an entrepreneur.' An entrepreneur would go find what needs to be found, install it herself, and get the thing working again."

The ability to have a handle on every aspect of your business is essential, agrees Crystal Johnson. "That's the one thing that people don't understand. When you own a small business or any business, you have to understand the different facets because you may have to step in or need to delegate to people and tell them exactly how you want something done. In order to do that, you have to understand it yourself, which means you probably have to have been in the trenches at some point."

To keep costs manageable, Crystal had to learn to create lush, beautiful interiors on a budget. "To buy things, I wouldn't go to Neiman Marcus! One of my talents is the ability to make something *look* like a million dollars. To do this, I would go to regular retail stores and search out quality products that were reasonably priced."

The profits from her first design show helped pay for the costs of setting up her first retail store, including the build-out, furnishings, and $25,000 worth of inventory. To save money, she was the general contractor on the site, getting all the permits and inventory in place.

"I had two part-time employees, because at that point I was still doing design and retail. But I also worked in the store," Crystal notes.

"It goes back to capital. I don't think we would have made it if we had to pay for all the services and support that we needed. Anything you can do yourself, or the people around you can help you do, you want to get it done that way. The technical part alone—networking our stores, for example—would have been very expensive for us. Over the years I've saved a lot of money doing my own website and my own ads. You can get caught up in 'Oh, let's just hire this person to do this or that.'"

PITFALL #6:
Not Valuing Your Time Highly

There's a flip side to thinking you have to do everything yourself, however. That is, at some point you need to start putting a value on your time. If you analyze your day, you may find you're spending 80 percent of your time doing routine tasks. By training someone to take them over, you can focus 80 percent of your time on building client relationships and long-range planning.

"The smartest move I made within the first year was probably to hire an administrative assistant and other people," says Lisa Druxman. "I finally realized that I spent an incredible amount of time on bookkeeping issues and that's far from being my area of expertise. We're talking about a woman who barely balances her own personal checkbook! So I started to realize that, even though I don't pay myself much, there's value to my time and only so many hours in the day.

"So it's not that you're merely delegating things so that you can eat more bonbons. You're delegating so that you can fill your time with what you really excel at. The biggest aha! moment for me financially was to realize I'm going to make more money by hiring a bookkeeper and an assistant than what I'm spending to do it."

When Brenda Newberry started focusing exclusively on building her business, everything started falling into place. "In the first days, I was contracting myself out and I was spread awfully thin. In fact, our best year in the beginning was after I stopped doing outside work and decided to concentrate on the business. I started meeting people, joining organizations, completing paperwork for certifications, and then things started to click even more. But it wasn't until I said to myself, 'OK, this is real, I'm doing it' versus 'Well in case it doesn't work, I at least have this job.' When you're straddling, you reach a point where you have to stop doing that. And I think you need to determine that point early on."

PITFALL #7:
Not Pricing Properly

Women actually have a higher success rate at running businesses because they are very service oriented. At the same time, as many studies have shown, women tend to undervalue their time, talent, and expertise when it comes to pricing and negotiating their terms for performing a service or selling their products. Fall into this trap and you can find it hard to dig your way out.

"Our experience is that women tend to ask for less from everyone than they should," notes Monica Doss, the president of the Council for Entrepreneurial Development. "In general, male entrepreneurs are more direct: they'll ask for more money and for more from their employees. Women, oftentimes because of their training and backgrounds, are a bit more tentative. Some of the data that's been gathered by women's networks validates this. If you put two people in a room with the same business plan and ask them how much money they need, a woman will ask for much less."

Knowing how to price your product and service fairly and profitably is a survival skill that every small-business owner needs to acquire. And learning how to price based on value offered, not time expended, is an art that many people have not mastered. Yet this is especially critical if you're offering a labor-intensive service. Ali Brown, the Internet marketing specialist, recalls her own business breakthrough: "My life changed the day I stopped selling my time and began leveraging my knowledge."

Pricing a product accurately so you can operate profitably is also key. This is an ongoing issue for Ronnie Fliss of Fat Murray's. "When I was starting my business I talked to a man who is the largest importer of Italian wine in the U.S. The first thing he said to me was, 'If you're going to do this, you have to know down to the penny what it is costing you to make a cookie—a cookie! And he was absolutely right! You have to watch your ingredients, your packaging materials, all your labor costs, and figure all that in to know what profit you can make on a cookie. You don't want to do this and not make money! So I was constantly reevaluating. As dairy and cheese costs went up, I had to incorporate that into my prices.

"I can set a price point, but the market will drive it. If it's too expensive, it's going to sit, the retailers will be unhappy, and the product will expire. If my dog cookies get stale, retailers lose and then I lose their business. And the margins are very narrow. I have to be constantly aware of what's going to sell and what consumers will pay for it, so I can still make a profit on it—and stay in business."

The counterpart of underpricing is overservicing your clients. Clients will be both the joy and the bane of your existence. You will be tempted to do everything for them, to provide service well in excess of the fees they are paying. Yes, you need to provide the very best client service you can, but not to the detriment of your own marketing, networking, and planning. You always need to be concerned about what's next once a project is completed, and you may not be able to do that if you're devoting more time than necessary to your clients. The chance to work with clients you like is a wonderful gift, but realize that enthusiasm and friendship must sometimes take a backseat to business. Giving 110 percent is smart; giving 200 percent is self-defeating!

PITFALL # 8:
Spending Too Much on Advertising

Not only do you have to find creative ways to get the word out, but you also need to ensure that people are listening. Many entrepreneurs caution against spending too much of your budget on advertising. For

Sarah Levy's bakery, it was word of mouth that proved most effective. For Crystal Johnson, it was finding the right location for her store, which meant healthy walk-in traffic.

"Advertising is a vicious cycle," warns Sarah Levy. "Once you start advertising in one place, people will call you constantly about buying ads. I personally don't think advertising is worth the money at all. You really have to look at it carefully because it's very expensive and it can really put a damper on your budget."

Crystal Johnson couldn't agree more. In the years since she's launched her business, she's steadily built her marketing skills and learned how to negotiate the worlds of promotion and advertising. "Marketing talent? That was something I didn't think I possessed," says Crystal. "I never thought of myself as a salesperson, but, given the level of passion I feel, it's just natural for me. I actually had to learn the importance of PR and marketing and advertising and what they can mean to my business. It wasn't something I took in college or learned at my former company. But if you don't market your business, no one else will. And no one will do it as effectively as you can, even if you pay them very well."

In her first year, Crystal didn't do much advertising at all. "I didn't feel comfortable writing checks for print ads when I didn't understand how they would work," Crystal points out. "I'm glad I didn't. We spent time researching the best avenues for marketing and advertising for the following year. I remember people saying, 'We see you everywhere!' Our TV commercial was one of our best advertising vehicles and it wasn't one of the first things that people suggested to me."

While a TV ad proved to be a winner for her interior design business, Crystal went this route *only* after she'd carefully investigated the benefits and learned about the costs on her own, so she could be fully informed and on top of the process. "I think it's a money pit," Crystal says of advertising. "They're vultures—the radio stations, TV stations, magazines, newspapers. Everybody was telling me to take out an ad and saying, 'We can bring you this or that audience.' But it just wasn't making any sense to me. I was saying to myself, 'I don't read this [publication].' I was my target demographic, so I know what I would do and wouldn't do."

Even for expert marketers, doing promotional tasks on their own behalf can be a daunting prospect. This is one area where it often pays to get some expert advice. That advice can be expensive, however, so before you pay an outsider to do the work for you, take some classes at your local community college or an inexpensive seminar that focuses on marketing strategies for small businesses. Become familiar with the tools of the trade, so that when you do hire someone you'll know how to manage them effectively.

PITFALL #9: Not Trusting Your Gut

One thing you'll probably never be shy of is advice—solicited and unsolicited. Sometimes everybody around you has an opinion and you need to tune them all out and go with your gut. Still, it's easy to find yourself relinquishing your powers to people who seem to know more about your business than you do. All too often, when you rely too heavily on outsiders to make major business decisions for you, you'll find that the advice you receive is too broad to meet your specific needs. Not only is taking this approach expensive, but it also can give you a false sense of security.

Remember, no expert you hire is ever going to have the emotional or financial stake in your business that you and your family have. Outside advisers always operate from a distance—and their meters are always running. So don't disempower yourself. Yes, you may need some advice and experienced guidance, but, in the end, you are the single best judge of what your business has to offer and how it should be run.

Suzanne Lyons and her partner ran headlong into this issue when they decided to open a low-budget division of their company, Snowfall Films. "Just because we had done four movies with bigger budgets, we thought, 'Oh, this part is going to be pretty easy—if we've done that, we can do this.' We didn't realize how dramatically different the lower budget world was. There were aspects of it that we didn't know, so we brought in a company that we thought knew more than we did and listened to them. If we'd listened to our gut response, we wouldn't have had the problems we did. Anytime we've relinquished our power, we've had problems. Trust your gut and heart."

The key lesson that Suzanne learned is that *she was really the best expert* when it came to her business. And *so are you*. When you go out on your own, it's natural that you may feel some uncertainty and insecurity about what you're doing. You may even think that since you lack experience as an entrepreneur, you need help from all sorts of "experts" to launch yourself. You may be tempted to hire other people and you can easily forget that you are in the driver's seat.

"People look at life in different ways," points out Crystal Johnson. "You can tell someone, 'I'm having a tough time. I'm thinking of giving up,' and they'll say, 'Well, yeah, maybe you should give up,' because that's what they would do. You have to have confidence in yourself."

Sometimes staying true to your vision results in a big hit to your bottom line. That's what happened to Ronnie Fliss, who lost a very large client because she stuck to her guns. "In that last year he was 10 percent of my business and I'm still very sad about it," she says. "He wanted me to use sugar coating on the cookies and I just can't give that to dogs, so he went to another source. That was very anxiety provoking, because when this client was buying from me, I knew that a $3,000 to $4000 order was coming in every two months. It was a very nice source of income. But I had to stick to what I believe in. My product has no preservatives, no sugar, no dyes or coloring. I just can't give dogs garbage."

PITFALL # 10:
Not Thinking Enough about the Big Picture

It's easy to lose your way when your mind is mired in the details of what needs to get done right now. But it's important to step back periodically and look at the big picture to see whether you and your business are headed in the right direction. You need to create a road map to your future. "The day-to-day things that need to get done, that's the doingness. That will look after itself," says Suzanne Lyons. "But it's the bigger picture, the context of it all, that I think is important.

"The biggest piece of advice that I would offer would be to create a really long-range plan so that you're not just looking at what you're going to do two or three years from now, but you're also asking, Where do I want to be ten years from now? The farther out I look, the bigger I become in the future. That means that in the present, I can manage my fears, moods, emotions, and concerns because I'm focusing on my long-term commitment to succeeding."

Staying focused on the big picture can give you the fuel you need to take risks and step out of your comfort zone. Staying small and acting small won't. "I remember years ago," recalls Marlene Waldock of First Impression Communications, "reading an article in *Inc.* magazine on risk that said, 'If there is no anxiety, then the risk you are taking is not worthy of you because there is no risk at all.' Anytime you are going to step out of your comfort zone and do something different, you will have a certain level of 'Can *I* do that?' It happens to everyone who takes this step. It doesn't matter how successful they are or have been."

It's also important to have a clear sense of what you really want out of your business, and that means clearly defining your goals. What do you want to happen? What are your terms of success?

Becky Rohrer, for example, never planned on getting rich from her bed-and-breakfast. "I was very clear on what my goal was, which was to be able to stay home with my son and have a business that could help me decompress, and that was exactly what happened. I kept reminding myself of that when I hit tough spots. I'm asking, 'Why am I doing this? I'm beating my head against the wall. I need a new car, and that's not in my budget.' That's when my mother reminds me, 'You never said you were going to get rich; you wanted to be happy. You have been happier than anyone I've ever known doing this business. Look at all the wonderful people you've met, look at the great child you've raised because you've been able to stay home with him. A lot of people look at you and think you have it made!'"

Quick Tips

Avoid Pitfall #1: Romanticizing
Take off the rose-colored glasses. Flexibility is great, but it comes with choices.

Avoid Pitfall #2: Bad Help
Find advisers you can rely on—and don't skimp on legal advice.

Avoid Pitfall #3: Bad Networking
Don't confuse networking with selling. Create circles of influence.

Avoid Pitfall #4: Burnout
Don't put your needs last! Take care of yourself: recharge to renew.

Avoid Pitfall #5: Misspending
Give up the grandiose! Stay lean. Spend lean. Image is just that—image!

Avoid Pitfall #6: Misusing Time
Don't get trapped in trivial pursuits. Consider hiring an administrative assistant.

Avoid Pitfall #7: Underpricing
Price smart so you can stay profitable. Love your clients, but serve them wisely.

Avoid Pitfall #8: Costly Advertising
Promote your business yourself. Learn how, and you'll reap amazing benefits.

Avoid Pitfall #9: Lack of Self-Trust
You know the most about your business. Don't give away your power to "experts."

Avoid Pitfall #10: Thinking Small
Don't hitch your wagon to a fence! Think big, aim high, act successful!

Chapter 10

Welcome to Your New Life!

Believe in yourself, your vision of your business,
and what you want it to be.

—CRYSTAL JOHNSON

We've been on a long journey together, haven't we? It hasn't always been easy for you, we know. Sometimes, you've felt tempest-tossed, anxious, and fearful. But we hope you haven't felt alone—and that you've found wise counsel and warm comfort in these pages. As we look back on all the stories we've told, all the ideas we've shared, and all the pitfalls we've worked hard to help you avoid, this whole venture seems almost overwhelming to us. Birthing the elephant seems to describe perfectly what we've been through together!

We hope you'll welcome this wonderful new life that you're creating—or summoning up the courage to leap into—with open arms! How brightly your light shines as you boldly take charge of your gifts and your dreams! What an inspiration you promise to be to those around you who secretly hope to find the strength to follow in your footsteps! As you move forward, here are a few parting thoughts to speed you on your way.

- ***Don't let a lack of confidence get in the way of your ability:*** Change can be daunting, but the status quo can be worse. Remember that even positive changes are stressful and are made most successfully one small step at a time. Nurture your self-esteem. Acknowledge and build on the experience, talent, and resources that you bring to your venture. Bolster your self-confidence through research, networking, and family support. Don't let fear hold you back—harness it and let it energize you and push you to do more and be more.

- *Don't let your age keep you from taking the plunge:* You're never too old or too young to strike out on your own. Some of the women we interviewed were in their forties and fifties when they started their businesses. Wherever you are and whatever you've been doing, if you find the drive within you to embrace the entrepreneurial life growing stronger and stronger, then go for it! Don't let the opportunity slip away because you think that time has passed you by. As one woman told us, "I never wanted to look back and say, 'I could have, should have, would have.'"

- *Find a way to fund your business that meets your comfort level:* When it comes to money, start small and build slowly. This may mean delaying your launch for six months or a year—or teaming up with a seasoned business owner to learn the ropes. Whatever route you take, remember that your energy and creativity, not dollars, will drive your start-up's growth. As most seasoned entrepreneurs will tell you, money is the by-product of a successful business, not its engine.

- *Know what money means to you:* Whatever your attitude, come to grips with it early, because it will influence how persistently you pursue your new-business goals. Work hard to separate your feelings of self-worth from your net worth. Give yourself the gift of time, renew your personal relationships, and strengthen your family connections. All these steps can enrich your life and validate the choices you've made.

- *Cultivate your connections to the outside world—they're vital:* See everyone you meet as a potential client. Attend meetings, help out on a committee, or run for a board position. Take classes at the local university; teach if you're qualified. Work out at a gym that caters to businesspeople. Look for help outside your field: make it a point to reach out to people in other lines of work—and compare strategies and successes. Be coachable; let people know that you're ready to listen and learn. "Talk to people, talk to people, talk to people!" That's the best advice one entrepreneur said she had to offer.

- **Share your success stories:** Everyone likes to hear a success story. Being part of one is even more satisfying. So keep the people who've helped you up-to-date on what you're doing, and brief them on any big wins you've had. The more ownership they take in your success, the more involved they'll be in helping you keep it going and growing.

- **Give back as you grow:** Virtually every woman business owner we interviewed has reached out to give back to her community or to a nonprofit that she cares about. Whether it's helping teens or women looking for work, as Bobbi Brown does, donating furniture to Katrina victims, as Crystal Johnson has done, creating a special candy to raise funds for children, as Sarah Levy did, or mentoring other aspiring entrepreneurs, as Liz Lange and Brenda Newberry enjoy doing—giving back is one of the most rewarding aspects of business ownership.

- **Give what you need:** One entrepreneur, Sharon Joseph of Harlem Lanes, shared one of her success strategies: Whenever she feels she's lacking something in her business, she turns around and gives that same thing away to someone else. And somehow, whatever it is—an idea, marketing support, a helpful lead—seems to come back to her. And sometimes, it happens in amazing and wholly unexpected ways. Try it and see!

- **Stay lean:** Yes, the entrepreneurial life lets you control certain aspects of your work; you'll be able to draw the picture instead of fitting into someone else's vision. Remember, however, that you aren't the boss, your business is. Employees add a whole new level of responsibility and complexity to your venture. Before taking on a full- or even part-time employee, look into other alternatives, such as contracting or clustering or finding a virtual assistant. Stay as lean as you can for as long as you can—that's the advice many women entrepreneurs offer.

- *Stay focused:* Growth comes from adversity, from change, from mistakes. Don't be too hard on yourself when you take a wrong turn. Don't dwell on your failures. Devote your energy and concentration to what you're doing now, not to what went wrong yesterday or what's going to happen tomorrow. Try to be "in the moment" as much as you can.

- *Stay curious:* Things that divert your attention may provide the inspiration you need to broaden or even change the original mission of your business. As your venture takes on a life of its own, you'll discover new skills and interests. Don't brush these aside or consider them distractions (unless they're really getting in the way of fulfilling client commitments), because it's in these areas that growth can often be most rewarding.

- *Finally, have faith in yourself and your goals:* Launching a new business is a lot like setting out to sea. As you leave port, the crowds cheer, the big whistle blows, there's a great feeling of purpose and excitement. Then you settle down to the task of keeping the ship running and pointed in the right direction. For many entrepreneurs, this is the most dangerous time of all—when the first flush of enthusiasm wanes and reality sets in.

Staying the course—staying true to your goals and to yourself—is perhaps the greatest challenge you'll face in the transition to entrepreneurial life. Tenacity in pursuit of the outcomes you hold most dear is the mark of the true entrepreneur. Perspective is gained only through experience, but you'll never gain the wisdom that experience offers if you don't follow your dreams. And when those dreams are realized, be sure to share your success and strength with others following you on the road to entrepreneurial success. Then cast your eye toward the horizon once again and dream another big dream. Bon voyage!

* Resources *

The Abilities Fund: Offers direct loans, business plan development, and other start-up support to entrepreneurs with disabilities.
www.abilitiesfund.org

American Home Business Association: Offers essential and innovative services, products, and guidance to entrepreneurs.
www.homebusiness.com

Bizy Moms: This site is for self-driven, energetic, entrepreneurial moms who are launching franchises.
www.bizymoms.com

Business Network International (BNI): Offers members the opportunity to increase business through networking and formal relationships.
www.bni.com

BusinessNation: This site offers sample business letters and forms, local business resources, and small-business links.
www.businessnation.com

BUZGate: A global resource network for small businesses.
www.buzzgate.org

Center for Women's Business Research (CFWBR): The go-to source on the trends, achievements, and challenges of women business owners.
www.cfwbr.org

Center for Women's Leadership at Babson College: Promotes the advancement of female entrepreneurs through education and research.
www.babson.edu/cwl

Count Me In: The leading national not-for-profit provider of micro loans, mentoring support, and business education for women entrepreneurs.
www.countmein.org

Direct Selling Women's Association (DSWA): Meets the needs of independent direct sellers through training and professional direct-sales guidance.
www.mydswa.org

Entrepreneur.com: This hub site offers resources and newsletters on franchises, home-based business start-up success, and marketing.
www.entrepreneur.com

eWomenNetwork.com: A network of female business owners with access to each other's offerings, skills, knowledge, and resources.
www.eWomenNetwork.com

Forum for Women Entrepreneurs and Executives: Women accelerate success through networking, educational events, and peer-to-peer meetings.
www.fwe.org

Franchise Solutions for Women: Entrepreneurs receive weekly support, educational seminars, and solid referrals.
www.womensfranchises.com

Golden Seeds: A venture capital group that identifies and supports women's enterprises with high growth potential.
www.goldenseeds.com

The IndUS Entrepreneurs (TiE): A network dedicated to mentoring, networking, and educating budding entrepreneurs through workshops and meetings.
www.tie.org

International Homeworkers Alliance (IHA): Provides work-from-home job listings and telecommuting job opportunities.
www.homeworkers.org

iVillage: Provides access to information for "mompreneurs" and other small-business owners through its Work from Home site.
www.iVillage.com

Job Accommodation Network: A free consulting service providing customized self-employment assistance to people with disabilities.
www.jan.wvu.edu

JumpUp.com: A free website created by Intuit to provide resources and start-up support to entrepreneurs and small businesses.
www.jumpup.intuit.com

Ladies Who Launch: Through its events, e-newsletter, website and incubators, LWL helps women exchange products, services, and ideas.
www.ladieswholaunch.com

LeTip International: Members exchange valuable business tips and work to provide each other with professional business leads.
www.letip.com

Meetup: A site that offers small-business networking and support. *www.meetup.com*

Minority Business Entrepreneur: A magazine targeting issues of importance to minority and women business owners. *www.mbemag.com*

Mompreneurs Online: Offers networking, resource center, mentoring, and articles for at-home entrepreneurial moms. *www.mompreneursonline.com*

My Own Business: This site allows entrepreneurs to get a quick, easy start through its free "My Own Business" Internet business course. *www.myownbusiness.org*

National Association for Female Executives (NAFE): The largest U.S. women's professional/business owners' group, offering resources and services. *www.nafe.com*

National Association for the Self-Employed: Provides a broad range of benefits and support to help small businesses succeed. *www.nase.org*

National Association of Women Business Owners (NAWBO): The only membership group sharing resources across all industries. *www.nawbo.org*

National Business Association (NBA): Offers members support programs, cost- and time-saving products, services, and valuable resources. *www.nationalbusiness.org*

National Federation of Independent Business: NFIB gives members access to many business products and services at discounted costs. *www.nfib.com*

National Foundation for Women Business Owners: A leading source on trends, characteristics, and challenges of women business owners. *www.nfwbo.org*

National Multiple Sclerosis Society: Provides advocacy, information, and work-related support to people living with multiple sclerosis. *www.msandyou.org*

Online Women's Business Center: The Small Business Administration (SBA) site for training, loan programs, and free online courses for women. *www.onlinewbc.gov*

Powerful You!: National networking group with local chapters; offers programs and support to help women build their businesses.
www.powerfulyou.com

Service Corps of Retired Executives (SCORE): Premier source of free small-business advice on business plans, marketing, and increasing cash flow.
www.score.org

Small Business Benefits Association (SBBA): Offers small businesses tools and support to succeed in today's competitive business climate.
www.sbba.com

SME Toolkit United States: Offers a variety of assistance with financing, alliances, and Internet growth.
www.smetoolkit.org

Springboard Enterprises: Organization dedicated to accelerating access to venture capital for high-growth women's businesses.
www.springboardenterprises.org

U.S. Chamber of Commerce: The Chamber's Small Business Center offers tool kits for start-up support, employee screening, and other resources.
www.uschamber.com

U.S. Women's Labor Bureau: The Bureau sponsors public conferences, seminars, and workshops across the country for women entrepreneurs.
www.dol.gov/wb

U.S. Small Business Administration (SBA): Counsels, assists, and protects the interests of small businesses.
www.sba.gov

VocationVacations: Offers short-term immersion with expert mentors in a wide range of fields to allow people to test-drive new work options.
www.vocationvacations.com

Women-21.gov: Offers key resources, online programs, and networking opportunities for small businesses to reach their maximum potential.
www.women-21.gov

Women for Women International: Provides microlending support and start-up training to disadvantaged women globally.
www.womenforwomen.org

Women Presidents' Organization (WPO): Offers members newsletters, referrals, and an annual conference.
www.womenpresidentsorg.com

WomenandBiz.com: An e-zine focusing on women entrepreneurs, marketing, family businesses, and start-up resources
www.womenandbiz.com

Women's Leadership Exchange (WLE): Women who support the growth of women-led businesses in all sectors.
www.womensleadershipexchange.com

WomensBiz.US: A free online magazine for women business owners at every stage of development.
www.womensbiz.us

Young Entrepreneurs Network: Educates, guides, and supports aspiring young entrepreneurs
www.youngandsuccessful.com; www.ysn.com

* Notes *

✳ Notes ✳

✳ Index ✳

N

Networking, 73, 181–83, 195–96
Newberry, Brenda, x, 13–14, 59, 68,
    99–100, 117–18, 148, 165,
    167, 169, 179, 185, 186–87,
    196
Niche marketing, 128

O

Obsession, with an idea, 65
Opportunity
    creating, 34
    lack of, 67–68
Overspending, 48, 52–54, 60, 104,
    106, 184–86, 188–90

P

Panic, 143–44
Partnerships, 76–77
Passion
    importance of, 12–13, 18, 86–87
    transforming, into performance,
        122–24
Paycheck mentality, giving up, 47–49,
    60
Performance anxiety, 135–36
Physical challenges, facing, 26–28
Pitfalls, avoiding, 178–93
Powerful You!, 78
Pricing, 187–88
Problem solving, 152
Professionalism, 72–73, 129–30

Q

Quitting. *See* Fall-apart phase

R

Renewal, importance of, 172–73
Research, 75, 79
Resiliency
    importance of, 14–15, 151
    strengthening, 151–53, 155
Richards, Gail, 165
Riggs, Jennifer Lovitt, x, 51–52, 56,
    72, 76
Rituals of completion, 114
Roadblocks. *See* Fall-apart phase
Rohrer, Becky, x, 16, 17, 28–30, 34,
    42, 59, 64, 84, 147–48, 150,
    157, 162–63, 173, 181, 192
Romanticizing, dangers of, 179–80

S

Safety net, financial, 55
Schoenfeldt, Beth, 9
Scribner, Patricia and Adam, x, 16, 17,
    50–51, 54–56, 66, 85, 96, 163
Seasonal businesses, 171
"Secret motivator," 146
Self-confidence
    creativity and, 56
    importance of, 194–95
    increasing, 160
Self-discipline, 72
Self-doubt, 136
Self-reliance, 161
Self-talk, 175
Self-worth vs. net worth, 43, 60
Siebert, Al, x, 14–15, 151, 152
Slow periods, 171
Small Business Administration's
        (SBA) Office of Women's
        Business Ownership, 78
Spitz, Karen, x, 64

* About the Authors *

KARIN ABARBANEL is an entrepreneur, marketing communications consultant, and expert on women's career and lifestyle trends. She is the author of *How to Succeed on Your Own* and three other how-to guides. In addition to acting as the "Corporation to Cottage" spokesperson for Avon Products, Karin has been a guest speaker at a wide range of organizations, including Columbia University, Equitable Life, and the National Association for Female Executives. Her corporate background includes more than twelve years with Booz Allen Hamilton, the global consulting firm. Karin received her MA from Columbia University, and her BA from Middlebury College. Karin lives with her husband and son in Montclair, New Jersey. *Visit www.aceyourstartup.com.*

BRUCE FREEMAN, nationally known as the Small Business Professor, is a syndicated small-business columnist for Scripps Howard News Service. An entrepreneur, he is the president of ProLine Communications, a successful marketing and public relations firm. Bruce serves as an adjunct professor of marketing and entrepreneurship at Kean and Seton Hall universities. He received his MA in public administration from Long Island University, and his BA from Binghamton University. Bruce lives with his wife and two daughters in Livingston, New Jersey. *Visit www.smallbusinessprof.com.*

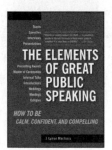